Praise for the novels of Glenda Larke

GILFEATHER

"Like *The Aware,* the action and the setting are well articulated and balanced. The pace is fast moving and the plot has a few twists and turns that left me gasping." —*Visions*

"The pool of main characters in this series may be small, but they are interesting and well developed . . . The Isles of Glory trilogy is a satisfying read." —*The Star* (Malaysia)

THE AWARE

"Witty, gritty, and enthralling." —Trudi Canavan, author of *The Magicians' Guild*

"Memorable fantasy . . . part mystery, part political intrigue, part love story, and many parts rollicking adventure." —*The Courier-Mail* (Brisbane)

"An experienced and gifted writer . . . A rip-roaring tale that kept me engrossed from start to finish . . . richly visualized world-building . . . harrowing ordeals that left me cringing." —*Visions*

"[Larke] proceeds to skillfully subvert the tropes of traditional fantasy." —*Andromeda Spaceways*

Ace Books by Glenda Larke

THE AWARE
GILFEATHER

GILFEATHER

BOOK TWO OF THE ISLES OF GLORY

GLENDA LARKE

ACE BOOKS, NEW YORK

THE BERKLEY PUBLISHING GROUP
Published by the Penguin Group
Penguin Group (USA) Inc.
375 Hudson Street, New York, New York 10014, USA

Penguin Group (Canada), 90 Eglinton Avenue East, Suite 700, Toronto, Ontario M4P 2Y3, Canada
(a division of Pearson Penguin Canada Inc.)
Penguin Books Ltd., 80 Strand, London WC2R 0RL, England
Penguin Group Ireland, 25 St. Stephen's Green, Dublin 2, Ireland (a division of Penguin Books Ltd.)
Penguin Group (Australia), 250 Camberwell Road, Camberwell, Victoria 3124, Australia
(a division of Pearson Australia Group Pty. Ltd.)
Penguin Books India Pvt. Ltd., 11 Community Centre, Panchsheel Park, New Delhi—110 017, India
Penguin Group (NZ), Cnr. Airborne and Rosedale Roads, Albany, Auckland 1310, New Zealand
(a division of Pearson New Zealand Ltd.)
Penguin Books (South Africa) (Pty.) Ltd., 24 Sturdee Avenue, Rosebank, Johannesburg 2196,
South Africa

Penguin Books Ltd., Registered Offices: 80 Strand, London WC2R 0RL, England

This is a work of fiction. Names, characters, places, and incidents either are the product of the author's imagination or are used fictitiously, and any resemblance to actual persons, living or dead, business establishments, events, or locales is entirely coincidental. The publisher does not have any control over and does not assume any responsibility for author or third-party websites or their content.

GILFEATHER

An Ace Book / published by arrangement with the author

PRINTING HISTORY
Voyager Books edition / 2004
Ace mass market edition / November 2005

Copyright © 2004 by Glenyce Noramly.
Maps copyright © by P. Phillips.
Cover art by Scott Grimando.
Cover design by Annette Fiore.
Interior text design by Stacy Irwin.

ISBN: 0-441-01348-1

ACE
Ace Books are published by The Berkley Publishing Group,
a division of Penguin Group (USA) Inc.,
375 Hudson Street, New York, New York 10014.
ACE and the "A" design are trademarks belonging to Penguin Group (USA) Inc.

PRINTED IN THE UNITED STATES OF AMERICA

10 9 8 7 6 5 4 3 2 1

This one is for you, Natasha,
with love, and thanks
for being exactly who you are

THE ISLES

Surveyed by the 2nd Explor.
Ex. Kells 1782–1784.

THE MIDDLING ISLES
Discovered by Sallavuard i. Rutho, 1780.

The Keeper Isles

Bethany Isles

BRETHBASTION

Breth Island

YENETH I.

THE HUB

BETHANY HOOD

IDIS IG.

FIFTH SPOKE

AYNN I.

ABAN I.

TENNOR I.

XOLCHASBARBICAN

Xolchas Stacks

CIRKASECASTLE

Cirkase Islands

PORTH

Mekaté Island

The Stragglers

MEKATÉHAVEN

SLLUP I.

STRAGGLERFORT

The Dustels

SPATTSHIELD

The Spatts

THE SOUTHER ISLES
Discovered by Sallavuard i. Rutho, 1781.

OF GLORY

Calment
Major

TINA I.

CALMENTCITADEL

FIRST BANK

ELIEN BANK

FEN TOWER

Fen
Island

QUINDIN I.

TANTA I.

THE NORTHER ISLES
Discovered by Huwight, 1781.

Calment
Minor

QUILLER
HARBOUR

Quiller
Island

SCALE OF NAUTICAL MILES
0   50   100   200

STATUTE MILES
0   50   100   200

ISLAND MILES
0   50   100   200

N

© P Phillips

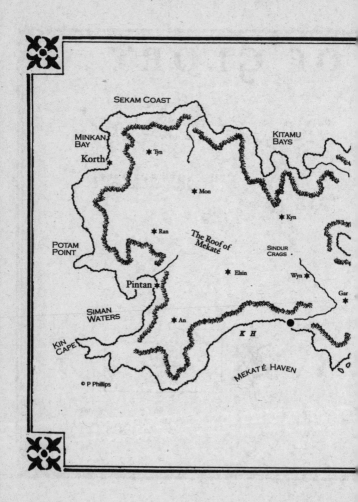

MEKATÉ ISLAND

Discovered by Sallavuard i. Rutho, 1781.
Surveyed by R.V. *Horn*. 2nd Explor. Ex. Kells 1784.

Rattéspie

KILGAIR MASSIF

PORTH

FLOATING MERE

Amkabraig

Niba Water

POINT NIBA

Lekenbraig

MORDON COAST

Ansin

MORDON REACH

Tel

IKAN BAY

CAPE KAN

EZUN I.

GORTHAN SPIT

Creed

Gorthan Docks

SCALE OF NAUTICAL MILES
0 5 10 15 20 25   50

STATUTE MILES
0 5 10 15 20 25   50

ISLAND MILES
0 5 10 15 20 25   50

N

THE PEPPERS

THE MOLAR

THE TOOTH

THE BEAK

THE TALON

THE CLAW

THE KNUCKLE-
BONES

TEMPLE OF
THE WINDS

THE FANG

Xolchasport

THE MILKTOOTH

THE SKINNY NECK

XOLCHASBARBICAN

THE GRAINS

THE FIN

THE CRUMBLE

THE CRUMBS

N

- - - - Route of the Stack Race
mmmm Bridge
——— Slide Rope

THE WALL

INNER XOLCHAS STACKS
Discovered by Sallavuard, 1638.
Surveyed by the U.S. *Explore* Ex. 1842.

SCALE OF NAUTICAL MILES
0   0.1   0.5   1

STATUTE MILES
0   0.1   0.5   1

© P Phillips

ISLAND MILES
0 0.1   0.5

ACKNOWLEDGMENTS

A number of people, from all corners of the world, have helped to get me and this trilogy to this point, and my thanks go out to you all:

First and foremost, to my agent, Dorothy Lumley, in the UK. Without her persistence, you would never be reading this. Thanks, Dot, for having faith in me, even when I had none in myself.

To Trudi Canavan in Victoria, fellow Voyager author, plot-hole finder *par excellence,* for her input and for cheering me up when I needed it.

To Russell Kirkpatrick in New Zealand, also a Voyager author, for thoughtful, invaluable commentary and for his ability to heal a writer's insecurities with such good humor.

To all the other regulars in the chatroom: Gisty, Cando and everyone else who offered encouragement and made me laugh over the months when I was writing this book.

To all those who answered my questions on the Voyager message board with wit and wisdom, and who helped me choose the titles.

To Perdy Phillips in Fremantle for the wonderful maps that made me want to go there.

To the Gilfeather in Glasgow who wasn't offended when I told him that his name just begged to have a lead role in a fantasy novel: thanks, Matt, for the loan!

To Colin in Scotland, webmaster, for his time and humor.

To Selina in Virginia for reading the beginning of the manuscript in Glasgow one Christmas.

To Greg Bridges for the evocative covers and Kim Swivel for the copy edit.

And, finally, to Stephanie Smith and the team at Harper-Collins Publishers Australia: Fiona, Linda, Gayna and all those I haven't yet met, for helping to make this book what it is.

A letter from Researcher (Special Class) S. iso Fabold, National Department of Exploration, Federal Ministry of Trade, Kells, to Masterman M. iso Kipswon, President of the National Society for the Scientific, Anthropological and Ethnographical Study of non-Kellish Peoples.

Dated this day 28/2nd Single/1793

Dear Uncle,
I do apologize for my lack of correspondence recently; I have been busy preparing information sheets for the Ministry. They are thinking of funding a fleet for a trade journey to the Isles of Glory! You can imagine my delight. I would love to be able to say that our bureaucrats have finally realized that official commerce with the Glorian Archipelago would be lucrative—and that if we don't step in, there are other mainland nations who will (the Regal States spring to mind)—but alas, I understand that the whole idea is prompted more by pressure from the League of Kellish Missionaries. The religious parties are just cloaking the expedition in the guise of a trade mission in order to obtain government financing, which, as you know, is constitutionally denied to non-secular projects. They have the ear of several cabinet ministers, I believe.

My own feeling, by the way, is that missionaries will find the Glory Isles a difficult ground to plow for souls. As you may remember from the earlier papers I have sent you, they already have a monotheist religion with a network of priests, called patriarchs, and a lay brotherhood, collectively called the Menod (short for Men of God), that is pervasive throughout the Isles.

Anyway, please find enclosed the next of the conversations for your perusal, translated as always by Nathan iso Vadim. These are from a different narrator, a medic, originally from a rural community of herders who live on an islandom called Mekaté. I do not think he would have talked to us at all if Blaze had not twisted his arm. I can't say I liked him much. He was always polite, if somewhat irascible, but somehow I could not rid myself of the feeling that he found me secretly amusing. However, judge for yourself. As usual, there has been little editing of the conversations. We did not try to reproduce any approximation of his accent in the body of the text, for fear readers would find it tedious. It is hard to know how to achieve that anyway, when you are dealing with a translation. These highland herders roll their "r" sounds in a tiresome manner, although some find the musical lilt of their speech attractive. In the translation, Nathan has rendered the man's direct speech as something akin to our own Kellish highlanders.

Extend my fondest affection to Aunt Rosris, and tell her not to jump to conclusions. She will know what I mean! Anyara and I are both mature adults and are very much aware that an ethnographer such as myself, given to long absences on exploration, would probably make a wretched husband. It is not a situation that either of us have resolved to our satisfaction as yet.

I remain,
Your obedient nephew,
Shor iso Fabold

CHAPTER I

NARRATOR : KELWYN

I FIRST MET BLAZE AND FLAME THE DAY before I murdered my wife. The evening before, to be exact. And now it seems I have to tell you about it. Believe me, I wouldn't be recounting any of this, except Blaze insists I must. She says it's important that you Kellish people understand the Isles, and maybe she's right at that, because, as far as I can see, none of you seems to have displayed any great insight as yet, for all that you have been coming here ten years or more . . .

All right, all right. Blaze complains I've gotten tetchy in my old age. I'll begin properly.

It was in the taproom of an inn in Mekatéhaven, on one of those hot, humid nights when the air seems so thick that it's hard to breathe. I remember the sweat crawling down my back to make a wet patch on my shirt. I actually had a room upstairs, but it was an airless cubby-hole I wanted to avoid. It overlooked the wharves, where ships fidgeted endlessly at their moorings and sailors and longshoremen squabbled all night long, so I'd decided to spend the evening in the common room. I had no intention of being sociable; I was mired so deep in my own troubles that all I wanted to do was nurse a tankard of watered-down mead and wonder what in all Creation I could do to solve problems that were all but insoluble.

My immediate difficulty was that I needed to go to the Fellih Bureau of Religious and Legal Affairs, and it had closed for the day. Until they opened in the morning, I wasn't going to be able to find out what had happened to my wife.

In the meantime, worry lurked in the pit of my stomach like over-spiced food promising unpleasantness. All I had at that point was a piece of paper telling me that, as the husband of Jastriákyn Longpeat of Wyn, I was expected to present myself as soon as possible at the Bureau. It was an imperious summons and there was no overt reason why I should answer it. Neither Jastriá nor I was a Fellih-worshipper and neither of us ever had been. Moreover, Fellih-worship was not an official religion, and the leader of the faith, the Exemplar, had no official status on Mekaté Island. The Havenlord himself was Menod and, as far as I knew, so were most of his court and his guard.

Nonetheless, the summons had given me a bad feeling and I hadn't hesitated: I set off for Mekatéhaven immediately. I even brought my selver all the way downscarp—which would be much frowned upon by the elders of my tharn if they ever found out—so that I could travel more quickly. The journey had still taken me a couple of days, and when I arrived it was to find the Bureau closed for the day.

So there I was, sipping my mead and paying no attention whatsoever to the other occupants of the inn. Trying, as much as I could, to ignore the fact that I was surrounded by dead wood. Trying even harder to ignore the smell of the place: the sharpness of coal smoke, warm toddy and spilled wine permeated everything inside; the muted scent of mold, mangrove mud and damp sails wafted in from outside. I was vaguely aware of a group of people playing cards on the other side of the room, of several merchants discussing business near the door, of a woman sitting alone at the table in the far corner. Apart from that, I was oblivious. All I could think of—with a mixture of exasperation, love and frustration—was Jastriá. What in the wide blue skies had she done this time?

"More mead, Syr?" The barkeep hovered at my elbow with a jug.

The title he gave me was not one I was entitled to, and I was sure he knew that. I shook my head, wishing he'd just go away.

But business was quiet, and he was talkative. "Just come down off the Sky Plains, have you?" he asked, stating the obvious. I had a selver in his stable and I was wearing a tagaird and dirk, after all.

I nodded.

"You must be tired. Can I ask my wife to get you a meal, maybe?"

"I'm not hungry." I made a gesture of negation that would have set my tankard flying if he hadn't grabbed it in time.

He set it carefully back on the table. "Ah, you're finding the heat and humidity oppressive, I suppose. You Sky People do, so they tell me," he added, cheerfully mopping up the spilled mead that had slopped on the table.

"Ye get other Plainsmen in here?" I was surprised. Not too many selver-herders ventured down off the Plains, and with good reason. Who wanted to suffer the appalling weather of the coast voluntarily, not to mention the filth of its streets and the narrow-mindedness of its townsfolk? We were all Mekatéen, but the selver-herders of the Sky Plains and the town dwellers and fisher folk of the tropical coast had little in common.

"Sky People here? Oh, sometimes, selling selver wool or paying taxes," he said, deliberately vague, and I realized he had not expected me to take him literally. I smothered a momentary irritation. We relied so much on smell on the Roof of Mekaté, it was sometimes hard to use and to understand the conversational gambits and niceties of the coast. I still made mistakes; coastal folk often found me abrupt, even rude, and their courtesies were often just lies to me.

He must have taken my question as an indication that I wanted to talk, because he leaned in closer and said in a conspiratorial whisper, "Have you noted the Cirkasian beauty in the corner?"

I hadn't, not really, but after I glanced at her I doubted that he'd believe that. The woman sitting alone in the corner was astonishingly beautiful: gold-blonde hair, with eyes the color of the sapphires we used to pick up sometimes in the streams of the Sky Plains. Her one flaw was that she had only one arm;

the other ended just above the elbow. She was wearing traveling garb stained with salt water. She smelled of salt and fatigue
and some faint animal scent I didn't know, all laced through
with a strong aroma of perfume. One of those over-spiced
tropical scents: chypre? Patchouli? Spikenard? I wasn't sure.

"Now what's a sea-dream like that doing in a bar alone at
night?" the barkeep asked. "That's what I'd like to know."

I shrugged and he sighed. "Business just gets worse and
worse," he continued, leaning into the table, his rotund belly
coming to rest on the planks. "It's the Fellih-priests to blame.
They don't like drinking. They don't like card-playing. They
don't like music. They don't like dancing. Or whoring. Or
gambling. Or just about anything that's fun. Which I wouldn't
mind, if they kept their ideas to themselves, but no, they have
to make non-worshippers feel guilty about doing those things,
and believers who indulge just get thrown in jail. It's got so that
when a bunch of them walk in for a meal, the drinkers leave."

I was startled. Things hadn't been that bad last time I was
on the coast.

I didn't travel all that much any more, not since Jastriá and
I had parted, but I was a physician and there were certain
herbs and medicinal ingredients that could only be procured
away from the Sky Plains. The lowland forests of Mekaté may
have been no more than a narrow trim to the highlands, a ruffle between the bottom of the scarp and the sea, but they held
a diversity of plant life that was both breathtaking and invaluable to a herbalist. And so I made the journey down to the
coast at least once a year, either buying from medicine shops
or collecting my own plants in the forest. I tried to keep the
trips short: what I saw along the Mekaté coast invariably
broke my heart.

The barkeep rambled on. "You Plains people have more
sense. You don't worship the Fellih-Master, do you?"

I shook my head, snorting at the thought of selver-herders
bothering with the doctrine of Fellih. We were far too pragmatic; far too content. Oh, Fellih missionaries had attempted
to penetrate the Plains with their ideas, as had the Menod, but
they had all met with a rock-solid wall of indifference and had
eventually taken their concept of God, sin and the afterlife
elsewhere.

I was still wondering how to get rid of the barkeep when one of the card players called for a round of drinks and he levered himself upright to attend to them. I decided to finish my mead and go up to my room, but, while I was sipping the last of the drink, I smelled something that seemed out of place. Feathers. I could definitely smell feathers, and an inn room late at night seemed an odd place for a bird.

Idly curious, I glanced around. It was a while before my eyes saw what my nose had identified: a nondescript blackish sparrow-like creature sitting on the rafters near the table where the card game was going on. I didn't know the species, but it surely didn't belong in a taproom. It seemed restless; I could see it cocking its head to look down from its perch, and occasionally it would shuffle its feet and flick its wings. Once it even flew across to one of the other beams, and then back again. Obviously the poor thing had become trapped inside the room and didn't know how to get out. I empathized.

The players at the table were noisy. Three or four of them were well on the way to being drunk, two of the others were arguing amiably about the previous hand and whether it had been luck or skill that had resulted in the sole woman among them winning a handsome amount of money. I had never played cards and didn't understand the conversation, but it seemed to me that there was an odd sort of tension in the group. Someone wasn't happy with having lost, and the woman was uneasy, although she hid it well. Suspicion tendrilled in among the sounds, pungent in a way that was quite different to the sharp tang of the ale in the casks along the wall or the bitters stewing in the brewery room out back.

I began to pay attention. I sat up and edged myself along the bench, thinking to leave for my room quietly and unobtrusively. Instead, I managed to topple what was left of my drink onto the floor. No one among the card players even bothered to look at what had caused the noise. It was definitely time for me to leave.

As I bent to retrieve the tankard, one of the card players, a young fellow with a strident voice and a drink-flushed face, flicked some money into the center of the table and said, "Your bet, sister. Match that, if you can."

The woman looked up at the rafters, apparently considering the bet, then laid her cards facedown with a shake of her head and a smile. "No," she said. "I think not. This pot is yours, my friend. In fact, it is time that I went to my bed."

"Wait a moment." Another of the players placed a hand over hers as she reached out to gather her own money together. "You can't win all that money and then just walk out of here!"

She stared at him, all hint of the smile gone. If I had been one of her companions, I would have been worried; there was something about her that made my nose tingle. "Oh, but I think I can," she said, removing her hand. "If you don't want to lose, then you shouldn't play. Th—"

She never finished what she had been about to say. Even as I rose to leave, the main doors to the inn were pushed open and a crowd of people surged in.

Not customers, that was immediately apparent. One of them wore blue robes, stacked shoes and a cylindrical hat with a small brim—Fellih-priest garb; I knew that much. The rest looked like thugs; they carried long wooden cudgels with rounded ends. The priest scanned the room with a glance, then gestured toward the card players. The cudgels moved to surround the table. The silence in the taproom was instantaneous. The merchants just melted away, leaving by a side door. The Cirkasian woman didn't move, and neither did I.

The card-playing woman *did* move, but her movement was so controlled and unobtrusive I doubted the newcomers noticed. She placed one hand on the hilt of the sword in the scabbard that was hanging on the back of her chair. I was intrigued; I had no idea that there were women who used swords. I hesitated, torn between drawing attention to myself by leaving, or simply staying put.

The barkeep spoke up. "Syr-priest, I beg you, this is a respectable house—"

The priest withered him with a look. "Respectable establishments do not allow gambling."

One of the young men at the table rose to his feet, belligerence in every nuance of his stance. "Syr-fellih," he said, "what possible business do you have here?"

"The Master's business," the priest replied, and his tone had all my senses tingling. "You have broken your faith with the Fellih-Master, lad." The "lad" in question must have been all of twenty-five, so that was an insult there to start with. "Show me your thumbs."

The man reddened from the neck upward and I could smell both his fear and his resentment. Reluctantly, he held out his hands. The Fellih-priest glanced at them and nodded to the cudgel-wielders. "And the rest of you," he said to the card players.

One of them answered calmly, "That will not be necessary. We freely admit it: we are all Fellih-worshippers here, except for the lady. And we have indeed fallen from Fellih's grace tonight. For that I apologize. We will abandon this place of iniquity and go home chastened, to pray for Fellih's forgiveness." He rose and bowed deeply in the direction of the priest. Only then did I notice that he too wore the high-stacked shoes of the Fellih-worshipper. In fact, they all did, except the woman.

If he thought that would be an end to it, he was mistaken. "I think not," the priest said. "The penalty is more than penance, lad. It is imprisonment and a fine."

The resentful one said hotly, "You overstep your mark, Syr-priest! I am the son of the Burgher Dunkan Kantor and my friends are—"

"No man and no man's son is above the Master's law." The priest nodded once more to the cudgel-wielders. Within seconds the young men were hustled outside, their protests ignored. The priest turned his attention to the woman. "And you," he said. "Let me see your thumbs."

I thought for a moment that she was going to refuse, but there were still four cudgel-men behind the priest and finally she shrugged and held out her hands, one at a time. The priest nodded, satisfied. He looked back at her face; then, without warning, he reached out and brushed the hair away from her left ear. It was bare: she lacked a citizenship tattoo. The subtleties of the physical differences between people from different islandoms was beyond me, but something in her looks—she was tall and tan-skinned with brown hair and startlingly green eyes—told him she was the result of inter-island mixing.

"Halfbreed," he hissed, and the hate in that one word left me gaping. How could one despise another simply because of an accident of birth?

"That's right," she said calmly. "And I arrived in Mekaté only this evening." She was lying, I could tell, but I doubted anyone else could. She was as unruffled as a mountain tarn. "The law says the citizenless may have three days' residence before they must leave."

"You have corrupted our young! Card-playing!" His bile was a tangible thing that made me flinch.

She gave him a flat stare. "I don't remember having to teach them how to play. Or how to wager their money. They seemed to be well acquainted with the procedure before I arrived."

"Your behavior is typical of the improperly bred and we don't want your kind here. Show me your branding."

I winced at his tone, at the smell of his barely leashed fury. She seemed unworried by the way his eyes narrowed and his voice flattened, but his words stilled her nonetheless. My breath caught in my throat. She had a magnificence about her, a dignity that transcended her situation, that made him look like what he was: a small and petty man. But there was more than dignity; there was a deep and abiding anger that made her seem dangerous even without a sword in her hand. The tension in the room ratcheted up a notch. Without a word, and with a controlled economy of movement, she untied the top of her tunic and bared her back so that he could see the mark there. It was an ugly thing, a scar in the shape of an empty triangle, burned deep into the skin of her shoulder blade. It had not healed well and the skin around it was puckered.

She readjusted her tunic. "Forgive me," she said, and her irony was mere surface covering to a deep churning rage, "I did not know gaming was against the law here. It was hardly obvious. With your leave, I shall be on my way." She turned away from him, perhaps to pick up her sword harness.

What happened next was so swift that the warnings shouted by myself and the Cirkasian were too late. The priest made a sign to one of the four remaining cudgel-men and, as quick as a spitting selver, the man brought the club down on her head. She had warning enough to turn so that much of the force of the blow was taken on her shoulder. Even so, she came up groggy and at a disadvantage. Or I thought she did, but a moment later I wasn't so certain. As she reeled, one of the other men tried to throw her, hard, into the wall. She ducked down, as if staggering, and somehow the fellow pitched right over her back. Before he hit the floor, she straightened and it was his head that collided with the stones of the wall, not hers. He was out cold. It all looked accidental, but something about the fluid grace of her moment had me wondering. Still, she was pale enough and had to prop herself against the wall in order to stand. A trickle of blood matted the hair over her temple. I doubted that her dizziness was feigned; she was close to blacking out and action had made her feel worse.

I stepped forward in protest. "Wait a wee moment," I said to the priest, "that wasna necessary! Ye have hurt the woman and she was offering no resistance. I am a physician; allow me to examine her. Him too," I added as an afterthought.

The priest looked at me coldly. "We need no heathen medicinemen interfering here."

"They may be concussed—"

"Do you dare to countermand me, herder?" he asked, his distaste clear. He signaled to the remaining cudgel-wielders. One of them grabbed her arms and forced them behind her back; another had her in manacles before she had time to protest. They'd obviously done this kind of thing before, often. The priest gestured and they hustled her away through the outside door. Beside me the Cirkasian was also on her feet, her face as pale as a meadow snowbell. The priest turned back to us. "Your thumbs," he said to us both.

I blinked and blundered on: "She needs attention—" I went to shoulder past him, but he blocked my way with his hand upraised. "Then let me tend the man," I said, indicating the fallen thug who was only now beginning to stir.

"Your thumbs," he snapped. There was so much authority in his tone that I halted.

The Cirkasian shrugged and held out her hand. He looked, nodded in satisfaction, and turned his attention back to me. I had no idea what he was looking for, but let him look anyway. He seemed satisfied and said, "You are both strangers here. Follow the example of the pure of heart and you will be welcome on the coast. Be not seduced by the sins you have witnessed in this mire of immorality tonight." The smell of his sincerity cloaked him, wisping through the air in swirls. He *believed* what he was saying. Behind him the dazed thug staggered to his feet and looked around to locate his friends.

"Oh, I dinna think there is any chance of that," I replied without inflection. "They are not sins I would want to emulate."

He hadn't the imagination to hear sarcasm. He inclined his head and strode to the table where the money from the card game was still piled up in heaps. He took out his purse and scooped up the money in the center. There wasn't all that much there; most of the cash was in the separate piles belonging to the players, but he ignored all that and strode out of the inn. He also left the halfbreed's sword, which was still hanging on the back of the chair.

I took a step toward the cudgel-man, intending to offer my help, but he bolted out of the door. The Cirkasian sat down at the gaming table in silence. I turned back to the barkeep. "What was all that about thumbs?"

"Oh—Fellih-worshippers: they have their thumbs tattooed with blue circles, at birth or conversion."

"And if a man changed his mind about his beliefs?" I asked.

He looked at me as if I were too innocent to be real. "Once a Fellih-worshipper, always a Fellih-worshipper. It's not a faith you can ever leave. Not alive, anyway."

"That . . . that's unbelievable. Parents can sentence their children to a lifetime of commitment?"

He shrugged to indicate that he shared my lack of understanding of that rationale.

"And the woman's brand on the shoulder?" I asked.

"That's to show she has been made barren. They castrate halfbreed men and sterilize the women, then brand 'em to show it has been done."

"They? *Who* does?" I had heard of the practice, come to think of it, but for some reason or another I'd thought it had fallen into disuse.

He shrugged as if the question made him uneasy. "Authorities. Here it's the Fellih-priests or the Havenlord's guards. It's the law in all the islandoms, though I've heard the Menod patriarchs preach against it."

"That's barbaric!"

"Plainsman," he said kindly, "you best go back where you belong. The world's too bad for the likes of you."

I grimaced. He was probably right at that. I glanced over at the gaming table, about to remark on the money left there, only to find it had vanished. The Cirkasian was walking toward us, the other woman's sword in her hand.

"Ye canna do that!" I blurted without thinking.

She looked at me, innocently bewildered. "Do what?"

"Take all their money."

"What money?"

"The money they left on the table."

"The priest took it."

"He only took part of it!"

I looked at the barkeep, wanting him to support me, but all he did was stare back in a puzzled fashion. "The priest took it," he said. "He took it all. I saw."

The Cirkasian nodded. "Where will they take the card players?" she asked.

"To the Fellih Bureau of Religious and Legal Affairs," the barkeep said. "There are cells there. Tomorrow they will come up against the Fellih magistrate. There will be lawyers for both sides who will quote the Holy Book, which is, of course, the inspired word of Fellih, and the one with the best quotes wins his case."

I gaped. "That's absurd." I was not all that familiar with the concepts of courts, lawyers and magistrates—we did not have such things on the Sky Plains—but even so, what he said seemed ridiculous.

"Not to a Fellih-worshipper," the barkeep replied. "They believe Fellih is omnipotent and cannot make mistakes. So, if the magistrate and the lawyers pray for guidance, which they do, the result must be the wish of Fellih. Simple logic." He snorted. "Which is one of the many reasons I'm a Menod, rather than a Fellih-worshipper."

I warmed to the man, but I didn't want to get into a religious discussion. Up on the Sky Plains, we didn't believe in any gods at all, which seemed much more sensible. I looked back at the Cirkasian. "And ye maintain ye didna take the money? And what about the sword you're carrying?"

She looked startled. There was a pause, and then she said, "I am not stealing the sword."

I blinked, confounded. The weapon was in her hand, after all, but she spoke with an honesty that was bewildering in light of the evidence.

She nodded to us both and headed for the stairs.

I looked back at the barkeep, but his garrulity seemed to have vanished. In fact, he was edging away as if he was having second thoughts about my inoffensiveness. I said goodnight and headed for my room as well—perplexed, but aware that it would be stupid to make a fuss. None of it was my business.

I was halfway up the stairs when I felt I was being watched. I turned to look, and the single eye that met mine belonged to the bird. The same bird as had been on the rafters, but it had moved to the newel post. It stood there regarding me until I turned away and resumed the climb to my room. I had a strange feeling that I was way out of my depth; a bird should never have had the emotions I could smell in that one.

CHAPTER 2

NARRATOR: KELWYN

I WAS AT THE FELLIH BUREAU OF RELI-
gious and Legal Affairs early the next morning, my anxiety
pungently tangible, at least to me. To my surprise, there was
already a crowd of people gathered in front of the building.
Most of them seemed to be well-dressed merchants in the
company of their wives and servants. Some of the women
were weeping; the men were as somber as their clothes. They
stood about talking while they waited for the office to open,
their hands fiddling with their prayer beads, their feet shuf-
fling in their uncomfortable shoes.

"What's going on?" I asked a man across the road who was
selling snacks of grilled sea-snails, fresh from the coals. The
smell was pervasive and made the end of my nose twitch.

He shrugged indifferently as he stirred the snails on the
wire grill, rolling them about with his spatula. "They arrested
some of the sons of the merchants last night for gaming. The
parents have come to get them released."

I watched the people milling around. One woman near me
hugged another, moaning, "Leeitha! Haven't I always *told*

him to be a good boy? I forbade him to go out at night and he wouldn't listen!"

She was dressed in red, with a blue shawl flung over her shoulders and leather sandals on her feet. As she was a woman, no one cared if her feet were contaminated by the dust. Men—whether priests or laymen—had to wear the high-stacked shoes, and were not permitted to touch the soil or earth, or wear any bright color other than blue. They weren't supposed to walk about the streets alone either; in fact, their Fellih-faith obliged them always to be in twos or groups, sup-posedly to ensure the good behavior of each individual. Re-strictions placed on a Fellih-faithful woman were not as stringent, as long as she did not commit adultery or tempt the menfolk with her behavior or dress. Jastriá had once explained that anomaly to me. It stemmed not from a more liberal atti-tude to women, but from a rather nasty aspect of the religion: women were not considered worth troubling oneself about. The Fellih-Master was contemptuous of women, and the Holy Book was full of tales of their empty-headed, superficial fem-ininity that was capable of neither piety nor scholarship. A woman, it seemed, went to paradise only if her husband accu-mulated sufficient merit in his own life to take her along with him. Rich women, therefore, often married more than one spouse in the hope that one of them would prove man enough to get her to heaven. (Jastriá had remarked with a cynical laugh that such pragmatism showed the intelligence of women, rather than a want of it.)

"You're going to have to wait if you have business with the Exemplar," the snail-seller told me as I watched the crowd. He snipped off the tip of a snail shell and sucked the animal out of its home with a loud slurping sound. "Aaah, delicious. Sure you won't have one?" I shook my head. "The Exemplar will have to clear all the spoiled brats of these merchants before he bothers to get to the case of one of the Sky People." He gave a snort as if to say he didn't think much of Fellih-worshippers. "Be careful, Plainsman; it doesn't do to bruise the skin of Fellih-priests."

"At least ye feel free enough to criticize," I said, and moved downwind of his grilling molluscs. Burned flesh always made me feel a shade queasy. I was thinking that my rash intervention the night before may well have already bruised the sensitivities of at least one priest. I had to hope I didn't come across that particular man again.

"The Havenlord of Mekaté still guarantees the religious freedoms of all Mekatéens," the seller agreed. "I wouldn't like to be one of the Fellih-faithful, though. They have their own legal system and it's onerous on them that believe. Makes life bleeding difficult for the poor sods. Are you *sure* you don't want some snails? Absolutely fresh. They go onto the coals still slithering." He waved one under my nose, holding it by a feeler. It was still alive.

I stepped back hurriedly, banged into something and apologized before I realized that I was saying sorry to a post driven into the ground. The snail-seller grinned. My ears burned. It's one disadvantage of being red-headed and pale-skinned: when you flush, it's very noticeable.

I went to find a quiet spot to wait.

I WAS FINALLY USHERED INTO THE EXEMplar's office several hours later, glad not to have come across the priest I'd seen the night before.

It was only with considerable restraint that I was able to conceal my distaste for the room. No pollarded branches had supplied the timber for the furniture; the size of the table alone appalled me. Whole trees had been slaughtered, just to give this one man his office. It was an effort to hide my revulsion at so much needless death. As if to emphasize the waste, there was an open shutter behind the desk and the window looked out onto a row of trees, aging giants that were all that was left of an ancient forest. They were festooned with life. Ferns and orchids grew in the crannies, creepers and vines draped the boughs, lichens patterned bark that doubtless crawled with insects and lizards—a blatant living fecundity that made the office seem even more of a sepulcher.

I stumbled over a colorful woven mat as I came forward. The Exemplar of Religious Law, a small and clean-shaven man, waited patiently for me to recover my balance and approach his desk. As his religion decreed, he wore robes that covered him from neck to wrist and knee, with his legs left bare below. The blue color of the robe was supposed to symbolize the heavens, just as the raised shoes were supposed to lift him away from the earth. His priestly hat was ridiculously tall, to symbolize the reaching up toward the Fellih-Master above. It was tied under his chin with a big black bow.

"My name is Exemplar Dih Pellidree," he said, politely cool. "Be seated. You wanted to see me?"

His clerk had already given him my name, so I said, "Aye. It's about the woman who was once my wife: Jastriákyn Longpeat of Wyn." I sat down, almost overturning the chair in my nervousness at his indifference. I could smell it on him; around him. He wished me gone. He thought me tiresome.

"Ah. Yes, the clerk brought me the file. What about her?" He retrieved a folder from the pile on the desk and began to thumb through it.

"Syr, I know nothing. Is she here? It was your office that suggested I needed to see you."

"Oh, yes. I remember the case now. She is here, in the jail below." He steepled his hands, tapping his fingers together. "It is my unpleasant duty to inform you, Plainsman, that she has been tried for the sin of adultery."

"Tried?" I stuttered, trying all the while to get my mind around what he was saying. I wasn't sure that I understood the word.

"In the religious court."

"She is to be punished?"

"She has been sentenced to death by dilapidation."

My breath caught. "*Death?* For adultery?"

"That is correct. Such a death is mandatory under the circumstances."

He could not have amazed me more. I felt as if I'd taken a blow to the stomach. I had to grope for words, for some kind of sense in something that was, at its core, quite senseless.

He waited, still polite, and remote. Disinterested. I searched the air for something, anything that would tell me what to do, or say, or ask. With no clues to help me, I forced myself to think. "Adultery?" I asked finally. "In that case, if anyone has been wronged it would be her husband. What has this to do with you?"

His eyes flashed. "The Fellih-Master, holy be His name, has

been wronged. The Master hates all iniquity, and illicit sex is a fearful sin in His eyes. Your wife is to face the ultimate penalty."

This can't be happening. I strove for calm, for logic. For some way to stop the unthinkable. "She is one of the Sky People. She doesna belong to your faith. How, then, can she have sinned by your faith?"

Once more the eyes sparked, but he kept a tight hold on his emotions. I smelled nothing. "When a heathen steps into our lives, then he or she is governed by our laws. This is our right, granted us by the Havenlord, and the Fellih-Master."

All I could manage was a stupefied: "Stepped into your lives?" I simply could not imagine Jastriá involving herself with the Fellih-faithful. Their beliefs were all that she despised.

"She seduced one of the faithful."

My heart sank within me. *Oh, Creation, Jastriá, what have ye done?* I swallowed, still groping for sense, for something that would stop this lunacy. Selverspit, think of something! *Speak wool to the weaver, music to the piper, love to the wife . . .* Play their game, if that's what it takes. "Jastriá is no longer married to me, so she can hardly have committed adultery."

"You have divorced her? Where are the papers?"

"We dinna use papers on the Roof of Mekaté, Exemplar Pellidree. I have, er, not stayed with Jastriá for several years past; by our customs, that means we are no longer wed."

"That is not sufficient to satisfy Fellih law."

"Ye dinna recognize our customs? Good then. We were wed by such customs. There were no papers then either. By your definition, therefore, we were never wed. Ye can't bring a charge of adultery against a woman who never married."

"You play with words, herder! And you also play with the truth. Your wife has fornicated and will be punished. Anyway, that she was perhaps not married is irrelevant: she seduced one of the faithful! She was caught in the act with him, not even under a roof like decent people, but outdoors, without shame, rutting like an animal in the grass. Her lover was married, even if she was not. She has been tried and sentenced and there is no turning back from that." By his tone he implied that he cared little, and was surprised that I did, considering the circumstances. I caught a whiff of indignation, but little else. "Time is short for her," he went on. "Her execution will take place at sunset, outside in the square."

"Sunset? *Today?*"

"Today."

"Creation's birth!" I sat there in the chair opposite that sanctimonious priest and felt myself to have been gutted. Finally I did manage to say, calmly enough, "Do ye never temper your decisions with mercy, Exemplar? Ye call your God Fellih-Master the Merciful. Is this mercy?"

"Do not question the ways of the Fellih-Master, heathen." Both his voice and his body odor signaled warning.

"What about Jastriá's lover? Is he also to be murdered?"

"I don't like your choice of words, herder! The man has already suffered the penalty for his crime. He was tried and executed for an illicit relationship with a heathen."

I took a deep breath, trying to calm the sick tumult inside me. "Is there no way I can stop Jastriá's execution? Or at least delay it?"

"None. The religious court's decisions are never reversed. How can they be? They are only made after invoking the Fellih-Master's guidance and can therefore never be wrong. The only reason your wife is still alive is that it was deemed reasonable you be informed before she dies, as you are an injured party and are responsible for your wife's affairs."

I felt all the color leave my face. "Do ye mean to tell me that I have ensured Jastriá's death by coming here?"

The Exemplar shrugged. "We would not have put off the execution for much longer anyway."

I sat for a moment, incapable of speech. Finally I managed a few forced words. "Jastriá. Can I see her?"

"Certainly. It is right that you should; an adulteress should be made to confront the man she has wronged and face his chastisement. I shall have someone escort you down to the cells." He rang a bell on his desk and gave the order to the man who answered it.

I rose, but it was an effort: my legs no longer seemed to belong to me. I paused on my way out and turned back to look at the Exemplar. "Dila—dilapidation," I said. "What is it?" My voice did not seem to belong to me either: it was another person speaking, the words coming to me from a long way off.

Dih Pellidree looked up from the papers on his desk. "Oh, stoning," he said, indifferent to the last. "Death by stoning."

I staggered, my body unable to function as my mind tried to accept the reality behind his words.

Pellidree wasn't even watching me. He was putting Jastriákyn's file at the bottom of the pile, taking up the next one on top. Next file, next crime, next punishment. All in a day's work. I wanted so badly to kill him, to rid the world of his smug sanctimony. For the first time in my life, I desperately wanted to annihilate another human being from Creation's living.

"This way," said the Fellih-worshipper who was going to guide me to the cells. He had to take me by the elbow and pull me gently from the Exemplar's room.

THE CELLS WERE LARGE AND DRY AND plain. There was a sizable grille set in each door, and we would have to talk through this. I did ask to be allowed entry, but of course the request was rejected. I was thoroughly searched and then my guide left me. There was another guard on duty there, seated at a table at the end of the cell block, so I wasn't unsupervised.

I looked in through the grille. There were two women in the cell: one was the card-playing halfbreed; the other was Jastriá. They were both seated on the single woven mat the room contained. The other woman had just said something to make Jastriá laugh, and the sound of her laughter brought back a flood of haunting memories, all the more poignant now I knew she was so close to death.

Jastriá . . . wild, opinionated, wonderful woman—and she was to be slaughtered in a barbaric way by a barbaric religion, all for the gift of her body to some unknown man. Creation, but the two of them had paid a high price for their passion.

"Jastriá," I said, and she looked up.

I knew from her smell that she had not expected me. *"Kel?"* She came across to the door, only half believing what her senses told her. "I thought I scented ye earlier, but I didna believe it!"

"They sent a message to the Plains, telling me to come. So I did."

She looked at me with troubled, dark-ringed eyes. "Oh, Kel, I'm so sorry. Ye shouldna have . . ." She swallowed. "Have they told ye what happened? They are going to kill me, y'know."

I nodded. "Jastriá, how could ye have been so foolish?" I hadn't meant to say that, and I would have taken the words back if it had been possible. She was going to die and I was reproaching her. I combed my fingers through my hair in a gesture of frustration at my own lack of thought.

She gave a tiny laugh. "Ah, y'know me, Kel. Anything for excitement, for a thrill. I had to live life to the full, taste everything, drink at every cup. It was fun while it lasted." That last was a lie and we both knew it. It hadn't been fun, but a desperate attempt to find a peace of mind that had always eluded her. She raised a hand to her head to pull out the comb that kept her hair piled up, and the red mane of it tumbled free.

"I tried," I said. "I tried to get them to change their minds, but, Jas, they didna want to listen."

"Did they say when?" she asked. She sounded much calmer than I felt.

I paused, letting her inhale first, so she could sense the bad news that was coming. A Sky Plains politesse, that: as if anyone could ever be prepared for what I had to say. "They say . . . this . . . this evening. At sunset, outside in the square."

She shrugged carelessly but the wave of her emotion caught me, pinioned me where I was: fear, horror, bitterness, resignation. I could taste it all in the back of my throat as I breathed. Through her shock she said at last, "What of it? It's no kind of life here in the jail anyway, not for someone born on the Plains."

I found I had to ask. I wanted answers. I wanted desperately to understand. "Oh, Creation—why, Jastriá, *why?*" What had made her leave me, leave the place of safety I had made for her amid the filth and stink of the coast? What made her so disillusioned with life that she didn't care if she died? She was only twenty-nine years old!

She looked at me with something close to pity. "I couldna stand it, Kel. I had to be myself, not the curds set in the mold, the same as everyone else. There is part of you that can understand that, isn't there? That's why I wed you!"

I stared at her and wondered if I understood. Perhaps Jastriá had seen more in me than was really there: perhaps she thought she had found a soul to meet hers, to meet her wildness. She thought I had the same rebel's heart that she had. But I wasn't a rebel at all. I didn't want to break the mold; I wanted to fashion new ones. I didn't want to fight the tharn elders; I wanted their approval for new ways. I achieved no satisfaction from shocking my family, from hurting those who loved me. All I wanted was to find a way where I could live within the restrictions without going mist-mad. I wanted to make the Roof of Mekaté a better place to live in. Jastriá had wanted to destroy it. She'd called me spineless. I'd called her reckless. She'd said I was an animal that was too dead to skin. I'd said she was like a grass-lion cub baying at a moon and expecting it to crumble.

Yet it was true that I was not set in the mold of the average selver-herder of the Sky Plains. I was a physician, an herbalist and chirurgeon, trained by my grandparents and my parents and my uncle. I rode the Plains—as all my House did—delivering the babies, tending the ill, stitching the wounds, prescribing the cures. From the time I was old enough, a lad wearing his first tagaird and dirk, I had accompanied my uncle to the coast to buy the drugs and plants we used. As an adult I'd developed a strong interest in the mixing of medicines and the use of herbals, and I'd obtained permission from the elders of my tharn to come to the coast whenever I needed, to search for ingredients. I was even given a portion of the Sky Plains treasury gold to do it. And so I had done what few Plainsmen ever did: travel. True, I'd never left the island of Mekaté, but I'd escaped the rigidity of a Sky Plains existence in a way that was open to very few. In a way, it was that escape that had kept me sane.

After our marriage, I had taken Jastriá with me of course, thinking it would cure her of her restlessness, of her dissatisfaction. But nothing satisfied Jastriá. She was scornful and scathing when we were on the coast, yet whenever we went back to Wyn she fought everything and everyone. I tried to understand, and part of me did. But the rest of me just cried out at her: why can't you be content with the good things? Why can't you conform in order to preserve what is valuable? If everyone went wherever they wanted, and did whatever they wanted, the fragile world of the Plains would disintegrate. There *had* to be rules.

In the end, the tharn—my tharn—had cast her out. Exiled her for a year, as punishment for transgressions. I had loved her enough to go with her, to set up a home on the coast. I paid for it by selling my services to coastal people, and I thought we would manage to scrape by. But the first time I left her to go upscarp to visit my family she disappeared. She left me a brief note and walked out.

I spent weeks looking for her. And after that I searched every time I returned to Mekatéhaven. I'd never found her.

And now she was sitting in a jail cell, asking me if I understood why she had been so restless, so unable to settle.

I said, "Understand? Partly. A little. After all, I never wanted to sit at home and be my father all over again. But, Jas, ye've just killed yourself! Was it *worth* it?"

"Y'know, I dinna care," she said. "I thought being free to do what I wanted would solve everything, but it never did. Because I was never free, not really. The Sky People despised me because I *wanted* to be different; the coastal people despised me because I *was* different. It just seemed that there was nowhere I could be happy."

"The man—" I began, and then couldn't think of any way to ask her.

"The man they caught me with? He was paying me for it, Kel. I didna even know him."

I felt sick and turned my face away.

Smelling my revulsion, her anger spilled over. "I'm glad to die. D'ye hear me? Glad!"

I didn't know what to say. I knew I'd failed her. I'd felt helpless during the years of our marriage, and I felt helpless then as I faced her through the grille of her prison. "I'm sorry," I said; inadequate words for an overwhelming situation.

She gave a sigh. "It doesna matter. I shouldn't have wed you. I shouldn't have wed anyone. I don't know what I should have done: there's no cure for corrosion of the soul. 'He who spits at the sky, gets it back in his face.' Well, it was my choice to spit at the sky."

"Is there naught I can do? We shouldn't be talking about

you dying. We should be trying to find a way to stop it. Do ye know anyone here that I can go to?"

She slipped her hand through the bars and placed her fingers over my mouth. "Stop it, Kel. This is not something ye can cure with one of your potions."

"Creation, Jas . . ."

We stared at each other, breathing in our mutual despair and horror, feeling each other in ways that coastal folk never know, every subtlety written in the air between us, to be read with every breath we took. For my part, all I had to say was there, stripped bare of soft words or social niceties: guilt, love, grief. I knew her own regret, her sadness, her intense smoldering rage. I smelled the traces of the spark of passion that she'd once had for me, long ago.

We had been so young then.

I looked over her shoulder and glimpsed her cellmate. The woman was leaning on the far wall of the room, arms folded, head cocked. She must have heard every word.

Jas stirred, sighing. "Kel, there is one thing ye can do for me."

"Aye."

"It may be the hardest thing I've ever asked of you."

I paused, cautious, not wanting to fail her again. "What is it?"

"I'm afraid of what they are going to do. They say . . . they say it can be a slow death. And painful."

"Ye have heard?"

"The stoning?" She nodded.

"I, I could give ye something to take, if they let me back in; a drug . . ." But then they'd only search me and take it away. Her aroma told me she was thinking the same thing.

"I'm told that it is the privilege of the wronged husband to, er, to throw the first stone." She cleared her throat. "Ye . . . ye are a strong man, Kelwyn."

The vomit rose in my throat. *No!* Not that. *Never.* I choked back bile.

"Please, Kel."

"Ye don't know what ye ask of me. I am a *physician*. And once I loved ye above all others . . ."

"Oh, I know. But I am selfish as always. And afraid. I wouldna ask it of a lesser man."

She was manipulating me, just as she had done a thousand times. There was no way she could not have known what she asked of me; no way at all. There was even a trace of something unpleasant in the smell of her. But what could I say? I touched her face through the bars, trying to muffle my pain so she would not sense it. "If . . . if they allow it."

"Promise?"

"I swear."

"Ye're a good man, Kel. Ye deserved better."

But I doubted it. I'd failed her, and I knew it.

She said, "Go now. And may ye always be at one with Creation."

I almost choked as I gave the salutation to the dying: "Return to Creation in peace." I withdrew my hand and gripped the bars, reluctant to go.

Behind her the other woman stirred herself and came forward. She nodded to me, her face calm. "Go on," she said. "Try to see the Havenlord. Or his Chamberlain." She slipped an arm around Jastriá's shoulder.

I nodded. "I will. And ye, are ye all right? Ye seemed concussed last night."

"Yes, I think I must have been." She smiled wryly. "Otherwise I wouldn't be locked up in here. Have you seen the blonde Cirkasian woman this morning?"

I shook my head and turned to go, but the guard at the end of the passage called out, "Hold it! You have to wait for an escort." He rang a bell on his desk to call another guard. "Wait where you are."

I sat on the bottom step of the stairs and waited, head in my hands. I felt so utterly helpless and so much to blame. Yet where had I gone wrong? I didn't know. I didn't know what I could have done to make Jastriá happy, yet there must have been a way. I'd just never seen it.

A minute or two later a guard came down the stairs, but he was escorting someone else: the Cirkasian. She was still dressed in traveling garb, in defiance of Fellih preferences for skirts, and she had the other woman's sword strapped onto her back. I was so embattled with my own emotions that the incongruity of her presence there, of her *armed* presence, of the fact that the other woman had asked about her, scarcely registered.

"Someone to see the halfbreed," the escort said to the guard in the passage. He looked at me. "You're ready to go back? Well, you can wait till this Cirkasian is finished and I'll take the two of you out together. Stay where you are." He turned to the Cirkasian with an anticipatory grin. "I have to search you, you know."

I watched with growing mystification as he went through her belt pouch and then patted her down, thoroughly rather than intrusively, all the while ignoring the sword as if it weren't there. She slipped it off while he was looking into the pouch and dumped it to the side of the cell door. It lay apparently unobserved by either of the guards. He continued to grin with obvious enjoyment as his hands roved over her body; she was merely stoical. When he had finished, he pointed to Jastriá's cell. "In there, lass." He gave her one last smirk and went off to join the other guard. I just stared at the sword, mesmerized. What in Creation was going on that guards allowed a visitor to come into a jail with a weapon? They could hardly have missed it: it was so huge it almost dwarfed the Cirkasian.

The halfbreed had taken Jastriá's place at the grille. The Cirkasian picked up the sword and passed it to her, harness and all. The hilt barely fitted through the bars. Then she took something out of her pouch and passed that over too: it looked like a small piece of metal with a hook at the end. The guards, busy with their own conversation, took absolutely no notice.

The halfbreed said, rather ungraciously, I thought, "What took you so long?"

"Well, hello, nice to see you too," the Cirkasian replied. "And thanks, Flame, for risking your neck and bringing my sword into the jail under the noses of the guards."

"Shut up, Flame," the woman said amiably. "That redheaded Plainsman behind you is listening to every word."

"Doesn't matter. He's one of the Awarefolk anyway."

The halfbreed indicated for the Cirkasian to get out of her way so that she could view me where I still sat on the stair. "No, he's not," she said.

"Yes, he is."

"No, he's not."

"Yes, he is. Blaze, he can see the sword. And he saw all the money I swiped from the card table."

She was diverted. "Oh, good, you got that, did you?"

"Most of it, yes. I let the Fellih-priest take some. I thought he might be suspicious otherwise."

The halfbreed returned her gaze to me. Her name, Blaze, suited her. "He's not one of the Aware, Flame. I recognize Awarefolk, sort of. I can sense my kinship to them. And that bushy red fellow is no Aware-kin of mine."

"Well, he can see straight through my illusions."

"Really?" She frowned, still looking at me in an interested fashion.

If I hadn't been trying to come to terms with all that had happened to me that morning, I might have said something, might have been indignant that they were talking about me as if I weren't there, able to hear all they said. But as it was, their conversation—and their names—just seemed weird, and in my devastation I couldn't bring myself to care.

Flame shrugged. "It doesn't matter. He's not going to say anything. He tried to help you last night. Don't you remember?"

"Vaguely. I was a bit woozy."

"Yeah, Blaze the famous swordswoman letting a thug with a cudgel get the better of her. That was a memorable moment."

"All right, all right, so sometimes I'm as brainless as a lobster in a pot. I know. I don't need to be told, damn it. My shoulder is aching like hell as a consequence and I have the grandmother whale of all headaches. And how come you didn't help anyway? Some friend *you* are!"

"It all happened so damn quickly. And then I thought the priest might have been one of the Awarefolk . . ."

Blaze pulled an aggrieved face. "So? What's life without a gamble or two?"

"A lot more peaceful! It was your damn gambling that got us into this predicament in the first place!"

"Hey, how else were we going to eat? I didn't see you offering to take a job washing dishes or scrubbing floors."

The Cirkasian raised an eyebrow and, unexpectedly, Blaze grinned.

Flame didn't grin back. Instead, she asked soberly, "What do they have planned for you, do you know?"

The halfbreed's voice filled with laughter. "I'm being deported on a ship bound for Gorthan Spit tomorrow morning."

The look on Flame's face was comical. "After all the trouble we took to *leave* that sodding place?"

"Ironical, eh? Anyway, I thought I'd get out of here this evening around sunset." She dropped her voice to the barest of whispers, but I had excellent hearing in those days. "My cellmate is to be executed in public in the square outside this building at dusk. I think people will be distracted by that, don't you?"

I turned my face away, sickened, and stopped listening.

MEKATÉHAVEN ALWAYS SMELLED. IT smelled of charcoal burning, of smelters and ironworks; it stank of smoke and grime, of fish-fertilizer in sacks waiting for export. Along the sluggish river that meandered in and out of the boroughs, the sewage-tainted mudflats reeked of offal. The city squatted on the land as if it had come to feed there: ugly, cancerous, obscene. Year by year it spread outward, oozing into the forest to despoil everything in its path. It sucked in the beauty of the land and spat out the purulence of middens and cesspools and slag heaps.

I often wondered how any human being could sanction the building of such an abomination, and how, once they had built it, any could want to live in such a cloaca of filth.

It had also once been crime-ridden; but, to give Fellih-worshippers their due, that had altered as they gained religious ascendancy in borough after borough. Their charitable endeavors had alleviated much of the penury that had fueled the crime; their cudgel-wielding guards had soon made any deviation a risky undertaking.

On my early visits to the coast, I'd avoided the city as much as possible. On Jastriá's exile, I had lived there for three months, until she disappeared. It had not been an experience I savored and I'd found it hard to understand how she could indeed savor it, how she could even think of finding a niche for herself in a part of the world that also harbored so much dirt and ugliness, not to mention Fellih-worshippers with their harsh, unrelenting faith. I'd failed to recognize that it was not Mekatéhaven that attracted, but rather the Sky Plains that repelled, and adventure that beckoned.

Of course, there were other religions besides Fellih-worship in the city, and other people too. The Havenlord for one, and he ruled the islandom and the islanders, Fellih-worshippers and Plainsmen included. Unfortunately I had no idea how a humble selver-herder physician was going to get to see the nation's ruler, or his Chamberlain, in just under seven hours.

I tried, Creation how I tried, with every weapon I could think of: bribery, cajolery, lies, the truth. It was no surprise to me when I failed.

A PUBLIC EXECUTION, IT SEEMED, HAD ITS own perverse attraction. When I arrived in the city's main square that evening, it was alive with people, not all of them the Fellih-faithful. They eddied around, whirlpools of excitement, of obscene expectation. I had been naive enough to think that it would be a somber occasion, a suitable atmosphere to mourn a tragedy. Instead, it had the air of a carnival: the crowd smelled of lusts and fervor, of the sheen of sweat and throbbing animation, of an animalistic greed for the sight of blood.

There was a stake driven into the earth at one end of the square, and a bucket stood by it, filled with sand to spread on the blood afterward. There were piles of stones everywhere, and there was the laughter of boys who had collected them. There were no female Fellih-worshippers in the square; this was a man's work, for a man's religion. Small groups of people of other faiths kept well back, scattered along the rear of the crowd. They, at least, seemed subdued.

A bell was ringing to signal sunset, but there was abundant twilight yet when they brought her to the stake. She looked regal, my Jastriá. Regal and proud. *I* was certainly proud of her. She wore a long shift and her hair fell about her shoulders just the way she liked to wear it. She held her head high and walked unaided to the post. Her glance raked the crowd, unflinching, until it found me. She gave the smallest of smiles and stood calmly while they tied her and left her there to face death in the circle of men. The crowd didn't close in on her; they wanted room to do their work, room to see, room to gloat. Their emotions overwhelmed me: I felt every nuance through their odor, the stink of a corrupt humanity.

Near me, one lad said to another, "Aim for her nose. I'll bet you anything I can hit it before you can."

The other laughed and selected a stone from the pile in front of him. "You couldn't hit anything smaller than an ox's arse from this distance."

A third scolded them. "Watch it. Someone might think you're really gambling and then you'd be the ones in trouble! Anyway, you shouldn't go for the face first. The Fellih-preacher I heard speak last night says you should break the legs first. Then the body. The face should be last."

"Why? asked the first.

"Cos it takes longer that way, and hurts more. He says sinners should take a long time to die. Then they have time to reflect on their sins and, anyway, if their death is painful, it acts as a—a whadd'ya call it—*deterrent* to others."

I couldn't bear to listen and moved away.

A moment later the Exemplar Dih Pellidree came forward to stand beside Jastriá, followed by other priests teetering on their stacked shoes. Acolytes in black followed, each carrying a basket of five large stones for use by the priests themselves. A man next to me, seeing I was a non-believer, took it upon himself to explain. "They get to throw before we do. It's their privilege, like. One of the perks of being a priest, I suppose. You know the Sky Plains whore, herder? She's a pretty one, that's for sure."

I didn't reply. The Exemplar recited the crime and the verdict, then intoned prayers to the Fellih-Master. He poured perfumed oil onto the ground at the end of each verse. All for Fellih the Wise, Fellih the Magnificent, Fellih the Just Judge. When he had finished, Jastriá spat on the ground.

A gasp went up from the crowd, then an angry muttering.

The Exemplar looked at me. I unfolded my arms and held up a hand to show him the stone I clutched. "It *is* your privilege," he said, inclining his head to cover his surprise. He had not expected me to claim the prerogative of a wronged husband.

"Hey," the man next to me said, grinning, "your *wife*, eh? Go for it, herder! The bitch deserves it!"

I stepped forward, flipping the rock in my hand to assess its weight. How many times had I done just that as a boy guarding the selver herds against the grass-lions of the sky meadows? It had been important for us to throw accurately. Essential even, because the Sky Plains people did not kill. Anything. Ever. So a boy learned to place a thrown rock just so, whipping it into a grass-lion's flank with just enough power to hurt; never enough to maim or even wound.

A frisson of anticipation rippled through the crowd like a wind-wave across the grass. I smelled it, a sourish, sweaty reek of misplaced lust. I met Jastriá's gaze and saw beyond the defiance, saw all the things I didn't want to see: fear of dying, sorrow at a life that had brought her little happiness, the resignation of defeat, anger. There was no love there; and no irresolution.

I saw her lips move and knew the words she spoke: "Creation take me. *Now*, Kelwyn." And the look she gave then was for me, and me alone. It chilled me to the core with the message it carried: it was everything I didn't want to know.

I whispered her name and thought, *Creation forgive me.*

I drew back my arm. And time seemed to slow, or is that just in my memory? I thought I saw the stone leave my hand and spin. Once, twice, three times, as it traveled across the square. I had not the slightest doubt of what it would do; I knew the power of my throw, the trueness of my eye. As a child, I had always been the one with the longest range, the most accurate throw. I seemed to spend an age watching the stone turn in the air. Was it possible that I heard the crunch of bone as it hit? Because that is what I remember.

Jastriá slumped at the stake, still with that half smile on her face, her crushed temple slammed back into her skull. The wound was a desecration, ending her beauty as well as her life in a welter of blood and brains and bone splinters.

Shredding my innocence. *How did you know I could do it, Jastriá?* How did you know that I could so easily leave behind all it means to be one of the Sky People? You knew me better than I knew myself.

I turned away, revolted, a different man to the one who had entered the square that evening. A man who knew he would never feel the same way about himself again. I pushed my way through the crowd. They stirred around me like a swirl of water caught in the confines of a river pool. They clinked their stones and muttered their anger at being denied their fun, at being cheated of the sight of a slow agony, cheated of the chance to mete out the just punishment to the heathen sinner. Those farthest away closed in and I knew they wanted to hurt me too, to express their frustration.

I raised my selver whistle to my lips and blew hard and long. Those who were closest hesitated, not understanding: the whistle had no sound to human ears. Those who saw my face tried to edge away. And on the outskirts of the crowd there was screaming as Skandor appeared. I didn't blame any who wanted to give him a wide berth. Skandor, when riled, dribbled bile and curled his lips to bare yellowing teeth. The result looked formidable. He *was* formidable—he could hawk up and spit greenish foul-smelling bile with pinpoint accuracy to fifteen paces away, and no one ever wanted to be hit by selverspit. It itched and it stank. It stank for *days*.

I had left him loosely tethered to one of the huge trees at the back of the Bureau of Religious and Legal Affairs, loose enough to pull away in case I needed him in a hurry, for just such a moment as this. He came trotting in, looking for me, shoving people out of the way to the left and right with his neck, bad-temperedly nipping at those who were too slow, flinging his head sideways.

What I had not bargained for, not in any of my most far-fetched contingency plans, was that when he arrived he would have someone on his back.

CHAPTER 3

NARRATOR : KELWYN

WITHOUT SELVERS, THERE WOULD NEVER
have been Sky Plains people.

Not much grows on the Roof of Mekaté. It is high enough
above sea level, thousands of feet in fact, to escape the tropical heat, but the ground is just rock, covered by the lightest of
soils. Yet it rains on the Roof, a lot. I've been told by sailors
that Mekaté is in the path of both a warm ocean current from
the southwest and winds from the same direction, a combination which brings moist clouds all year round. The Scarps
force the clouds upward and, as they cool, they drop their burden as rain. It is said of the weather on the Sky Plains that if
you can't see it raining, it's only because the mist is too thick.

The selvers, fortunately, thrive on the dampness and the
variety of grasses that cover the high meadows and Plains
people thrive on the selvers. Their dung gives us fuel for our
fires and manure for our crops. Their hides provide us with
leather, their wool gives us our clothing and blankets, their
bones supply the material for needles and brooches and count-
less other items. Their milk gives cheese and butter and curds.
Their iron-hard hooves can be carved and honed into knives

and all kinds of utensils. We never deliberately kill them, of course—the Sky Plains people never kill anything willingly—but we are a pragmatic folk, and a selver that has to be put down because of injury, or that dies of old age, is used right up to the last eyelash.

You've never seen one? Ah. Well, imagine the body of a sheep—a shaggy, very large sheep, mind—the legs of a Keeper Isles pony, the cocked tail and ears of a deer, the snout of a goat, and the neck of—well, I'm not sure what else has a neck like a selver. A long, straight, perpendicular neck. Not at all like your Kellish horses. And they are covered in matted wool, not hair. All shades of brown, gray, black or white, or a combination of more than one of those colors.

Every person of the Plains who is old enough to walk owns at least one selver, and those we ride we usually have a special affinity for, but in many ways they are hard animals to love. They are cantankerous and tetchy, given to biting and spitting and sideways neck-butting. They are also rather stupid and not particularly loyal. Skandor was the best one I ever owned, because he had a modicum of intelligence. He was good at responding to a selver whistle, although it didn't matter too much to him who was blowing it. He did, however, hate to be ridden by anyone but me, which was one reason why the sight of someone else on his back as he came through the crowd toward me rooted me to the spot in astonishment.

It was the woman called Blaze, who should still have been in prison. Mind you, she wasn't exactly riding him—he had decided where he was going and nothing short of a broken leg was going to stop him—but she managed to stay in the saddle. She even looked reasonably at home there. She was wearing her sword in the harness on her back.

When she reached me, Skandor came to a halt, so she leaned forward and stretched out a hand to help me mount.

I didn't take it. I growled, "What the darkmoon hells are ye doing on my selver?"

"Can we discuss that later?" she asked. "I think you really should get out of here. This crowd is a flight of wasps looking for something to attack. I suspect they have you in mind."

She was right, so I took her hand and she hauled me up behind her. I grabbed the reins from her and dug my heels in, hard. Skandor took exception, and spat as he wheeled. The crowd scattered hurriedly as they were showered with foul-smelling slobber. An oversized dog with huge feet leaped into the confusion and snapped at a man who had a rock in his hand. The fellow dropped the rock and ran. The dog turned his attention to an approaching Fellih-priest, who made the mistake of trying to hit the animal with his staff. The dog sprang up and ripped the sleeve of the priest's robe from shoulder to wrist, growling all the while. The man fell in the dirt and a gasp rippled through the crowd, growing into a squall of sound that spread outward. I didn't understand until I remembered that Fellih men were not supposed to touch the earth, especially not if they were a holy priest.

"Oh shit!" said the woman, ducking as someone threw a stone. It missed and she slapped Skandor hard at the base of the neck. He took the hint and lunged to greater speed.

"Where's my bag?" I growled. I had left it tied to Skandor's saddle and it wasn't there anymore. It had been replaced by someone else's.

"Back where you tethered the beast."

"I'm surprised ye aren't covered in spit." I was peeved with Skandor. Confound the animal; he was supposed to be *mine*. He ought not to have allowed himself to be stolen. Just then someone leaped up, grabbing for the reins, and Skandor redeemed himself with a sideways swipe of his neck that sent the man spinning away. Another spray of bile followed the arc of his swing. The crowd shrieked and scattered once more.

"He does spit a lot, doesn't he?" she remarked. "I guess I didn't give him time to object."

As we were already at the edge of the crowd, I yanked Skandor toward the rear of the Bureau of Religious and Legal Affairs. Another stone flew by my head, grazing my ear. Fortunately the next rock landed on Skandor's rump and he fairly flew down the street, leaving the crowd behind. The rest of the missiles fell harmlessly onto the roadway.

I guided the animal along the side of the building and we thundered past the archways of the courtrooms. The street was deserted; probably everyone was at the execution. It was even quieter once we reached the trees at the back of the building. I reined in where I had tethered Skandor and, sure enough, my bag was there. So was the Cirkasian woman. She had her own pack on her back.

"This is as far as you go," I said to the woman in front of me. "I dinna want to know what ye were doing with my mount; just get down and leave me be." Reaction had set in; all I wanted was to be left alone. To grieve. To come to terms with what I had done. To leave this wretched city behind and never return. I had to steady my trembling hands against my thighs.

I don't know what might have happened next, but the choices were suddenly taken away from us. A loud bell began ringing, and it was accompanied by a frenzied shouting. I thought it was something to do with me, with what had happened in the square, but Flame said, "*Charnels!* Blaze, they've found out you escaped. Let's get the tarnation out of here!"

Even as she spoke, she threw my bag at me. Without thinking, I dropped the reins to catch it. Blaze reached down to take her hand, to haul her up behind me. "Hey!" I protested. "What in all the wide blue skies do ye think ye are doing?" As I said the words, Flame mounted and Blaze grabbed up the reins and dug her heels in.

Just at that moment, half a dozen guards, led by a priest hobbling along as fast as he could on his silly shoes, ran out of the building toward us. The guards all carried pikes; fortunately none of them had a bow. Selvers are large and strong, but three people on Skandor's back—two of them as large as Blaze and I were—was pushing the limit more than a little. He shook his neck and jibbed. The priest shouted at us not to move. To my horror, I realized it was the same one who had been at the inn. The guardsman in front charged at us with his pike extended. And I didn't have control of the reins. That darn woman did.

She hauled the selver around; Skandor spun on the spot and the pike swung past his shoulder, missing us all by inches. I stuck out a foot as we spun and caught the guard on the chest. For a split second our eyes met, and then he went tumbling to the ground. All three of us lost balance and almost came crashing off Skandor. Blaze levered herself back into the saddle by pulling on the pommel and brought me up with her. Skies, she was strong, that woman! I grabbed at Flame behind me and wrenched her upright as well.

The rest of the guards were almost on us and Skandor wasn't moving.

"Flame!" Blaze snapped. "Do something, you sylv-soaked idiot!" Just what she expected the one-armed Cirkasian to do, I had no idea. She herself was busy with the reins, trying to get Skandor moving. She yelled, "And you, red-man-whatever-your-name-is—get my sword out!"

The nearest guard was almost in a position to swing his pike at us. I tried to haul the sword out of the scabbard on Blaze's back. It was too long. I had to stand up in the stirrups to extract it, which I managed to do by kicking Blaze's-feet out first. I almost dropped the weapon before I realized that this was something that needed two hands, and then I came close to decapitating first Blaze, then myself. Once I had it under control, just, I really didn't know what to do with it, and ended up waving it in a halfhearted manner at the guard. I may not have looked all that formidable, but the sword did, and he jumped back.

Blaze twisted back and grabbed it from me, cursing my ineptness in a few ripe words. Then, with what seemed like effortless ease, she bent and swung the weapon, not at any of the guardsmen but at the priest, who was trying to catch hold of the reins. I cried a protest, but I did her an injustice. She didn't try to kill him. Instead, with remarkable precision—seeing as Skandor was wheeling around at the time—she inserted the sword beneath the hat ribbon that was tied in a bow under his chin. The ribbon parted and the hat tumbled, to be trampled beneath the selver's hooves. And Blaze laughed. The priest purpled, incoherent with outrage at her deliberate mockery.

By this time, all the other guards had caught up and, although Skandor had finally decided that Blaze really did mean him to move, he didn't have a way out of the threatening circle of men.

"Take them from all sides at once!" one of them shouted.

Suddenly, without any reason that I could see, all the guards advancing on us stopped dead, faces registering puzzlement, then the beginnings of fear. Several others raced up and careened into them from behind. A sweet smell wafted around us, potent and tantalizing. Patchouli? What *was* that aroma . . . I'd smelled it back at the inn. The same large dog that had attacked the priest appeared out of nowhere and added to the chaos by snapping at the guards, taking a chunk out of the man on the ground and then worrying the priest's hat. When a guard raised a sword to slash him from behind, the dog didn't notice—yet the sword stroke never came. The guard inexplicably paled and dropped his weapon. Blaze finally managed to get Skandor sorted out and the selver shouldered his way past men who seemed half stupefied. At the last minute, Blaze bent low in the saddle and scooped up the priest's hat from the ground with the tip of her sword. We headed up the laneway at a canter with her brandishing the speared trophy like a captured battle standard. Skandor didn't even labor under our weight. Behind us the guards and the priest stared at our wake in apparent confusion.

"What did they see?" Blaze asked, sounding interested.

"Nothing much," Flame replied. "I just blurred us a bit to start with, then added a few flames and a monster or two. Enough to get us out of there." She sighed. "I've just broken the law of the Isles again: that will *never* count as justified use of magic."

One more thing I didn't understand. I opened my mouth to say something, then realized I didn't have any idea of just what I wanted to say. Blaze threw away the hat, then handed me the sword and I went to slip it back into its harness. For some reason that was even more difficult than extracting it: I nicked myself, jabbed Skandor with the point—which brought his head around with an indignant snort—and scraped Blaze's head with the hilt before it finally dropped back where it belonged.

"Confound it, Blaze," Flame was saying in an irritated fashion, "did you have to play with that preacherman's hat? We could have been killed while you were having your bit of fun!"

"He had his henchman hit me with a cudgel, Flame, and then had me thrown in jail. Believe me, I was tempted to do a whole lot more than ruin his hat, the sanctimonious bastard." She looked back over her shoulder and grinned. "Did you see the expression on his face as we rode away?"

Flame giggled. I felt as if I had ended up in the company of a couple of madwomen from the local borough hospice.

I waited until we had put some distance and many corners

between us and the guards before I reached around Blaze and hauled on the reins. Skandor obligingly stopped. We were outside a godown on the river and the light had finally dimmed in the sky. A lamplighter had just passed and oil lamps glowed and flickered on their poles. Most people were indoors having their evening meal at that hour, and we seemed to be unobserved—except by the dog, now sniffing around the feet of the selver.

Blaze turned in the saddle. "Something the matter?" she asked.

"Get down," I said, my anger barely under control. "Both of you."

"All right," she said, "but can't we just go on a little further first? We're too close to that festering Bureau of Religious Hypocrisy and Legal Lurger-shit for my taste."

"Get down," I said coldly. "Just get down and leave me be."

"Tsk, tsk," Flame said at my back. "Now what's put you all in a pother? We just—"

Blaze hurriedly interrupted. "Flame, the man has just been forced by those canting hypocrites back there to kill his wife. He's entitled to be a little testy."

I exploded. "*They* did that to me, and to her, aye. What *you two* did to me is something else entirely. Have ye only the brains of a burrowing worm that ye canna see what ye've done? *I'm Mekatéen.* I have to live in this islandom and ye've just made me a fugitive, on the run from the law for assisting in a jail-break! The priest can find out my name from the inn register. And I've just learned what happens to Sky Plainsfolk who interfere in Fellih affairs. My wife *died* back there. All because she lay with a Fellih-worshipper! Now what d'ye think they'll be doing to a man who helps someone break out of their jail?"

Both of them sat absolutely still. "Oh, charnels," Flame said in a small voice. "I'm sorry. I guess I didn't think. And I . . . I didn't know about your wife. That was her in the cell with Blaze? I didn't know."

I turned back to look at her, and came nose to beak with a bird sitting on her shoulder. It looked like the one I'd seen back in the inn. I had no idea where it came from, or when, or why. I felt the whole world was splintering insanely apart.

Quite spontaneously, Flame lay her face against my back, flooding my senses with her sympathy. "I am so, so sorry," she whispered.

The odd gesture almost unmanned me. It was all too much: I wanted to break down, cry, give way to that ball of guilt inside me. I wanted to rage at them, shout, shake some sense into them. Instead, I took a deep, calming breath and switched my attention to Blaze again. She was still twisted around in the saddle, looking back at me. She nodded, apparently agreeing with Flame's sentiments. "We didn't mean to involve you," she said. "We just wanted to steal your mount. But when I got up on its back, it took off into the square and there wasn't a damn thing I could do to stop it. Is there anything we can do to make it right?"

"Give yourselves up, perhaps?" I snarled. "Ye could start by explaining to the Fellih-guards what happened."

"Er, short of that." She had the grace to look sheepish, but it was clear she had no intention of endangering her own freedom to ensure mine.

I ground my teeth in helpless frustration.

She said, "We'll leave you, if you insist. We need to get to the nearest ghemph enclave. Would you know where—?"

"If ye think a ghemph will help you, you're mist-mad. They *never* break the law."

"I still need to find a ghemph. I need some information that they might be able to supply." Her look was steady. She wasn't begging so much as expecting me to oblige.

"Creation, but ye have a *gall* to ask me to do anything!"

She nodded, silent this time.

I gathered up the reins again. "It's on my way," I said with a sigh.

I could not believe how fast my whole world had come tumbling down around my ears.

THE GHEMPHIC ENCLAVE WAS SMALL: about ten houses on the banks of the tidal river that slithered, with seeping incontinence, through the outskirts of the city to the sea. The whole area was surrounded by brackish pools that filled and emptied with the tides, a watery web of channels hidden from the sun by mangroves. A lacework of interlocking branches and arching roots formed a tangled, swampy barrier that protected the enclave from sight. They liked their privacy, ghemphs. And they didn't seem to mind the mosquitoes either.

Nearby ran one of the two paths that climbed from Mekatéhaven up the Scarps, and hence to the Roof of Mekaté, and the ghemphs had erected a sign on that path pointing to the entrance of the smaller trail that led into their settlement. We stopped by the sign while Blaze shone her lantern on it to check that we had the right place. It read: *Ghemphic Tattoos.* No price mentioned, but then the cost of a tattoo was standard throughout the Glory Isles and it didn't matter if it was a rabbit with a cheap mother-of-pearl body like mine, or an expensive aquamarine iris in a tattooed eye like the Cirkasian's. You were given the tattoo and jewel that matched your citizenship and that was that. In fact, the only good thing that most people ever said about the ghemphs was that they were incorruptible. You couldn't bribe them, no matter how much you offered.

The issue of citizenship did not bother us much up on the Sky Plains, but I had heard enough to know that life could be tough for those without it. Being without a tattoo marked you as citizenless, having no status and no rights. You could be legally hounded out of an islandom. Those who survived did so mostly on the wrong side of the law, or as outcasts on places like Gorthan Spit.

We left the main path and headed up the trail, still using the lantern. It must have been close to midnight by then, although I couldn't be sure of the time because it was impossible to see the sky. Too much smoke and foulness in the air, as there often was in Mekatéhaven.

The dog continued to follow us, snuffling around Skandor's feet or disappearing into the undergrowth, only to return a while later with muddy legs and his tongue hanging out. He had feet that were more like those of a grass-lion: padded things the size of a large round cheese, which had me wondering if he really was a dog. He had a peculiar gait: his hindquarters always seemed to be trying to overtake his front on the right-hand side, which was disconcerting. You could never be quite sure if he was heading straight for you, or somewhere else. He was a scruffy animal, with patches of uneven hair and bare skin as if he had been partially mowed by an army of skin-mites. Just looking at him was enough to start me itching.

Blaze drew Skandor to a halt. "These are their houses?" she asked me. The buildings at the end of the track were all in darkness, as could be expected at that time of night, and under the trees it was well nigh impossible to see.

"I suppose so," I replied. "I've never been in here before. Are ye going to wake somebody up?"

"That won't be necessary," a voice said out of the gloom. "Are you wanting a tattoo?"

"No," Blaze said. "Just a ghemph. Or, perhaps, one of the elder ghemphs."

There was a short silence. Then, "I am one of the elders here."

Blaze slid to the ground and handed the reins to me. Wordlessly she held out her right hand, palm upward, to the shadowy figure that stood in front of one of the houses. She raised the lantern to illuminate whatever it was she held. I caught a flash of gold. The ghemph looked and hissed in a breath of surprise. Whatever it was she'd shown him, she had astonished the breath out of him, but he made no move to take the offering. "Who did that?" he asked. I actually hadn't the faintest idea of his gender, and my sense of smell told me nothing. Ghemphs had no real odor; they were as neutral as morning dew.

"Eylsa," she said. "Who also honored me with her spirit name."

"An honor indeed," he whispered. "And you have come to tell me of her death."

"Er, yes. Did . . . did you know her?"

"She was not my pod-sibling. We never met."

Blaze nodded, but I'm not sure that she understood. She said, "It is late. I have many things to say, but perhaps they can wait till morning. Is there somewhere we can shelter for the night?"

He seemed taken aback, as if she had asked for something beyond his ability to supply, but he said finally, "There's the barn, yonder." He nodded to a structure we could just see at the back of the houses.

"That will be fine."

"There's some feed and water for your beast there. Do you have water for yourselves?" he asked as he led us up to the building and opened the door.

"Sufficient for tonight," she replied.

"Then I will bid you goodnight." He bowed and melted away into the darkness. I did not see which house he entered, if any. I had not seen him well in the dark, but it seemed to me that he had been wet, and that what I had taken to be clothing was no more than a loin cloth or a towel. Which seemed odd. Why had he been taking a bath outside in the dark?

The barn was large enough for us to bed down on straw, and for Skandor to be sheltered as well. There were a couple of goats and numerous chickens, and once the latter had recovered from the nervous shock of being sniffed at by a large canine, we all managed to settle down for the night. Just before I closed my eyes, I said, "That *is* your dog, isn't it? Because he's not mine."

Blaze laughed in the darkness. "Yes. That's Seeker. He's half Fen Island lurger, a water canine."

"Huh. Just thought I'd check."

Flame grunted. "See, Blaze? He doesn't much like the oversized flea-hound either."

"Ingrates," she said indignantly. "That animal bit numerous Fellih-worshippers on our behalf today."

I supposed she was right at that. But it didn't make the beast any more appealing.

I WOKE LONG BEFORE DAWN FROM A TORtured dream I couldn't remember, didn't *want* to remember. Skies, the reality was bad enough. That look she had given me. The moment when the stone had hit. The *sound* of it, the smell of her blood. And she was gone, by my hand, the fragile wisp of her that was life, now no more.

Jastriá. How could I have failed her so badly?

I unrolled from the tagaird I was using as a blanket and went outside. It had rained some time during the night and the air had freshened. There were even patches of clear sky, with stars shining. It was a double moon month, and I walked in the moonlight along a path beyond the last of the houses through the mangroves to the edge of the river. There was a jetty there, with steps leading down to the mud beneath, but no boat in sight. And no place to tie one up either, which was odd. There wasn't much water as it was low tide. I sat on the end of the jetty, surprised to find how much noise there was in the exposed mudflats: sounds of slithering, of snapping crab claws, of mud-skipper tails slapped in territorial warning, a hundred different messages I heard but couldn't interpret.

I tried to think what I'd done wrong; why I had never been able to help her. There didn't seem to be any answers and all I ended up doing was crying: great heaving sobs that came up from some dark place and ripped me apart.

Absorbed in my grief, I didn't scent Blaze's approach. Didn't hear her either; for a large woman she could pad as silently as a grass-lion through a meadow. I only knew that she was there when she slipped an arm around my shoulders as she sat next to me. She let me sob myself out, then handed me a kerchief to use. A practical woman. I needed it by then.

"I don't believe there was anything you could have done to save her," she said when I had finally calmed. "She wanted to die: it's as simple as that."

I felt stripped bare before her, and didn't care. I asked in a whisper, "But *why*?"

"Sometimes," she said carefully, as though she had thought deeply about this on other occasions, "sometimes there are people who are born into the wrong world. They strive to make sense of it, but can't. Some then seek a solution by trying to change the world: they are the revolutionaries. Then there are those who try to mold themselves to fit the expectations of others. They end up being as unhappy as a crab trying to walk straight because they are not true to themselves. Many of those, like Jastriá, finally run away, thinking that they will find a place that does not try to mold them to what they are not. This dream of freedom is usually an illusion, especially when they take their problem with them. Jastriá's problem was that she did not know how to control her own fate. Her tragedy was to be a woman without skills, for there are few chances for such a woman to escape. Men often have more options."

"What should I have done?" I asked, not really expecting a reply. The question was for me, not her, but she answered it anyway.

"The problem was not yours," she said, more in irritation than kindness. "It was hers. And in the end she could only find one way to solve it. That was her weakness, not yours."

"She spoke of this to you?" I was hurt. Jealous even.

"Yes, indirectly. We talked of many things. She knew she was about to die. She wanted someone to understand, and I was there."

I had a blinding moment of truth. "She could have gone with you, couldn't she? She could have escaped too. Ye offered it! Skies above, she *refused* the freedom ye offered."

Blaze looked at me with compassion. "Yes."

I shuddered, my whole body crying out against the thought. "All that afternoon, I ran around trying to find someone who would listen, someone who had the power to stop the stoning. A Menod patriarch. The Commander of the Guards. The Chamberlain. The Havenlord. And all the while she had the means to escape *and turned it down*." I felt an enormous bitterness toward Jastriá, and struggled with it. She was *dead*: how could I be angry with her? But I could, and was.

"It was her choice," Blaze said.

I stared at her, channeling my anger at someone who deserved it least. "Ye couldna persuade her? Did ye even *try*?"

Her eyes flashed, but she answered calmly. "I threatened to knock her unconscious and carry her out over my shoulder. She said if I came near her, she would scream and tell the guards I had a lock-pick and a sword. So I let her be. She wanted to die more than I wanted her to live, and that's a truth."

It was too; my nose confirmed her honesty.

It took me a while to put into words something that had been nagging at the back of my mind: a canker that wouldn't go away, no matter how much I tried to ignore it. "I canna help thinking that . . . that she wanted me to be the one to kill her because . . . because—" But I couldn't put the thought into words. It was too terrible.

At first she didn't know what I was talking about. Then she looked startled. "You mean, not because she was afraid of the pain, but just in order to hurt you?"

I nodded and tried to explain, aware all the while that I was talking to a woman who carried a sword that was quite obviously not an ornamental item of dress. "To kill another person is the worst thing that one of the Skyfolk can do. It is the one crime that is punishable by permanent exile. We dinna even slay the mice on the Sky Plains. Even worse for *me* to do so, because I am a physician, a healer, dedicated to *saving* life." My voice dropped to a whisper. I could barely get the words out. "Killing her has . . . has blemished my soul. Blemished it forever. She *must* have known it would do that. Blaze, what did I do to her that was so terrible she thought I *deserved* this?"

She considered that and I could smell the contempt that tinged those thoughts. She believed I was taking Jastriá's tragedy and turning it into my own, for some perverted reasons of my twisted soul. She did not say: this isn't *your* tragedy, you bastard, but I saw the sentiment there in her eyes, I smelled it on her skin. Her contempt had an aroma like burning oil.

I didn't blame her. She didn't know me, she didn't know Jastriá, she didn't know the Skyfolk, she quite possibly killed people for a living, and she hadn't seen the last look that Jastriá gave me in the seconds before she died. In her last moments, Jastriá had been triumphant, and it was the kind of triumph that a winner displays to taunt a hated opponent. She had believed that she had won a battle I hadn't even known was being fought. I felt gutted.

In my heart I knew that I had to find the answer to the question I had asked Blaze. Even with it, I was not sure I would ever know any peace; without it, the pain would never end.

I didn't know then, of course, that there would come a time when the death of one woman would seem paltry; a triviality, when compared to the thousands of innocents who were to die, and die horribly, by my hand. I, who had never wanted to kill at all, ended up killing more people than anyone has ever been able to count. The peace I sought after Jastriá's death became an elusive dream that has tormented me for a lifetime.

I WENT BACK INTO THE BARN TO FETCH
Skandor and bring him out to feed. I took him along the river-

bank some distance and tethered him in a spot where I was sure he wouldn't be seen either from the road or the river. By the time I returned, the ghemphs were up and about, and one of them was talking to Blaze and Flame. I wasn't sure whether it was the same one we had met the night before; it was hard to tell. They all dressed the same way, and there was not all that much difference between them. They had a grayish cast to their skins which became progressively darker from the head downward until the bare webbed feet, which were a deep charcoal color. They had no hair anywhere on their bodies, and I could never sort out which of them was male and which female. Some had more wrinkles than others; whether that meant they were therefore older I could only guess.

As I came up, Blaze turned to me and said politely, "Kelwyn, this ghemph is the most senior elder of the enclave. I'm sorry, I don't know your family name to introduce you properly. Jastriá only referred to you as Kelwyn."

"Gilfeather."

Her eyebrows shot up. "You wouldn't be related to *Garrowyn* Gilfeather, would you?"

"Skies, ye know my uncle?"

She started to laugh. "Jumping catfish, I've only ever met two Mekaté Plainsmen in my life and they happen to be *related*?"

I shrugged. "The wonder of it is that ye met *any* Plainsmen. Verra few of us come down from the Roof of Mekaté. If ye were going to meet one, then either my uncle or I would be likely candidates. We come down because we are both physicians, in search of medicines and herbs."

"You don't have his thick accent."

"I prefer to be understood when I am away from the Sky Plains. Uncle Garrowyn is a contrary old buzzard who prefers to confound." I turned to the ghemph. "I must thank ye for the use of your barn. I shall leave now; I have no wish to bring trouble down on your heads and I'm thinking I'm not popular in Mekatéhaven this morning."

The ghemph held up his hand. "We would be honored if you would linger long enough to partake of our morning meal. We have cooked especially to suit the taste of humans."

I blinked and looked at Blaze, wondering what in the world

she had shown the ghemph the night before to warrant all this. Ghemphs hardly spoke to humans, and when they did, it was out of the necessity of business, not social conventions. In their speech they were usually monosyllabic, not convoluted. And they *never* invited people in to eat.

Blaze, blandly innocent, returned my look. "I'm sure he can, er, linger a while longer."

I should have refused. I should have just said my good-byes and gone. I opened my mouth to do so, in fact, but Blaze got in first. She said to me, "I never really did introduce myself. My name's Blaze Halfbreed, born citizenless in The Hub, on the Keeper Isles. My friend is Flame Windrider of Cirkase. And I am truly sorry for what we have done to you."

I looked at her then, really looked at her, for the first time. She was a large woman, broad-shouldered, with a mass of shoulder-length hair worn plaited at the nape. I count myself a tall man, but she was taller. No one would have called her beautiful, but she had a presence that commanded respect, and those eyes of hers were far too shrewd to be anything but disconcerting. She may have apologized for involving me in her affairs, but she did not look apologetic.

"Sorry? Ye would do exactly the same thing again," I said bluntly, and knew it for a truth.

Flame opened her mouth to say something indignant, but that blessed bird was back on her shoulder and when it jumped about, chirping, she closed her mouth. The bird and I looked at each other and a shiver went up my spine. I wanted to get out of there as fast as I could.

I turned back to the ghemph to say so, only to find that we were suddenly surrounded by ghemphs. They had brought out chairs and a table and were covering it with dishes of steaming food. Before I knew it, I was gently coaxed into sitting down and something hot was poured into a mug and shoved into my hand. I gestured in protest, spilling much of the drink over the table, but all the ghemphs except two had vanished. One, the elder I had been introduced to, sat down opposite Blaze; the other slipped into the seat next to me.

"What is it you want to know?" the elder asked without preamble.

I stopped protesting and started to clean up the mess I had

made, using the seaweed napkin beside my plate. At least, I thought it was a napkin; later I saw the ghemph next to me nibbling at his, so maybe it wasn't.

Blaze put her mug down, and that was when I saw the palm of her hand. There was an inlay of gold in the skin there, a curlicue of some kind, undeniably the work of a ghemph tattooist. That must have been what she'd shown him the night before. I was still gazing at it, wondering just what I had got myself into, when Blaze replied, "I am looking for a dunmagicker of great power. One of the names he uses is Morthred, Red Death, and the last I heard he was heading for Mekaté. Apparently he has an enclave of dunmagickers somewhere in the islandom. Many of them are subverted sylvs: he has the power to change the silver-blue magic to dun-red. To make dunmagickers out of sylvs."

The ghemph did not look happy, but he didn't look surprised either. "What is your interest in such occurrences?" he asked at last.

"We wish to stop him. We have . . . scores of a private nature to settle, but there is more to it than that. He must be stopped before he gains more power to do greater damage. He hankers after political position and came within a lobster's whisker of achieving ascendancy over Castlemaid Lyssal, the heir to the Cirkase Islands. He also tried to murder Ransom Holswood, the heir to the Bethany Isles." She paused a moment to drink from the mug and her eyes glazed over in shock. At a guess, whatever was in it tasted awful. I had been about to drink mine, and hastily put it back on the table untouched.

"Isn't this task more suited to the sylvs of the Keeper Isles?" the ghemph asked.

"They are also interested in finding the dunmagicker, of course. But only the Awarefolk can bring him down, because only the Awarefolk are not affected by dunmagic. Only the Awarefolk can *see* dunmagic."

"And you are one of the Awarefolk?"

"I am. Flame is sylv."

I listened to all this with growing skepticism. My uncle Garrowyn had often regaled the children of the Sky Plains with tales of magic, of the sylvs who tricked people with illusions and healed the sick with their minds; and of the wicked dunmagickers he had met and vanquished on his travels. I'd grown out of believing such tales.

"And why do you think we ghemphs can aid you?"

"Because when people live too far away from your enclaves and cannot bring their newborn to you for tattooing, you go to them. There is not a remote place in the whole of the Isles of Glory that you do not visit—except Gorthan Spit. You are in the best position to notice anything that is not . . . right. Not as it should be."

He inclined his head, acknowledging that as a truth. "We do not normally concern ourselves with the affairs of men. We make the tattoos for your citizens so that your rulers can impose their rules and their laws, but these things are not our . . . not our domain. All we have ever wanted is to be left alone."

Flame spoke for the first time. "Do you really believe they, the dunmagickers, will leave ghemphs alone if they are in positions of power? Eylsa was killed by dunmagickers. Murdered. They don't like anything or anyone they can't control. You ghemphs are too independent, and they would see that as a threat. Besides, Blaze told me you can't be magicked. They hate people they can't magick."

Blaze, holding up her marked hand, added, "This is what Eylsa made with her blood as she lay dying. I think you know that must be a truth."

The ghemph elder didn't reply.

Flame sipped her drink, apparently without ill-effect, and ate heartily from several of the dishes. I forced myself to take some food: it tasted vaguely of what I imagined was fish and, as far as I could discern, mangrove mud. When I tried to wash it down with the contents of the mug, I almost choked. At a guess it was vinegar, flavored with seaweed.

The second ghemph, the one sitting next to me, turned to Blaze and said quietly, "Eylsa was my pod-sister. We grew up together. I wish to thank you on behalf of the pod for the care you must have bestowed on her in order for her to honor you as she did. We would breach for you."

Blaze looked blank. "Breach?"

"We would honor you."

"It was I who was honored," Blaze said. "I have lost a true friend." It was hard to believe that such a statement could be true, and yet Blaze's distress was real: I smelled it, as potent as whatever it was I had just drunk. She genuinely grieved for the ghemph, for a being of another race, beings that, as far as I knew, had always kept themselves aloof from human attachments.

"Porth," the ghemph elder said suddenly. "It has to be Porth."

Blaze frowned. The name obviously meant something to her.

"Where's that?" Flame asked.

"It's an island off the northeast coast. I killed a dunmagicker there . . . oh, about seven or eight years ago," Blaze replied, sounding offhand, as if she were mentioning that it rained a lot, or something equally innocuous. "He had set himself up as the island's governor. He even started a school for young dunmagickers on mainland Mekaté, which we had to clean out a year or two later. Some of them escaped and we never did find them. What have you been hearing from Porth?"

The ghemph frowned. "Rumors mostly. One of our folk was at a place called the Floating Mere, in order to tattoo babies at the villages around the lake there. She said the people were frightened. They spoke of all sorts of things: of lake spirits, of strangers, of a village on a lake island that no one heard from anymore."

"She went there, to the island?"

"Oh, yes, of course. It was her duty, you understand. She found no children, none at all. The villagers were sullen and asked her to leave. She was glad to do so; she said the place was full of wrongness. It is the only place I have heard about where there has been an occurrence of . . . oddity."

Blaze's frown deepened. "Eylsa told me magic does not affect ghemphs, but can you see it? Would that ghemph tattooist have seen dunmagic enslavement, for example?"

"We do not see the colors or smell the magic the way the Aware do. But she should have sensed its . . . vibration. However, she is very young. It was her first journey, and it is possible she did not realize what it was that she felt."

"Thank you. I think we need to go there. But we have a slight problem with the Fellih-priests in Mekatéhaven, which might make it difficult for us to leave here by boat. Is there an overland route to some other port besides Mekatéhaven?"

The ghemphs both looked at me.

Reluctantly, I said, "The only way is up onto the Roof and down the other side, to Niba Water. There's a port there called Lekenbraig, and a packet boat that goes to Porth from there."

As if on cue, Flame and Blaze both smiled.

"Oh, nay," I said, looking from one to the other. "No. Absolutely no. I'm not taking the two of you *anywhere*!"

A letter from Researcher (Special Class) S. iso Fabold, National Department of Exploration, Federal Ministry of Trade, Kells, to Masterman M. iso Kipswon, President of the National Society for the Scientific, Anthropological and Ethnographical Study of non-Kellish Peoples.

Dated this day 49/2nd Single/1793

Dear Uncle,

Thank you for the note. To answer your question: yes, to hear Gilfeather talk so casually of his meeting with ghemphs was indeed a shock, and probably one of the most cogent arguments that ghemphs were real and not a part of the cultural imagination. Gilfeather is, after all, a man of science, a medic, and for all his Plainsman upbringing in a remote mountain area, a man of education and learning. And yet, we still need to explain why we see no ghemphs in the Glory Isles now, why—if they did exist—they left behind no artifacts, why there are no written records with regard to them, why people are reluctant to speak of them. As I have said before, the matter needs more study.

As for your second question: no, I did not personally speak to any of the Fellih-faithful. They are, in fact, rather rare nowadays, as the cult has lost favor. Even the Mekatéen Havenlord has, I believe, curtailed their power. My feeling is that Tor Ryder, as his own influence increased, had a lot to do with that. But more of that later.

On a personal note, I spent the week before last with Anyara in County Assels. We stayed with her aunt and uncle (Sheveron i. Trekald, whom I think you know), after which I returned to the city to continue organization of the new voyage. I haven't received the letter of appointment yet, but have been asked to proceed with arrangements, so I assume it will come. Nathan has agreed to return to the Isles as my translator, but I am having difficulty finding an artist. Anyara, bless her, of-

fered her services! Of course, I would never countenance such a thing, even if we married first. The journey is too rigorous for one of the fair sex. She is, however, just as excited as I am about the idea of new explorations of the Isles of Glory, even though I do believe she will miss me. She has made me promise that if I do go, I will see Blaze again, if she is still alive.

I must cut this short: someone has just delivered a packet of papers. Forms I must fill in, in triplicate, for the order of scientific supplies. I am having a new spyglass made, and one of these new-fangled magnifying tubes as well, for looking at plant specimens and insects.

Warmest regards to Aunt Rosris.

Your dutiful nephew,
Shor iso Fabold

CHAPTER 4

"THAT WAS THE WORST MEAL I'VE EVER had in my life," Blaze remarked as we trekked upward from the foot of the Scarps. "If that's what ghemphs believe our cuisine is like, I think I'd rather have theirs."

"I've heard they eat everything raw," Flame replied. "Bones and all. But I didn't think the food was all that bad. The drink was odd-tasting, that's all."

"*Not all that bad?* Flame, it was vile! You have the palate of a bottom-feeding catfish!"

"Nonsense. My palate was nurtured by the best palace chefs in Cirkasecastle. And look who's talking anyway. I saw you eat lugworms stewed with jellyfish tentacles when we were at Cape Kan!"

"I was hungry. After a couple of days at sea on the back of a sea-pony, any eating-house at all looked good to me, and that was the only one there was."

"And it only had one dish on the menu, I noticed. And *you* should have noticed that I did *not* partake of it!"

I had finally realized that their casually flung insults were actually friendly banter. It had taken me a while to wake up to that; it was not a conversational style that was popular on the Sky Plains. Fortunately, however, my family circle did include Garrowyn Gilfeather who—with what I assumed to be a certain amount of avuncular affection mixed in with the exasperation—had been known to call me "a fire-headed gangling disaster with two left feet and all the dexterity of a selver learning to tat milk-jug covers."

Blaze and Flame, I decided, were lovers. I could scent their affection for one another. It did not worry me; on the Sky Plains, such relationships were not regarded as something sinful. It happened, it was accepted, and perhaps the only universal attitude was one of mild pity. To have children was considered a great joy for Plainsfolk, and the fact that some couples were unable to have that joy because of the nature of their coupling was considered sad for all concerned.

I was far more worried about my personal situation. I could scarcely believe that I had somehow become entangled in such a mess. And things had worsened before we left the ghemph enclave. I had intended to head off up the Scarps, alone. I had planned to travel as quickly as possible on Skandor before the Fellih-guards were able to cut me off. But in the end, we all left the ghemphic enclave together in a desperate hurry, just ahead of pursuit.

While we were still eating the ghemphic breakfast, a youngster rushed up shouting something in their incomprehensible tongue. The ghemph elder translated quickly, even as he hustled us away from the table: "There's a group of Fellih-guards sailing up the inlet on the tide and they have some of the Havenlord's troops with them."

I didn't wait. I didn't even say thank you. I raced across to the barn, picked up my pack and Skandor's saddle, and headed straight for where I'd tethered the selver. When I took a quick look over my shoulder it was to see Flame and Blaze pounding after me, and Seeker lolloping after them. The boat was not yet in sight, so there was a good chance we'd be able to flee unnoticed.

I suppose I could have leaped on the selver and just left them behind. It occurred to me, though, that if I did, they would probably be captured. And if they were caught, who knew what story they would tell of my involvement in their jail-break. As it was, once I was up in the saddle, I hesitated just long enough for Blaze to catch my arm and haul herself up behind me. I hid a sigh and waited for Flame as well.

Fortunately, I knew the general area as I had often collected medicinal plants around there. I guided Skandor into the forest at a trot and we didn't slow down until I was sure there was no pursuit. When we emerged onto a narrow track that ran through bamboo groves, I brought Skandor down to a walk. I insisted on silence, more because I just wasn't in the mood for talk than for reasons of security, but I didn't tell them that.

The bamboo was routinely cut by village folk for poles, but we did not see anyone that day. About three hours later, when we reached the canopied forest on the other side, we refilled our drinkskins at a forest stream. I dug up some tuber roots we could roast later on, because none of us had any food in our packs. Four hours later we were climbing up the track that led to the Roof, where, simply by looking down, we could be sure there was no one following us. We had all dismounted by then, and I rested Skandor by leading him—and that was when Flame and Blaze started up their conversation about ghemphic food.

Flame was finding the climb tough. She obviously wasn't used to a life of hardship. Her one remaining hand was soft and white, not the hand of a woman who'd done the housework or tilled the fields. I wondered just how long ago she'd had her other arm amputated. I'd seen the stump that morning when she washed at a stream, and it looked as if it had been healed several months.

I wanted to stride out ahead, leave them behind and be darned to them both, but the physician in me was made of softer stuff. I suspected that the Cirkasian was by no means fully recovered from whatever trauma she had been through. There was something in her eyes, a bruised look, that said more even than the way she lagged behind. And then there were the traces of pain I smelled behind that enigmatic aroma of hers. She had been hurt, and hurt badly, in ways that had nothing to do with her physical trauma. She constantly chatted to that bird of hers until I wondered if she was quite sane.

When we came out onto a grassy ledge where Skandor could feed, I called a halt. Flame gratefully flung herself down on the grass. Blaze was far more cautious. I saw her looking around, studying the ledge, visually surveying the trail up, gazing down on the way we had come. Only then did she unstrap her sword. She didn't take chances, that woman, and I wondered about her history. She was much more inscrutable than Flame: most of the time I had no sense of her. She was one of the few downscarpers I'd ever met who could, if she wished, contain her feelings so deep no scent of them leaked into the air.

I took our bags from Skandor's saddle, loosened the saddle girth and turned the animal free to graze. "We'll stay here an hour," I said and then went to look over the edge. We were already high above the coastal strip and the excrescence that was Mekatéhaven. From this height it was possible to see the scars on the land that they had made with their city and their quarries and their mines and their forest plundering. There was a pall of filthy air drifting over the buildings and out to sea; where the river disgorged itself into the ocean, there was a swathe of muddy water slicing knife-edged into the blue before opening into a fan of brown curds.

"They make a mess, don't they?" Blaze said at my side.

Flame rolled over on the grass to have a look. "Great Trench below, I've never been up this high before in my life. Everything is so *small*! Are we almost at the top?"

I shook my head. "Ye're not even halfway. We will have to sleep along the track somewhere."

She shuddered. "I hope we can find a decent-sized ledge then. I'd hate to roll off during the night. Blaze, I told you we should have taken a boat. I could have used illusion—"

"That would have weakened you."

"And climbing a bloody big mountain doesn't?"

Blaze ignored her. "How long will it take us to get to the other side of the Roof of Mekaté, and down to the coast?"

"Depends on whether ye have selvers to cross the Plains," I said. "Ten days on foot across the top maybe, if ye kept the pace up. And then another couple of days to get down to the port, Lekenbraig."

"We have coin to hire beasts."

"The money ye stole from the card players," I said flatly.

"That's right." She looked at me, curious. "They were rich, spoiled brats who needed a lesson. Money meant little to them and I had no qualms about transferring some of it to us when we were penniless and hungry. I was cheating, you know, even before Flame stole the money, although I doubt that I needed to. They were charnel-rotten card players." She quirked her head at me and held my gaze with a flat look. "Are you really an upright man, Kelwyn Gilfeather, or are you just another righteous hypocrite?"

I tried hard to quell my anger. "We dinna steal in the Sky Plains. And ye will find it hard to buy anything either. We dinna use money."

Her disbelief was obvious.

"Why use money when there is naught to buy?" I asked by way of explanation. "Everything is supplied when needed. If I need a new tagaird, someone will weave me one. When the weaver's children are sick, I will tend them. When a bridge needs repair, the whole tharn will come to do it. And when we have need of something only available downscarp, then we can apply for money from our Sky Plains treasury to buy it."

"Where does that money come from?" Blaze asked, still skeptical.

"Tharns sell their excess wool downscarp."

"Tharn?" Flame asked.

"Village, I supposed ye'd call it. Ten houses grouped together. A tharn is the unit that runs a thousand selver, one hundred animals to each house. Usually ten people to a house. So, there are about one hundred Plainsfolk to a tharn."

"And a tagaird?" Flame persisted.

I fingered the length of twilled material I wore over my trews and shirt. It served instead of a coat or shawl, and doubled as a rain-cloak or blanket when needed. "This. The garb of the Plainsfolk, worn by men and women. Old-fashioned folk like my Uncle Garrow wear only undergarments beneath, but I prefer it worn with trews."

"Selver wool," Blaze said, fingering the cloth.

I nodded. "This particular twill pattern marks the owner as

someone from the Gilfeather House. And the combination of dark green and red is unique to my tharn."

She raised her eyes as she took in the implications of that. "Hard to be anonymous on the Plains, eh? So tell me, how do we survive upon the Roof of Mekaté if we cannot buy what we need?"

"If they like ye and trust ye, they will give or lend ye what ye need. If they don't like you, then ye'll be escorted to the scarp edge and told to leave."

"Garrowyn said it was paradise."

I raised a disbelieving eyebrow. I knew my uncle.

"He also said that paradise has to have rules. And one man's paradise can be another man's hell," she added.

That sounded more like him. "My uncle always did gab too much. He only ever stays at home for a month or two at a time. And then he is off again. That in itself runs counter to custom. They make an exception for him because of his healing skills; he *says* he travels the world to enrich his medical knowledge. I suspect it's more because he finds the Plains too restricting. However, he teaches us much each time he returns, so his eccentricities are tolerated." I paused, then elaborated. "The truth of the matter is that we live in a fragile place and we only survive because we have restrictions, rules we must follow. Aye, 'tis paradise, but a paradise we could destroy in a moment if everyone did as he wanted. That's the paradox of the Sky Plains. Paradise comes at a price, and a few would say that the price is hell."

When I finished, they were both silent. Then Flame held up her amputated arm. "Tell me, Kelwyn," she said, changing the subject, "what do you see?"

I didn't know what she meant. "Your arm?"

She nodded.

"It has been amputated above the elbow. Not so verra long ago. It has healed well."

Flame looked at Blaze. "See, I told you."

I don't know what she did next, but she did something, because Blaze flinched away as if someone had thrown something at her head. The only thing I was aware of was an intensified aroma around Flame. She always smelled to me: a sort of perfumed sweetness that was tantalizing because I could never quite name it. Right then, it was strong, almost sickly, but I still couldn't say what it reminded me of, if anything.

"He's Aware," Flame said. "He knew my arm was an illusion. And yet he didn't see the sylv ball I just tossed at him. He didn't duck."

"*I* did, though," Blaze said and frowned. "I saw the magic around it, and that was enough to make me want to dodge. He didn't see anything at all. He didn't even blink." She looked at me in wonderment.

"What ball?" I asked.

Flame shook her head, disbelieving. "He saw nothing? Not the illusion, nor the sylv glow? What kind of person is that?"

"A rational human being?" I suggested.

"He can't be faking it, can he?" Flame asked, apparently still dubious.

I gritted my teeth. "Ye know something? I am finding it verra irritating to be talked about as if I didna exist. And I am beginning to think the both of you are mist-mad. I dinna believe in magic because there is no such thing. Ye're both too old to believe in spells and the reality of superstitions and myths and legends. Next ye'll be telling me the Dustels disappeared because of the actions of a dunmagicker, as the coastal storytellers say."

The bird on Flame's shoulder flew straight at me, chittering.

"Ruarth!" Flame admonished. It flew back to her shoulder and sat there. I swear it glowered at me.

Blaze smiled in my direction. "Watch where you put your feet, Gilfeather: try to keep them out of your mouth. Ruarth is a Dustel Islander. He doesn't take kindly to the contention that there are no dunmagickers. In fact, we all believe that this particular dunmagicker we are chasing is the actual sod who sank the Dustel Islands beneath the sea."

"Blaze!" exclaimed Flame. "You shouldn't be telling him about the Dustel Island birds!"

Blaze gave her a broad grin. "What does it matter? He doesn't believe a word of it!"

I'd had it with them both. They were making fun of me, and I didn't deserve that from either of them. I scrambled to my feet. "Time to get going again."

Flame groaned. "That wasn't a full hour," she complained.

"Probably not," I agreed and smiled in a way that must have resembled the grin of a hungry grass-lion. "I just canna bear to listen to your inane conversation any more."

I spoiled the line by forgetting that I had loosened Skandor's saddle girth. The saddle slipped as I mounted and I ignominiously measured my length on the ground.

I tended to do things like that. A lot.

BY THE TIME WE HAD FOUND A PLACE TO camp that night, it was raining. Not hard, just continuously. I managed to get a fire going in a hastily constructed rock fireplace. For fuel, I pulled out some old selver dung from the mats of grass around us. I roasted the tubers and we had a substantial meal, if a bland one. The only means we had of keeping the rain off, though, was the thin waterproof cover I had in my pack, made of felted and oiled selver wool. It was made for one person, not three, so we had to sit close together, knees up, backs to a rock, with the cover rigged overhead. It was a situation that invited serious talk, so I was unsurprised when Flame said, "I really am sorry about your wife, Kelwyn. And sorry that we made such a mess of things for you. Is there nothing we can do to help put things right? Maybe we could write a letter once we are safely off-island."

"Naïve, Flame," Blaze interrupted. I had the idea that she used that word quite often where Flame was concerned. "They are hardly going to take much notice of a letter from a jail-breaker and her female accomplice telling them we forced Gilfeather here to help us."

Flame sighed. "No, I suppose not."

Blaze turned to me. "Would they really come after you, all the way up here? Or is it just us they are after?"

"Oh aye, they'd come. It's me they want as much as you two."

When she looked skeptical, I explained, "Ye've got to understand the relationship we selver-herders have with the authorities on the coast. We pay tax to the Havenlord, in the form of cloth that we weave from the first shearing of the season's selver kids. The wool is fine; they call it wool-silk and it's verra much sought after." I fingered the sleeve of my shirt.

"This is wool-silk. In return, we are left alone. No one is permitted to set foot upon the Roof without our agreement. We apply our own laws, handle our own affairs, educate our own children. Of course, once a year the ghemphs come up to tattoo our newborns. There is a catch though; we have an understanding that the moment any of our folk go down the Scarps, they are treated like any other coastal citizen, and they canna expect to run to the Roof for sanctuary either, if they do something wrong.

"But it's more than that too. In a strange sort of way, the coastal folk are wary of us. They fear us. We are taller than they are, stronger in build. We are uncanny to them, with our red hair and beards, our fair skins and odd way of speaking, and what they regard as our godless ways, for we worship no gods. Most of the land of Mekaté belongs to us, not them. They live around the fringe of this island, clinging to the coast as precariously as ferns on a cliff side. They seem to want constant reassurance that we will not come rampaging down off the Roof to sweep them into the ocean.

"So, aye, they would come after me, even if ye were not with me, as a matter of principle. And once they have me, they will enforce the law to the limit. I knew that for certain from the moment the ghemph told me that the Fellih-guards had the Havenlord's men with them. The Havenlord is backing the Fellih-worshippers. And they were quick too: they must have made a decision last night to sail after us in the hope that they could cut us off."

Flame swore, using a lewd expression that had me blinking in surprise. She was oblivious to my reaction and added, "This really is rotten, then. I am sorry."

"They can't have known we'd be in the ghemphic village, surely?" Blaze protested.

"No, of course not. It's just that the village landing there is the closest one to this upscarp trail. Doubtless other guards looked for us elsewhere."

Flame's pet bird, now sitting on her knee, chirruped. She said, "Ruarth wants to know what you'll do now. Will your people hide you?"

"I don't know. And dinna ask me to believe in talking birds," I said in disgust. "Just because I come from a nation of herders doesna make me stupid, or poorly educated, or gullible."

There was a moment's silence. Then she said in tones that sounded dangerously taut, "And just because I talk to a bird makes me neither a liar nor mad. Maybe I will find it hard to prove that I understand Ruarth, but I can prove that *he* understands *you*." The smell of her anger blasted me.

"Watch it, Flame," Blaze said, and I felt her amusement, "a while back you didn't want him to know about Dustel birds . . ."

But I had riled the Cirkasian and there was no stopping her now. "Well, it's time he found out. We're going to be traveling together."

"Ach, nay, we're not!" I said.

She went on relentlessly, but she was talking to Blaze, not me. "Blaze, we've wrecked his life. He's got to come with us, what else can he do? We have to help him, and maybe he can help us. After all, he's impervious to sylvmagic. Maybe he is to dunmagic too." She turned back to me. "Tell Ruarth to do something. Something a bird can do, of course. Anything at all."

I looked back at the bird. The sun had not yet completely set and I could see him well enough. He regarded me with a bright blue eye and cocked his head. "Verra well," I said, never doubting that I could thwart whatever trick she had in mind. "Flame, close your eyes and stay absolutely still and quiet. You too, Blaze." Flame shrugged and did as I asked. Blaze grinned in appreciation of the precaution and did likewise. I said, "Ruarth, fly down to my left hand and peck me five times."

He didn't wait. And he didn't restrain himself either. My left hand was resting on my knee and he pecked at it savagely. Five times. Then he stood there and looked at me, while my carefully thought-out world came crashing down around my ears for the second time in two days.

"Oh dear," said Flame contritely, when she opened her eyes and noted the blood he had drawn. "Ruarth, that was not nice." She looked at me apologetically.

Beside me, Blaze started to laugh.

CHAPTER 5

NARRATOR : KELWYN

TO BE HONEST, I TRIED NOT TO THINK about Ruarth at all. Or sylvmagic. Or dunmagic.

I slept fitfully and, once we started upward the next morning, I strode off ahead of the women, hauling Skandor behind me, and didn't wait for them when they dropped behind. Blaze, of course, could have kept up with me easily, but she matched Flame's pace. I preferred to walk on without either of them. Occasionally the dog, Seeker, would gambol up, all feet and lolling tongue, to check on me, but other than that I was alone with my thoughts. With Jastriá. With that last look she had given me.

I arrived at the top of the Scarps about mid-morning. It was still misty, which was normal up on the Plains. It hadn't dissipated even by the time Blaze and Flame caught up.

"Do we wait for it to clear?" Blaze asked, looking ahead into the whiteness. The darn woman wasn't even breathing hard.

"Ye could be here for days. Nay, we'll walk on."

"But there doesn't appear to be a path."

"There isn't. There are no paths on the Plains. No roads. No tracks."

"*None?*"

"None. Except for a few stepping stones going from house to house in each tharn. In fact, while ye are here, ye must abide by our customary rules. Don't walk in the footprints of the person in front. This is to make sure that no track is ever made."

Flame's eyes widened. "What's the matter with tracks?"

"As I said before, this is a fragile place. Only meadow grasses and sedges grow here, and it rains often, sometimes verra heavily. If there is no grass, all the soil is washed away. Erosion is the true enemy of the Plains. So we dinna make paths. Ye will not walk behind me, but beside, and ye will take care not to scar the land."

She looked apprehensively into the mist. "That's all very well, but how do we find our way?"

I pointed. "My tharn is five hours' selver ride, at a canter, that way. Even in the thickest of mists I wouldna lose my way, because I can smell it."

"Does it smell so very bad?" she asked innocently.

I was completely unable to tell if she was serious or teasing. "It dinna smell bad at all. It smells of roasting bread, and dried selver dung burning sweetly in the fireplaces; it smells of the flower dyes our neighbors mix for the wools; it smells of the griddle cakes my sister-in-law has just cooked on the stove top."

"And you smell all that through the mist?"

"I'm joking. It's too far to smell aught. Tharn Wyn is more than a day's walk from here, and we will be traveling at a walking pace even if we take it in turns to ride Skandor. Plainsmen have good noses, but not that good." The smell of those griddle cakes was tantalizing. I was hungry already, but I wasn't about to give too much away.

"So, how *do* you find your way through the mist?" Blaze asked.

"I know every blade of grass twixt here and home, I promise you. Flame, ye ride for a bit."

She winced, rubbing her thighs eloquently. "I'd rather walk. I can heal myself, but it's tiring."

I didn't like the look of the shadows under her eyes. "Ride," I said. "Ye'll find it much more comfortable when there's only one person on his back, not three."

She opened her mouth to protest, but Blaze supported me, and Flame rode. Blaze matched her steps to mine. "Can Plainsmen really smell better than other people?"

I shrugged noncommittally. "How would I know? I only know my own nose."

She persisted. "Tell me, what smell do you associate with Flame?"

"Sweetness," I said. "But today she hasna used her perfume. For which small mercy I am verra grateful."

"That's no perfume," she said, "that's sylvmagic. You don't smell it now because she has dropped the illusion of having a real left arm."

I winced. "Please. No more of this nonsense."

"A great many people believe in magic, Gilfeather."

"That dinna make it true. A great many people believe in the Fellih-Master, and believe that he would have been pleased by Jastriákyn's death. Dinna make it true."

"What *are* the religious beliefs of the Plainsfolk?"

"We have none, not really. We believe that we are part of the world. We believe we must hand it on to our descendants just the way we found it. When we die, we are buried and eventually become one with the land. That way, as part of the land, we bequeath ourselves to the care of our descendants. And, as part of the land that feeds them, so we will care for them in turn."

"No heaven, no hell? And you don't believe that it was a god, a creator, that put you here in the first place?"

"No. Why should it be a god? Or any being? We just are. We live, we die, and the cycle goes on. We look forward to the time when we are the land. We think of it not so much as a death, but as a gradual rebirth into the land that has nurtured us, and so into every birth that follows us. We believe in the consciousness of the land, of a kind that is unknowable to us until after death. Death is not an end, it's just a different state, so different that there is no point in even thinking about it."

"You believe that your ancestors are part of you now?"

"In a way."

"No worship, no gods, no temples, no patriarchs?"

"Nary a one."

"Sounds like my kind of religion." She smiled at me, but there was something wistful there, almost tragic. She shrugged it off and changed the subject. "Are you still denying Ruarth can understand us?"

I shook my head. "Nay. I'm no daft, I can see he does. And old Skandor here comes when I whistle. But that doesna make it magic. Maybe it's just that Ruarth's species is— different. So, there are sentient birds. I have no doubt there are many wonders in this world that I have not yet traveled far enough to see, and maybe many of those I will find hard to believe in too."

"You're a stubborn man, Kelwyn Gilfeather."

"I'm a physician, a man who studies the science of healing. I like to see the facts before I prescribe the medicine."

She glanced sideways to make sure that Flame and Skandor were not becoming lost in the mist. "You have not traveled far enough, herder. Not nearly far enough."

I grunted and brought the conversation to a close by pulling the end of my tagaird up over my head, against the dampness of the mist. There are many things one can say with a tagaird.

THE SUN BROKE THROUGH THE MIST JUST before we reached Wyn on the afternoon of the next day.

In a perverse way, I was glad of that, for it enabled me to show them that the Roof of Mekaté was one of the most beautiful places in all the Isles of Glory. I don't know why I wanted them to like my land, but I did. Perhaps it was simply to show Blaze Halfbreed that I, at least, didn't need to travel far to see the best of the world.

And the Roof of Mekaté was surely that. We called it the Sky Plains, but in reality the place was not flat. There were rolling hills and rocky creeks; crags and boulders sculpted by the wind and rain; there were vast meadows that bloomed with color, different colors for different times of the year. Right then, it was a sea of pink bells and gray catkins. As soon as the sun came out and the mist wisped away into nothingness, the white daisies growing in between the pink and gray opened their petals and it was as if the meadows were repainted before our eyes. Whenever scudding clouds covered the sun, the daisies closed in moving, living artistry.

We were at the top of the slope that led down to the stream known as Wyn Spill. The houses of Wyn were arranged along the stream, five on each side, the front doors just far enough away from the water to escape any storm flooding. The backs of the houses were built into the slopes in order to have the least possible impact on the landscape. The front room of each house projected out, but had a roof that was topped with sod and planted with the few grain and vegetable crops that Plains people cultivated. A stone footbridge crossed the stream from one side to the other, and there were stepping stones from one house to the next and leading to the bridge.

"That's it?" Blaze asked at my side. "That's Wyn?"

I felt piqued that she was unimpressed. "Aye, that's it. In fact, that's all ye will ever see here on the Roof of Mekaté. There are no towns, just tharns. And each has ten named Houses. And there's never more paths than those."

"Where are your selver herds?"

"Out grazing. We dinna bring them to the tharn, except for the few that we are milking. The herders look after them day and night, taking them from one area to another so that they dinna mark the landscape. We all do our share of herding." I turned to look at them. "Ye must be especially careful at the tharn not to damage the soil. Dinna leave the stone paths if ye go to visit another house."

"What about Seeker? Will he be welcome?" Blaze asked.

Flame snorted. "As if that walking mange-mat would be welcome anywhere."

I hesitated. "We dinna keep pets. And we dinna have the food for an animal as big as that. In fact, we dinna eat meat, as a rule."

Blaze rolled her eyes. "What *do* you eat, then?"

"Milk, cheese, curds, berries, nuts, sourdough from tuber flour, selver placenta in the birthing season—" Flame made a strange strangled noise, so I stopped. "It's verra good for ye," I told her.

"I'll bet," she said.

"Yeah," said Blaze, clapping her hands twice at Seeker. He

gave her a keen look, as though to see if she really meant it, and then slunk away.

The darn animal made me feel guilty. "I'm sorry."

"He's part lurger. They are hunting animals. He can look after himself."

We started down the hill, and one of the tharn children, the leatherman's son Haidwyn, saw us. He raced along to tell my household that I was home. I had no doubt that they already knew; it was a family joke that my mother could smell me from one side of the Plains to the other, but tharn children loved to be the first to spy visitors or returning travelers.

Even though I had only been gone six days, by the time we reached the front door, my whole family was gathered in the living hall to greet me. I went from one to the other, touching their cheeks with the back of my hand, in order of precedence, as was customary: my grandmother, my father, my mother, my uncle, my brother and his wife. The other two members of our House, my cousin and her husband, must have been on the rotated duty of herding the selvers. I turned to indicate Blaze and Flame. They stood awkwardly in the doorway behind me, feeling out of place, and doubtless absorbing the strangeness of the lacquered room with its sparse stone and wool furnishings.

"I have brought two downscarpers onto the Plains," I told my family, in formal declaration of my responsibility for Blaze and Flame. "They have need to cross the Roof on their way to Lekenbraig. This is Blaze Halfbreed, and that's Flame Windrider behind her." I didn't mention Ruarth, who sat unobtrusively silent on Flame's shoulder. I introduced my family by name and their relationship to me, ending by saying, "And I think ye both know my uncle, Garrowyn. Uncle, when did ye return? Ye must have passed me by in Mekatéhaven."

He gave that smile of his, with its lurking cynicism. "Aye. I spent a couple of weeks collecting plants on the coast on my way home. I arrived in Wyn yesterday. I understand ye went downscarp at the request of the Fellih-Exemplar, Kel." He inclined his head to Flame. "Glad to see ye're thriving, lass. Seems the butcher did a right good job there."

Flame frowned. "Butcher?"

Blaze interrupted; rather hurriedly, I thought, "Nice to see you again, Garrowyn. And I'm sure the state of Flame's arm has much to do with your skills."

Garrowyn gave a knowing smile and then turned to me. "What did the Fellih fanatics want, Kel?"

I paused to give them warning, to alert their senses, then said, "They have killed Jastriákyn for the crime of lying with one of their own."

The ripple of shock went through them all; I smelled the impact of it in them. Jastriá had been gone four years, but her absence had left a void that had never been filled, and created a thorn that had never stopped pricking. At least I could put an end to that now. I looked at my brother, Jaimwyn, and his wife, Tessrym. "Out of death comes rebirth. I will not bring another wife to this House; the birth is yours." Tessrym, who was already over thirty, started to cry and Jaim put his arm around her. I had granted them permission to have a child, relinquishing my own rights to the tenth place in our household for my own partner. At that moment, I did not think it a sacrifice, but still I felt the shriveling of hopes and dreams. I severed something with those words, and knew I would never get it back.

My grandmother smiled, a radiant smile that lit her face from within. " 'Tis well done, Kel. We grieve for ye, but a birthing will bring joy to this household."

I returned her smile, knowing how much it saddened her to know that her longevity was preventing others from having children. It was not unknown for an elder to walk out into the cold of a stormy night, hoping to end their life and thus bestow on loved descendants the right to conceive. It was not a fate any of us wanted for her.

My mother laid a sympathetic hand on my arm, enough to tell me of her love and concern, then turned to Blaze and Flame. "Come, your clothes are damp, I can see. I will lend ye both a dry tagaird and show ye where ye can wash and change. And by the time ye have done all that, there will be a meal on the table."

I nodded my thanks to her, acknowledging her hospitality. Then I, too, went to clean up.

As I looked around the room that had been Jastriá's and mine, I tried to see it through the eyes of strangers. The room itself was carved out of the hillside in two levels, each sprayed with lacquer to seal it. The lacquer came from the bones and horns of selvers and, after generations of annual respraying, was as hard as sword-steel, in spite of its soft honeyed glow. There was a window dug through to the outside hill slope, with panes of semi-translucent lacquer. There was no bed, but the upper level of the room, which was at hip height, was where the bedding was put: soft selver pelts and wool blankets. At the other end of this raised area was the pile of my extra tagaird, trews, shirts and undergarments. A simple room, with no adornments, no cupboards, no chairs. I wondered what Blaze and Flame would make of it. My mother had put them in my cousins' room, and it was identical.

Jaimwyn came in, bringing a washbowl and towel. "Ye'd better clean up here: the lasses are in the washroom."

"Thanks."

He noted my abstraction and said, "Ye're thinking of Jastriákyn."

I hadn't been, but I did the moment he spoke her name. I saw her in my mind's eye, draped voluptuously on the bedding, beckoning me; I smelled her sex and her passion once more, saw the way she had of tossing her hair and playing with her tagaird and the ties of her shirt in order to tempt me.

"Aye," I said. "There was a part of her that will be hard to forget."

"I appreciate your decision not to wed again yet. Are ye sure, lad?"

He often called me lad, doing it to tease. I was thirty, the elder of the two of us. "Aye. I'm no hankering to marry another."

"Ye should. 'Twas not the wedding that was at fault; 'twas the bride."

"Speak no ill of the dead, Jaimie."

"Nay, I'll no do that. 'Tis not ill I speak, but truth. She was wild, and she brought that side in ye to the fore. Ye would have settled better, had ye wed a different lass. Someone like my Tess."

I just stopped myself shuddering in time. Tess was outwardly attractive but she had the soul of a pedant, the imagination of a selver tick, and absolutely no sense of humor. The only thing that made Tessrym smile was the sight of a well-cooked dish, or a well-woven cloth. Quickly I stripped off my tagaird and shirt, and bent to wash.

He continued, oblivious, "I love ye dearly, brother, but your wild ways have given me many frets."

Still dripping water, I stared at him in astonishment. "Wild ways? What wild ways?"

"Oh, come now, ye know what I mean. Ye're like Uncle Garrow, always hankering to go downscarp. And then when ye're here, ye're always experimenting with your herbs and your potions, and reading your textbooks, even though ye are already the best physician we have on the Roof. 'Tis more than is normal, lad."

"Ye may be glad enough of my skills when a bairn of yours falls ill."

He shrugged, and gave a sheepish grin. "Oh, aye, I'll grant ye that. Which is why I'd not chide ye. But it frets me, nonetheless, for I dinna see ye happy, lad. Ye dinna fit the mold."

Fit the mold. Creation, how often had I heard that expression as I grew up. "Ye've got to fit the mold, Kel." "Dinna break the mold, lad." "Ye've got to learn to find your place, and ye'll not find it unless ye fit the mold."

I said irritably, "I'm a Plainsman, Jaimie. I belong here, and there's naught I've ever done that has broken a single tharn rule since I was a lad." Not while on the Sky Plains anyway.

"Nay, of course not," he said hurriedly. "I'd no accuse ye of such, ever. But for most of us the mold is a comfortable place to be. That's as it should be. It grieves me that ye have never found it so." He changed the subject, aware that there were places I did not want to go. "That lass ye've brought back, the young one, I've never seen such beauty." He rolled his eyes upward.

I tried to match his mood. "And you a married man! Shame on you. Here, hand me the towel."

He threw it across. "Tess would scratch my eyes out," he said regretfully. "But in truth, if ever a lass could tempt me, that one would. Pity about her arm." He clapped me on the back and left the room.

No sooner had the thick wool door flopped back into place than it was lifted again. It was my mother. She stood there for a moment, unmoving. I knew what she was doing: taking in the smell of me. They have a saying on the Plains: there's nowhere to hide from a mother's nose. Whoever first said that had a mother exactly like mine; she'd been the bane of my adolescent existence, knowing exactly every time I lusted, and after which lass . . . "Ye're in more trouble than ye're saying," she said bluntly.

Mothers. "Maybe." I went and touched her cheek, trying to reassure her, but doubtless my scent told her a different story. She could have said much, but that wasn't her way. She let me sense her love, her support, her troubled concern. She surrounded me with the smells of my childhood, the safety and love that had been mine. But she couldn't hide from me the other thing she felt: fear. I smelled it skittering around the edges of her thoughts, like a mouse afraid to come out into the open. "Be careful," she said at last. Then she touched my cheek in turn, and left the room.

As she went, Garrowyn arrived. I gestured him inside, and wondered who'd be next. My mother's fears had left me unsettled and I suspected I was going to feel even worse by the time Garrowyn had finished with me. I selected a clean undershirt and pulled it over my head.

"Ye've brought us a nest of vipers, laddie," he said. He ran a hand through his hair in a gesture that had become mine as well. Sometimes I thought we were a mirror image of each other, separated only by time: I was the man he had been thirty years before. We both had long noses, hair that looked like shorn selver wool before it was carded, beards that grew every which way and skin that freckles attempted, with near success, to cover completely. Garrowyn may have been more grizzled, and I may have been taller and broader, but the resemblance was such that there were many who mistook us for father and son.

"Nest of vipers?" I repeated. "Ye mean the women?"

He nodded. "Up to their bonnie eyebrows in magic."

I groaned. "Not you too. Uncle, ye'll no be telling me that all those tales ye spun to us boys were *real,* will ye?"

He shrugged. "Who knows what's real and what's not? Sure, I canna see magic meself, nor can it harm me. But I've seen folk hurt by it, hurt direly, including yon Cirkasian lassie. And I've seen others deceived by it, seeing things that are no there, or no seeing things that are. Mayhap ye have to believe in it, to have it affect ye. I dinna ken. I can smell it, that's for sure. And I dinna like what's done with it. The Keepers, with their illusions of sylv, twist the minds of those who oppose them. And the dunmagickers kill and maim and pervert. I fear them, laddie, for all that they canna touch me. They are souls of sickness, with a sickness that is too evil to mend."

" 'Tis a disease, then?" I asked, still striving to find some rational way to account for these tales of magic.

He shrugged. "Aye, that it could be. But I've not found that it pays to investigate. Yon Cirkasian had a dunmagic sore in her arm that was subverting her to evil."

I was scornful. "Ye mean affecting her personality, no more than that, surely."

He ignored my attempt to make science out of fable. "So she had the arm cut off. I helped, and then scarpered. I thought to come home and rest here nice and quiet like, till all the frets had died down and the dunmagicker had moved on, and what do I find? My nephew turns up on the doorstep with the same two female maelstroms in tow! When I saw them there, I felt fate had us in its grip and it willna let us go till the rills and becks run dry." He sighed. "There are some people who attract strife, like Sindur Crags attract the lightning. And you've brought not one, but two of them into this household, laddie."

"They're just *women*," I said. "Not the plague."

"Those two are trouble. I dinna ken what it is that a dunmagicker uses—magic, disease, mesmerism, poison—but I ken that Flame was infected, and that the halfbreed thwarted the dunmagicker. Wherever he is, whoever he is, those two bonnie lasses will be the folk he hates most. Ye watch your step, laddie. Dunmagickers are famed for their notions of revenge for even the wee bittiest of slights."

"This particular one: they seem to think he's on Porth. They want to go after him." I picked up a clean tagaird.

"Let 'em. And quickly."

"Aye, I will. But my troubles are not with a dunmagicker, Uncle. It's the Fellih-priests who are after my hide." I began to pleat and wrap the tagaird, dismayed to find some of the hidden hooks seemed to be in the wrong place. I had evidently lost some weight while I was downscarp.

He looked up, frowning. "Ye'd better tell me what ye've been up to, Kel. That sounds serious."

"It is." I tucked in the cloth as I related the bare outline of all that had happened to me in Mekatéhaven. By the time I was finished he was actively trying to dampen down his emotions so that the rest of the house wouldn't be swamped with evidence of his agitation.

"Oh, Creation, Kel. That's one hell-bound mess ye've got yourself into. The Fellih-worshippers will be up here in the shake of a selver's tail, protesting and demanding we hand ye over, all of ye."

"They dinna know we came upscarp." A stupid remark, and he gave it the scorn it deserved.

"Of course they ken! Where else would a Plainsman go with a selver? But that's no the worst of it. Have ye told anyone about how Jastriákyn died?"

"Blaze knows. She heard Jastriá ask me to do it. And she saw my face afterward. And I'm sure she will have told Flame by now. They have no secrets, those two."

"Dinna tell any of our folk, Kel. None of them would understand."

"But she was going to die anyway. Slowly, horribly, with them making a *game* of it."

"Aye, lad, I ken. But that's no what people would have a problem with. What will stick in their craw is that *ye could do it.* D'ye understand me?"

I thought about that and then said slowly, "They will think I am some kind of monster. Prone to violence."

"*Capable* of violence anyway. And that's enough. Lad, belief's always what has kept us intact and apart: belief that we are better people, that we have a better way of life. Folk here look at the two of us askance already, because we leave the Roof from time to time. But they tolerate it, because we are physicians and they need our medicines. But if they ken that ye can kill, ye are finished here. Forever."

I sank down on the bed, head in hands. "Is that the truth? Even though she was going to die anyway?" I whispered. An unnecessary question. I knew the answer. In my heart, I had known it even as I made my decision to kill her. I just hadn't wanted to face it.

"Aye. I fear so, laddie. Dinna tell even your own kin what happened in that square. Not ever. And ye had better hope they dinna hear it from others either. Mum's the word, Kel. *Forever.*"

CHAPTER 6

NARRATOR: KELWYN

IN SKY PLAINS HOUSES, THE LIVING HALL ran the width of the house, and it was the only room that was at all large. At one end there was the slow-burning stove made of stone. All the household cooking was done here, using selver turds as fuel. The heat generated was channeled to stone piping that warmed the house and provided hot water to the washroom. In the center of the room was the sunken dining area, designed to eliminate the need for chairs. The table was a long stone slab placed on stone pillars. At the other end of the room were the lacquered shelves, hewn from the earth and stone of the hill slope, which contained the family's wealth: the books of learning accumulated over generations, all written on selver vellum. In a place like The Hub, there were printing presses and printed books; but on the Roof of Mekaté, everything was still hand-written. In our house, this area was also the place where Garrowyn and I kept the rows of smoked bottles, bought in Mekatéhaven, for our medicines. Here, too, was the stone bench where we mixed and pounded our herbs and potions.

When I came back out into the living hall, Blaze was already there looking at the books. My mother, my grandmother and Tessrym were busy with the cooking; my father and brother were out at the stream, pumping up water to the house cistern and talking to Garrowyn. Doubtless he was telling them about how the Fellih-worshippers were after Blaze and Flame and me on account of the jail-break. I went to join Blaze.

"You have an impressive number of books," she said. "Is every tharn house like this?"

"Aye, indeed. Here in Gilfeather house, books are mostly on topics to do with herbs and medicines and illness, because we are a physician family. Every house has its speciality. Every tharn has its weaver, spinner and leatherworker houses, of course, but physician houses are rarer. We tend the sick in all the tharns in this area of the Roof. It is the same with many other specialist houses: potters, tinkers, dye-makers and so on—one house serves an area."

She replaced the book she had been looking at. "And if a member of the potters' house were to marry into a dyemakers'?"

I stirred uncomfortably. The question seemed innocent enough, but I smelled a trace of underlying scorn, and the idea that she dared to scorn us rankled. "The speciality goes with the house, not the family. So does the name, actually. Everyone who lives here is a Gilfeather for as long as they live here, no matter what house they were born into. Mostly a man or woman will seek to find a mate from the same trade. If not, then one of them must change their interest. No exceptions. It was one of the . . . problems for Jastriá. She was from a lacquer-makers' house, but she hated that. When we married, she said she'd be a midwife, but she wasna suited to it. She wouldn't study, she wasna—wasna *tactful* with patients. She didn't pull her weight."

"And she had no choice?"

"The only choice ye have is whether the man moves to his wife's house, or she to his, or they both go somewhere entirely different. But that depends also on which house has a room. There can never be more than ten people to a house."

"But you can build a new house, surely," she said.

"We dinna do that."

She stared at me for a minute. "And I don't suppose you ever start new villages either."

I shook my head. "The Sky Plains already runs the maximum number of selver possible. There can be no more tharns, or we will all suffer."

"Hence what you said to your brother. You gave him permission to start a family. The whole system is very . . . rigid." Her expression was neutral, but she couldn't hide the traces of her disapproval from my nose.

"Ye may think so, but think also on this: no one goes cold or unloved or hungry here. Not ever." The words were said without particular thought, but I didn't need to be sensitive to see that I had struck a chord with her. She gave me a sharp look, as if to ask: *How did you know that?* And it was then that I realized her childhood must have been an impoverished one. I hurried on. "There is almost no crime on the Sky Plains. No murder, no theft. Because there is no poverty, no want, no neglect."

"And no freedom."

I shrugged. "Which is more important?"

"Perhaps you should ask Jastriá?"

I felt as if I'd been slapped, and I stepped away from her.

She was instantly contrite. "I'm sorry; that was crass. I did not mean to be hurtful."

"No? What were ye doing, then?"

"Speaking my mind."

"Aye. I noticed."

"It may give you an insight, perhaps, to what motivated her."

I nodded, deciding she was probably telling the truth. She was blunt, this halfbreed woman, but I doubted that she was mean-spirited. I looked away, fiddling with the mortar and pestle on the counter beneath the shelves. "I would ask something of ye and Flame, if I could. I would rather that not one learned of the exact manner of Jastriá's death. Of my . . . part in it. Could ye no mention it?"

"You did not need to ask that," she said quietly.

I reddened. Somehow, when talking to Blaze, I had a genius for blundering about like a newborn selver foal trying to stand. She intimidated me.

"How long do you think it is safe to stay here?" she asked, changing the subject.

I looked out of the door to where Garrowyn was now talking to a group of people: one representative of every House, at a guess. "I rather think my uncle has just been telling most of the sorry tale. Doubtless my father will have something to say about it over supper." I looked back at her, suddenly irritable. "I wish ye had found a better way to raise money than gambling."

"So do I. I didn't set out to upset the Fellih-worshippers."

"Did I not hear ye say ye arrived on Mekaté by sea-pony? If ye needed money, why did ye not sell the beast?"

"We were exhausted by the time we made landfall at Cape Kan. We just rolled off the pony onto the beach, and it swam away. Believe me, that was not one of my finer moments."

I almost laughed. It was nice to know she could also make major mistakes.

"She blames me, of course," Flame said, coming up behind me. "Something about the person who has the responsibility of driving the beast ought never to have the bother of tending it. That's the passenger's job. Or so she informed me as the wretched animal frolicked away through the breakers. Of course, it was a shade too late then . . ." She grinned, but that changed to a frown as she remembered something. "Hey, Blaze, what was that remark Garrowyn made about a butcher?"

"Ah, nothing. Just an expression, I suppose."

Flame was relentless. "You aren't going to tell me that the man you paid to cut off my arm was an incompetent chirurgeon with a reputation for slaughtering his patients, are you?"

"No, not unless you want me to," Blaze said blandly.

Flame opened her mouth, closed it again while she tried to make head or tail of what Blaze meant, then said, "I sort of recall him saying something about cutting off his wife's arm."

"You were delirious."

Flame continued to frown, trying to remember. The look she gave Blaze was full of suspicion. Fortunately for Blaze, just then my mother beckoned us to the table. As I went outside to call in my father, Jaimwyn and Garrowyn, she directed the two women to their places. With my cousins away, there was space for an extra two.

The early part of the lunch went smoothly enough. My mother, without being asked, placed a small bowl of water and some seeds on the table at Flame's elbow for Ruarth. I couldn't help wondering if he was going to disgrace himself by making a mess on the table, and kept sending sidelong glances his way until Blaze raised an eyebrow at me. Skies above, how did she always seem to know what I was thinking?

"Ye are lucky," my father commented as the last of the dishes was served up, "we have meat today. One of the Tomwyn House selvers died yesterday, and the carcass was divided among all the tharn households."

Blaze, who had been about to swallow a piece of the stew, almost choked. Flame lowered her spoon back to her bowl.

"Died of what?" Blaze asked, offhand.

"Ach, old age, I think," my father said. "But dinna fret, my wife knows exactly how to tenderise an old selver."

"I thought you were all vegetarians," Blaze said to me, expressionless.

"We just don't kill for food. But if the food dies of its own accord, why waste it?"

A peculiar look flicked across her face. "Why indeed?" After that, neither of them ate much of the meat, but concentrated on the sour curds, watercress, sourdough and butter. That was fine with the rest of us: selver meat was a treat we did not get often.

Halfway through dinner, my father brought up the matter of what had happened in Mekatéhaven, as I knew he would. "Garrow has told me that the Fellih-worshippers were looking for ye in the city," he said to Blaze.

She nodded. "I'm afraid so."

"We have talked this matter over—all the Houses have, I mean."

"We don't want to bring trouble to your tharn."

"Oh, the trouble will come, owing to the involvement of my son. That canna be changed now. We will not shield ye, that is decided. But we have no love for the Fellih, not after what they did to one of our Skyfolk." He meant Jastriákyn, of course. "We will help ye on your way. Are ye *sure* ye will no have some more meat?"

"No, thank you. When would you like us to leave?"

"There is no need to scurry till we have warning. Jaim will

fetch some selvers off the meadows for ye to ride, and my wife and Tess here will prepare provender for ye to take."

"Hard cheeses," my mother said, "sourdough, things that travel well."

"That's very kind of you."

My father continued, "When ye get to the Scarps above Niba Water, ye just release the animals. They will return of their own accord. There's no point in taking them further."

"You mentioned a warning?" Blaze asked.

"Aye. We always have warning. As soon as the Havenlord's guards and the Fellih-priests arrive on the Roof, they will go straight to Tharn Gar—they always do. The coastal folk willna know where Tharn Wyn is, even if they ken Kel's tharn from his name. They will ask Gar, Gar will send us word, while they delay them. The coastal folk will not have mounts, ye ken, and will have to hire them, and guides . . . there will have to be negotiations. Ye will have plenty of time to flee. But dinna expect us to tell falsehoods for ye. We will tell them ye were here, and we will tell them where ye are going, if they ask. However, I shouldna fret that they will catch up with ye."

Blaze said, "Don't tell me, I can guess. Plainsmen guides have a distressing tendency to get lost."

"Something like that," my father said with a twinkling smile at her. He liked her, which surprised me. My father did not usually take to downscarpers. He sipped some hot milk, watching me over the rim of his cup. His aroma thickened, warning me of what was to come. His sorrow washed over me, almost choking me with its intensity. "Ye, though, Kel. That's another matter. I'm sorry, lad, but the tharn has decided to exile ye."

I felt sick, but I said nothing.

Flame and Blaze looked startled. "Just like that?" Flame asked.

"Aye. We have to protect the tharn and the peace between coast and Sky Plains."

My mother sought my hand and gripped it across the table. "For how long?" she asked my father.

"At least a year, better two." He sighed. "Garrow will give ye contacts all over the Isles. Ye can work as a physician and chirurgeon wherever ye are, ye ken that. Your uncle has money to get ye started. Ye can take Blaze and Flame to the coast first, and then be on your way quickly to another is-landom, before word gets to other coastal towns that ye're a wanted man. We will explain to the office of the Havenlord what happened, that ye didna mean to get involved with the affairs of off-islanders or law-breakers." He cleared his throat and glanced apologetically at Blaze. "We will try to unsully your name, Kel. Write to us when ye're settled, and we will let ye know when ye can return. Dinna fret, the rest of us can manage the sick, even if Garrow leaves again. Tess is becom-ing a fine midwife, ye ken, and she has a way with the bairns."

I nodded. It was fairly much what I had expected after speaking to Garrowyn, but it hurt nonetheless. As long as two years away from the Sky Plains? The idea was appalling. I took care not to look at Blaze, afraid that I would be unable to keep my rage from showing on my face. I put my spoon down; I had no more appetite.

AFTER LUNCH, JAIM TOOK THE VILLAGE hack and rode off to look for our flock. He would do it by smell, because they could have been anywhere. We all recog-nized the smell of our own herd, of course. My mother bustled around, giving orders to Tess and my father, taking refuge in action so that she didn't have to think. My grandmother napped in front of the fire. Garrowyn and I sat down for a long talk while he tried to instill in me in an afternoon everything I needed to know about living off-island. I felt as if I had just fallen off a selver, but hadn't hit the ground yet. Sooner or later there was going to be an impact that was going to hurt like the end of Creation; in the meantime, there was just a continual feeling of impending disaster. And yet, there was part of me that was excited. Here was a chance to see other parts of the world, to search for new herbs, new cures; to talk to other healers. Even Garrowyn's rather pessimistic view could not wholly dim that excitement.

"'Tis no as easy to make a living as a physician as your fa-ther thinks," he warned. "Folk with money can afford sylv healers, and believe me, many of them do a better job than the likes of us, especially if the patient goes to them for treatment early enough. That leaves the poor, and they dinna pay much. Obviously. 'Tis one of the reasons I went to Gorthan Spit. There are no sylv healers there, so ye get the wealthy as well. However, I wouldna recommend that place. Not now. Nay, go to Breth Island. I'll give ye the name of a woman there who will help set ye up. Ye can have my medicine chest."

"Where is it?" I asked.

"I left it in Mekatéhaven, with a friend, as usual." The chest was huge, far too large to lug upscarp every time he came back.

I grunted. "Somehow I dinna think I will be returning there in a hurry."

"I can get her to send it on. Look, I have another friend in Amkabraig on Porth. A real fine lassie called Anistie. Ye'll get to Amkabraig anyway; the inter-island packet boats from Lekenbraig call in there before proceeding on to Xolchas Stacks and hence to Breth. I'll get my chest sent to Anistie by sea. Let me write out her name and how to find her."

"No, Uncle. That would mean ye'd have to ride downscarp to Mekatéhaven to arrange it all, and I'm not sure that's a good idea right now."

"Nay, nay. I'll pay one of the men they send after ye to deliver the letter to my friend in Mekatéhaven."

I stared at him in disbelief. "Ye'll *what?* And what if he reads the letter?"

"Ach, laddie, give me a skerrick of credit, will ye no? I can word it so that it doesna give anything away. Besides, they'd never think I'd be so gormless as to give them a letter that concerned ye."

I threw up my hands in a gesture of defeat. Garrowyn always had been impossible. My life seemed to be out of my hands, and it appeared that I was going to be stuck in the company of Blaze Halfbreed far longer than I would have liked.

"Ye'll like Anistie," he went on. "And ye can spend your time there profitably; ye can poke your nose into the papers and such that she has of mine."

"Papers?"

"Aye, a collection I've made over the years. Never could be

bothered lugging them all the way upscarp, so I left them with Anistie Brittlelyn. Besides, having them there gives me an excuse to drop in on her once in a while. A wise lass, Anistie." He winked.

I ignored that. "So what kind of papers are we talking about?"

"They're on magic mostly. Especially dunmagic. It has always fascinated me. Have ye never wondered where magic came from?"

"No. I canna say I have. What did these papers of yours tell ye?"

"Oh, I've not read most of them. Always found other things to be doing at Anistie's, ye ken."

"I think you're a rogue, Uncle."

"Aye, of course. Never said I was aught different. Rogues have much more fun; ye should think on that occasionally, Kel. Ye're far too serious a lad for your own good, ye ken."

"Uncle," I said, "I think I want to go for a walk."

He looked up from his writing of Anistie's address, almost protested, then nodded. "Aye," he said. "Ye'll need to say good-bye to the place, I suppose. And I'll hunt out some ordinary clothing for ye. Mayhap it would be better that ye didn't wear the tagaird while ye are traveling in the Mekaté Isles; it will set ye apart too much, and somehow I think that's not what ye need."

I nodded, but I didn't really listen.

I left the house and started walking up the hill behind the tharn. Memories came tumbling in with every step I took: riding on my father's back as he went to find wild mushrooms; running hand in hand with my mother just for the fun of it; racing Jaim downhill and tumbling head over heels into the daisies; making love to Jastriá behind the crags at the top of the slope in the heat of the afternoon. Memories of smells: meadow flowers dotted with pollen-covered bees, wet selvers in the rain, ripe cloudberries damp with mist, the clean new-scent of freshly dyed tagaird flapping on the line in the breeze.

Jastriá had given it all up willingly, because she had wanted freedom. Because of her, I had all the freedom I didn't want.

I sat down at the top of the hill, closed my eyes and drank

in the smells, the redolence, as if I had to absorb enough to last a lifetime. I wanted to remember it all.

It was Seeker that broke through my concentration, that returned me to the present. He shoved his damp snout into my face and licked. He smelled strongly of fish. I opened my eyes and looked at him. He was the ugliest dog I'd ever seen, and he managed to look absurdly pleased with himself. He'd caught a fish and had laid it on the grass next to me. Once he was sure I had seen it, he proceeded to dismember it with surprising dexterity, carefully filleting out the backbone and the fins. When he'd eaten half of the fleshy parts, he offered me a piece. I declined, so he ate the rest with relish. I was used to the dogs of Mekatéhaven, but this fellow wasn't like them.

Come to think of it, nothing in my life at that point in time was quite what it seemed to be on the surface, not even our impending departure.

I CAME ON DOWN THE HILL AND WENT to pack as much of my medicines and equipment as I could take. While traveling by selver it didn't matter, but there was going to come a time when I would have to carry everything on my back, so I was as ruthless as I knew how to be, especially when I eyed the size of the cheese that my mother was packing.

By the time Jaim came back the next day with the two extra selvers, I had everything done. Garrowyn had given me money and addresses and directions and enough advice to last a lifetime. Father had given me his best dirk, my mother had produced her enormous packs of food for each of us, which was the best way she had of telling me how much she cared. She was not an articulate woman, my mother.

I turned the dirk over in my hands. The short blade was made of downscarp steel; the handle was selver horn so old it was black. It was an all-purpose tool rather than a weapon. We did not need weapons on the Plains. I nodded my thanks to my father, smiled at my mother and wondered at the lump in my throat.

All that remained was to say good-bye . . .

Blaze held the bridle of her mount, trying to make friends, but the beast dribbled bile and kept baring his teeth. Flame regarded her own selver with a dubious expression, and said that, although she had ridden Keeper Isle ponies in Cirkase as a child, she'd already found out that wasn't much use when it came to riding one of our hacks.

I was helping to saddle the selvers, when Tess said, "There's someone coming."

My father raised his head from the girth he was tightening. He had the best nose among us, and he added, "From Gar. Madrigogar Elsin's eldest son."

He was right, of course; he always was. It was Deringar, one of the resin-makers of Elsin House, a man of my age, and he came thundering down to the tharn with a disregard for the slope that had us all gaping. He drew rein only as he came to the first house, and even then he rode along the stepping stones, an enormous breach of good manners that had my father darkening with anger, and my more astute mother turning white. Garrow and I exchanged glances. Blaze caught the look and her eyes narrowed. There wasn't much that escaped her. The houses of the tharn emptied as everyone came running out; there could have been no one who was unaware of Derin's turmoil by the time he pulled up in front of me.

I resigned myself and the grief I felt was heavy enough to paralyze.

Derin stared straight at me as he spoke. "There is a delegation of officials from Mekatéhaven: twenty men. They say they are after three law-breakers, and one of them is ye, Kel Gilfeather of Wyn."

I was silent. *Twenty* men?

"They bear the Havenlord's seal, and they have orders to bring ye back down."

I nodded, knowing there was more.

"We will delay them till morning." He turned to look at my father. "Torrwyn, we of Gar demand Kel's life exile from the Sky Plains."

My father's jaw dropped. "For aiding these lasses?" he asked, incredulous. "'Twas a minor thing that he had little control over."

"Nay, he has not told ye the truth then, Torr. It was his hand that flung the stone that took the life of his wife, or so one of the Fellih-worshippers told us. And the man had no idea of the gravity of what he said! 'Twas a mere remark made in passing, that Kel must be a strong man to have such strength in his arm. We confirmed the story with the others in the group." He stared at me, as if he was seeing me for the first time in his life. And we had played together all our lives, herded our flocks together, giggled about lovemaking and girls together as we grew. "Ye're a people-killer, Kel, and we of Gar want naught of ye here. Not ever."

I turned to my father and tried to defend myself. "They were going to kill her slowly. I wanted to save her the pain."

My mother collapsed. Garrow caught her as she fell, lowering her to the ground. My father didn't even seem to notice. He was staring at me, his aroma blank of emotion. Derin turned his mount and rode away, more circumspectly than on his arrival. Tess gave me one horrified look then said stiffly to her husband, "Come inside, Jaimie." He shook off her hand as it plucked at his arm, and went to help Mother instead, but he didn't look at me. Tess turned on her heel and went inside; if there had been a door to slam, she would have slammed it. Her revulsion hung in the air behind her.

I said to Blaze, "We'll go now."

She nodded and went to help Flame mount. I tied the last package to Skandor's saddle and turned to Jaim. "Is she all right?"

He was kneeling beside our mother, taking her head onto his lap, but he didn't reply to the question. He asked instead, "It's *true*, Kel? And ye a physician?"

I nodded and he looked away. There was no explanation he would ever understand.

Garrowyn said, "She'll be fine, lad. It's best ye go now."

My father caught my bridle as I mounted. "Lad." We looked at each other in mutual pain. I wanted to ask: how can it make such a difference? I wanted to say that I was still his son; wasn't I the same person I had always been? But I was afraid of the answer.

"Write," he said at last. "Always write, for your mother's

sake." And I knew then that it did make a difference to him, and always would.

I nodded. I said to Garrow, "Give her my love."

And so it was we left Wyn.

I wonder sometimes what the Plainsfolk would have thought had they known what happened to me after that; if they'd come to know that in the end I became one of the greatest mass killers of all Glorian history, rivaling even Morthred himself. Perhaps they would have nodded sagely, and said, Well, we knew he had it in him, didn't we?

Letter to T. iso Tramin, Lecturer (Second Class), Mithodis Academy of Historical Studies, Yamindaton Crossways, Kells, from Researcher (Special Class) S. iso Fabold, National Department of Exploration, Federal Ministry of Trade, Kells.

Dated this day 2/2ndDouble/1793

My dearest Treff,
So you have become intrigued by the new hero in my Glorian tales, have you? I had to laugh when you wrote that you wish you could be a historian in the Glory Isles as life seems so much more interesting there! And I always thought there were far too many battles and tales of conquest in our own history . . .

I wish you could meet Gilfeather. He is still a great big bear of a man, in spite of his years, with a gray thatch of hair and grizzled beard now, of course. I think in his younger days he was probably quite imposing, at least when he wasn't tripping over things. He still does that. He spilled hot tea all over Nathan on our last visit and ruined two sheets of notes. He is treated with a strange mix of reverence, awe and fear by the people in the town where he now lives, a place called Osgath, on Arutha Island. (You won't find it on the early Glorian-made maps but it is marked on some later Kellish ones I have.)

I'm afraid I never did take to him much, and I don't think he had much time for me either, but I must admit that by all accounts he was a fine medic in his time. He was the founder of the local medic school in Osgath and is still the equivalent of our Chirurgeon Emeritus there. People come from all over the Glory Isles to study at the school. His reputation as a physician, though, is still tainted by his history. I've heard him referred to as Gilfeather of the Massacre.

Anyway, Tramin, I'm sorry, but you will have to wait your turn for the next set of translated Glorian papers.

My uncle has them at the moment. I know Gilfeather's remark about being a mass killer has intrigued you and you want to know more. You shall, you shall, and then you can judge for yourself.

When are you next coming down from Yamindaton Crossways? There is a new drinking shop in the city which is all the rage at the moment. They serve something called chocolate, a sort of brown syrupy stuff that comes from The Spatts in the Glory Isles. Quite, quite delicious. Ironical, isn't it—I never drank it in Spattshield, but I have become quite addicted at this shop just around the corner from my rooms in the city. I shall buy you a cup . . .

In friendship,
Shor

CHAPTER 7

I KNEW THERE WAS NO REASON TO FLEE as if every grass-lion on the Roof was nipping at our heels. We Sky Plainsfolk did not give up our own so easily, no matter what they had done. Yes, the people of Tharn Gar would agree to guide the guards; yes, they would bring them to Tharn Wyn, and in Wyn my father would tell them we had gone to the coast. The guides would then offer to show them the way we had taken, but it would be a tortuous route they followed. By the time they reached the far side of the Roof, days hence, we would be long gone.

However, all that did not mean we had time to dawdle, especially as I needed to drop by Tharn Kyn to see Jastriá's family, which was some distance out of our way. We had to proceed briskly, which wasn't always that easy. Blaze seemed to have a natural seat and told me matter-of-factly that she had stolen rides on Hub ponies as a child, and ridden everything in the years since, from sea-ponies to Keeper donkeys, from Fen buffalo to Calment's mountain choats. I didn't know what some of those creatures were, but it didn't matter; it was obvious she would manage. Flame was another matter. She had not yet accustomed herself to the loss of the limb; worse was the fact that she clearly didn't like being so far away from the ground. She clung grimly to the saddle and seemed determined not to complain, so I left her schooling up to Blaze, but it meant our progress was halting.

No sooner had we left Wyn than Seeker appeared and fell in alongside Blaze. I was in no mood to talk and stayed ahead, slowing every now and then when I could see they were dropping too far back.

When it started raining in the late afternoon on that first day, I stopped and we set up camp at the base of Sindur's Crags, where there were scattered boulders to offer a windbreak. At least now we had a proper selver-hide shelter to keep the worst of the water off, and warmer bedding, courtesy of my father.

It was Blaze who hunted out dung from the grass and got the fire going. By the time I had the shelter properly rigged and the selvers hobbled and turned loose, she had water boiling. Still later she was handing me a meal she had cooked in the ashes; I am not sure how she did it, but somehow she had melted cheese inside an outer jacket of bread. I hadn't been hungry, hadn't wanted to eat at all, but the smell was seductive and I ended up finishing all she gave. My mood, however, remained dark, and immediately afterward I lay down under the shelter, well-wrapped against the cold, and went to sleep.

I woke halfway through the night. It had stopped raining and the double moons were up, almost touching, or so it seemed—one silver, one gold, a combination which gave a blue-greenish sheen to the world. It was almost light enough to read by. I felt the lingering remains of the dream I had been having; no, not dream: nightmare. Jastriákyn standing on the roof of our family house, surrounded by Fellih-priests who were throwing dried selver pats at her. She was screaming out to me for help and I was calling to her: "Don't worry, Jastriá, I will save ye." She smiled at me, happily. And then I picked up a rock—

I rolled out of the extra tagaird I used as a blanket and stood up, feeling sick. Seeker looked up expectantly but I ignored him. I walked down the hillside a way, and then seated myself on a boulder, hugging my knees. It was a cold night, but I hardly noticed.

How long before I learned to live with what I'd done? I couldn't even imagine coming to terms with it. *I'd killed my wife.* The woman I had once loved so deeply I would have died for her. The woman I had once envisaged as the mother of my children. The woman I had once desired so much that the thought of ever sleeping with another had been anathema. The woman who had ended with a deep need to punish me for what I had done, or not done.

A woman whom I had not known at all.

Seeker came and laid his chin on my knee and whined. I patted his head absently, and he slobbered in gratitude.

"I don't much like dogs."

Startled, I looked up. I had been so absorbed in my own troubles, I hadn't been aware of Flame's approach. For once, her bird was nowhere to be seen. "But somehow," she continued as the animal turned his dribbling attentions to her, "I've become quite fond of Seeker. I don't tell Blaze that, of course. It's a secret: mine and Seeker's." She rubbed him under the throat and he whacked me with his tail. It hurt and I had to push him away.

She seated herself on another rock, but she didn't look at me. "I guess you don't feel like company right now, but I felt I had to tell you how sorry I am that they found out about how Jastriá died. I couldn't sleep either." She shook her head and added, "I keep on saying sorry to you, even when I know apologizing doesn't help, not even a smidgeon."

I didn't reply, so she went on, "When I decided to go after Morthred, I thought it was just him and me. That nothing I was going to do could possibly make the world any worse; that it might just conceivably make the Isles a better place. But because I made that decision, I have wrecked your life. Your family were so kind to us, and now they are wretched because of what they have learned. It would not have happened if we had not stolen your selver. There's nothing I can say to make things better for you, but I do want you to know that I would change it all back again if I could."

I spoke then, more in surprise than anything else: "It was *your* idea to go after this Morthred? Not Blaze's?"

"No, it was mine. Blaze came along because she couldn't

bear the idea of me going off alone after that bastard. She has her own wounds to salve, but I doubt she would have bothered if I hadn't stepped in with my plans first."

I found myself having to rearrange my ideas about her. "Why?" I asked. "What is so important that ye had to go after him?"

"There's a very obvious reason. Ruarth. While Morthred is alive, Ruarth and many other Dustel Islanders remain as birds."

I nodded, trying to accept that outrageous notion as fact, and failing. I could accept that Dustel birds were sentient, but the idea that they would one day change into men was preposterous.

"But there's more than that too. There's something . . . It's as if . . . Morthred . . ."

But whatever it was she wanted to tell me, she couldn't find the words to say it. Looking back later, I realized how close she came in that moment to telling me something that would have saved us so much heartbreak and pain. Something that would have changed the future for all of us. It wasn't that she wanted to hide the truth, of course; it was just that she had not yet recognized it. She felt something, but it was too nebulous to be articulated. And by the time she realized what it was, it was too late . . . and that was her tragedy.

Finally, when she did speak, I suspected it was not what she had started to say. "He is very powerful. My sylvmagic is nothing compared to his power. When we last saw him he was weakened, it's true, but I don't think he will stay that way for long." The smell from her was strong: loathing, fear—a turmoil of emotion so potent it shocked me. "Most bad people have good in them. And so does he. He is even aware of the good place within himself, and he gleefully tortures that place just as he tortures others. He told me once that he'd had a happy childhood, until the rest of his family was betrayed and murdered. Perhaps it is that memory, of what he once had, that makes him what he is now. He's mad, Kel. With a terrible madness. He doesn't like killing people, because that just puts them out of their misery. If he could, he would have every citizen of the Glory Isles live in terror and pain and guilt and despair for eternity, so that he could . . . gloat. And yet even as he does all those terrible things, he suffers himself . . . He is a tortured, twisted human being, so deformed in soul that it would be an act of mercy to kill him." She took a deep breath, as if an effort was necessary for her to breathe at all. "D'you know, he almost turned me into one of his own kind. Twice. Do you know how a sylv would feel if they were subverted to dunmagic?"

I shook my head. I didn't even *believe* in magic. Although . . . why hadn't the guards seen her pass Blaze's sword through the bars into her jail cell? Why, later on, had the guards not been able to stop us escaping?

She continued, "The very feel of dunmagic hurts us. Sears us. A subverted sylv would have to live with that physical pain. But that's nothing compared to the rest of it. Far worse is the fact that the sylv would remember who he— who she had been. She would remember her own beliefs and personality, even as she acted in ways which were the antithesis of her sylv self. She would happily kill her own loved ones, grieving in agony as she did, but be unable to stop the new dun side of herself. Healing her, changing her back to sylv, would be theoretically possible, if the dunmagicker who had subverted her died. But the dunmagic itself would never allow her to become a sylv again. Because the subverted one would *be* a dunmagicker herself, she would use her dunpower to *stay* a dunmagicker, with the sylv locked away inside, unable to break out. She would never allow others to heal her. Never be able to obey that part of herself that *wanted* so desperately to be sylv again." One of her hands gripped at Seeker's hair so firmly that he whined; she didn't even notice. "I can think of no greater horror. It would be far, far worse than death." She shuddered, shudders that racked her as if she was fevered.

I stared at her, appalled, unable to speak.

Oh, Creation, I thought. He raped her. Or worse.

With a depth of intensity that was frightening, she said, "I want him dead, Kel. I want him dead so badly it almost consumes me." She gave me a weak smile, apparently realizing from the expression on my face how impassioned she had been. "Well, you *did* ask."

* * *

IN THE LATE AFTERNOON THREE DAYS
later, we came across a flock of selvers, herded by two youths
from Tharn Kyn. I remembered them vaguely from a summer
festival gathering the year before; one of them was related to
Jastriá. They were delighted to see us; a month's stint herding
can be monotonous, even for those Plainsfolk who never han-
kered after another way of life. They greeted me, introducing
themselves as Corkyn and Belankyn, but their eyes never left
Flame the whole while. They tried to be polite, but they were
finding it hard to put two coherent words together. After no
other company except each other and selvers, any woman
would have looked good; for two adolescents barely eighteen
years old, Flame Windrider must have looked like a sea-
dream visitation. Blaze, with her enormous sword, they were
more inclined to treat with dazed respect.

We had our evening meal, supplemented by the fresh milk
the lads gave us. Blaze and Flame were happy to rest: in fact,
Flame was so sore by this time that she could barely move after dismounting. When I offered her some liniment, she
smiled and remarked that she was quite capable of healing
herself, thank you. Fortunately the two lads were only too
happy to wait on her hand and foot, tending to her mount and
bringing her hot water to wash. Blaze just watched cynically,
rolling her eyes at me after one of the youths offered to mas-
sage Flame's back as I rode past, on my way to Tham Kyn to
see Jastriá's parents.

My meeting with the members of the Longpeat House was
trying for us all. Jastriá's parents were loving people, but with
no understanding of their daughter or the cause of her troubled nature. They had been happy that she had married, saddened that it had not solved her problem, devastated when she
had been exiled. They loved her and now they were heartbro-
ken when I told them she had died.

The worst thing of all was that behind their grief, I smelled
the traces of something else: relief. One small unworthy part
of them was glad that she was gone, because that meant peace.
Peace for her, peace for them. It sickened me, it demeaned
them, and for a fleeting moment I hated everything about the
Sky Plains. Jastriákyn had deserved better.

Early the next morning, in an even worse mood than when

I'd left, I rode back to our camp. As soon as I arrived, we said good-bye to the two lads, who seemed remarkably cheerful, seeing that the weather was wretchedly gray and soggy. In fact, it started to rain again as we rode away, and it was a miserable ride, drizzling the whole day long and not clearing until late evening.

I hardly said two words all day, and the weather had even dampened the normal bickering that Flame and Blaze seemed to so delight in. It wasn't until we were setting up camp in the evening that they started up again after Seeker, wet and muddy from a roll in a boggy patch of ground, shook himself all over Flame and splattered her with mud that had a distinctly malodorous pong to it.

She gave a yelp of dismay, whacked Seeker's rump with the parcel she had been dragging out of her pack at the time, and wailed at Blaze, "That's it, Blaze! Either that misbegotten bag of halitosis learns some manners, or he is *grilled* tonight, over the coals, for supper!"

"Can't do that," Blaze said with deadpan seriousness. "Gilfeather here won't eat anything that's deliberately slaughtered."

"He'd better watch it or I'll be gnawing on his ribs tomorrow for breakfast."

"Gilfeather's ribs?"

"Seeker's, you dolt of an Awarewoman!"

The object of her ire slunk away and hid himself behind Blaze, or tried to; difficult because he was an enormous animal. Blaze looked down at him with a sigh. "You great big lug, you are supposed to protect me, not the other way around. Now, if you could only learn to run off all the lovelorn men that hang around Flame over there, you might just earn your keep! Last night I hardly slept a wink. Flame, that's not the *bread* that you just thwacked the animal with, is it?"

Flame looked down at her hand. "Oh. Well, yes, it is, actually. Never mind, it is wrapped. Sort of."

Blaze sighed and took the battered parcel from her.

I continued to erect the shelter for our camp, and thought over their conversation one more time. She didn't mean, she *couldn't* mean—I looked over at Flame, and blushed at what I was thinking. Not *both* of the lads, surely. Besides, didn't she prefer women? Blaze saw my blush and gave me a quizzical look. I flushed deeper and got on with the job. I most certainly wasn't going to ask. I said instead, "I have some ointment for Seeker. I made it up back at home, but I forgot to give it to you. It will help clear up that mange of his. At least, I think it will. It works on the selvers when they have skin problems."

I COULDN'T SLEEP AGAIN THAT NIGHT. IT was becoming a habit and I wondered if I should resort to a sleeping draft. Instead, I rose about an hour after I had turned in for the night, intending this time to go for a long walk. The moons were shining, both on the wane as we headed for the darkmoon month, but nonetheless still bright in a sky that seemed to have washed itself clean of clouds.

I hadn't gone far when I realized that I was not alone.

I turned around to find Blaze following me. I suppressed a sigh. Sometimes it seemed that these two women were Creation-bent on irritating me. "What is it?" I asked when she came up, aware that I sounded snappish.

She noticed, of course. "You don't sleep," she said. "And when you do, you are restless. I thought maybe I could help."

I wondered if she was offering herself, but withdrew that thought almost as soon as it occurred. There was no hint of sexual invitation. "What do ye mean?" I asked neutrally.

"Well, I've been thinking. Now that I have seen how you lived in Wyn, now that I've met your family, and having talked last night to those two young idiots from Kyn, I've been able to put it all together with things that Jastriá said to me. I think I have a better understanding of her. I think I know what motivated her."

I turned to continue walking and she fell in at my side. "I think you were right: she did want to hurt you."

"Oh, aye. I know that much. She wanted to hurt me as best she could. But what did I do to her to deserve that?"

"Deceived her, perhaps. Unintentionally, but it was still a deceit. She saw how you escaped to the lowlands to keep you sanity; she saw Garrowyn, who traveled even further. She thought she could persuade you to take her away, completely away. But you wouldn't be honest with yourself. You still aren't."

"What's that supposed to mean?"

"Kel, look at youself. And look at your brother. Jaimwyn's a physician, just like you. He mixes medicines and rides out to treat people, but you don't see him traveling downscarp. You don't see him trying new things, looking for new herbs, new treatments, new cures. You don't see him playing with fire and marrying a woman like Jastriá, with her wildness and passion. You and he are oceans apart. He's happy to stay in Wyn, to do what your father did, and his father before him. Happy to marry a woman like Tess. But you aren't the kind of man to sit in Wyn for the rest of your life, any more than your uncle was. Jastriá saw that; she saw in you what she saw in herself. She saw the desire for new things, for new challenges. She saw the passion. She expected you to rescue her from the sameness here that stultified her.

"Instead, you kept coming back to Wyn. Settling down, or pretending to. I think it made her deeply angry that you wouldn't acknowledge what you really were: a rebel, like her."

I wanted to give way to rage, to throw the lies back in her face, to say *I'm not like that!* But I couldn't. Deep in my heart I knew that all these years the only thing that had made Wyn pleasurable—or even bearable—had been knowing that sometimes I could leave it. And that was hardly a normal Plainsman's way of looking at his home. I just hadn't been brave enough to say it, or to take my needs to their logical conclusion and do what Uncle Garrow did, and live most of my life away.

Finally, I said softly, "Jastriá begged me, often, but I kept on coming back, bringing her back with me. To where it was safe. There's a kind of seduction in that, ye know: safety, certainty, always knowing what to do and how to do it. Ye dinna have to think. I just didna have the courage to leave . . . knowing that if I did, there would be no certainties. No safety. I loved her, but I didna love her enough to give her what she wanted."

"I think it's what you want too. And *that's* what embittered her."

"Well, I've got what I want then, haven't I?" I said, bitter in my turn. "So tell me, why do I feel so bad?" I didn't expect an answer, and I didn't get one.

We walked on in silence for perhaps a mile before I said slowly, "And so she punished me. She refused the chance ye offered her to escape, and instead forced me to kill her. Which gave her the added satisfaction of revenge on me, because she felt I had betrayed her."

"I think so. She felt there was no—no hope. And she was very angry. It wasn't your fault."

"Ye just said it was."

She grabbed me by the arm, bringing me to a halt. "No, I didn't. I gave you an explanation." She pulled me around to face her, forced me to look her in the eye. I had to look up. She said, "Jastriá was an adult. She was old enough to make her own decisions. She could have made a decent life for herself away from the Sky Plains. She was intelligent and personable and she wasn't destitute. She chose her path to ruin with her own self-destructiveness, and like a fish caught on a hook, she had to blame the fisherman, not herself. *It wasn't your fault.*"

I turned to walk on and she strode after me. "Gilfeather, I know what you are going through."

"How can ye possibly have the slightest ideas? I *killed* my wife!"

She made a conciliatory gesture with her hand. "All right, so I've never killed a husband. Not yet anyway. But I did kill Niamor—a friend, a man I liked and respected, for all that he was a rogue. It was only . . . only a month ago, back on Gorthan Spit."

The bitterness spilled over. "So? Ye carry a sword, woman! Doubtless ye've killed a lot of people! I assume ye make a *business* of it."

"I don't kill my friends, as a rule."

Her voice shook and I was so surprised, I stopped walking and looked at her.

She took the opportunity to explain. "He'd been attacked by the dunmaster and left to rot to death. I can't imagine a worse way to die. He asked me to kill him, so I did."

To my utter amazement, I thought I saw the glint of a tear on her lashes. Creation, these two women confounded me every time I thought I had them worked out. First Flame, whom I had thought was as soft as selver butter left in the sun, revealed herself to be the prime mover behind the plan to rid the Isles of a man who was supposedly a dunmaster, a powerful, evil sorcerer. And now Blaze, whom I had thought was as hard as selver horn, cried over the death of a friend, and cared enough about my despair to tell me . . .

She said, "It isn't something you get over easily. It isn't something you'll ever forget. I thought it might help if you knew that someone else understands."

I was oddly moved. "Aye," I said, finally managing to be gracious.

We turned and started to walk back toward the camp.

She said, "And thank you for the ointment for Seeker. It was kind of you. And I marvel that you thought to do something like that in the midst of all of your troubles. You are a remarkable man, Kelwyn."

"No. I'm a healer, that's all. And that animal has a skin problem."

"Thanks anyway," she said, and then screwed up her nose. "What *is* that aroma around here? I don't remember smelling that earlier this evening."

"Moonflowers. They only blossom at night, and only in doublemoon months. The smell is supposed to be an aphrodisiac, and honeymooners often choose to herd the selvers so that they can find patches of moonflowers to lie in . . ." I stopped, embarrassed. It wasn't what I wanted to be talking about with her.

She laughed. "Then we had better hope that there are none back near where we are camped."

I smiled at her. "No, I couldn't smell any there. I suspect it is more myth than medical fact anyway. Although—"

"Although what?"

"They have an interesting way of propagating. Come. I'll show ye."

I followed the strongest aroma, stumbling clumsily in the gloom, until I found a patch of moonflowers capping the top of a rise like snow. There was a breeze blowing, wafting the scent aloft, ideal conditions for the fertilization process. The female flowers stood tallest, with their creamy translucent petals spread like sails to catch the wind; around their feet the tiny, whiter male flowers, thousands of them covering the low bushes, seemed to watch and wait.

"They are lovely," Blaze said, "although a little overpowering."

"Look," I said.

A puff of wind caught one of the female flowers and it detached from the mother plant, breaking its scent glands wide open. The wind wafted it high into the air as the smell strengthened. In answer, hundreds of the male flowers sprang into the air, impelled by aroma-stimulated triggers.

The air swirled with a storm of white petals. For a while they drifted this way and that, at the mercy of the breeze, until at last one male flower brushed up against the petals of the female. The creamy petals enclosed the smaller blossom in a fond floral embrace. They drifted on, gently spun on the wind until they were out of sight. The pungency of their aroma lingered in the air.

I heard Blaze release the breath she had been holding. "Yes, well. I can see why it might stimulate a few randy young selver-herders into passion." She looked back at me, and we stood there gazing at each other for a long moonlit moment. It was an instant in time that could have gone either way, then something about her stance told me that, although she would not have been averse to lying with me in among the flowers, it wasn't really me she wanted to be with. I felt sharp disappointment, shocking myself. Till that moment I hadn't considered Blaze in those terms. Yet now I found myself wanting her, needing her comfort, her companionship, her tenderness. The idea of possessing such a woman, of being possessed by her, was overwhelmingly attractive.

Creation, don't be stupid, I told myself crossly. It's Flame. Blaze prefers women. She wants Flame, but Flame prefers men. That must be it. That's sad. If you want to bed anyone, my lad, you'd better start hankering after the Cirkasian.

She'd probably do it too, if her activities with the lad—or lads—from Kyn were any indication.

With one accord, we turned and made our way back toward the camp. "You will have to tell me what it is about you and smells," she said after a while.

"What's there to tell?" I asked lightly, and then spoiled the moment by blundering into a prickle bush. I swore and stopped to extricate myself. "We Plainsfolk have strong noses, that's all."

"Better noses than eyesight," she remarked, watching my ineffectual efforts with the hooked thorns of the plant, locally know as the wait-a-while. "A little more than that, I think. I am not cockle-brained stupid, Gilfeather. You know things that people oughtn't to know. It is magic?" She came over to help me unhook the thorns from my tagaird.

"There's no such thing," I said, irritated once more. "Our noses are different, that's all. As ye must have noticed, all Plainsfolk have noses which are straight and unusually long. Inside, the structure is verra different from other peoples of the Isles. Or so Garrow tells me. I have actually not dissected cadavers of downscarpers, but he has. He doesn't seem to have the same problem with cutting into dead bodies as he does with living ones. He says that anatomically our noses are more complex, with more nerve endings. And ye can hardly have failed to notice that the tips of them tend to twitch slightly when—when they are stimulated."

Finally free of the bush, we started off again. As if on cue, Seeker bounded up, leaping around like the overgrown puppy he was. He'd been killing again: his snout was bloody. I warded him off and then added, "There's naught more to it than that. Our sense of smell is more acute than yours, that's all."

"So acute that you can tell when people are approaching your village? And even what village they come from? Even exactly *who* they are?"

I stared at her, surprised. *Selverspit.* She had managed to infer a great deal from a few stray words of my father's. "We dinna speak of such things to downscarpers," I said finally.

"You may as well tell me. I have seen too much, heard too much, deduced too much. Even Garrowyn gave things away when he was treating Flame, back on Gorthan Spit. He could smell dunmagic. And you weren't joking when you said you smelled your village through the mist. Kel, don't *ever* make the mistake of thinking that because I am large, and female, I also have the brains of a beached whale."

"Oh. Er, no. Of course not. It's just that we, er, dinna like to—" I shut up again. "Oh, Creationless *hell*."

"We have to talk," she said.

Seeker, excited by my tone, was trying to jump up and lick my face. Exasperated, I asked, "Why in all the blue skies do ye keep such a daft dog?"

"He reminds me of the reason I am going with Flame to kill a dunmaster," she said with perfect seriousness. "Every time I look at him I am reminded of his previous owner, a lad called Tunn. You *will* talk to me, Gilfeather, and you will help us."

I looked at her in shock. "Help ye kill someone? Are ye out of your mind, then? I'm a physician and a chirurgeon. I *cure* people, not kill them." Then I remembered Jastriá, and reddened.

"I'm not asking you to kill anyone."

"Ye are asking me to help ye, and ye have murder on your mind."

"Not murder. Execution of a killer. The worst the world has ever known. Tunn was one of his victims: a child given a dun whipping and then left to die in agony."

I was stilled by the seriousness of her tone. "I'm a physician," I muttered, but the words seemed to lack force.

She threw up her hands. "I'll be a clawless crab. *Another* damn peacemonger! What is it about me, that I am a magnet for people who think we should have polite conversations and sip tea with the villains of the world? We *will* talk," she added again. "I promise you."

CHAPTER 8

NARRATOR: KELWYN

THE PEOPLE OF THE SKY PLAINS MAY HAVE condemned what I had done, but they were true to the unity of our people and the customs of the Plains. Six days later we left the Roof of Makaté without the Fellih-worshippers and the Havenlord's guards ever having caught up with us, and I knew that we had the guides from Tharn Gar to thank.

At the top of the Scarps we loosed the selvers, still wearing their saddles and loaded with our warm bedding and felted shelters. I lingered a moment to watch them disappear into the mist, and felt as if they carried part of my heart away with them, a part I would never know again. And so I suppose it was, for I never did see my father again, or speak to my mother, or joke with my brother. I never did look down on Wyn once more, or ride a selver over the Sky Plains, or smell the moonflowers under a doublemoon sky.

I turned away and started after Blaze and Flame on our way downscarp, a man who had lost part of himself. And for a moment I hated the two women who had brought me to this.

It was not an easy trail: it was not as well used as those that went to Mekatéhaven. This path wound down in tight zigzags to a narrow plain and hence to the port called Lekenbraig at the head of Niba Water. I'd been there once, but had never had a hankering to return. Most of the forest around it had been totally eradicated, slaughtered in order to mine the sand underneath. The sand was apparently heavily laced with alluvial tin that was used to make pewter, and to get at it, the trees and all that lived in them had been wiped from the face of the earth. When I'd passed that way last, I thought I'd caught a lingering aroma of a complexity of life that no longer existed, as though the clean-washed sands could not entirely rid themselves of their fecund past.

Even this time, as we came lower and lower and the mist cleared, the devastation gnawed at me. Knowing how vibrant the life of the coastal forests could be, I found it hard to disregard its total desecration with equilibrium when the result was spread out beneath us like a vellum map.

"What's the matter?" Blaze asked as we finally traversed this desert the next day, following a dusty trail from the foot of the scarp toward the distant town. "What's upsetting you?"

"The mining," I replied tersely. "D'ye know how much they killed to do all this?" I waved a hand at the sea of sand interspersed with ponds of lifeless water.

"You are upset about the death of *plants*?" she asked, puzzled.

"That's right. And each one of those plants teemed with life. It's all gone."

She looked at me blankly, struggling with the concept that a man could be upset by what happened to nonsentient life. "Does it matter?" she asked finally.

"The destruction of life and beauty always matters," I said.

"We need the tin."

"My people need no tin."

"Not everyone can live the way the Plainsmen do." She stopped short, aware of her unintended cruelty. *Jastriá.* "I'm sorry. There are no easy answers, Gilfeather."

"I will say it's hotter without the forest," Flame said, placating. "Much hotter than around Mekatéhaven where there were more trees. How far to this Lekenbraig?"

"Another day on foot," I replied.

"Then what?"

"We buy tickets on the packet boat for Porth."

"How long might we have to wait?"

"I think it's a matter of luck. There is a fair amount of trade between Porth and Lekenbraig, and the merchants travel to and fro. More to the point, though, is what will happen when those behind us follow us down, as they will once they realize we must have left the Roof of Mekaté. They could catch up with us while we wait for the packet."

I had tried to insist that we make ourselves a little less memorable. I was wearing Garrowyn's traveling garb which was nondescript and patched. I'd stained my red hair brown with the juice of keth berries—more usually used to draw patterns on the stoneware back in the tharns of the Sky Plains— and I had shaved my beard, but there was nothing I could do to disguise the reddish freckles that covered my skin. Being freckled was just part of being a Plainsman. Flame had obligingly tucked her golden hair into a scarf and wore her tunic unbelted—as if that could hide her attributes. But there was nothing much Blaze could do to disguise her height and her green eyes. She absolutely refused to wrap her sword and harness in her cloak, and snapped at me when I suggested it. I suppose that from a distance she could easily have passed for a man, and Seeker added authenticity to that role; he wasn't the kind of animal a woman usually had as a pet.

Both of them protested that there really was no need for all these precautions when a few illusions would work just as well. I took no notice. And I ignored the amused glance they exchanged. It was harder to ignore the sudden return of that sweet smell around Flame every time we passed someone.

We continued trudging on through the heat and the dazzle of sand, regretting by the minute that it hadn't been possible to bring our selvers with us. Around midday we stopped for a rest beside one of the ponds, glad to have found a straggly tree that offered some shade. "You're right about one thing, Gilfeather," Blaze said as she flung herself down on the sand at the edge of the water. "This place is dryboned-awful. Reminds me of Gorthan Spit. Do you think the water is all right to drink?"

She didn't wait for my answer, but drank anyway. We had no fuel to boil it and we were all thirsty. As she sat up again afterward, chin dripping, she fixed me with a look that told me that this time I was not going to wriggle out of what she had in mind: a serious talk. I had dodged it so far by always pressing us onward every time she brought the subject up, until Flame had told her to tie a knot in her tongue. "Every damn time I want to rest, you start in on Kel, and he jumps up and tells us to hurry on. Can't you please keep your mouth shut? I need to sit down for once and be able to relax!"

This time Blaze was not going to take my evasive tactics for an answer. "I want to know about the Skyfolk's sense of smell, Gilfeather. It might be important to us. And I want to tell you about sylvmagic, because you need to understand what it can do."

I had a drink, then went to sit with my back to the tree before I answered. "We dinna like to talk about our abilities to downscarpers. Our sense of smell is our defense."

"I'm willing to swear that anything you say won't go any further."

"Me too," Flame said. "If only to make sure that we have this conversation at last, and get it out of the way."

"There's naught to tell, really. We just have a better sense of smell than anyone else."

"How good?" Blaze asked, her eyes skewering me. "What can you smell right now?"

"First, what can ye smell?" I countered.

They both took a deep breath. Disconcertingly, so did Ruarth. He was sitting on top of Blaze's pack, taking an intelligent interest in everything, as usual.

"Seeker," Flame and Blaze said simultaneously, and burst out laughing. Flame added, "So what else is new? The wretched animal always stinks."

"Is that all?" I asked.

They tried again. "The ointment I've been putting on Seeker," Blaze said. "My own sweat. Your sweat. The watery smell of the pond. That's all, I think."

"The tree," Flame added. "There's a smell of resin or sap or something."

"Anything else?"

They shook their heads.

"What about you?" Blaze asked, still curious. She wanted to know.

"Everything around us," I said. "The sand, our bodies, the tree, what's in our packs. There are some ants in the tree bark." I nodded to the track we were following. "There's some folk up there. Not Sky People, obviously, but I would know that anyway, by their smell. We smell quite different, perhaps because usually we dinna eat meat. Some of these folk are women. There's at least one still nursing a bairn—I can smell the lactation. One of the adults has bad teeth. There's an animal . . . an animal that eats plants. An ox, I suppose. They use them around here to pull carts. And there's several cats. Some chickens. There's probably a house of some kind, because I can smell food being cooked . . . Fish. Seaweed. Tomatls."

"How far away?"

I shrugged. "Depends on the wind. Maybe a mile. Beyond them, way beyond, is the sea. I can faintly smell that, if I concentrate. The strongest odors of the port: fresh tar, wet sails, water-soaked hulls. And the stench of the city. That's worse: charnel houses, middenheaps."

"So you really could smell your tharn through the mist! Don't you get overwhelmed?" Flame asked, fascinated. "Smelling Seeker here is bad enough; I can't fathom just how awful it must to be able to smell *everything*." She intrigued me, this lass from Cirkase. She seemed to see so much of the world, of life in fact, in terms of how it affected others. Blaze wanted to know how to make use of my talents; Flame just worried about me.

"Hmm," Blaze agreed. "A simultaneous whiff of every latrine in Lekenbraig would be hard to take, I imagine."

"It's like, oh, background noises. As we are talking now, ye dinna hear the leaves in the tree rustling in the breeze over your head, or the cicada singing. It's there, but ye filter it out. 'Tis the same with us. I dinna want to smell the latrines, so I block the stench from my consciousness, if not from my nose."

"So how is this a defense for the Plainsfolk?" Blaze asked.

"No one can ever creep up on us unexpectedly. Just as a loud noise would wake you in the night, an unexpected smell would wake me, or a whole tharn. Which came in handy on occasion in the past, when downscarpers attacked, thinking to seize our land or our herds."

"Of what use is a warning if you won't fight anyway? You don't, do you?" she persisted.

"No. We've never had to. We melt away into the meadows. We whistle in the selvers. A whole herd of selvers obeying sounds that no man can hear can be verra, er, intimidating. And they dinna like strangers. You don't know how odd it was that Skandor let you ride him that day . . . Anyway, no interloper has ever tarried on the Plains. We have never been conquered."

"Do you recognize individual people by smell? Your father did, didn't he?"

"Oh, aye. Ye may never forget a face; we never forget a smell, and everyone is unique. If I were to meet you again in ten years, it would be your body odor I would remember. Ye have an unforgettable aroma, Blaze Halfbreed."

Flame giggled. "Maybe he's telling you that you stink, Blaze."

She ignored her. "No, Gilfeather, it's got to be more than that. Garrowyn once said he smelled fear. You not only smell people; you smell their intentions. Their emotions."

Flame looked startled. "You mean you could tell if I, er, liked you or not?"

I grinned.

She was indignant. "That's downright embarrassing."

"Dinna fret. It is not all that subtle. I could tell if ye disliked me strongly, or wanted me strongly. Or if ye wanted to hurt me. The shades in between are not always all that clear."

Blaze cocked her head thoughtfully. "What about lies? Can you tell if someone is lying?"

"Sometimes." I hesitated. "Well, most of the time, if the lie was spoken maliciously, in order to deceive. But then, so could ye, I imagine. And ye have a nose that doesna smell a thing unless it's sitting on your lap."

She smiled faintly, acknowledging the indirect compliment. "I think you're a dangerous man, Kelwyn Gilfeather. I think you know far more about me than I would like you to know."

I smiled back, as bland as I knew how to make it. She was going to be much more cautious around me in future, but it wouldn't do her any good. My nose told me more about people, even about her, than her eyes and instinct told her about others.

"You must be one helluva doctor," she said softly. "You can smell disease." Trust her to go directly to what was important. In the Sky Plains, we went to the patients and told them they were ill, not the other way around. "So," she said thoughtfully, "once we are in Lekenbraig, you will be able to tell us when our followers reach the town?"

I nodded. "Aye. I have their smells in my memory. Ye dinna ken, but their guides from Gar brought them quite close to us several times, then veered away and went elsewhere." It had been deliberate; I knew that. The guides had wanted me to know that I was at their mercy. That I owed my freedom to their magnanimity. Yet they also wanted me to know the men who followed us, because I was a Plainsman, and those who followed were not.

"How many of the others altogether?"

"There are two Fellih-priests and ten Fellih-guards, plus eight of the Havenlord's guards. The Gar guides will no follow us down, of course."

"You can tell the difference between the Fellih and the Havenlord's men?"

"Oh, aye. Those stupid hats of the priests smell when they get wet. Besides—"

"Yes?"

"Religious fervor has a certain odor. When they pray, I can tell. Shall we move on now?"

"No, not yet," Blaze said, to Flame's undisguised relief. "I want you to know about what Flame can do. What any sylv can do. And why we don't have to worry too much about being followed, as long as you have warning of when they are around, which you evidently can have. We will make a good team: a sylv for illusions, two Aware to see the magic, one of them a bird for spying and the other a sword for tight spots, and, lastly, a nose for just about everything else."

"I am *no* part of any team," I said, appalled. "Let's get that firmly fixed in your head. I am going to Amkabraig on Porth to pick up a trunk of medicines when it arrives, and from there I will catch the packet to Breth. That's *all*. I am not interested in what ye're doing. Ye ruined my life between the two of you, and the sooner we part, the better."

She was unperturbed. "Nonetheless, I want to show you what sylvmagic is all about."

"Maybe a demonstration is what he needs," Flame suggested. They exchanged smiles and I had the horrible feeling that I was somehow at their mercy. I could smell them savoring the moment.

WE WALKED ON IN THE HEAT. EVEN Seeker drooped as he trotted from one pond to the next, drinking copiously at all, taking an occasional swim to cool down and then coming back to shower us with water. A few miles down the road, we came across the small settlement that I had smelled: a huddle of homes made of tar-paper haphazardly tied together and anchored down with rocks; a good wind would have disintegrated them, and possibly did from time to time.

"This will do," Blaze said. "Let's convince this barnacle-skulled unbeliever that magic exists. Hide us, Flame, and you do the talking."

"I trust there's none of the Aware down there?" the Cirkasian asked her.

"Not that I can sense."

There was a sudden sweetness in the air; that same cloying scent. "I'm ready," she said, "let's go."

The closer we came to the huts, the stronger that smell became; I hadn't the slightest doubt that it was somehow emanating from Flame. In her sweat? I wondered. How? *Why?* The man of science in me was intrigued.

A few snot-nosed children were playing in the dust outside the huts as we came up. One of them had a chest problem that would be the death of him within months unless he was treated. Wheezing, he ran into a hut as soon as he saw we were going to stop, and shouted for his mother. "Ma, ma, dere's a lady here!" It wasn't a woman who came out in answer, though; the hut disgorged five or six men. They were all gaunt fellows, beaten down by a lifetime of poor nutrition and constant work. From my previous visit to this area, I knew enough to guess that they were dulang-washers. After most of the readily available tin was extracted, poor people moved in with their sieve-stands and flat dishes, called dulangs, to re-sift and wash the sand left behind, collecting the tiny granules of tin not extracted the first time around. It was hard, back-breaking work for little return.

Blaze grabbled Seeker by the ruff with one hand and me by the arm with the other, and pulled us both back a little, away from Flame. I opened my mouth to mutter a warning that I didn't like the smell of these people, but she shushed me with a gesture, slipped her pack to the ground and extracted her sword from its scabbard. Not one of the group of men even looked her way; they were all gazing at Flame. Well, that was not unexpected. Most men would.

Flame smiled, apparently unfazed by the lack of welcome we were getting. "I wonder, my good men," she said pleasantly, "whether you could tell me if I am on the right track for Lekenbraig?"

"Well, lookee here," the largest one of the group said with a grin that was definitely predatory. He smelled like a grass-lion that's spotted its dinner. "A pretty lass that's all alone. Now whadd'ya make of that, lads?"

"Leave the girl be," a voice said from the doorway. It was a middle-aged woman with several children clinging to her skirts. Her request sounded more like a whine than an order, and she was ignored.

"Shall we ask the lovely one to linger a while?" one of the older men suggested. He reached forward to touch Flame, but somehow he misjudged and his groping hand clutched at nothing.

The others assumed he was teasing Flame, but I caught the whiff of the fellow's surprise in my nostrils. I stirred uneasily. The whole scene was making me feel uncomfortable. Beside me, Blaze remained quiet, the point of her blade on the ground between her feet, one hand on the hilt, the other still gripping Seeker. I could not smell any emotion at all from either her or Flame. They were both as calm as a pond on a windless day.

"Tell you what," the large man said, "we'll give you the answer if you'll give each of us a kiss."

One of the others guffawed. "I know where I'd like her to kiss me," he said, and accompanied the words with a gesture just in case no one understood his joke.

I made a move to step forward, but Blaze grabbed me, jerking me back. I tripped and sat down hard on the ground, all the air whooshing out of my lungs. For the next few seconds I made fish-like gobbles and observed all that happened through a blur of tears.

Flame, with a casual movement that he must surely have seen coming, kicked the man between the legs. I couldn't understand why he didn't dodge. Predictably, he doubled up in agony.

"There?" she asked politely.

The woman hustled the children back into the hut. Incomprehensibly, the men were all ignoring Blaze, Seeker and myself. I was heaving in air in gasps; Blaze was having to keep a firm hold on the dog—he was eager to enter the fray, and his teeth were bared in a way that predicted a nasty future for any adversary—yet none of the men even looked our way. Blaze helped me to my feet. "Sorry. Didn't mean to flatten you," she said in my ear.

The men gazed down at the injured man, perplexed, as if they could not understand how he had ended up on the ground. The leader, the large fellow, ignored his friends and made a grab at Flame. She side-stepped unhurriedly and strolled over to where we stood. The sweet smell was almost overpowering.

And still the men didn't look our way. They didn't even seem to notice that Flame had walked away from them. The leader swiped the air in front of him and then recoiled in horror. One of the others shrieked. Another, slightly braver, made a tentative movement to touch something that he apparently saw in front of him. When he couldn't catch hold of it he screamed out, "It's a ghost! Look out—she'll suck the spirit out of you!" Without further thought, they all ran. A couple vanished into the huts, the rest scuttled around to the back.

"Let's go on, shall we?" Blaze asked calmly.

"So," I said as we started up the track again, "what do ye say happened back there?" I tried to sound unfazed, but the truth was I was shaken.

"Flame made an illusion of herself that looked real. At the same time, she blurred herself and us. We weren't exactly invisible: if their attention hadn't been focused on the illusion, they may even have seen us, which is why I held on to my sword. Better to be safe than sorry."

Flame added. "The illusions, of course, are not real. I could have made them almost solid, had I wanted, but it takes a lot of energy. Easier to make them of air, so when the men reached out to touch what they thought was me, their hands went straight through the illusion."

"In the meantime," Blaze continued, "her real self spoke to them, her real self kicked that man. He didn't see it coming because he was focused on the illusion. Those are two of the aspects of sylvmagic: illusion and blurring reality. Clever use of illusion can fool someone into believing all sorts of lies. The third aspect is warding; the fourth healing. And there are a few other odd things that sylvs can do. Create a sylv light, for example. It glows like a lantern, but can't be seen by anyone else unless they are Aware. Useful talent, that. Dunmagic goes still further, into other realms: destruction, disease, coercion. Nasty stuff."

My interest quickened, although I was still reeling from the impact of all that I had seen. "Tell me about healing."

Flame nodded. "A sylv can heal other people to a certain degree. It's draining, though. If the illness is severe, it's best done using more than one sylv. And we can't cure everything. We can do a lot for ourselves, from within. We can even stop conception if we want, which comes in handy." *Especially if you're raped.* The words hung in the air between us, unspoken.

"And what's warding?" I asked.

"The ability to put in place a barrier of sylvpower, through which neither dunmagic nor anything living can pass. Except the Aware, of course. We found out, though, that the dunmaster doesn't seem all that bothered by wards; he's too powerful. Or he was. I couldn't defend myself against him; it seemed as if much of my sylvtalent just faded away when he was near. I couldn't ward at all, and even my illusion of having an arm was hard to maintain. That was not a nice feeling." The sweetness had already diminished, leaving only traces. As her past memories churned, I also caught the mustiness of her fear.

I thought back to what had happened at the huts. There had to be a scientific explanation: there was no such thing as magic. Mass hallucination. It had to be some kind of hallucination. The sweetness . . . it was exuded by Flame and it had some hallucinatory properties. Some abnormality in the metabolism of the sylvtalents . . . chemicals in the sweat. My mind raced. The so-called Aware, and we Sky Plains dwellers, were immune to the effect, so we didn't see the illusion. That would explain a lot. That was why the priest had not taken all the money from the inn table; why the guards had not seen Flame give Blaze the sword in jail; why we had been able to escape so easily after the stoning of Jastriá.

But it wasn't magic; it was science. It had to be.

"Why do I get the impression that we haven't convinced you of anything?" Blaze asked after a while.

"There's some kind of rational explanation," I said.

"Yes," she agreed. "And it is this: there is such a thing as sylvmagic."

I didn't answer.

"Trench take it, Gilfeather, you are as stubborn as one of your damn selvers!"

She was right: I was stubborn. However, as we walked on, I felt uneasy. It was hard to explain just how Flame could control someone else's hallucinations. Moreover, something had happened during Flame's demonstration that I had not liked. It took me a while to put my finger on it, and when I did, I liked it even less. At some point when she had been fooling them with her illusion—the hallucination—there had been a jab into my consciousness that had pained me, a sharp prod of something unpleasant.

If I had not been a man of science, I would have called it evil.

A letter from Researcher (Special Class) S. iso Fabold, National Department of Exploration, Federal Ministry of Trade, Kells, to Masterman M. iso Kipswon, President of the National Society for the Scientific, Anthropological and Ethonographical Study of non-Kellish Peoples.

Dated this day 14/2nd Double/1793

Dear Uncle,
I enclose another packet of translated conversations for you. Hope you continue to enjoy Gilfeather's account as he blunders along, trying to make sense of the world he now has to live in. As much as I didn't like him, I still found myself empathizing as I listened to his tale.

I am thinking of giving a paper entitled Medicine and the Glory Isles: Shamans or Scientists? *at the Annual Convention of our Society this year, as a continuation of the subject of my spring meeting presentation. I know it will interest you, at least, for you asked about how efficacious Glorian medicines were, and whether our sawbones could learn anything from their medical practices. When I consider that old fuddy-flopping quack who administered to me here when I was suffering from that fever a couple of months back, I rather think the answer must be yes!*

However, I also know that the medics trained at Gilfeather's hospital put much emphasis on things which seem quite worthless: extreme cleanliness, for example, scrubbing themselves and everything else in sight, as if that matters to the progress of an illness or a birthing. Special diets are another favorite. I guess that's not much different from Aunt Rosris and her possets and soup! And they have one absolutely revolting practice that I heard of: using live maggots in a wound. Cobwebs and mold are used in other treatments. I have no idea how anyone could be stupid enough to think any of that helps.

People from the Keeper Isles are full of tales of sylv

healing, of course, and how miraculous it was, but when I asked for proof they just said it doesn't happen anymore. Really, they are like children sometimes, full of tales of long ago when things were magical.

What did you think of Kelwyn Gilfeather's explanation of the sylv–dunmagic phenomenon? A medical problem! Interesting, eh? I liked his theory when I first heard it; it seemed to me that it would explain so much. But more of that later on.

I have just received good news: the return voyage to the Isles of Glory is officially confirmed for RV Seadrift, RV Windrift, and a naval brigantine, KN Warrior, and I have the letter appointing me to head the ethnographical team again, as well as making me the overall Scientific Comptroller! The bad news is that we will have a huge complement of missionaries, even Aetherialia nuns, over all of whom I will have no control. Two more ships, both merchantmen, have had to be commissioned just for them.

It will be at least another four to five months before the fleet sets sail . . . and so much to do in the meantime.

My fondest love to Aunt Rosris.

Your dutiful nephew,
Shor iso Fabold

CHAPTER 9

NARRATOR: KELWYN

"I THINK IT WOULD BE A GOOD IDEA IF YOU learned how to understand Ruarth," Blaze remarked as we trudged along the trail toward Lekenbraig. "And it would help pass the time."

I looked around us. In all directions, nothing much more than a vast expanse of blinding white sand and one barren pond of dark water after another. Then a shimmer of tar-papered poverty as another village straggled into view; or the occasional dulang-washer working knee-deep in water with his sieves and dishes, body burned black by a relentless sun; or a broken bole of a forest giant, stark remnant of a once great forest. They were scenes emptied of all joy; portraits that seared my Plainsman's soul.

Anything to take my mind off the horror of that landscape. "Aye," I said. "A good idea." I wiped my face. Although the day wasn't windy, somehow we were all covered in a fine film of dust. Perspiration made trails on our faces like rills down a hillside.

Flame explained the rudiments of Dustel bird-talk. "You have to watch in order to understand," she said. "It's largely a sign language, conveyed as much by stance, or wing and foot movements, or the angle of the head, as by sound."

She ran through the basics, and the bird on her shoulder cooperated in the demonstration. At first I found that uncanny. It made me uneasy, as if the laws of the natural world had somehow been subverted. So I tried to stop thinking of Ruarth as a bird, and thought of him as something else instead: a Dustel, sentient like us, but a being who could not speak as we did. It was easier that way. By the end of that first day, I found I could understand a whole slew of common phrases, things like: "I don't know"; "yes, of course"; "I'm hungry"; "turn left here"; "look over there." I knew now that a partly open beak accompanied by a sideways tilt to the head was a grin; when accompanied by a cocked tail as well, then it was a laugh. More complex conversations involved song: trills and tone and pace. That was much more difficult for someone who had always thought that one bird sounded very much like another.

That night we slept on the ground near a pond; the following morning we walked on into Lekenbraig, our Dustel bird language lessons continuing apace. Blaze, I discovered, was still learning as well, and the lessons developed into a mildly combative competition between us: I was trying to catch up; she strove to keep ahead. It was our way of continuing our clash without actually discussing the real issue: whether or not I was going to help them rid the world of a dunmaster.

We finally arrived in Lekenbraig in the late afternoon, just as I was mastering the complexities of wing-stretching and adjectives. Our first inquiry in the city, made by Blaze while cloaked in the illusions of a Fen Islander man, was about the packet boat. The news was not good: it seemed likely we would have to wait more than a week. The direct packet—and there was only one since the second had recently had its masts ripped out in a whirlstorm—was not in port. The through packet, the one that went on to the Xolchas Stacks and Breth, was fully booked for another two sailings.

We took rooms at an inn near the waterfront, with a view that looked out onto one of the wharves. It was noisy, it was smelly and it was cheap. I hadn't been there ten minutes before I felt myself sliding down into a depression as deep as the night of a darkmoon month. I was assailed by stench: dead fish, tar and hemp, whale oil, human excrement, stale semen on my pallet, cheap perfume on what passed for a pillow, boiled cabbage everywhere in the inn, dog's piss and tomcat spray on every street corner. And human emotion. Raw and uncurtailed: human fury and despair, lust and avarice; you name it, I could smell it, intense and all-pervading. It was always hard to take at first when I descended to the coast. At home, knowing the skill of our neighbors' noses, we Plains-folk kept our passions furled tight inside our hearts and minds. On the Plains, we murmured; in the coastal cities, humanity roared.

I flung myself down on the bed and was overwhelmed by a feeling of loss: I was exiled for the rest of my days. There was no going back to the predictability of the Roof of Mekaté, no return to the life I had once led. The pure smells and fresh aromas of the Sky Plains were now only a memory. *Jastriá, ye've had your revenge.*

I had never before felt so wretchedly sorry for myself.

When I did not go down for dinner, as we had agreed, Blaze came and knocked on my door. I knew it was her, my nose told me that, but I didn't stir. She knocked again, louder, and I ignored it still. I should have known better: a moment later she had slipped her sword in the space between door and jamb and forced up the latch.

I stayed where I was, on the bed with its miserable thin pallet, its lack of linen and its single dirt-encrusted blanket. The only light in the room was what came in through the glassless window from lamps outside, where chandlers' supplies and tin ore were being delivered to a cargo ship tied up opposite. "D'ye always feel ye have a right to enter a room, even when it is latched?" I asked without looking at her.

She ignored that. "I brought you some goat's milk," she said. "And some bean curds stewed with lily petals. Oh, and an omelette. And seeing that I have been good enough to go to all that trouble to get you food you will eat, you will be good enough to eat it."

I sat up, ashamed, reddening under her scrutiny even as I answered grumpily, "Aye, *ma'am.* Ye sound like the old dame in our tharn who used to teach the young'uns their alphabet." I lit the stub of a candle while she dumped her purchases on the room's one other item of furniture: the wash stand.

"I'm not going to let you sulk. Besides, I have to talk to you."

"*More* conversation? And what if I am too crabbit for talk?"

"Crabbit?"

"Bad-tempered."

She shoved a plate into my hands, and I had to admit it smelled appetizing. I tried some of the omelette, without mentioning that most Skyfolk regarded eating eggs with the same distaste we had for eating animals slaughtered for food. I told myself the embryo had died long before it was cooked, and pragmatically ate it all.

"Flame and I had dinner, thanks for asking. She's gone to sleep."

I ignored her sarcasm.

"She's still weak. We have hardly had time to rest this past month."

"I could make up a tonic. How long ago was her arm amputated?"

She thought back, counting up the days. "I'm not exactly sure . . . I was in a dark hell-hole of a pit for part of the time and I've never asked anyone how long we were in there. The amputation must have been done at least ten days before we left the Spit, probably more like twelve. Then we took a day to get down the length of the Spit on the sea-pony, another three days at sea, another ten to get from where we landed to Mekatéhaven, two days in the city, a day in the jail—how long since then?"

I counted in my head. "Sixteen. No, seventeen." Which meant it had been just eighteen days since I had first clapped eyes on them in the inn in Mekatéhaven. It seemed like half a lifetime.

"Um, that makes it about forty-six days."

I stared at her. "It's got to be longer than that, surely? That arm is well healed."

"Sylv healing," she replied. "Councillor Syr-sylv Duthrick worked his magic on it, after some persuasion. And Flame herself, of course, once she was strong enough."

I thought about that, wondering if a patient under my care

would have done so well. What did these sylvs know that I did not?

Blaze continued to fret. "Still, I worry about her. It's been unpleasantly stressful ever since we left Gorthan Spit. Before that, what she went through was sheer hell, of course. And I need her strong again. We'll need her illusions to keep us safe and to fight this dunmaster. I wish she'd rest somewhere for a while, just to recuperate. But, for all her whingeing about rest breaks, she seems . . . driven. It worries me. It's as if she feels there is very little time, that if we delay, something terrible will go wrong. I think she's weaker than she makes out." She started pacing the room.

I gave a mocking smile. "Dinna tell me Blaze the Sword-wielder believes in nebulous 'feelings' . . ."

"I've learned to listen to them sometimes, yes. Because they can be a mirror reflection of what is happening around us. And right now I think Flame knows something deep inside her that none of us is consciously aware of. I wonder sometimes if she hasn't still got some of the dun contamination within her. Morthred's contamination. A subverted sylv is . . . attracted to the person who subverted them. After planting his evil inside them, all Morthred had to do was wait for them to come to him, apparently of their own free will. Flame told me that, back on the Spit. It was what she felt."

"And ye think it's what she feels now?"

"I don't know. She is no longer subverted . . . everyone assured me of that, including Keeper Councillor Duthrick. But perhaps there is some . . . some residue left . . . ? Maybe that is why she is so anxious to face Morthred again."

"Ye're Aware, or so ye tell me. Would ye not see the dun if she still had it?"

She stopped pacing and mused, "I would have thought so. But I can't sense anything tangible. There's no dun color about her now, none. But then, I'm not omnipotent. I couldn't even tell a pregnant woman her baby was a sylv."

I expressed an interest in that, so she told me about a sylv woman called Mallani, who had wanted to know if her child was sylv or not. "It was strange," she said as she finished, "the placenta was so rich in color, it was almost more dun than sylv. I suppose it is possible that the baby only became sylv during the birth process, because of what was pumped into it through the placenta. Or maybe I just couldn't sense the child while it was still inside its mother."

"So maybe your Awareness is not so aware after all?"

"Oh, shut up, Gilfeather! I thought we'd managed to convince you that there is more out there than just science and laws of mathematics. When are you going to open up your mind to the reality of magic?"

"About the same time as I get over losing my home and my family and my life, I imagine."

That gave her pause. We glared at each other in heavy silence for a while, then I added, "Seems ye will be stopping here a wee while anyway, as we wait for the packet. Flame will have time to build up strength. But did ye not say that her magic wouldna work against the dunmaster? That he is too strong? So how do you expect to defeat him?" I still didn't believe all they'd told me about magic, of course, but I was interested in their plans.

"Warding didn't work. But illusions did. At least when he wasn't expecting them, they did. And now, well, he *was* weakened . . . I'm hoping he's taking a long time to recover, although we can't count on it. The sooner we tackle him, the better. Maybe that's why Flame is so driven. All we need is a few illusions from her to allow us to get close to him, and then we have my sword to finish him off. But she needs to be strong. A small illusion—like building an illusory new arm— is easy, but hiding us, or disguising us: that takes real power and is hard to maintain over a long period of time without growing exhausted."

I must have looked skeptical, because she added, "I think I need to tell you the whole wretched story."

"Ye don't have to tell me anything," I said impatiently. "In a week or so, the packet boat is going to sail away from that wharf and we'll all be on it. A week or so after that, we shall disembark in Amkabraig, and we need never see one another again. Which will suit me just fine."

"You are ungracious."

"*Ungracious?* D'ye blame me? If it weren't for you two, I could have ridden out of Mekatéhaven without half the Fellih-priesthood and the Havenlord's troops on my tail!" I could still be a Plainsman, living on the Roof of Mekaté. I tried to push the bitterness away and concentrated on the bean curds. They were good.

"I want to tell you a story, whether you want to listen or not."

I shrugged. "Go ahead. I imagine it will be entertaining, if nothing else."

"Flame's real name," she began, "is Lyssal. She is the Castlemaid of Cirkase . . ."

I had speared some sea-lettuce and it was on its way to my mouth when she said that. I dropped the lot back on the plate and gaped at her. "The *heir* to an *islandom*?"

"And you," she added, "ought to be able to tell that I am speaking the truth." She came and sat next to me on the bed. "I want to tell you who I am, who I was, all about us, and why we're going to look for a dunmaster . . ."

And she went on to tell me the story of what had happened to them all on Gorthan Spit.

The tale was a strange one. It seemed that Flame ran away from Cirkase with Ruarth because her father wanted her to marry the Islandlord of Breth. The Keeper Isles had pushed the match because they wanted to please both Breth and Cirkase in order to gain a trade advantage. As wildly unlikely as it sounded, they were trying to buy—from those two islandoms—the ingredients for a black powder that was the ammunition for cannon-guns, a new weapon they had developed. In fact, the Keepers, under a Keeper Councillor named Duthrick, were so keen on finding Flame that they were prepared to hunt her down.

And the hunter they'd sent was Blaze.

At the same time, Duthrick himself was looking for a dunmaster called Morthred and the sylvs he had subverted. On the island of Gorthan Spit, the hunters and the hunted met up. There Flame inadvertently attracted the attention of Morthred. She was abducted, raped, and had to have her arm amputated because of a dun infection. Blaze, and a Menod priest called Tor Ryder, came to her aid, only to end up in trouble themselves. That was where the ghemph, Eylsa, was involved; she was instrumental in freeing Blaze—but died in the process.

Shortly afterward, two Keeper ships attacked the village of Creed, Morthred's dunmagic enclave on the spit. Morthred and his henchman Domino managed to escape the attack by fleeing to Gorthan Docks on a sea-pony. There they seized the *Keeper Liberty*—which had just arrived bearing Keeper sylv reinforcements for Duthrick—and forced the ship to sail for Mekaté.

Not long afterward, Blaze enraged Duthrick by wresting Flame away from him, and the two women headed after Morthred.

I had to believe the tale, or rather I had to believe that she thought it was the truth. I could scent no deception, although I was aware that there were some evasions. She didn't tell me, for example, how she felt about Patriarch Syraware Tor Ryder; I only found *that* out much later. The rest was spread out for me to absorb as I would. When she had finished, it was long after midnight.

There was a silence as I thought about all she had said. She didn't ask for my comment or pester me for my reaction, as most women would have done; she simply walked to the window and looked down on the darkness of the wharves.

"How did ye know the dunmaster headed for Mekaté?" I asked.

"He'd made the mistake of telling Flame he had another dun enclave there. Once Creed was in ruins, it seemed logical he would try to get to it. In fact, he went to Mekatéhaven first, to revictual the ship. By the time we'd walked into the port from Cape Kan, the vessel had been and gone. A local merchant, one of the Awarefolk, even told the port authorities that the ship and its crew were all drenched in dun color, but the harbormaster was an idiot and while he dithered, the *Keeper Liberty* sailed. That's when Flame and I decided to go to the ghemphs—and ran afoul of the Fellih-priest instead."

"So," I said, "ye earned the enmity of a Keeper Councillor. Is that likely to be a problem in the future?"

"Yes. Syr-sylv Ansor Duthrick is not a forgiving man, and he is powerful in The Hub. Well connected too. His wife is a right proper bitch from a well-bred sylv family."

"He sounds like a fool to me. Why did he not have Flame under better guard?"

She turned, grinning. "Because he thought I'd already left the Spit with Tor."

"It's an interesting tale, I'll give ye that."

"Think about it, Gilfeather. I'll say goodnight now. It's late."

After she left, it was a long time before I was able to sleep. I lay awake trying to decide how much was true, and how much was self-deception. Dunmagic sores, for example. Perhaps they were just some kind of gangrenous infection? Perhaps this Morthred had a way of infecting people, and it was the infection that changed personalities? That story about the baby born to a Keeper sylv on Duthrick's ship . . . an infection, passed from mother to child? That was an interesting observation about the color of the "magic" she observed . . . And wards? What were these wards—these webs made of magic light—that Flame had been unable to cross? Had she been somehow mesmerized, first by Morthred in Gorthan Docks and Creed, and then by Duthrick on board his ship? Some Sky Plains physicians made use of mesmeric suggestion to relieve pain, and I knew it could be amazingly effective. Or was it just the power of suggestion? Tell someone the ward was there, and have them believe it enough, maybe they would not be able to pass through it . . .

There had to be a rational explanation. The world was a truly wondrous place—I knew that just from living on the Sky Plains—but it was the mystique of Creation that made it that way, not spells. To explain the wondrous, it was just a matter of finding the logic behind all the small miracles that made up our lives.

Still, it *was* a long time before I fell asleep.

THE WHARVES OF LEKENBRAIG WERE IN A continual hustle of activity. There were ships berthing and unloading and departing all the time; a nonstop flow of vessels and goods and sailors. I suppose it was to be expected: each side of Mekaté was cut off from the others by the steep walls of the Scarps; each coastal bay was divided from the next by tropical forest, much of it indented by swamps and tidal inlets and mangroves. The easiest way to get yourself or your goods from one place to the next was by sea.

Trade and packet boats circled the main island of Mekaté both clockwise and counterclockwise. Ships left Lekenbraig on the international trade routes as well: the wharves here were the center of the Mekatéen trade with Xolchas Stacks, Breth Island and The Hub. The third group of boats in and out of the harbor were those of the fishing fleet; like most people of the Glory Isles, or at least those of coastal regions, Mekaté-folk ate seafood every day.

As soon as she realized just how busy the port was, Flame determined to find a berth for us on a cargo boat to Amkabraig, the southern port of Porth, instead of waiting for the packet. "Because," she remarked to me in Blaze's hearing, "Blaze will be as grumpy as a starving shark if she has to wait in this dump a week or two doing nothing."

"So patience isn't my strongest virtue," Blaze admitted. "You'd better hope we're successful."

They left the inn after breakfast the next day, together with Seeker, apparently in the guise of husband and wife taking their dog for a stroll. Ruarth also flew off, saying that he was going to see if he could find more Dustel birds. It seemed the birds had dispersed throughout the archipelago after the is-lands were sunk, and their descendants could now be found scattered in all islandoms. Ruarth was hoping there was a flock or two in Lekenbraig; if so, he would have an instant source of information.

I stayed in my room while I waited for them all to come back. I made up a tonic for Flame from the medicines I had with me, and spent the rest of the time writing down as much as I could remember about the Dustel bird language, and then watching the ordered chaos of loading and unloading cargo beneath my window. I was fascinated by the sails of the local ships: they were colorful, woven from flat strips in intricate patterns of scarlet and gold, turquoise and purple. I had seen such before once or twice, but I was more used to the dull-colored canvas, made from tropical hemp or Fen Island flax, of the inter-island vessels I had seen in Mekatéhaven.

Around midday the others all returned, reporting varying degrees of success. Ruarth had found a small group of Dustel birds. *Rogues,* he said, *but happy to be useful to a fellow Dus-*

tel. Blaze, on the other hand, had found out that no one wanted to offer any of us a berth.

"Why ever not?" I asked over lunch, which we all had in the taproom downstairs. "We have money to pay!"

"It took ages to find out," she said, "and it was Ruarth who finally extracted the information from his new Dustel acquaintances. It seems that the packet boats, all of them, including the ones on the circular routes around Mekaté, are owned by one large extended family called Dendridie. As you can imagine, they are exceedingly wealthy. They are also staunch Menod supporters of the Havenlord, and they have managed to have a law enacted in Mekatéhaven that forbids any ship other than a packet boat from taking paying passengers. If they do, the owner could lose the whole ship to the Havenlord's coffers, and the captain would be banned from sailing again. Needless to say, I couldn't find a captain or a ship's owner who would take that risk. Apparently it simply doesn't pay to tread on the toes of a Dendridie."

Ruarth started chittering, far too fast for either Blaze or me to follow.

"Did you get all that?" Flame asked when he had finished. We both shook our heads.

"He says that he thinks he can persuade a couple of young Dustel fellows to hitch a ride in the rigging of a cargo vessel to Porth, especially if we can hide some food for them on the ship somewhere. Once on Porth, they can start hunting for the dunmaster, do some on-the-ground spying, then meet us when our packet berths in Amkabraig and tell us all they've found out."

Blaze was cheered. "Would they really do that?"

Dustels hate dunmagickers, Ruarth said simply. He followed that statement up with something I translated as, *And they particularly hate this one, for obvious reasons. Anyway, if others won't go, I will go myself.* Flame fidgeted a bit at that, but she was wise enough not to say anything. I didn't think Ruarth would take kindly to being told what he could and could not do.

"All right," Blaze agreed. "That sounds like a helpful idea. But only if one of them is Aware. It would be too risky otherwise."

"If ye are right in what ye believe," I said, and I was careful with my wording, "Morthred obviously knows that Dustels became birds—he's the one who caused them to be that way." Even if I were to believe in magic, I would have had my reservations about the truth of that. The Dustel Isles had vanished some ninety or more years earlier. That would have made Morthred well over one hundred years old, but for the time being, I let the contradiction ride. "So would he not be suspicious about seeing such birds on his doorstep?"

"He knows the *original* Dustel Islanders became birds," Flame said, "but it is unlikely he knows their descendants are sentient. It is a well-kept secret, known to few. Hurry up and finish your lunch," she added. "Otherwise I am going to lose my hold on my illusion. And I don't know how we would explain the sudden change in our appearance."

As we all rose to leave, Blaze said quietly, "We still have a week or more to stay here, and I am afraid that means being inside most of the time. We don't want to tax Flame and we dare not go out without the illusion. I hope this won't bore you, Gilfeather."

"I'll live." I didn't bother to explain that it wouldn't be boredom that was a problem; it would be learning to live all over again with the daily assault on my sense of smell. And coming to terms with the knowledge that I could never go back to the Sky Plains.

THREE OR FOUR DAYS LATER THE FELLIH-priests, Fellih-guards and the Havenlord's men who had been following us arrived in Lekenbraig. I didn't see them, but I did smell them. They slept that night somewhere on the other side of the city, and the next day they started methodically searching. Ruarth flew out, after obtaining the general direction of their presence from me, and located them. By the end of the day, he was able to tell us where they were lodging: at the barracks of the city's town guard. Worse, they had enlisted the aid of the town guard. There weren't just twenty men looking for us now, there were something like a hundred and seventy. On a more encouraging note, he told us that two Dustel Island birds

were only too delighted to make the journey to Porth. Moreover, there was a ship leaving that very night with a cargo of
hempen rope for the shipbuilding yards of Amkabraig . . .

Flame located the ship, blurred herself and had food secreted all over it in a matter of minutes. When it sailed with
the tide just before midnight, the two birds were huddled in
the crow's nest.

On the morning of the day after, some of the Havenlord's
local guards arrived at our inn, looking for us. It seemed that
they already knew there were three inn guests who had booked
tickets on the next packet. They obviously had their sources of
information. The innkeeper came upstairs to tell us, politely,
that the town guard wanted to make our acquaintance, and that
they were waiting downstairs in the taproom. A glance out of
the window showed me that there were also guards on the
wharf; presumably a precautionary move to make sure we
didn't try to escape before they had checked us out.

Blaze looked unruffled. I hoped that she appeared that way
to the innkeeper as well, but I couldn't tell. He would have
been seeing Flame's illusion and I was completely oblivious
to what that was. All I saw was her polite nod to the man, as
she said, "We will be down directly." She turned to Flame.
"Hand me my coat, dear, will you?"

Flame—in her role as wife—obliged, but it wasn't the coat
she gave Blaze; it was her sword. As I drew in a sharp breath
at their audacity, the innkeeper nodded and left. Blaze held
open the door for us to leave. "Say as little as possible," she
told me as I brushed past her. "Flame will have trouble changing your accent."

I nodded, muttering, "Ye're mist-mad, the two of you."

Ruarth added, *Let's hope there are no Awarefolk among the
soldiers, or you'll all be up to your necks in guano.*

There were six guards waiting for us down in the taproom,
and several others hanging around just outside the door. Blaze
came down the stairs without hesitation, Flame immediately
behind her. I hung back a little. Ruarth disappeared up into the
rafters. It was only then, when I saw him up there watching us
from his vantage point, that I realized just how Blaze had
cheated at cards: that darn bird had been signaling to her what

everyone had in their hand. Creation, but they were an audacious trio. It was no wonder they had managed to mire themselves in trouble.

"I believe you wanted to meet us, guardsman?" Blaze asked the officer in charge, with just the right mix of imperiousness to an underling and courtesy to a stranger. "My name is Ducrest. This is my wife, Lyss. The other man is my servant. Is there some kind of problem?"

The guard in charge shook his head. "Sorry to have troubled you, Syr. We are seeking some fugitives, but you are obviously not them. We will not disturb you any further." He bowed, and gave a hand signal for his men to leave. They turned away to obey, all except the youngest, a small lad who could not have been more than fourteen or so. We all noted the expression on his face: he was looking at us as if we each had two heads. Blaze smiled at him.

Fortunately none of the other guards noticed. The officer in charge swept out past the boy, leaving him still standing there gaping, and the other guards followed.

Blaze swore under her breath.

"Aware?" Flame asked in a whisper.

Blaze nodded. Flame signaled Ruarth. He chittered something, and flew out the door after the boy when the lad finally gathered his wits and ran out.

I drew in a breath and felt the same thing that I had felt out on the road, the day Flame had spoken to the dulang-washers. That same feeling of dread, of pain, of something fundamentally *wrong*.

"Let's sit down and order a drink," Blaze said, unperturbed. "Ruarth will give us warning."

I almost choked as I groped for equilibrium. I finally managed to say, "If the lad's Aware, don't ye think we should be running?"

She shook her head and sat down at one of the tables, signaling for service as she did so. "In my experience, most tight spots melt away if you don't run. Running just tells everyone that you're guilty, and that it's probably worth their while to run after you. Three ciders, please." This last was for the serving girl.

"You'll have to get used to Blaze," Flame told me kindly.

"Traveling with her is sort of like hitching a ride on the back of a shark. While you hold on tight, you're fine; it's only when you fall off that you find yourself in deep water."

"That's wonderfully comforting," I said. "While the shark's pals are ripping my feet off, I shall console myself with the thought that I am perfectly safe from the one I am riding upon." Flame laughed. I took a calming breath; the awful feeling of wrongness had finally vanished.

The girl brought our drinks and I stuck my nose in the glass and wished I was just about anywhere else.

Twenty minutes later Ruarth returned and flew in to sit on our table.

Nothing to worry about, he said.

"The boy is Aware, though, isn't he?" Blaze asked.

He chittered. *Very much so.*

Blaze frowned. "He'd hardly sympathize with us. He's a guardsboy! Why didn't he tell the officer that we were lying?"

I lost much of Ruarth's answer, and Flame had to translate. It appeared that Ruarth had followed the lad and the other guards along the waterfront to the next inn, which they had searched as well. The boy had simply not spoken to any of the other guardsmen during that time, not about anything.

"I suggest we leave," I said. "Now."

"How did the lad smell to you?" Blaze asked me.

"Like he'd been tossed widdershins from a selver," I said. "He was shocked, bemused, muddled. Once he starts thinking straight, he'll act, surely."

"If we leave now, we'll instantly be objects of suspicion," Blaze said, still calm. "We stay."

"That's foolhardy," I said. But nonetheless, I admired her coolness. Did nothing *ever* ruffle her composure?

"No, it's not. Listen, I doubt that lad has ever seen sylvs or sylvmagic in his life, or, if he has, only from visiting Keepers. He'll either be too scared to report it, for fear he'd be accused of imagining things, or else he will associate the way we look—covered in the silver of Flame's sylvmagic—with Keepers. And no one messes with Keepers."

I downed the last of the cider. "Ye'd better be right, Blaze. Because if ye're wrong, ye'll have quite a burden on your conscience as we all languish in a Fellih prison."

Flame gave a snort. "You don't have to worry, Kel. She's relying on my illusions to get us out of any trouble she gets us into, as usual. Such is my fate, I fear: to be constantly rescuing the damsel in distress . . ." She grinned at Blaze, who rolled her eyes.

I stood up. "I'll be in my room if the bottom falls out of the world," I said sourly. "Come and tell me, Ruarth, when it's time for me to start panicking."

Back in the room, I dragged the bed over to the window so that I could sit there and keep an eye on the inn entrance. I was genuinely expecting the guards to return, full force; instead, three hours later I saw the lad coming back. He was no longer dressed in uniform, and he scuttled along as if he had a spitting selver on his tail.

Oh *hells,* I thought, here comes trouble.

CHAPTER 10

NARRATOR: KELWYN

DEKAN GRINPINDILLIE WAS BORN IN A simple one-room house on stilts on the tidal mudflats of the Kitamu Bays. When the tide went out, the mud beneath was exposed: a gray expanse of glutinous shore that may have looked solid, but would have been a treacherous graveyard to anyone unwise enough to set foot on it. No one came or went from the Grinpindillie household except by boat.

The house itself, built of driftwood, was hardly more than a shelter. It contained nothing that could be called furniture, except for a clay fireplace for cooking and a barrel for collecting rainwater, and it stood over a fish trap of mangrove wood. When the tide came in, fish were funnelled by lines of stakes into a woven trap beneath the house; when the tide went out, Dekan's father, Bolchar, climbed down a ladder to hook up the catch from the mud. Dekan's mother would then gut them, and salt and dry what they could not eat. Once a month, Bolchar would row his skiff to the coast where he would collect driftwood for fuel and, in a nearby village, exchange salted fish for vegetables, the occasional piece of old clothing, or some other necessity.

For his first seven years, that was all Dekan, or Dek, as he was called, knew of life. He helped his mother evaporate sea water for the salt it contained, then prepare the salted fish, laying the fillets out in the sun, bringing them in again before it rained. His entire existence revolved around keeping out of the way of his vile-tempered father—difficult when there was nowhere to run to—and listening to the stories his mother told him.

When he was seven, his father took him to the shore for the first time, on one of his monthly forays. Dek, however, did not get to enjoy the hospitality of the village: Bolchar put him to work gathering the driftwood along the edge of the mangroves. Thereafter he always accompanied his father, and gathering the fuel was his job. No matter how much he collected, his father was never satisfied, and inevitably he was cuffed about the head as a result.

Visitors to the house were a rarity; neither of his parents had family that visited, or friends. Perhaps once or twice a year a sudden squall would drive a fishing dhow to shelter under the house, and the fishermen would mount the ladder to sit on the floor and wait out the storm. His mother would make them a hot drink of seaweed brew and his father would talk about how bad his catch had been.

It was no life at all for a growing boy, but Dek became aware of that fact only because his mother was a storyteller.

Her name was Inya. Once it had been Syr-aware Inya Grinpindillie. Once she had been a pretty girl, the youngest child of loving parents with a big family. Her father was a Mekatéhaven merchant, one of the Awarefolk who applied his Aware talents to doing business with sylvs, trading linen which he imported from Keeper-owned businesses on Breth.

Inya was spoiled and cosseted, and she loved nothing better than to sit in the square outside their house and listen to the professional storytellers every evening. In the normal way of things, she would have married a merchant's son, lived in a mansion somewhere nearby, and raised her own family. Her father, though, was in no hurry to marry off his youngest and favorite daughter, and she was content for it to be that way. When she was nineteen, she pestered him to take her with him on his next buying trip to Breth: she ached to see another islandom, to have an adventure. He was content to yield, and they sailed together on a cargo ship that he half owned. The voyage was uneventful as they sailed west, rounded Kin Cape and headed up the west coast of Mekaté. Somewhere north of Minkan Bay, however, they were caught in an unseasonable storm that broke the main mast and sent the crippled boat reeling eastward along the Sekam Coast, at the mercy of the wind and tide.

Inya was below decks when the ship finally foundered on rocks north of the Kitamu Bays. The hull was staved, and she was thrown into the water as the ship broke up. She was injured: her face ripped open and her knee crushed. She clung to the wreckage, alone in a turbulent sea, flung eventually into the calmer waters of the Bays. Bolchar spotted her as he was rowing his skiff back from the mainland to his stilt-house the next day. He took her in, and never let her go.

It was easy at first. She was hurt and weak from pain and immersion and loss of blood. She lay on his pallet, took the fish soup he offered her, and drifted in and out of delirium. When she recovered, she could not speak. Her mouth had been ripped open in a tear that split her cheek; it was weeks before she could form any recognizable words, and even then her speech was distorted. Her knee was beyond repair, and she would drag her leg at a twisted angle for the rest of her life. When she finally pulled herself up from the pallet and looked out on the world that was not hers, she wept. By that time, she had seen the covetous shine of Bolchar's eyes. She knew she would never escape. She knew what was going to happen to her.

There was no point in resistance; Bolchar was strong enough to do whatever he wanted with her body. If she acquiesced, at least she wasn't beaten. Once Dek was born, Bolchar had an added lever to manipulate her; all he had to do was clip the boy over the head, and she was willing to do anything to placate him.

She had no mirror to see her face, but she saw the looks of the fishermen who occasionally came to the house. She saw their irritation when she tried to make them understand her clumsy, distorted speech. She heard one of them laugh once, and call her the halfwitted wife of the madman. Even were she to escape, what would become of her? She had no future. But her son would have one . . .

She lived for Dek, determined that when he was eventually old enough to fend for himself, he would escape this life. She poured her stories into his willing ears so that he would be prepared for the world he would find away from the Kitamu Bays: stories of her old life, of her family, of the great trading houses of Mekatéhaven. Tales of adventure and magic that she had heard from the professional storytellers of her youth. Stories based on the politics she had heard discussed around the dinner table. Anything and everything she could remember.

Dek absorbed it all. If sometimes he had trouble sorting out the truth from the fiction, he could hardly be blamed: he had seen none of it firsthand. He didn't even know what it was like to be Aware; there was no magic in the Kitamu Bays for him to be aware of—no sylvs, no dunmagickers.

When he was twelve, Inya told Dek to escape next time he went to the mainland with his father. She told him to get to Mekatéhaven, to go to her family. He refused to leave her. It became a litany she whispered in his ear each time he left; he always came back. Then, one day when he was almost fourteen, he returned to find she was gone. Vanished, leaving no traces behind to tell him what had happened.

He didn't need them. He knew. After he and Bolchar had gone, the tide would have retreated, leaving behind its gray expanse of mud so deep it could easily swallow a man. Or a woman jumping down into it from the house windows high above . . .

And he knew why she had done it: so that he would leave.

His remorse was intense, but his anger was more focused. The next time Bolchar and he went ashore, Dek pushed his father out of the boat, knocked him unconscious with an oar, and drowned him. His only regret was that he had not done it earlier, in time to save his mother. He rowed the boat to the coastal village where he told the headman that his mother had fallen from the hut, his father had tried to save her, and they had both perished in the mud. He gave up the skiff and the hut with its valuable fishing trap to the villagers, in exchange for a boat ride to the nearest large town, Lekenbraig.

Lekenbraig overawed him. As much as his mother had explained what town life was like, he had not grasped even the most elementary of impressions. The noise, the bustle, the sheer size and solidity of buildings, the numbers of people, the smells, the choices: it was all enough to start him trembling, and he did not stop shaking for almost a week.

He followed the advice of the fishermen who had taken him to the city, and went to the town guard for help. The officer in charge was a kindly man with a son of the same age. He listened to the lad's tale—fortunately Dek had enough sense to stick to his story about the deaths of his parents—and took the boy under his wing. Letters were written to Mekatéhaven, with the purpose of finding Inya's family; in the meantime, Dek bedded down in the barracks and became the guard's mascot. Who could resist a lad who didn't know how to eat an egg or use money, who had never sat in a chair, drunk from a bottle, pumped water from a well, worn shoes, patted a dog or heard a cat purr? They weren't unkind, but Dek was soon a source of endless amusement to the guards. He learned to keep a vacuous grin on his face while he hoped that they would tire of fooling him with things he did not know.

In time, word came back from Mekatéhaven. It had been seventeen years since Inya and her father had disappeared, and while Inya's brother, who now headed the family, was willing to admit that this orphaned boy might well be Inya's child, he did not think anything would be gained by his arrival at the family home in Mekatéhaven. However, the brother was a generous man. He suggested that he would pay for a place for Dek in the town guard, and provide him with a lump sum of money to set himself up with the clothing and such that he needed.

The guard officer recommended that Dek accept the offer. "Your uncle's under no obligation to provide for you," he explained to Dek. "Your mother may have been entitled to part of her father's estate, but you can't prove that you are her son. And you are illegitimate anyways. You had best take the money he offers and be a guard as he suggests."

Dek had little experience in judging people. He had really only ever known two people in his whole life: his father, who had beaten him regularly and never shown him the slightest affection, and his mother, who had loved him enough to die for him. He knew nothing of peole who lay somewhere between those two extremes, but something told him that the officer meant well. He accepted the advice and joined the town guards. In a small act of homage to his mother, he took the name of Grinpindillie as his own.

The first year had been a long one as he endured an endless stream of practical jokes at his expense. Gradually, though, he learned not to believe everything he was told. He learned enough about his new world to fit in.

That, however, was not the end of his problems. It was all very well for a fourteen-year-old lad to be a guardsboy; it would be quite another matter to have a young guardsman who was no taller than the chest ties on his superior's uniform, and it was clear to the guards that Dek had not grown at all in the year he had been with them. Although better food had fleshed him out a little, and training had built muscle, he simply had neither the stature nor the height to be a guardsman. The guard's commanding officer agreed to wait a little longer, but the truth of the matter was, if Dek didn't grow soon, he would have to find another home.

This was the state of affairs for Dek when the guards were ordered out to help look for some wanted fugitives: a halfbreed woman with a sword, a red-bearded Sky Plainsman and a beautiful blonde woman who may have been a Cirkasian.

When Dek entered a waterfront inn that was supposed to be housing three people who had bought tickets on the next packet to Porth, it had seemed a routine inquiry. They'd heard nothing to suggest that the three would-be travelers were the fugitives they were looking for, so it was with considerable surprise that he saw that very trio—the halfbreed, the Plainsman and the Cirkasian—coming down the stairs into the taproom. Worse, the halfbreed was gripping her sword by the hilt, and she looked at ease, as if she knew exactly how to use it. "I believe you wanted to meet us, guardsman?" she asked. "My name is Ducrest. This is my wife, Lyss. The other man is my servant. Is there some kind of problem?"

Dek stared at her. She was pretending to be a man, and no one seemed to notice. He gaped.

Bender, the guardsman in charge, shook his head. "Sorry to have troubled you, Syr. We are seeking some fugitives, but you are obviously not them. We will not disturb you any further." He bowed, and gave a hand signal for all the guards to leave.

Dek couldn't move. He saw the silver-blue color playing over the skins of all three of the people. It was beautiful, a glow of light that twisted and changed from one delicate hue to another. *This is sylvmagic,* he thought. This was what his mother had told him about.

He knew he should have told Bender. But then the large woman looked at him, looked straight at him, and smiled. He felt it as an acknowledgment. As if she had spoken aloud: *We are kin, lad, you and me.* She may have been wearing a sylv illusion, but he *knew* she wasn't sylv. She was Aware.

And so was he.

In a state of shock, he turned and walked out of the inn.

For the rest of the day he trailed around after the other guards, but with his mind elsewhere. He tried to remember all he could of what his mother had told him about sylvs and Awarefolk. She called the Aware "her" people. And she admired sylvs, and wished that she'd had their power. "Then I would never have had to stay here," she had told him. "I could have escaped any time I liked . . ."

Dek didn't like the idea of betraying an Aware woman or sylvs. He didn't like it at all. And he needed friends desperately. When the guards returned to the barracks, off duty at last, he took the opportunity to change into his one set of ordinary clothes and return to the inn. One part of him was as scared as a mudskipper in a heron's beak—he knew enough to know that sylvs were powerful people with powerful connections. The other side of him was excited at the thought of being one of the Awarefolk, of meeting someone else who was too. He hadn't even known that he *was* Aware until that day! He could hardly stop shaking.

AS SOON AS I SAW THE BOY HEADING FOR the inn, I went and banged on the door to Blaze and Flame's room. "The lad's coming to see us," I said.

"Thought he would," Blaze said. "Disguise me, Flame."

She stepped out onto the landing.

When the boy entered the taproom, he made straight for the stairs, but was arrested by the booming voice of the innkeeper. "Hold it, lad! Just where do you think you are going, then?"

Blaze interrupted from above. "That's all right," she told him. "The lad has come to see us." She smiled encouragingly, and Dek came on up the stairs.

He stood there at the entrance to Flame and Blaze's room and looked at us all. Belatedly, he snatched off his cap and turned it this way and that in his hands. "Me name's Dek," he said finally. "Dekan Grinpindillie."

Blaze gestured him inside. "Come in, Dekan. I'm Blaze Halfbreed. Over there is Flame Windrider, and the red fellow with the wild hair is a Sky Plainsman who goes by the name of Kelwyn Gilfeather." She didn't introduce Ruarth; a deliberate omission, I assumed. "You wanted to see one of us?" she prompted.

"You're Aware," he said, without preamble. "Same as me." He looked at Flame. "And you're sylv."

"Perhaps," Blaze agreed. "But what of it?"

"You're the crims they're lookin' for. I didn't say nuttin'."

"Thank you," Blaze said gravely.

There was a prolonged silence. He fiddled with his cap and shuffled his feet.

Flame took pity on him. "Come and sit down here, Dekan," she said, indicating the edge of the bed next to herself. "You're a brave lad to come and tell us this. How did you know we wouldn't magick you?"

"You can't," he said, confidently enough. "I'm Aware. Anyways, my ma always said sylvs are good people."

Blaze snorted in derision. "Sylvs, my lad, are back-stabbing, bottom-crawling tricksters for the most part, and I wouldn't trust them to do as much as tie my breeches. And *I* happen to like 'em."

Flame glared at her and turned back to Dek. "Suppose you tell us what you want, lad."

"I wanna go with you. They're gunna throw me outta the guard cos I'm too small. I wanna go with you and fight dun-magickers."

We were all taken aback at that. "What makes you think we're going to fight dunmagickers?" Flame asked.

"Cos that's what sylvs and Awarefolk do," he said, confident he was right.

"Er—" Flame was nonplussed. "Not always. But why don't you start at the beginning, Dekan, and tell us everything about yourself. Who are you? Where do you come from?"

And that was when he told us the story that I've just narrated.

When he had finished, Blaze looked across at me with a raised eyebrow. I knew what she was asking. "The smell of truth," I said. "Every bit of it."

Blaze raised her eyebrow a second time.

"Including . . . ?" She was asking me why he had told us so matter-of-factly that he had murdered his father. In all honesty, I had been shocked at his casual acknowledgment of patricide. He could have omitted that, as he evidently had hidden it from the fishermen and the guards, but he hadn't.

I shrugged. "No guilt." Bolchar had kidnapped and raped his mother, beaten them both and denied them dignity. He regarded the murder as a simple execution. Justice.

"Why do you want to fight dunmagickers?" Blaze asked him.

"Me ma told me that was what Awarefolk do."

"*She* didn't fight."

"That was cos she got stolen by my da. Otherwise she might of. *Would* of."

"All right," Blaze said. "I'll tell you this much: we *are* going to fight dunmagickers. Have you heard anything about dunmagickers on Porth?"

"They talk about it some, back at the barracks. They say it used to be dangerous to go to a place there, a town—I've forgotten the name—but then the Keeper sylv came and cleaned it up. That was ages ago, before I got here. Years back."

Blaze grunted. I discovered later that she had been the one who had done most to rid Porth of dunmagickers for the Keepers. "After that? Anything recent?" she asked.

He shook his head. "If anything happened there real recent, we wouldn't hear till the packet comes back. Can I go with you?"

"It's too dangerous," Flame said: "You need to grow up and become a fighter first, Dek."

"I'm nivver gunna be real big. But I'm Aware. That's good, isn't it?"

"Dunmagickers have lots of ways of killing people," Blaze said. "Not just using magic. Being Aware wouldn't help you then. In fact, it can even be a disadvantage; if someone hurts you, a sylv cannot heal you the way they could heal an ordinary person."

"I'm not scared."

"Then you ought to be."

"Oh." He deflated, and his bottom lip trembled a bit. Then he brightened. "But my ma told me a story about a syr-aware lord in olden times. He called all the sylv healers on his island together and got himself cured after someone ran a sword through his belly."

Flame laughed. "I know that one," she said. "It was the governor of Chis, a couple of hundred years ago. Chis is one of the Cirkase Islands. He told the sylvs they had better fix him up or his last order on earth would be to have them all executed. History says they did and he recovered. He *was* a real person, and he *was* Aware. My tutors made me learn all about his rule. He's famous for having invented the pendulum clock—"

Blaze gave her a flat stare and she subsided. "It's just a story, Dek," she said. "He might have recovered anyway. The real point is that dunmagickers are dangerous."

"I dunno what to do. I gotta go *somewhere*."

"Can you follow orders?" Blaze asked him.

"I'm a guardsboy. We don't do nuttin' 'cept follow orders."

"We'll buy you a ticket for Porth," Blaze said then, surprising us all. "Meet us at the dock before the next packet sails." She persuaded him to go back to the barracks and behave himself for the next few days, before ushering him out. No sooner had the door closed behind him than Flame and Ruarth both jumped on her indignantly.

"How could you *do* that?" Flame asked. "Don't you remember what happened to Tunn? He'd still be alive if you hadn't involved him in our affairs."

Blaze's face darkened. "Trench damn it, Flame, do you think I learned nothing from what happened to Tunn? I'm trying to help this boy, not kill him!"

I intervened. "Blaze is right, Flame. If she hadna said that, Dekan would have found a way to go to Porth on his own, and probably would have got himself into a whole lot more trouble."

"How could you possibly know that?"

"His intention to deceive was written all over him. I could smell it, as strong as that hot tar in a tub on the wharf outside." More intriguing was how Blaze, who didn't have my sense of smell, knew it. Sometimes she read people a darn sight too well.

Flame sniffed. "Oh," she said.

Ruarth fluttered and flicked his wings, following it with a few shrill notes. *That's a handy talent you have, Kel,* he said.

"Too good to be wasted," Blaze agreed. "We need you, Gil-feather. We don't know what we will be facing there, at this Floating Mere. You would give us the edge we need."

"I'm a physician," I told her coldly, "not a fighter. I am going to Amkabraig where I will wait till Garrowyn's medical chest arrives. Then I shall take the next packet out to Breth. If ye think I will do aught else, then ye deceive yourselves."

I turned on my heel and left the room to go back to my own.

While I was unlatching my door, Blaze came out into the passageway. "I've upset you," she said. "Damn it, Gilfeather, you're as sensitive as a pink anemone in a rock pool, flinching when touched."

I sighed. "Aye. Listen, Blaze. I still haven't learned to deal with the death I did cause. Dinna ask me to layer it over with others. Ye called me a peacemonger once. Ye had the truth of it: that's *exactly* what I am."

I went into my room and shut the door. I was shaking. Every now and then something would remind me and I was haunted once more by that moment when the rock left my hand and a life ended.

Jastriá. Wonderful, confused, troubled, infuriating Jastriá. Dead by my hand.

I leaned with my back to the door and wished I could be stronger.

CHAPTER 11

THEY WOULDN'T ALLOW SEEKER ON board the Porth packet. Apparently he rated as cargo, and had to be sent on a cargo boat, at extra cost, of course. Blaze took this in her stride. She sent the dog back down to the wharf and clapped her hands twice. He slunk away, tail between his legs.

We had two cabins on the port side of the vessel; Flame and Blaze shared one, Dek and I were in the second with two other passengers, sailmakers who were going to Porth to buy raw materials. Dek had turned up the moment the packet docked, his face shining in anticipation. Blaze, who didn't want to advertise the defection of a member of the town guard, bundled him down to the cabin immediately and told him to stay there out of sight. I suspected that Flame concealed him under the cloak of her magic as well because I could smell that sweet spice aroma, but it was frustrating not being able to tell for sure. Certainly, when I heard Blaze give a whistle a little later, and I spied Seeker slink up the gangplank, crawl behind the luggage of some other passengers and then accompany Blaze down to the cabin, none of the sailors took any notice.

I could convince myself that sylvs secreted something that produced hallucinations, but I still couldn't understand how Flame was able to control what others could see. I gathered from what the others said, that if a person was rendered virtually invisible, then to the Aware it appeared as if he was blurred by a bluish light or glow or mist, whereas to sylvs and ordinary folk, he more or less disappeared because he became difficult to focus on. When I asked Flame about the mechanics of it, she was vague; not, I think, because she wanted to deceive me, but because she simply didn't know.

"I focus on what I want to change or conceal, and how I want it to appear, and it happens," she said. "It takes a certain amount of concentration. Small things, like the illusion of my arm, I can maintain even while I sleep. Most things I have to think about. All the time. It's not easy." She gave a warm smile. "It's magic, Kel. There's no need to *worry* about it."

The ship was searched, thoroughly, by Fellih-guards and town guards before it set sail; they never gave any of us a second glance. There I stood, six foot of freckled, red-haired Plainsman (the dye was wearing off), and all they could apparently see was a nondescript servant (me) of a Keeper businessman (Blaze) and his wife (Flame). As much as I appreciated it, I didn't like it.

I DON'T REMEMBER MUCH ABOUT THE first day out of port. It was the first time I had been on board a ship, and I decided minutes after we left the sheltered confines of Lekenbraig harbor that it was likely to be the last. I never wanted to subject myself to such misery ever again. A little later I decided it was a moot point as I wasn't going to live through it anyway. Still later I didn't *want* to live through it. I had never felt so ill; never conceived that it was *possible* to feel so ill.

Hours later, having rid myself of the contents of my stomach an inordinate number of times, I managed to slip into an exhausted sleep.

I awoke in the morning amazed to find myself still alive, astonished to find that I actually felt human again. I even managed to make my way up on deck—weakly, but willing to take an interest in life once more. Blaze and Dek were already there, leaning against a railing and apparently enjoying each other's company. They weren't the only passengers who had emerged: five or six others were strolling about or chatting. Dek seemed to regard Blaze with an attitude that bordered on adulation, even though she had a habit of dashing his most-cherished delusions on a regular basis. "What d'you call your sword?" he was asking her as I crossed the deck.

She was bewildered. "*Call* my sword?"

"Yeah. Its name. It must have a name: is it a secret?"

"It's just a sword, Dek. Why in all the Isles should it have a name?"

"My ma used to tell me all the heroes had swords with names. Magical names sometimes, and if you didn't know the name, then you couldn't draw the sword . . ."

"It doesn't have a name. I don't name my boots either. Or my belt. Only my dog. Maybe I'm not a hero." She grinned on seeing me. "Glad to see you're still alive."

"I did wonder if I'd still be here in the morning. How's Flame?"

"Terrible. She fully expects not to move from the cabin for the voyage. I gather she's no sailor. She wasn't sick on the sea-pony though, but I guess that's different."

"I'll look in on her later. Although I don't know what I can do for her. I didna seem able to help myself."

"Cor—you was *putrid,*" Dek said. I had apparently managed to impress him with my ability to be sick. Perhaps that made up for the fact that I didn't wear a sword.

"If Flame is sick," I asked, "does that mean we are, er, exposed for what we really are?"

"'Fraid so. But I shouldn't worry about it too much. None of the sailors are going to do anything about it now that we've sailed. The worst would be that information would eventually get back to Lekenbraig that we escaped on this packet, but sailors have a habit of minding their own business. They probably won't tell."

I thought about that, and wondered just how long it was going to be before Garrowyn's medicine chest reached me in

Amkabraig. Several weeks obviously, probably considerably longer. Long enough for trouble to find me if it was coming.

"I'm going to see Flame," I said.

THE VOYAGE WAS NOT PARTICULARLY eventful. Several of the ship's officers gave us some suspicious looks, but no one said anything. Seeker came up on deck only at night and proved to be adept at keeping out of everyone's way. There was some muttering about a ghost dog on board, but it never came to anything.

Flame remained ill the whole way and lost weight. Seasickness, apparently, was one illness she was unable to self-cure. Fortunately she was at least able to keep liquids down, and we managed to stop her from becoming dehydrated.

Dek roamed the ship in some kind of boy-paradise. After a lifetime in a one-room hut, the vessel must have seemed spacious; after the regimen of a guards' barracks, the lack of supervision must have felt liberating. By the time we docked in Amkabraig, he knew the packet from crow's nest to bilge water, and was on first-name terms with every crew member and all the passengers who would deign to talk to him.

Ruarth spent much of his time watching over Flame, and pestering me to find some way to help her. When she slept, I dragged him off to teach me more about his Dustel tongue. I worked hard at it, intrigued by its complexity and the combination of body language and sound. In fact, the whole idea of a race of birds, scattered throughout the Isles, who traced their feathers back to the time when the Dustel Islands disappeared beneath the waves, fascinated me. I didn't *believe* it, mind. Not that they had once been human, I mean. From my reading, and from things Garrowyn had told me, it seemed to me that myths had a strange way of becoming real as the years went by. The Calmenters thought their mountains were coughed up by a dragon; the Fen Islanders believed that they were descended from fish-tailed creatures called merfolk; the Spatt Islanders swore that their islands were all that was left of a third moon that had fallen into the ocean. I didn't believe those stories either.

Blaze spent much of her time up on deck manipulating that

enormously long sword of hers, training, I suppose. The other passengers gave her a wide berth and muttered among themselves about a shameless halfbreed hussy. She must have been taught by a master, because I could see that she methodically worked every muscle group in her body. As a physician, I appreciated her fitness, and the dedication she devoted to it. I'm a big man, strong and fit enough, and as a Plains physician I rode a lot, but when I moved, I was much more likely to fall over any furniture within range than exhibit grace or agility. Blaze, on the other hand, was fast and lithe, moving with a fluidity and flexibility that was a joy to watch. When I said as much, she replied, "You are looking at what makes the difference between life and death in my line of work."

"Your line of work?"

She hesitated over that. I suppose it wasn't an easy question to answer now that she had left Keeper employ. "Problem-solver," she said finally. "Wandering adventurer. Dun-killer."

She said it flippantly enough, but somehow the words tore at me. I realized that in some ways we were no different. We were both being hunted. We were both homeless, condemned to a kind of exile. She wasn't permitted a home because of her citizenless status; I was banned from mine. There was an irony there, in that she had been the cause of my banishment.

My physician skills were required a number of times during the course of the sail. I couldn't do much to help with seasickness, any more than Flame could with her sylvmagic, but there were other ills. One of the children on board came down with the six-day fever; fortunately I caught it before it spread, and I had the means to treat it in my kit. One of the sailors fell from the rigging and broke his arm: a nasty break with a multiple fracture that exposed the bone. Removing splinters, setting the arm and sewing up the wound would have been routine on the Plains; on a heaving ship and with limited medication, it was more difficult, but I was fairly sure I had managed to save the arm and its future mobility. Blaze cheerfully acted as my assistant, took the blood in her stride, and was obviously fascinated by the mechanics of what I did. She asked intelligent, penetrating questions, and I couldn't help but think she would have made a fine chirurgeon.

After the surgery was over, she gave me a thoughtful look

that I was able to interpret as her rueful acknowledgment of an error she had made. I had a good idea what it might have been. "Why so surprised?" I asked, nettled, as we left the cabin, having done all we could for the patient. "I am a physician, after all."

She had the grace to be embarrassed. In the darkness of the gangway, I couldn't see her face, but I could smell her discomposure.

"I . . . oh hells, I'm sorry," she said. She halted, and the movement of the ship threw me against her. "Damn it all, Gilfeather, sometimes it's so bloody difficult being around you." She added as we disengaged, "You know far too much. It's hard to have a private thought when you can smell what I'm thinking! Beats me how in all tarnation you can stand it. Knowing what people feel all the time. Knowing if they like you, or hate you, or are amused by you. Feeling their antipathies for one another: it must be horrible."

"Ye get used to it. I've never known it any other way, y'know. And I don't know what ye're *thinking.* Only what ye're feeling. Ye were surprised, but I didn't know *why.*"

"Ah, that, It's only . . . well, you seem so clumsy. Always falling over things, dropping things, spilling things—but what I saw in there, just now, it was beautiful. Everything you did. So I was surprised. Sometimes . . . sometimes I'm like the tiddler in a tidal pool; thinking that's all there is, not seeing the ocean. That's what I was guilty of: I didn't see the whole you."

My breath caught in my throat. She was saying one thing, but her body was saying something more.

She laughed ruefully. "There you go again. You know what I'm thinking."

"Feeling," I corrected automatically, and then blushed red.

"Well, you're damn right, if you're thinking that I find you attractive now. I do."

The ship pitched and I lurched into her again. I braced myself against the wall behind her head and pushed myself away from her.

"But you're not going to act on it," she said with conviction as we straightened.

"And *ye* don't even have a good nose."

She laughed. "Instinct," she said. "And it tells me you aren't interested."

"Ye're in love with someone else."

"You know far too damn much, Kelwyn Gilfeather."

"Ye've already said that."

"Does it make a difference, knowing there's someone else?"

I nodded. "Aye. Aye, it does."

She shrugged. "He's not here, Kel. And never will be. And there are other things besides love. There's . . . companionship between people who like each other. Who are attracted to each other. Bear that in mind, if ever you reconsider."

I watched as she turned away and climbed the companionway up to the deck. *He? A man?* It wasn't Flame she had been thinking of? I felt a fool. In spite of my nose, it seemed I had completely misread her. I blushed deep red and was glad she was no longer there to see. I leaned against the wall and thought about what an idiot I was.

It had been a long time since I had bedded a woman. Since I'd had Jastriá in my arms. More than four years. Yet it seemed somehow . . . disloyal to be feeling what I was feeling just then. I sighed and wondered if I could buy some grog from the ship's crew.

AT LEAST THE PATIENTS HELPED TO KEEP MY mind off my future, and away from the niggling unpleasantness that never seemed to be far distant; that odd stab of something evil, the sick fear it engendered, that I could never quite shake.

The night before we sailed into Amkabraig harbor, I woke bathed in sweat, knowing that I had just experienced another such jab of horror; that somehow it had penetrated my dreams. I couldn't sleep after that, and rose to go up on deck. It was a lovely night: darkmoon and starlit, and the smells of the port were still far enough away not to impinge on my enjoyment of the scent of sea and spray and salt. I might have managed to push away that nebulous fear, except that a moment or two later Blaze also climbed up onto the deck. It was too much of a coincidence; I could only believe that her Awareness had attuned her to whatever had awakened me.

"What woke ye?" I asked.

"I don't know. I'm paranoid, you know; all it takes is a mouse and my eyes pop open. Sleeping with my mind alert to everything around me is all part of staying alive."

There was a poignancy there, that spoke of a life I could hardly imagine. What right had I to be bitter over what I had lost? At least I'd had it once. "Somehow I dinna think it's a mouse that has ye pacing the deck now, lass. Blaze, what does dunmagic smell like?"

She was quiet for a moment before answering. "Like nothing else on earth," she said finally. "It's not putrefaction, it's not like the normal processes of rot. It's just the smell of evil." That didn't help me much, and she must have sensed that, because she added, "The smell of wrongness. Of something that shouldn't exist, because it is out of kilter with order. There's no logic to true evil. Quite the opposite. And so it is with dunmagic . . . it smells wrong."

"I think I've been smelling it," I said soberly. "Every now and then. Just a whiff, and then it's gone, but it leaves me gasping. I think that was what woke me just now."

"Ah." She paused. "I haven't smelled anything untoward, although I have been sniffing the air, believe me. I thought that if Morthred passed this way he might have left his trail behind like the slug he is. In fact, he would have done, but it was weeks ago now. Too long ago for me to smell it. You, though; your nose is far superior to mine, so that's probably what you've got scent of: his old trail. Perhaps he was in Lekenbraig—maybe his ship was once tied up next to this one somewhere. Or maybe there was some other dunmagicker on board this vessel not long ago."

"Or it could be the residue ye mentioned, the traces of Morthred left in Flame."

"Perhaps."

It was all very logical. It fitted. It explained everything. It was so easy to believe.

The truth was so much more unpalatable . . . and so much harder to recognize. What fools we were.

* * *

"NOT LONG NOW," I TOLD FLAME. "WE ARE already behind the protected headlands of the harbor entrance; can ye no feel how the ship has steadied?" I was getting good at this sailing business.

She nodded weakly. "I don't know if I could have stood it much longer."

I was inclined to agree with her. She looked dreadful: thin, her hair lank and unwashed, her face drawn, great shadows under her eyes. For the first time since I had met her, I wasn't continually having to make an effort to ignore her beauty, her unconscious sexuality.

I said, "Blaze says ye'll all stay a while in the town so ye can recover some of your strength."

She gripped me by the wrist. "You are going to come with us, aren't you?" Her pleading eyes looked too large and luminous for her face. Ruarth, perched on the overhead lamp swinging from the ceiling, ruffled his wings in echo of her plea.

I shook my head. "No, Flame. This is not my fight."

"This is everyone's fight."

"I'm a physician," I said yet again. "Not a warrior."

"You're a selfish man," she told me. "Thinking of yourself and not others. Is that the mark of a fine physician? Have you any idea of how many people are dying, and dying horribly because of Morthred and his kind? How can any true man of medicine stand by and let that happen to truly good people?"

If it had been Blaze who had said that, I would have shrugged it off, but this was the first time I had ever heard criticism from Flame, and I flushed.

"You don't know what it's like to have a dunmagic contamination. You don't know the anguish. You haven't seen the deaths." Her tone was soaked with pain and bitterness and held a honed edge of contempt.

I flushed still darker.

Flame, Ruarth chided her.

She was instantly contrite. "I'm sorry, Kel. I shouldn't have said that. I am just so tired and sick and worried."

I mumbled something conciliatory and went up the ladder to the deck. Blaze was leaning against the railing, watching the land come closer. Almost all the passengers were lined up to watch as well, but not one of them was standing too close to her. Her antics with her sword practice during the voyage had cleared a permanent circle around her that no one broached without invitation. I came and stood next to her. "I think ye have a bad dose of the plague," I said.

It comes in handy sometimes." She sounded amused. "How's Flame?"

"Tetchy."

"Yes, I've noticed. She accused me of paying more attention to Seeker than to her, and she told Ruarth that he may as well go and sleep in your cabin if he wanted to spend all his time teaching you how to understand his tongue. I've never known her so inclined to snap and snarl."

"Ye've never been seasick," I said, and there was a wealth of feeling in that remark.

She laughed. "No, I haven't. And I've seen some rough seas. Sea trips bore me beyond measure: being cooped up in such a small space. Or they did until this one. Thanks for being such an interesting companion, Kel. I've enjoyed getting to know you."

I stared at her, surprised, wondering if she was being sarcastic, but both her expression and her scent were genuinely friendly. I managed to smile in return, then thought back over our conversations and realized we had done a remarkable amount of talking. There really is not much else to do on board ship. She had been intensely interested in life on the Sky Plains, wanting to know all about us, everything from marriage ceremonies to how to make selver cheese. She had been fascinated by my medical knowledge and we had spent hours discussing medicines, treatment and surgery. She had considerable knowledge herself, gleaned from her own voyages, and she wanted to know about the treatments that we used. When I asked her why she wanted so many details, she had given a wry smile and said, "Ah, in my line of work, you never know when a doctor's knowledge will be useful. Sometimes I think I've spent as much time repairing injuries in others as I have in inflicting the injuries on them!"

The knowledge flowed both ways. She had been to every islandom at one time or another and was full of tales that

were exotic fare to a Plainsman who had never been anywhere at all. She was funny and astute; she could be scathing
about stupidity or wise about people. Blaze Halfbreed might
have been formidable enough to scare away the passengers on
that ship, but she had a fine mind under that forbidding exterior. And at least she had given up calling me Gilfeather.
Sometimes, anyway.

Above us, sailors were scattering throughout the rigging as
sails were furled and the ship slowed. "I spoke to those sailmakers in our cabin," I said. "They are going to Amkabraig to
buy the plant strips they use to make sails like these." I indicated the colored woven material the sailors were now wrap-
ping along the yards. "They call it pandana. It is a species of
pandanus palm, that grows only on Porth and has become inexplicably scarce of late."

She paused. Then, "Why do I get the feeling that there's
more to that statement than what you just said?"

"Pandana is a water plant that grows on the Floating
Mere." And in the middle of the Floating Mere there was an
island that had no children, according to the ghemphs.

"Ah. And are these sailmakers going there?"

I shook my head. "No. They just want to get their share of
what's available in Amkabraig. Just thought I'd mention it."

Blaze nodded, noncommittal. A small boat approached
from the shore. "The pilot," she said. "I'll go and see if I can
persuade Flame to come up on deck." She turned to go, but
then turned back to me again, as if she had thought of something else. "We do need you, Kel."

"Ye have Dek and Ruarth for Awareness. They would be
far more use than me: I have no skills at all."

"We need your sense of smell. That's your skill, and it's of
vastly more use than Awareness."

"Blaze, for the last time, I'm a physician." I was tiring of
saying the same thing again and again. "I dinna kill people, or
help others to kill people. Even if they are dunmasters. I dinna
share your view of the world."

All the color drained from her face and for a moment I
thought she might fall. I reached out and steadied her. "What's
the matter?"

She took a deep breath and gave a weak smile. "Fleas coming back to bite the dog that bred them. I once said those words, 'I don't share your view of the world,' or something very like them, to someone else. It was my reason for leaving him. Life has a habit of mocking us, I find."

I was to remember those words in the coming days.

CHAPTER 12

NARRATOR: KELWYN

IT WAS HARD TO UNDERSTAND WHY, BUT I never felt comfortable in the inn Blaze found for us in Amkabraig. She'd suggested a hostelry that she had known from her last visit, and shepherded us unerringly there—not bad for someone who had not been on Porth in seven years or so. Because it was tucked away on the edge of town, the place was cheap; for the same reason, it was quiet. The innkeeper was also the local midwife, a likable woman called Maryn, who was happy to keep me fed with vegetarian food and ply us all with excellent spiced mead. The inn itself had a garden and bordered an overgrown cemetery, so the smells were more those of the countryside and were therefore less of an assault on the senses. It was even close to the contact Garrowyn had given me: Anistie Brittlelyn, to whom he was sending his medicine chest. Of course, there had to be a disadvantage or two: I had to share a bed with Dek, and the ceiling of our room sloped so steeply that I couldn't stand upright without bumping my head. Dek thought that was inordinately funny. He was also amused by the matting on the floor: made from the same flat pandana strips as the ship's sails, it was amazingly colorful and had zigzag designs so confusing they seemed to move by themselves if you stared at them for too long.

None of which was any reason for me to feel constantly uneasy, but I did. It was rather as if there was a hot-weather storm of forbidding intensity gathering just over the horizon, close enough that it could be felt even if it could not yet be seen. I even caught myself looking up at the sky sometimes, but of course there was no storm. I am not a fanciful man, and I knew there had to be a real reason for my unease; I just couldn't seem to find it.

It wasn't anything to do with the news given to us by the Dustel birds who were waiting for us when the packet docked, because I didn't listen to what they had to say, and I avoided Blaze and Flame whenever they discussed their intentions. I didn't want to know about dunmagic or their plans to combat it.

It certainly had nothing to do with Garrowyn's friend; Anistie was charming. She must have been close to seventy, and her face was meshed with wrinkles, but her rosebud mouth stayed in a permanently upturned smile and her dark eyes twinkled as if she had never known tragedy or disaster. She welcomed me into her cottage—a tiny two-room house overlooking an ocean bay beyond the cemetery—with a hug. "Any nephew of Garrow's is more than welcome!" she cried. "My, oh my, you *do* look like him!"

I was pressed to drink a cup of hot chocolate and eat some of her coconut cake, while I told her how Garrowyn was doing. At the same time I eyed the main room of her cottage. The stove and wash area were under a lean-to at the back, so the tiny main room contained nothing but a kitchen table, two chairs, a dresser, and a large—very large—book shelf. The shelves were crammed with books and documents and scrolls. When she saw me eyeing them, she said, "Oh, they aren't mine, dearie. They are Garrow's. He asked if he could leave them here, and he had the shelves made for them. He says he's going to come back in his old age and read them all . . ." She looked quite misty-eyed. "Such a fine figure of a man, he is."

"He gave me this letter for you," I said, bemused but smiling politely, and handed it over. The idea of Uncle Garrowyn being "a fine figure of a man" took some digestion.

She read it slowly, and blushed. "He's also very wicked," she added primly, but her aroma told me she was more amused than angry. "He says you might want to look at some of the books and documents while you are waiting for his medicine chest to arrive. I'm sure you're very welcome, any time you want. Seems a shame to have all this knowledge just sitting here, and no one gaining any benefit from it. I tried to read it myself, but most of it is as dry as sun-bleached coral, and far less interesting." She smiled at me. "So you come whenever you like, dear."

I promised I would.

I didn't think my unease had anything to do with Flame either. Once back on land and eating well, she seemed much better. Within a week, the color was back in her cheeks and her hair had regained its lustre. She was a little quiet, not responding to Blaze's banter in her usual way, but apart from that, I thought she was growing stronger day by day. I attributed her lack of vivacity to her worry about what was in store for them; and she was about to face the man who had raped her and infected her with some kind of terrible disease that had necessitated the amputation of her arm—that was surely enough to make any normal person a tad subdued.

I had not had to deal with much in the line of assaults and rapes. It happened rarely up on the Sky Plains, and usually involved a perpetrator who suffered from some kind of mental illness, but Garrowyn had told me a lot about his observations in other islandoms, and some of the problems created by such unspeakable traumas. Compared to the effect it could have on a victim's mind, I found Flame's courage astonishing.

Are you sure she's all right? Ruarth asked one day, after I had been speaking to her. He flew onto my shoulder as I walked outside to sit on one of the benches in the hostelry's orchid garden.

"She's fine," I said. "In fact, I would suggest that ye leave soon. Inactivity might be worse for her than waiting, ye ken, knowing all the while that she's going to face this monster of a man again. Besides, once the packet gets back to Lekenbraig with the news that we were on board, the Fellih-worshippers or the Havenlord's guards may come after us."

The tapboy, sent out to me by the innkeeper to take my order, stared at me open-mouthed.

I stared back. "So, what's the matter, lad? Have ye never seen a man talk to himself before?"

He continued to gape.

"Go get me a watered-down mead."

Ruarth flew down to sit on the wooden slats of the table as the lad hurried away. *I'm worried. She seems . . . different,* he said.

"She was raped. The trauma of what she went through: it will keep coming back. Ye canna expect her to be the same—"

You think I don't know that? I was there, remember!

I felt as if the ground had shifted beneath my feet. "Sweet Creation," I whispered, wondering if I had understood what he was saying. "Ye *saw* what happened?"

Not the first time. That was when she went down to the privy at the inn where we were staying. But when she didn't come back I went to look for her. I found her on the ground . . . And I saw Morthred's henchmen come and take her away. I followed.

He was silent then and the pause seemed to last forever.

Yes, he said finally. *I saw what he did to her, later that same night, in his house. I was there. I heard the things he said to her as he did it.* He cocked his head in the way birds have, so that he was looking at me with only one eye, but for once his gaze seemed entirely human. *He—he wasn't the only one either. They all . . .*

There was another long pause. I had to choke back an urge to throw the contents of my stomach into the bushes.

And then she went back to him again, you know, in Creed. Deliberately. To save Blaze and Tor. I was there then too. Night after night after night.

It was a long time before I could speak. I opened my mouth several times, but there were no words there to say. I remembered what Blaze had told me: Flame and Ruarth had grown up together. They were inseparable. And yet he had been powerless to help her, because he was only a bird, because the only person who could understand him had been Flame herself . . .

I tried to imagine how I would have felt if it had happened to Jastriá and me, with me powerless to intervene. It was incomprehensible. Pain beyond imagining. Something that

would diminish a man in a way only a man could truly understand. A man—or perhaps a male Dustel.

When the tapboy returned with the mead, I drank it
straight down.

Finally I said, "I canna think how ye have both endured."

One day, I will kill him.

Ruarth's declaration should have seemed ridiculous. He
was no bigger than the palm of my hand. His beak was shorter
than one of my fingernails. His claws were less dangerous
than a rose thorn.

Yet he said it with so much cold passion, as if it were a
stark statement of fact, that it didn't seem ridiculous at all.

MOST PROBABLY, MY UNEASE WAS
prompted simply because every so often I had that whiff of
something so strong it went beyond a smell and hit me in the
gut like a physical blow. Each time I smelled it, it seemed
stronger. More potent.

"Dunmagic," Blaze said. "One of them has been this way."

She said it, but I was fairly sure she didn't believe it. She
thought it was the remains of the contamination Flame had
suffered, a flare-up of something within her. Something Flame
was, in part, able to control. Something she would finally be
able to rid herself of only on the day that Morthred died.

JUST TEN DAYS AFTER WE HAD ARRIVED
in Amkabraig, while we were having breakfast in the orchid
garden, Blaze told me that they had decided to leave. "I'd advise you to move too, or at least to hide yourself," she said.
"Just in case the next packet boat carries a message to the
Havenlord's guards here, or the Fellih-guards, about us."

*If you like, my Dustel friends will hang around the wharf
when the packet comes in and see what they can find out,* said
Ruarth. *Birds that small and nondescript make good spies.*

I nodded and thanked Ruarth, knowing he was right. Porth
wasn't as tropical as the main island of Mekaté, but it was still
a warm place. Windows had no glass, only bars or louvered
shutters; small birds slipped in and out at will and nobody

thought anything of it. I said, "Garrowyn's friend, Anistie, has said I can come and stay with her if they are looking for me." I had been back to the cottage several times to read some of the contents of those shelves, but there was still no sign of Garrowyn's medicine chest. "Only thing is, it will eventually be difficult for me to leave on a ship for Breth if the Havenlord's guards are hunting me."

Flame poured herself a glass of sour milk curds. "If you wait long enough, we will be back again, and I can disguise you with illusion once more."

I blushed. It was an annoying habit; I was red enough without flushing like an adolescent girl. But there was Flame offering to help me, when I was refusing to help her, and it embarrassed me. Blaze, the wretch, sucked in her cheeks, enjoying my discomfort. She knew exactly what prompted my coloring up. Flame was puzzled, but Blaze could read me like a book. Dek, who could be indescribably dense, asked loudly, "Why are you turnin' red, Syr Gilfeather?"

"None of your business," I growled.

Blaze took pity on me and changed the subject. "D'you know, I really don't like these orchids." I looked around at the arbor we sat in: tied to every post there were boldly colored sprays in reed baskets. They were Maryn's pride and she spent several hours every day tending them.

"Why ever not?" Flame asked. "They are lovely!"

I pushed the pastries over to her, as a peace offering, and she took one with a smile for me. Had I been a younger, more impressionable man that smile would have had my knees melting into slush. As it was, I often found myself gazing at her for the sheer pleasure of it.

"Too blatant," Blaze said. "Too bold. Too big. Too solid. Too exotic. Like me. I prefer my flowers dainty and pink and perfumed. Everything I am not. Silly, huh?"

"*Pink?*" Dek asked, disgusted.

"Yes. And for pulling that face, my lad, you can go and hire us an ox-cart after breakfast. We shall go to the Floating Mere in style."

"That's not necessary," Flame said. "I can walk."

"Who said it was for you?" Blaze asked mildly. "Maybe I need it to save my aching knees."

"Don't you patronize me," she said, and followed this up with an epithet that had us all stunned by its vulgarity.

I knew that Flame could sometimes be foul-mouthed, a result of her childhood connection with Dustels, but I'd never heard her be quite so brutally coarse before. It was out of character, and we all stared at her in shock.

Flame! Ruarth chided.

"I'm fed up with the lot of you!" she cried. "Always talking about me behind my back." She shook an admonishing finger at Ruarth. "And you—you are *disloyal,* you lousy pile of feathers! You spend all your time with Blaze and Kel, and not with me." With that parting shot, soaked through with spite, she rose and left the table, pushing past the innkeeper as she went, upsetting the laden plate Maryn carried. Our pile of breakfast pancakes was only just saved from sliding off the dish by Dek's self-interested dive to save them.

"Hey, did you see that?" he crowed. "You all owe me! You would of all lost your breakfast if not for me."

Ruarth flew off after Flame and Dek busied himself with the pancakes as Maryn headed for the kitchen once more. Blaze looked at me. "It's getting worse."

I nodded. "Aye."

"She wasn't like this when you first met her."

"No."

"Cutting off her arm was not enough, was it? Not even the sylv healing by Duthrick and the others was enough."

"There are some illnesses that do return long after they have apparently been cured."

"Dunmagic is not an illness," she said acidly.

I shrugged. "Ye were asking for my opinion, weren't ye?"

She threw her hands up. "Trench save me from selver-herding physicians with the brains of a squashed ant!"

We stared at each other over the table and Dek watched, fascinated, even as he made inroads into the pile of pancakes.

"You *really* think dunmagic is an illness?" she asked after a prolonged silence.

"Aye, I do. I dinna know for sure, but that's what I think. And I think ye are right: she wasn't fully cured. There are diseases like that, many of them. Swamp fever, for example. It keeps on coming back in some individuals, for years sometimes, in spite of medicinal bark, especially in those who didna seek early treatment. Ye did say that Flame was treated some time after Morthred gave her that first sore."

"Yes. But she didn't have swamp fever. Kel, is she going to die?"

"How can I tell? I have no experience with dunmagic. Until recently I didna even believe it existed!"

She stared at me, a flat unfriendly look. "I'm not asking you because I think you understand dunmagic. I'm asking you because of your nose. I want to know what it tells you about her present state. About what is wrong with her."

I capitulated, and did what no physician should ever do: I guessed. "I don't know whether it will end up killing her, or whether she will finally banish it, but my medical opinion, based on my ability to smell, is that the disease is not at the moment in an acute stage."

Her eyes went steely. "Which, in plain language, means?"

"I dinna think she is going to die any time soon. Or even fall desperately ill any time soon. I think it is cyclical. It will come and go. She will have bad days and good days. My guess, and it is only a guess, is that ye will have time to do what ye want."

"We'd have a better chance if you were with us."

I stirred guiltily. She was probably right. "Blaze, ye can't expect me to help ye kill someone I don't know, who has never done me any harm. I dinna even really believe that killing him will make any difference to Flame's illness, although his death may enable her to focus on her infection. She needs to rest and take care of her health, not race across the country after a madman who raped her."

Dek's eyes went very large. We both ignored him.

"Maybe ye should try finding a sylv to treat her, if ye think that works."

"We have a sylv," she pointed out. "And she is trying. I think."

"Someone else? More of them? Ye said it took more than one person last time."

"Even if I could find any sylv healers, I couldn't afford them. Besides, Flame won't hear of it. She says she can take care of it herself. She just wants to go after Morthred and kill him."

"Then maybe that's what ye had better do, as quickly as possible. I'm sorry I canna help you more."

"You can, but you won't, you knuckle-headed bonesetter," she snapped. Then she added, more resigned, "I guess that's it, then. We'll leave tomorrow morning." She smiled slightly. "At least *I* believe that killing Morthred will cure her. Completely, and immediately."

She had forgotten that I could tell when someone lied.

THEY LEFT LATE MORNING. BLAZE HAD compromised: there was no ox-cart, but she had rented or bought a donkey which carried all their belongings and provisions. Flame must have apologized because the atmosphere seemed cordial as they left. I watched them go down the laneway out into the countryside and felt bereft, which was odd. They had caused me so many problems and all I could think of was that I was going to miss them: Flame with her kind heart and bravery and beauty; Blaze with her self-deprecating humor, her honesty and her confidence; Ruarth with his endless patience and a wisdom far greater than one had any right to expect from a bird; Dek, with his bright-eyed romanticism that transcended a horrific childhood. With a sudden pang, I realized they were *friends*. The only friend I'd ever had before was Jastriá, and I'd made the mistake of marrying her. And she was gone anyway.

I went and sat in the orchid garden and ordered some ale. A voice whispered inside my head: If ye feel this way, then surely ye have no right to let them go without ye . . . If ye were with them, they'd have a better chance. Ye'll miss her, the voice said. *Go after them, ye fool.* Go after *her*.

I drank the ale, and then had another. I was beginning to feel nicely maudlin.

Fortunately, before I could settle into feeling sorry for myself, I was called upon to stitch up the inn's cook, who had managed to slice off the top of her finger.

After that, word soon got around that I was a physician, and there was a trickle of patients every day wanting to see me. I had to make a few forays into the forest along the edge of the city to collect some more herbs, fungi and medicinal plants to replace my diminishing stock. I visited Anistie almost every day, drank innumerable cups of her hot chocolate, and ate my way through a variety of her home-baked cakes while I investigated Garrowyn's collection of papers. She was a comfortable woman to be with, Anistie. Her aroma was one of peace and contentment, a smell that reminded me of fresh apples and summer breezes. I found myself telling her the story of my exile and how Blaze and Flame had wanted me to accompany them to the Mere. She was not at all judgmental, but even so, I could not tell her about Jastriá, and what I had done. That was still too raw to share.

I was beginning to think that I would be able to fill the time I had left to wait quite adequately, and earn a little cash at the same time, as long as the Mekatéen guards didn't appear on the doorstep one day. Yet every now and then I would wander to the gate and look down the road they had taken, and wonder yet again if I had done the right thing, or just the expedient thing, because I didn't want to be hurt all over again.

When the next packet from Lekenbraig docked, the Dustels checked it out and informed me that there didn't seem to be anyone on board with orders for the Amkabraig guard, nor had any Fellih-worshippers disembarked. In fact, most of the talk in the port had been about the arrival of several Keeper ships. Apparently they'd been looking for a missing Keeper vessel, and there was some sort of diplomatic furore going on because the vessel had been found burned out on a Porthian beach. It was the *Keeper Liberty,* of course, the ship stolen by Morthred in Gorthan Docks once he'd escaped from Creed.

After talking to the Dustels, I heaved a sigh of relief that I wasn't being hunted down, at least not in Porth, and continued to stay at the inn.

As the days passed, I became more and more fascinated by what I was reading in Garrowyn's papers. Creation knows where he had collected it all from; Anistie said it was the result of years of visits. It seemed that her relationship with Garrowyn was a long-standing one. Certainly her voice softened when she spoke of him, and yet she seemed to have no illusions about him. "He's like a butterfly, flits from flower to flower," she said with total lack of rancor. "Sips and moves on, the old rascal. And he likes the older blooms. More honey, he says." And she chuckled as I blushed like an adolescent and returned to my reading.

There were scrolls of myths on how magic had come to the Isles, there were books of stories with magical themes, there were histories of how both sylv and dunmagic had been used and abused over the ages, there were medical accounts of sylv healing. I read how ancient gods from the sea had gifted sylv-magic to a few families among the first settlers of the Isles of Glory, and how some had not been content with that and had refined the magic into the more evil dun. Then, or so that particular tale continued, other gods—those of the sky—had given other families the gift of Awareness, so that they could fight dunmagic.

In the histories, I learned how the Keeper Isles carefully nurtured sylvs so that the number of people with magic abilities increased. This deliberate policy was almost five hundred years old, and it had worked perhaps because the Keeper Isles did not have a hereditary royal family wanting to limit powerful people, as had been the case in other islandoms.

Mostly, of course, I was interested in the medical papers. In fact, one of the first things I did was to skim everything that was in the shelves and separate those that pertained to sylv healing or the inheritance of magic. And I read my way through them.

SIX DAYS AFTER BLAZE AND THE OTHERS had left, Maryn was called out in her capacity as a midwife. I was in the garden at the time, reading, and she passed me on the way out. "Another baby on the way, I suppose," she said. "I've delivered seven this week, would you believe?" I grinned at her, and waved as she let herself out of the side gate.

The tapboy brought me another drink. I sipped it and read on for a half hour or so.

"Physician Gilfeather?"

I looked up in surprise; I had been deep in thought and had not heard anyone come in through the garden gate. A middle-aged man stood there, turning his hat in his hands: a merchant, I guessed, if his clothing was anything to go by. Then I noted his workman's hands, and wondered.

"Midwife Maryn asked if you would mind coming to see

her patient. She would like your advice. I will show you the way."

I stared at him in further surprise. Maryn, for all her amiability, had struck me as jealous of her status and had never included me in any of her house calls or discussed her cases or asked my opinion. I stood up. "Of course. I need to get my instruments and medicines. Wait here." I gathered all the things I might need from my room, and came downstairs again.

The man's name was Keothie, he told me. He was a glass-blower who owned a small glassworks nearby. I noted his barrel-chest and callused lips, perhaps both marks of his trade, although I knew little about the skill of glass-making. We didn't use much glass on the Sky Plains and what we did we bought from the coast. "Who is the patient?" I asked as we hurried through the streets.

"My niece," he said. "From the countryside. Just a child, you know; barely thirteen. Her mother sent her to us just a couple of months ago."

"What ails her?"

I sensed his hesitation. He wasn't about to lie, but he didn't really want to talk about it. Eventually he said quietly, "Poor wee mite. She was ill-used. That's why her ma and pa sent her to us. She's my wife's sister's child. Her name is Ginna. My wife—my wife says she is increasing." When I looked blank, he added by way of explanation, "In a delicate condition."

It took me a moment to understand what he meant. On the Sky Plains we didn't think pregnancy was something that warranted euphemisms. Inside me, my heart was plummeting. I knew *how* to induce an abortion, but it was not something we ever *did* on the Sky Plains; it was regarded as murder. It had been Garrowyn who had taught me several ways that it could be done, because he believed that there were times when cleansing a woman of an unwanted pregnancy was a blessing for everyone, although I don't think he'd ever tried it on the Roof. "Listen well," he'd said, "and learn. Ye never ken when ye might need a skill, lad." My own thoughts on the matter remained ambivalent. I would have preferred that my moral stance was never tested. I hadn't really thought it ever would be; it was the women of our House who dealt with pregnancies and births after all.

For a fleeting moment of cowardice, I wanted to do no more than go home. Go back to Wyn and somehow live there again, the way I once had . . . where life wasn't full of things that meant hard decisions.

"But it's more than that, you know," Keothie continued. "When she first came to us, she was quiet, cried a lot. Maryn came several times to tend her. We thought she was recovering . . . but lately, lately she has changed. She was always a quiet lass, well behaved, kind and dutiful. Now—now I hardly know her anymore. You'll see." He refused to say any more, and hurried on.

I knew I was in trouble before we reached his cottage. I could smell it: the wrongness. Dunmagic, if Blaze had the right of it. It seeped into me with every breath I took, flooding my body with pain. I wanted to reject it, to turn away and walk in the opposite direction.

"What's the matter?" Keothie asked as I started breathing in gasps.

"Allergies," I lied. "Naught to fret about." I stopped for a moment, trying to come to terms with what I was feeling. I couldn't let the wrongness swamp me. There had to be a way to deal with it, to stay in command, to dominate the pain. I steadied my breathing; forced it to an even and regular rhythm. "Go on."

The further we went, the stronger the smell became, until we stopped in front of a small house next to a larger building that smelled of charcoal and potash and other things I could not identify. I made him wait a moment on the cottage stoop while I composed myself, and used my sense of smell to prepare me for what awaited us within. There was no doubt: whatever that foul smell was, it originated from inside the house.

I allowed myself a moment of ironical appreciation; I'd rejected any notion of taking on dunmagic at Blaze and Flame's behest, and now here I was confronted with it by myself. "Let's go in," I said, and steeled myself against the pain that had already set my joints aching and my nasal passages smarting.

Keothie introduced me to his wife, a portly woman with huge apron-covered bosoms and ample buttocks, and she led us upstairs. Underfoot there were mats woven from vivid strips in intricate patterns, just like the ones in the inn. In the sickroom, the bed had been placed in the middle of the mats and the girl Ginna lay upon it, but with her wrists and ankles tied to the four corner posts. When we approached the bed, she snarled at us and shouted a string of obscenities. What made it even more horrible was that the words were childish. She was unfamiliar with adult curses or the swear words of city slums; the best she could come up with were words referring to common bodily functions. It was pathetic and heartrending.

Her lovely dark eyes looked up at me from under the curling lashes of a child; her mouth was small and pink, her cheeks still had the roundness of childhood. As I approached the bed, the air seemed to thicken, to be almost impossible to breathe. I was uncertain how long I could tolerate the stench.

I looked at Maryn and raised a questioning eyebrow. I could not trust myself to speak: pain and nausea were coursing through me in waves, cresting and breaking inside my body, no longer quantifiable.

"I've never seen aught like this," she said quietly, her deep worry showing in her voice and in her smell. "I don't know what it is." She pulled back the covers. Ginna writhed on the bed, but it wasn't pain or disease that made her throw herself around: it was rage. I could smell it, a louring cloud of hatred and terrible anger.

Maryn bared the girl's lower torso and I skimmed my fingers over her abdomen. I withdrew my hand hurriedly. It felt seared, but not from the heat of her body. From something else. "How many weeks pregnant is she?" I asked.

"About eighteen. The babe has quickened."

Garrowyn had warned me not to abort a bairn at this stage, saying he thought that it was too dangerous for the mother. So at least that was one decision I did not need to make.

I had to get out of there. I was suffocating on the smell of pain. I didn't want to stay there any longer listening to the stream of filth and vituperation spewing out of that child's lips. I jerked my head, indicating that we should all leave the room.

Back in the parlor-kitchen of the house, the girl's aunt and uncle eyed me anxiously. I had to put my hands on the back of a chair just so that I could stay upright. "What happens if she is untied?" I asked. There was blood inside my mouth; somehow, under the assault on my senses, I had bitten my tongue.

They exchanged furtive looks. "She tries to run away," Keothie said at last. "She says she wants to go back to the man who did this to her. It's—it's eerie. At first she was just so glad to have got away from him. In fact, if we understand the right of it, she escaped at terrible risk of her life after several days of ill-usage and imprisonment. She shuddered just to talk about it. Now she acts as if the man who did this to her is the one she loves, although she never uses that word. It doesn't make sense."

It didn't make sense to me either, but I couldn't help remembering all that Blaze had told me about dun subversion. "Is she a sylv?"

Once more they exchanged glances. "We are good God-fearing folk," Keothie said. "We don't hold with magic. The Menod do not think that it is godly to have such power, and we are Menod."

"Yet I understand that sylvs make fine healers."

"Yes, there is that, I suppose."

"So, is she a sylv?"

It was his wife who replied, wiping the sweat from her palms onto her expanse of apron. "Alas, there's a strain of sylvpower in my family, Syr Gilfeather. We do not encourage it. When her folk saw she could make illusions, Ginna was taught that she must not do such things. She was taught to suppress her magic and she did so willingly. She is an obedient, pious child. Or was."

"Where did she live?"

"Go on, tell him," Keothie's wife prompted. "If he needs to know in order to help, then tell him." She looked directly at me. "I'd do anything for my sister's child, Syr-physician. She was a lovely sweet lass before all this."

"Her dad's a matmaker," Keothie said. "He collects the pandana that grows on the Floating Mere, then strips the leaves down, dyes them and makes mats." He pointed to the matting we stood upon. "Those are his. When he brought Ginna here, he said that there were new people living on an island in the Mere. He said that he thought one of them had been responsible. He said there have also been people disappearing from the villages around the lake—girls. When menfolk hunt for them, they disappear too, until no one wants to investigate any more."

"Dunmagickers," I said.

"*Dunmagickers?* I didn't hear talk of that," Maryn said. "People were saying these strangers must have been calling up lake spirits. Or monsters that live in the lake. There have been myths of such for as long as I remember. Please, God, not dunmagickers again!"

"Again?"

"There was a dunmaster governor right here on Porth, in Amkabraig, seven or eight years ago, until the Keepers sent us help to deal with him," Keothie explained. "He would do anything to gratify his lusts. So many people died before they found out what he was. They say dunmagickers feed on pain and death . . ." His voice trailed away and her eyes widened. "*Ginna*—?"

"I think she has been raped by a dunmagicker. I think he has transferred his disease to her in a process called subversion. And I think her child has this illness too."

Keothie faltered. "D—disease?"

"It is my belief that dunmagic is a disease, I think both Ginna and her unborn babe are now infected. The burning feeling ye get: that's dunmagic, not fever."

They all looked at me in shock as the true horror of what I was saying began to sink in. "You mean," Maryn said finally, "that *Ginna* is a dunmagicker? And will give birth to another such?"

I think it is likely. Aye." The pain inside me was finally easing back to a more manageable level. I looked down at my hands still gripping the back of the chair. When I eased my hold, my fingers started trembling.

"Can't you *do* something?" That was from Keothie's wife.

"I have no experience with dunmagic. I am not one of the Awarefolk, so I canna even be certain that what I say is the truth. I would suggest that ye find one of them to confirm what I have said. And I would suggest that ye swallow your prejudices against sylvmagic, and get a sylv healer here to cure her. They may be able to do so, especially if ye dinna wait any longer."

"Awarefolk? Sylvs? This is Porth!" Keothie cried. "Who here has such skills? And if they did, how could I afford a sylv healer?"

His wife shot him a look that was brimful of contempt. At

a guess, I would have said that she thought Keothie had plenty of money, but a marked reluctance to spend it.

I said, "Ginna is a Porth-born sylv; where there is one, there will be others. I suggest ye look among the rich for practicing sylvs. I believe they are skilled at using their talents to increase their wealth. And if they are reluctant to cure your niece, point out to them that if they dinna do it, there will be two more dunmagickers let loose on the world."

"They may kill her!" the woman protested. "Do you know what sylvs say about dunmagickers?"

"Aye," I agreed and added brutally, "I know what everyone says about dunmagickers. But dying would be a better end for Ginna than what would happen if she is not cured. If I am right, ye must get sylv help and ye must get it verra, verra soon. Any later and she will resist all attempts at cure. It may already be too late. And now, ye must excuse me. I have to go." I didn't wait to hear out their protest and their distress; I had to put as much distance between me and the dunmagic as I could, and soon. I would never have believed that it was possible for my sense of smell to cause me so much pain.

Outside the cottage, doubled up in excruciating discomfort, I vomited in the gutter. After that I took a couple of deep breaths and leaned against the wall; it was covered with a flowering creeper and I buried my face in the blooms. I could still smell the stench of dunmagic, but at least it wasn't overpowering, as it had been inside. Behind me the front door opened and Maryn stepped out. "Syr?" she asked tentatively. "Are you all right?"

I nodded dumbly. Doubtless I had pollen all over my face, and smelled of vomit.

"You look sick."

I waved a hand at the house. "Dunmagic does that to me, evidently."

"It—it's that bad?"

I nodded again. "Aye," I said. "Aye, I think it is." I might not yet have known what dunmagic was, but one thing I had become totally convinced of that afternoon: dunmagic *was* evil. I lurched away and was sick again.

A letter from Researcher (Special Class) S. iso Fabold, National Department of Exploration, Federal Ministry of Trade, Kells, to Masterman M. iso Kipswon, President of the National Society for the Scientific, Anthropological and Ethnographical Study of non-Kellish Peoples.

Dated this day 24/2nd Darkmoon/1793

Dear uncle,
I received your letter expressing curiosity about the Keeper Isles and Syr-sylv Councillor Duthrick. You are right, of course, The Hub was the political center of the Isles of Glory in the 1740s, and the Keeper Council was at the heart of its power. Apparently, there was a saying in those days that goes like this: "When the Keeperlord frowns, the peasants on Fen Island wince" (Fen Island being the most remote islandom of the Isles of Glory).

Anyway, to satisfy your curiosity, I have asked Nathan to translate a conversation I had with Blaze on just this subject, and I send it to you here. It deals with what Duthrick did immediately after the events that took place on Gorthan Spit, and introduces you to the politics of The Hub. Of course, what Blaze relates of Duthrick's activities during this time is all secondhand—she herself was still in the Mekaté Islands at the time.

In fact, from now on, the translated conversations will be from both Gilfeather and Blaze. I have tried to keep them in chronological order as much as possible. I hope it is not confusing for you; I have put the name of the speaker at the top of each section.

Up to this point, I was quite impressed with Gilfeather's good sense. I appreciated the scientific bent of his mind, even though I may not have had much affinity for his personality. Unfortunately, in the end, my respect for him diminished. I felt he lost his objectivity, but more of that anon.

I thought my paper on Medicine in the Glory Isles *was quite well received, didn't you? Except for that very odd man from the Regal States, who seemed to think that imps—so small we can't even see them—are what make us ill. Anyara sprang to his defense afterward: her propensity to defend the underdog, or in this case, the foreign dog, can be either endearing or infuriating, depending on the circumstances!*

And I hardly thought that the Society's Annual Convention was quite the place for her to make the point that belief in magic could be equated with religious faith, even if it was only made to you and me and Nathan during the supper break. Bishop Khoran would have dragged her off to attend his "crisis of faith" classes had he heard her make that comment. I fear my lovely Anyara will never have the blessing of a religious aetherial, as I understand that only those with perfect faith ever see the transcendence of God. Anyara is always demanding proof, and while her belief never wavers, I am sure, she is also never content to take anything as a matter of faith.

I will admit that I find that defect of character disturbing. Aunt Rosris assures me that Anyara will grow out of it, but I am not certain. It provides me with a quandary which I must resolve before RV Seadrift leaves again for the Isles of Glory . . .

Forgive me, I ramble.

I remain,
Your obedient nephew,
Shor iso Fabold

CHAPTER 13

I HAD BEEN INSIDE THE SANCTUM OF THE Keeper Councillory in The Hub several times, courtesy of Duthrick, to make a personal report on something or other to the Council. They were not visits I relished: it entailed dressing up like a jester—Blaze Halfbreed wearing a skirt is a sight to behold—and being on my best behavior; that is, meek and polite. Not a role I ever played well.

Still, it was always an opportunity to see the inside of what has been judged to be the finest edifice ever built in the Isles of Glory, with considerable justification. The Councillory, lauded for its many towers and domes, presides over The Hub from the highest hill in the city. You've seen it, of course. The building is impressive enough from the outside; inside, it is awe-inspiring. The chamber walls of the Sanctum, inlaid with gold leaf and silver filigree, tower upward to a porcelain dome that seems to float, impossibly high, above. The blue and white patterns on the porcelain panels emulate a summer sky, each panel so skillfully placed that they appear seamless from below. The impression of an outdoor sky used to be enhanced by having live songbirds released inside the dome every time there was a meeting held there. I believe the birdsong was supposed to help inspire Keeper Councillors to enact noble legislature and pass just rulings. I also heard that, in order to ensure that there were no unseemly droppings cast during the course of meetings and that the singing would be prolonged and soulful, the birds were starved for a day or so before being released into the chamber.

I'll admit to being awestruck the first time I ventured in—I had to keep dragging my eyes away from the ceiling in order to answer the questions being addressed to me! One of the Councillors laughed at my naivety and murmured to his neighbor that this was what happened when you allowed street crud from the gutter to sully the Council Sanctum. I was only sixteen at the time, and if I'd been wearing my sword, he might have lived to regret his scorn. Fortunately for us both, swords weren't allowed inside the Councillory.

The padded seating of the Sanctum was arranged in semi-circular tiers to overlook the central meeting area. At a full Council meeting, with attendant scribes, secretaries and Awarefolk (to make sure that there was no illegal use of magic), the Sanctum could hold almost eight hundred people. At cabinet meetings, which only the Inner Council headed by the Keeperlord attended, just the central table was used. To ensure privacy at such times, four Wardsmen of the Council stationed themselves around the table and raised sylv wards so that no one could spy on the conversations. The table was a massive piece of furniture carved from a single kelmari log that was imported from the forests of Aban, one of the Bethany Isles. (It was a gift from the Bethany Holdlord at the turn of the century; the man had been angling for preferential trade status for his country at the time. He obtained the status he coveted, but it was short-lived; the Keeper Council soon courted other nations with similar promises. The Aban forests are all gone now, by the way, sold to the Keeper Isles and cut down to satisfy their love of solid furniture.)

Oddly enough, in the end it isn't the ceiling, or the crude remark, or the massive table, that I remember most today. It is the birds, with their endless songs of beauty, and their futile fluttering against the illusion of a painted sky.

* * *

BUT WE ARE TALKING ABOUT 1742, WHEN
the Keeperlord was a man called Emmerlynd Bartbarick. He
was old by then, having held on to power for almost twenty
years. He was unattractive in a culture which almost demanded physical beauty as a prerequisite for position. Of
course, most achieved the appearance of perfection with the
use of the sylvpower of illusion; Bartbarick eccentrically
scorned what he considered to be prodigal use, or abuse, of
sylvtalent, and bared his massive lantern jaw to all. He had a
sharp mind, plus administrative skill, financial acumen and
commercial sagacity, all of which accounts for his election by
his peers to the Keeperlord's post in spite of his jaw. He maintained his power as the Keeper Isles expanded its commercial
dominance throughout the Glory Isles and he himself became
the richest merchant who had ever owned a fleet of Keeper
ships.

His personal wealth was legendary, and so was his family
life. He married a fellow sylv's daughter, a girl just sixteen
years old, and rapidly sired a succession of fourteen daughters. Each of his offspring inherited his unfortunate jaw, and
every single one of them covered it up with illusion.

His fifteenth child was Fotherly Bartbarick, a lad destined
to be raised in a largely feminine household, spoiled by a dot-
ing mother and numerous sisters. Later, stories were rife
among Fotherly's contemporaries regarding his propensity to
bribe to gain favors, and to use his money to make life uncomfortable for those he perceived as thwarting him. To those
who did not know him well, he was often thought effete, ef-
feminate, and correspondingly foolish. He was, in fact, often
referred to as Foth the Foppish. It was an assessment that
many lived to regret making, for Fotherly was an unscrupu-
lous schemer, merciless to those who opposed him. His other
nickname, Bart the Barbaric, was much more apt. By the time
I first entered the Councillory, he was already a member of the
Inner Council, by virtue, some said, of the monetary induce-
ments he offered to other Council members, rather than as a
result of his father's patronage.

By 1742, it was clear that his father Emmerlynd, the Keeperlord, ought to be replaced by a younger man. His heyday was over; he shuffled when he walked, dribbled when he ate, and occasionally lost the thread of conversations. Fotherly's name was on everyone's lips as a possible new Keeperlord, but it would have been an idiotic choice; the man was not astute enough to maintain the Keeper Isles' burgeoning prosperity and military power. Some Council members recognized this. Before I left for Cirkase, and hence to Gorthan Spit and Mekaté, there were growing factions pressing Duthrick to stand at the next election. As much as I had ambivalent feelings toward the man, even I had to admit that he would have been a better choice than Fotherly.

Duthrick, however, was not a member of the Inner Council, although he definitely had the ambition to be so. His title was Councillor Executant, or "active" councillor; that is, one who was given assignments throughout the Glory Isles. That didn't mean that he had to perform these assignments in person; merely that he had to see that they were done. He had unofficial agents like me for most tasks, not to mention his own official staff, his own ship and an almost unlimited budget, all of which meant that he had power and influence. He was an attractive, urbane man with considerable charisma and intelligence, which earned him the support of a number of Councillors. Of course, he could also be ruthless in his efficiency, and arrogant in his power-wielding, traits that had gained him an equal amount of enemies. Enemies who were only too willing to shred him to pieces when he returned to the Inner Council to report that he had not found the Castlemaid, and that the dunmaster had escaped from his bombardment of Creed . . .

By the time he reached the Councillory, Fotherly and the elder Bartbarick had been primed and, from all reports, Duthrick had a grueling time standing before that kelmari table, during which he was denounced as an incompetent for having had the Castlemaid in his hands and then allowing her to slip away; grilled about his extravagant use of cannon powder, which was now in short supply, seeing as the Breth Bastionlord was not selling them any more saltpeter; accused of employing foolish females (me) instead of sylv armsmen;

chided for his dependence on Awarefolk of dubious origins
(me again); and severely chastised for the accidental killing of
a senior Menod patriarch (Alain Jentel), blown up in the bombardment of Creed, no less. It seemed that the Menod Council
had wasted no time making its protest to the Keeper Council
on that latter issue.

Duthrick emerged from the Sanctum some three hours
later in tight-lipped rage. His next appointment happened to
be with Syr-sylv Arnado, my mentor, who was supposed to be
reporting in to him on another assignment. Instead, poor Arnado was met by a man who was white with blistering anger.
Taken aback, Arnado could only listen as Duthrick paced his
office, pouring out his grievances against me and Tor Ryder in
a vitriolic spew.

Arnado was alarmed enough to sit down the next day and
write me a letter, telling me what had happened and urging
caution. *I've rarely seen a man hate another as much as that
man hates you,* he wrote. *Blaze, my friend, be very, very careful. He will do you whatever harm he can if ever your paths
cross again, and he is taking steps to make sure that they do.
He has put out an edict, addressed to all sylvs under the command of the Council, ordering your immediate arrest no matter where they might find you. That's right: believe it or not, he
is saying that the Keeper Isles have the right to arrest someone
in another islandom and bring them back here. Sounds like
kidnapping to me, but Duthrick seems to think that might is
right. Moreover, he has wrangled the offer of a huge reward
for either you or the Castlemaid. Blaze, you have shattered the
pride of an overly proud man: he will not forget it. Beware.*

*Oh, and he seems to have taken an inordinate dislike to this
Menod fellow by the name of Tor Ryder, who has just been ele-
vated to Patriarch Council. Duthrick has asked one of our colleagues to dig up some dirt on this man. I think he intends to
sully his name with the Menod if he can; I understand from
something Duthrick let drop in his anger that all this has something to do with you too? You have been busy, my friend . . .*

Unfortunately, the only address that Arnado had for me
was my lodgings in The Hub. As it would have been pointless
to deliver it there, he sent it instead to the only person he
could think of who might have known where I was: he sent it

to Tenkor Island, to the Menod, addressed care of Patriarch Tor Ryder. By the time it arrived, Tor was no longer in Tenkor.

Would it have made a difference, that letter of warning from a concerned man who had once taken me under his wing and taught me all he knew, had I received it much earlier than I did?

Unlikely. Yet it is little things like that—a delayed warning, a missed meeting, a mistaken message—that determine events, that shape lives; most of the time we are not even aware of their import. Sometimes you have to accept that you aren't the only master of your journey.

I SUSPECT THAT IT WAS THE VERBAL DRUB-bing that Duthrick received from the Inner Council that strengthened his resolve to become Keeperlord. He hated his humiliation and how better to avoid humiliation than to be the predator at the top of the reef? With single-minded dedication, he set about becoming the ruler of the Keeper Isles.

Most people would have started with the other elected members of Council. They were the ones who voted each year on who was to lead them, after all. But Duthrick was more subtle. He started with the people who had influence. The merchants of The Hub, who knew security meant prosperity. The great sylv families, to whom the thought of a dunmaster on the loose, subverting their own, was terrifying.

Duthrick visited them all, leaving behind a trail of rumor like a sea-pony leaving its sticky track. The reason the dunmaster had escaped, he said, was because the Keeperlord had not foreseen the danger. He had not given Duthrick enough resources to do the job properly. Duthrick achieved a great victory, but he had not been able to complete the task. It was a miracle that he'd been able to wipe out a huge dunmagic enclave with just two ships; the wonder of it was that he'd achieved as much as he had. He'd been thwarted by inferior staff, even having to make use of traitorous halfbreeds because he could not afford to pay for reliable armsmen and agents. In spite of this, he'd found the Castlemaid of Cirkase, only to have her snatched from him by the treachery of the said halfbreed.

The Keeperlord was old, he whispered to his most trusted friends. He dribbles, have you noticed? His mind wanders. Did you see how he addressed Syr-sylv Hathic by the wrong name at the gathering last week? Called him Hammerling, and Councillor Hammerling has been dead six years! We need a new man. Someone with drive and ambition, who has a vision for the Keeper Isles. Someone who is not afraid to use Keeper power. Not afraid to make use of cannon fire to show the Isles our Keeper justice. Are we going to let the Breth Bastionlord blackmail us as if we were as weak and pathetic as Spatt Islanders? Are we going to allow them to tell us what we can and cannot buy? Are we going to turn a blind eye while another dunmagicker enclave grows somewhere else? We are the strongest islandom this world has ever seen! We must have a leader to match our strength. A man who understands the commercial needs of a great people . . .

As I have said, he was a man of considerable charisma and charm.

People began to whisper that he was also a man of courage and foresight.

After a public cockfight one night along one of The Hub's back streets, there was a spontaneous riot against halfbreeds. Two citizens who were rumored, erroneously, to have halfbreed blood were killed, a row of shops was gutted by fire and a halfbreed beggar murdered while he slept.

And the name of Blaze Halfbreed became anathema to every patriotic citizen of the Keeper Isles.

In the meantime, I was still on Porth, without the slightest idea of the hell that Duthrick was brewing for my future.

CHAPTER 14

BEFORE GINNA, I HAD JUSTIFIED MY RE-
fusal to further involve myself in Blaze and Flame's affairs by
saying it was no business of mine, that Morthred hadn't done
anything to me, that dunmagic might not be as evil as they
said, that they believed things that were palpably not true,
such as the Dustel Islands sinking under Morthred's spells . . .
After Ginna, I would never be so impersonal about dunmagic
again. I might still not have believed that it was a supernatural
thing, but I would never again be able to think, with any ease,
that it was nothing to do with me.

Mind you, disease always smelled foul to me, wrong even,
but it had never smelled *evil* before. And whatever infected
Ginna was evil. It had no right to be in the world. I had caught
a whiff of that same evil in Flame, but it had been slight
enough for me to wonder if I was just imagining its vileness.
Now I knew. If that was what dunmagic was, then I wanted it
swept from the world.

If I'd seen Ginna before Blaze and Flame had left, things
might have been different, but they had left for the Floating

Mere ten days earlier. It was too late now; I would never be able to catch up with them.

And so I lingered on in Amkabraig, reading and waiting for Garrowyn's trunk.

IT WAS SURPRISING HOW CONSISTENT THE stories were, in a general sense, about the origins of magic. They all agreed that the people who came to the Isles, from some place far away, in order to escape the Kelvish, had no magic. It was given to them after they arrived, or at least to some of them. It was intriguing, too, that all the texts seemed to agree that it was some kind of misuse of sylvpower that had led to dunmagic. All the details in the stories could be different—they couldn't even agree on exactly who had gifted the magic—but those few points were always the same.

Especially intriguing were the more medical aspects of sylv and dunmagic. I pored over the medical papers Garrowyn had collected—he seemed to have found something in every single islandom—and compared them with the scrolls he had obtained from sylv healers. It was fascinating reading that spanned several centuries of study: a mix of mythology, superstition, supposition and science. The difficulty was in sorting out what was proven fact, and what was fable. Again, they all agreed on some things: once a dunmagicker, always a dunmagicker; sylvmagic was usually passed from parent to child; dunmagic was the more virulent. A dunmagicker of either sex always had dun children, but only ever seemed to have children if the woman was dun or sylv. When there was a liaison with an ordinary woman, no children were ever conceived, but then, if the texts were to be believed, that might have stemmed from the fact that ordinary women rarely survived a sexual encounter with a dunmagicker.

When sylvs mated with ordinary people, there was no absolute certainty the child would be sylv, although it did seem to end up that way, nine times out of ten. Having Awareness, on the other hand, seemed to be much more random, although it could run in families, and often seemed to be more prevalent in some areas than in others. However, there seemed to be no hard and fast rules: Aware children could be born to non-Aware families anywhere in the Isles.

Two weeks or more after Blaze and the others had left, I came across an interesting paper on dunmagickers entitled *A Treatise on Comparison: four case studies of dunmagickers as compared to known sylvs*. It had been written by a nonsylv physician in Quillerharbor a hundred years earlier, and it explained that a dunmagicker could do all the things a sylv could, although sometimes not as well. A dunmagicker's illusion could never match the grand scale possible for a sylv, for example. He could disguise himself with illusion, but little more than that. However, a dunmagicker could conjure up destructive magic, which was beyond a sylv's power. He could kill with dunmagic sores. And he could coerce, which seemed to be an ability to exert his will upon others. The Quillerman physician didn't seem to have much to say about dunmasters, and nor did anyone else, except that they earned the name by being noticeably more powerful than normal dunmagickers.

I sighed, and allowed the treatise to roll itself up on Anistie's table top. I leaned back in the kitchen chair and just at that moment Anistie came in from the garden. Her hands were still grubby from gardening and she carried a sprig of orchids for the table. "My, it's hot out there," she said, putting the flowers down in front of me.

"I'm sorry," I said, "I have been taking over your table—"

"Ah, it's good to have company," she replied. "How are your studies progressing?"

I sighed again. "Not so well. I was hoping to find something that would explain how to help my friend Flame. How to cure the residue of her dunmagic infection, but there is verra little about that. They speak only of sylv healing, but she had some of the best sylv healers in the Isles, and they still didn't rid her of all that infected her."

"That's sad. Will she die?"

"I didn't know. The awful thing is, I have this feeling that the solution is right under my nose. That I have read something, right here in one of these books or papers, that gave me the clue, but I just didna recognize it." I gave a disheartened shrug. "I suppose it doesn't matter all that much now. I'm not likely to see her again."

Anistie gave me a shrewd look. "You made a mistake there, lad."

I looked up, questioning.

"You should always follow your heart. And your heart told you they needed you."

"It's irrelevant now," I said, replacing scrolls and books on the shelves. "It's been, um, eighteen days since they left and I have no idea where they are."

"You could still catch them up," she said casually as she washed her hands and then filled a milk jug with water to put the orchid in. "They took the long way around, didn't they?"

I turned to look at her, not understanding. "Long way around?"

"Didn't you know?" she asked. "There are three ways to get to the Floating Mere. You can take a boat to the northern port of Rattéspie and travel up the Kilgair Slug. That's a river. But I wouldn't advise that; it would be too difficult to get a berth to Rattéspie. Then there's the way that your friends went: follow the road that skirts the Kilgair Massif, finally ending up at the Mere. But that way takes at least three weeks, more if the weather is unkind, which it usually is. The road curls through rugged country, up hill and down dale, and the mud is awful when it rains. And then there's the third way. You climb the Kilgair Massif and take a raft down the Kilgair Spill. Three days' walk from here to the river head, and two days down on the raft. Five days. Expensive, mind. Which is probably why it wasn't an option for your friends. But if you were to go now, you would arrive at the Mere at about the same time your friends will. No more than a day or two behind anyway."

I was stilled. For a moment I felt as if my heart had stopped beating. Only then did I realize how glad I had been that I didn't have to make a decision, or I thought I didn't have to, after I had seen Ginna. I didn't *want* to have to face anyone who had dunmagic. I didn't want to have to face up to the am- bivalent feelings I had about Blaze and Flame. I wanted to be able to walk away and say, "Well, it's too late to do anything now." And that option had just been removed.

I said weakly, "I still don't know how to help Flame."

"Yes, you do," Anistie said and her tone was implacable. "You just said you do, dearie, but you haven't recognized it yet. You just need to think about it, is all. Given time, your mind will make the right connections with the knowledge you have."

I dithered still.

She pushed me back into the chair and sat down opposite me across the table, and suddenly she was a different woman. Solemn, shrewd, a woman who was used to being taken seriously. "Kelwyn, I've been watching you, listening to you almost every day since you first came to Amkabraig. And it saddens me that you have been listening to neither your heart, nor your conscience. You have been exiled from your home with no hope of return. Your plans are nebulous, and flexible. Yet when you were offered friendship and purpose, you turned away from both. Kelwyn, nobility of purpose fires the soul with the will to live. And to recklessly discard friends is plain silly. Friends are all you have now; haven't you realized that?"

I was silent. She made it sound so simple, and it wasn't simple at all.

Or was it?

"I know you feel that killing a dunmaster is hardly the sort of thing a physician should be involved in. I would have felt the same way once. But then we had a governor right here in Amkabraig who turned out to be a dunmaster, not so very long ago. Nasty creature he was too. He first targeted the Awarefolk who might have warned others, killing them before they had time to realize what was happening. Next, he used coercion to seize power. Then he used illusive charm to establish his legitimacy. And finally he used force to maintain it. We suffered as a result, in ways I can't even begin to tell you. He was able to do all that because at first no one would stand up to him. Then, by the time someone did, he had enough acolytes and enough power to bring down opposition.

"Do you know who rescued us from the purgatory we had helped establish with our blindness and fear?"

I stared at her. She was still the same curly-headed graying woman with the sweet rosebud smile and the wrinkles, but she was also much, much more. I just hadn't seen it.

She answered her own question. "Your Blaze Halfbreed. Sent by the Keeper Council."

I stared at her. "Who *are* ye?"

"Right now? No more than you see: an old woman who loves her garden and her friends and the view from her windows. Who is content with her life, and enjoys the occasional visit from your rogue of an uncle. Who *was* I? Ah, that's another story. I was married to the man who was the deputy governor of Porth when the dunmaster came. A silly frivolous woman who didn't know how to be grateful for what she had, and who had to lose it all to know." I felt the wash of her grief, and then it was gone, replaced by her sunny smile. "Ah, listen to me, then! Getting maudlin about the past. No point in that. And you, my lad, you go back to the inn and you pack your bags and you go after them, along the Kilgair Spill. Friends are everything. And you need to be able to live with your conscience."

I felt a chill across my cheek. She was right. If I walked away from the whole dunmagic issue right then, I would have yet another guilt to agonize over. I had been a fool, so caught up on one moral question that I had ignored others just as potent.

I stood up and kissed her on the cheek. "Thank ye, Anistie. Garrowyn was right. He told me ye were a wise woman. Oh— what about his medicine chest?"

"It will be waiting here for you when you get back."

If I had any further doubts about whether I'd made the right decision, they disappeared on the walk back to the inn. For the first time in weeks, I felt at peace with myself.

CHAPTER 15

NARRATOR : KELWYN

I STOOD LOOKING DOWN ON THE KILGAIR
Spill and knew I must have lost all the good sense I'd ever
had. Did I really want to get to the Floating Mere in *that* much
of a hurry?

"Eight setus," the young man said.

I hesitated.

I was standing at the edge of a river pond. It was filled
from above by a burst of water out of the mountain rock face.
It was as if the river began its life by escaping imprisonment,
shouting its wrath in a rage of white foam and spray. In the
pond it hesitated a while, partially placated but still restless,
and then poured down the Kilgair Spill in corrugations, slipping between the rocks and boulders in anxious haste to be on
its way.

I'd spent three days climbing the Kilgair Massif, following
the donkey trail upward with other travelers, mostly traders,
just to get to this point.

"*Eight* setus?" I asked, and didn't have to fake my wrath.
Anistie had warned me that it was a costly way to get to the
lake, I just hadn't thought it would be this outrageous.

The man shrugged. "That's without illusion. You want illusion, it'll be an extra setu."

"No, I dinna want illusions," I snapped, even though I had no idea what sort of illusion he meant. Eight setus: that was a small fortune for a one-way journey down a river.

"That includes meals," he said. "And accommodation overnight."

"How long does it take?"

"Two days. But we won't be leaving today."

I couldn't help but look down at the cascade. And then at all the rafts floating in the pond, tied up to the jetty. They were just bamboo platforms, several layers built up to make floats which were then joined together by a floor of bamboo stems. If one of them hit a boulder, everyone on board could be thrown into the water.

"Ye want eight setus for riding *that* water on *that* contraption? It's a death trap!"

He grinned at that. "Is it now? You get what you pay for, Syr. Eight setus buys you a skillful poler: me brother, Mackie. Who's the best. And me as the front man. You want to die? Find yourself someone who'll do it for less. I've got a cousin who's just learning. Maybe you could try him."

It was pointless arguing, I realized belatedly. He knew there was no way I was going to trudge all the way back down the mountain toward Amkabraig and then take the long road around the Massif. I had come this way because I wanted to get to the lake quickly, and he knew it, even though he would not have known why.

I fumbled in my purse for the coins. "Why can we no leave today?"

"The water's too high. Too much rain in the mountains." He took pity on me and nodded at the river. "We don't make the descent till it's more manageable than that."

He grinned again. I sighed. People loved to gull the rustic mountain man from the Roof of Mekaté. Sometimes it seemed that bright red hair and freckles were equated with the simple-minded. "My name's Kelwyn Gilfeather," I said, indicating acceptance of a place on his raft.

"I'm Jakan Tassianie. See that place with the new thatch

roof over there?" He pointed at the muddle of houses on stilts strung along the pond shoreline. "You can bed down there, free, until we are ready to descend. Blankets are extra. Meals are five coppers for plain fare."

"Ye just said—"

"Food's free once the journey starts."

I sighed again, shouldered my pack and made my way to the building he indicated. It was a simple structure made of wood and it had woven pandana walls, a grass roof and a split cane floor. A single room and nothing else: no furniture, no privy, nothing. The village itself was not even as large as a Sky Plains tharn, although it did, it seemed, have a Menod priest. He was seated on the ground near the building, surrounded by all the village children, telling them a story. As I passed by, most of the kids turned to stare at me: the red hair, I suppose.

There were a number of other people already there in the building as I entered, all waiting for the river to fall and the rafts to start on their way down once more. They were mostly traders; men who had dragged their laden donkeys up the track with goods they wanted to sell, merchants for whom time was money.

Selver-herding, something all Plainsmen do throughout their working lives, usually breeds patience, but sitting in that ramshackle village waiting for the river to go down was hard. Now that I believed I had made the right decision, I just wanted to get there in time to be of some use. So that Blaze and Flame and Dek wouldn't have to face a dunmagicker without my nose to help them. And all the while I had that strange niggling feeling that there was something that I should know, that was desperately important, if only I could work out what it was.

FORTUNATELY, WHEN WE AWOKE THE FOLlowing morning, it was to find that the amount of water entering the river had fallen enough to make the trip possible. Jakan came to tell me to pack up and come down to the jetty, but when I got there, he tried to squeeze another setu out of me for illusions. "You'll get scared otherwise," he said, "and maybe do summat foolish. With illusions, the raft'll seem as smooth as a walking donkey."

"Why should I pay extra for something I can't even see?" I asked.

"Oh! You're Aware! In that case—" He shrugged. "No extra charge." He stowed my bag by tying it to the bamboo platform, and indicated where I was to sit. There were a number of rope loops tied along the sides and floor of the raft and he picked one of them up to show me. "Hold on to these when the river gets rough, and don't let go. Tuck your feet into them too." He grinned at me, daring me to ask what the odds were that the raft would be overturned. I didn't say anything.

The first of the rafts, with several traders and their wares aboard, started on its way and I watched as it navigated the drop out of the pond into the Spill proper. The raft *bent* under the force of the water.

A moment later the other passengers for our raft arrived. The first was a woman with two children and a large bundle. One of the children was a boy of about eight; the other was a baby. The woman said her name was Stelass, and she was taking her children back to see their grandparents on the Floating Mere. Apparently she had married an Amkabraig man, and hadn't been home for six years. She seemed completely unfazed by the idea of taking her two children on a hair-raising ride down a river liberally laced with rapids.

The other passenger was the priest. He, too, was on his way to the Mere, all part of his parish, I supposed. Just before he came on board, he removed the coral necklace that was a symbol of the Menod priesthood and stripped off his black outer robe to reveal ordinary traveling clothes. I wondered about that: did he expect to be tossed into the water and knew a robe was not the best thing to swim in? I was beginning to have even more doubts about this trip. He nodded politely to me, and we made a few innocuous remarks about the weather.

The trip was every bit as horrendous as I anticipated. Once we had left the confines of the river pool, we were caught up in the flow and traveled at frightening speeds, sometimes skimming on white water as light as swallows on air, sometimes squeezing between boulders and over cascades as recklessly as a torrent duck. Jakan stood braced on the front of the raft with a pole which he used to fend us off the rocks; occasionally he would kneel and use a paddle with furious energy to direct us away from whirlpools formed at the base of spillovers. Within a few minutes of setting off, we were all wet, soaked by spray, and we stayed that way the whole journey through.

I hung on to the ropes as if my life depended on it, which perhaps it did, but I was astonished by Stelass and her older child. They sat in the middle of the raft, and kept their feet hooked into the rope loops as Jakan had instructed them, but they only held on tight when either Jakan or his brother Mackie told them to, which was at the most dangerous moments. For the rest of the time they sat with their backs to the front of the raft, seemingly oblivious to everything around them. They could have been sitting in their own kitchen, chatting over the events of a normal, peaceful day. Even when the raft bounced on the rough water or they had to lean to compensate for the movement, they did it with a coolness that seemed foolhardy, at best. Mackie was creating an illusion, I could smell that much, but it seemed unbelievable that anyone could be so easily lulled into complacency as Stelass and her son obviously were. I looked back at the priest. Although he was calm enough, the way he watched the water betrayed him: he could see what was happening, just as I could. One of the Awarefolk, I assumed, although there was nothing about his smell to tell me, any more than there had been with Blaze.

Midmorning, at a riverside village, we stopped briefly to stretch our legs and give the two brothers a rest; at midday we stopped again, this time for lunch, prepared by the women of another village. There, I took the opportunity to ask the priest what the woman and her son were seeing that made them so calm.

He looked at me oddly. "They see a smooth river, gently gliding between the banks. No rocks, no boulders, no cascades."

"That's insane," I said. "Dinna they feel the bumps? Are they not wet by the spray?"

"Illusion is a powerful force in the hands of a skillful sylv."

"Then I am glad I am immune."

His gaze sharpened. "An interesting choice of word."

"I'm a physician." I must have sounded as grumpy as a drunk in the morning; that was pretty much how I felt.

"You are Aware?"

"Nay, just immune. I see nothing."

Just then we were called back to the raft and I didn't have a chance to talk to him again until we stopped for the night. The dinner we were served, like lunch, was mostly meat killed by the villagers and fish from the river. I couldn't bring myself to eat it, but fortunately I still had the remains of a hard cheese, a packet of dried bananas and some yam chips I had bought in Amkabraig. Together with the fried fern leaves supplied by the villagers, it was an adequate meal.

Afterward, when I was preparing to sleep in the hut given to us, the priest beckoned me out. He had evidently been attending to his parishioners, because he asked, "You said you were a physician? There's a child here needs some help. Some kind of nasty skin condition."

Nasty was an understatement. It covered the poor boy and was excruciatingly itchy, and of course scratching had made it worse. It was not anything I had ever seen before, but I knew that children of the tropical regions of Mekaté were prone to skin ailments, especially fungal ones. Unfortunately I had none of the correct herbs with me. I spoke at length with the boy's family, telling them which plants to seek and how to prepare the unguent and how to apply it. They seemed to listen carefully enough, so I could hope that he would be cured.

As we left their hut, the priest thanked me, adding, "Villagers in these remoter corners of the world never see trained sylv healers. Not, probably, that they would accept sylv healing anyway. They are conservative with their Menod faith, believing that magic is sinful. Our young raftsmen garner a few extra setus with Mackie's sylvtalent, but I wouldn't mind betting they don't tell their fellow villagers. These remote settlements have no ordinary physicians either . . . a great tragedy." The depth of his caring touched me: he was really concerned about these people, as if they were his own family.

"Ye canna take on the whole world," I said, and then could have kicked myself. It was none of my business. When would I learn to behave properly among people who leaked their emotions so blatantly all over the place?

The remark earned me another odd look. "Let's walk down to the river," he suggested. "I want to talk to you about this 'immunity' of yours . . ."

There didn't seem any reason why I shouldn't; he seemed a pleasant enough sort of fellow and his aroma was benign, so I explained how I could not see sylvmagic, neither the color of it nor its illusions, even though I could smell it. I didn't delve into the details of the olfactory abilities of a Plainsman, though.

"And you suspect that all Sky Plains people are the same?" he asked as we reached the river and sat down side by side on the jetty.

His genuine interest flattered me, and I plunged on with my theories. "Aye, although I canna prove it. I think it's an immunity we have, an immunity to a disease, which somehow manifests itself in an inability to see the sylv silver-blue, whatever that is, as well as an inability to see illusions. I suspect that I wouldn't respond to sylv healing either, and would walk right through sylv wards without even knowing they were there. Just like you Awarefolk."

He did not deny his Awareness, but he looked startled. "A disease? You think sylvmagic is a *disease*?"

"Aye."

He tried not to laugh. He was polite, this priest. "The Keeper sylvs would love to hear that." He smiled. "And what about dunmagic? Just a disease too?"

"Probably."

"Do you have any evidence? If it's a disease, then how is it transmitted? And why doesn't everyone contract it?"

"From what one of the Awarefolk, who was once present at a sylv woman's birthing, described to me, it seemed that the baby received its sylvmagic through its mother's placenta. It's all peskily hard to prove, though."

"That's an interesting theory. If it is a disease, then it could be cured, couldn't it?"

I laughed. "Not all diseases can be cured, y'know. Not even by sylvs, I think. At least not yet. Of course, I'm not convinced that there is such a thing as sylv healing. What puzzles me is the color Awarefolk see . . . what can that be? Some kind of skin secretion? And why dinna others see it?"

He stared at me, half intrigued, half bemused, as though he thought I were mad. "And dunmagic?" he asked. "What do you think about dunmagic?"

"I suspect they are one and the same."

"Pardon?"

"Sylv and dunmagic. One and the same thing. It was the description of the sylv woman's birthing that set me thinking along those lines. The Aware woman said that the sylvmagic was so concentrated in the placenta that it was almost dun-colored . . ."

"Now I *know* you can't be serious."

"Oh, but I am. I suspect that dunmagic is just a more severe presentation of the same disease. And that Awareness is a less extreme presentation of the immunity than the one I have."

I had rocked him. His shock flowed out from him in a strong aroma. He was silent a long time.

"It's one thing that can explain subversion," I said. "As far as I know, it can only happen to a sylv, not to one of the Awarefolk, or to an ordinary person." He was silent, so I started explaining. "Subversion is when—"

"I know what subversion is," he interrupted harshly. "I'm more interested in what you know about it."

"A dunmaster who can subvert an individual sylv by himself must be particularly diseased, I think. He contaminates a sylv with his own strain of the sickness—infecting the blood somehow? They become sicker, and then ye have a dunmagicker." I stopped, aware of his mental withdrawal. "Ye dinna believe a skerrick of it."

"I'm a priest," he said slowly. "And a man who's seen a lot of magic over the years. Both good and bad. I've killed dunmagickers, believing I was doing something right, believing that it was the only way to fight a great evil that should never have been born into the world. Now you tell me dunmagickers might be what they are because of a disease. That it's not their fault; that one day they could even be cured. That's a . . . disconcerting thought for one of the Menod." He turned to look at me. I couldn't see his expression, but I could smell his distress. "I'm not a man of science. I tend to look at problems from a spiritual angle, and by preference I seek spiritual solutions, although I am pragmatic enough to seek other answers if the spiritual does not provide a solution. God, after all, gave us our brains to use.

"I think you have given me much to think about, Plainsman. Tomorrow you must explain to me just how you know as much as you do about subversion. Right now, I think I have had enough surprises. I am going to go to bed."

He stood up, a tall, dark man, broad-shouldered, with the ear tattoo of the Stragglers.

That was a description that had been given to me before . . . "Oh, Creation," I said in shock, rising to my feet. "Ye are no Porthian parish priest!"

He turned back to face me, puzzled. "I never said I was."

"Ye're Tor Ryder, aren't ye?"

He stilled. "Now, how in all the seas of Glory did you know that?" he asked softly.

"She . . . she described ye . . . I just didna expect to see ye here. She said ye were going to the Spatts . . ."

"Blaze," he said even more softly. "You know Blaze." The wave of pain from him was so intense that it took my breath away, and yet his voice remained steady and calm. "Is she well?"

"I—last I saw, aye. A few weeks back. In Amkabraig." Selverspit, he *loves* her. The idea was distinctly unsettling. A *priest* and Blaze? *This* was the man she had referred to when she spoke of loving someone?

"She's still there?"

I shook my head. I was having to struggle to find words and didn't know why. "Nay. She and Flame and Ruarth have gone on to the Floating Mere."

He nodded as if he'd expected that, but was more than glad to have it confirmed. "Tomorrow . . . tomorrow you can tell me just who the hell you are. But not now. Not now . . ."

He walked away back to the huts, unconsciously trailing pain through the air behind him.

CHAPTER 16

NARRATOR: BLAZE

SO IT IS MY TURN TO TELL THE STORY again, is it? I hope you credit what I have to say, as I understand that you don't always believe what Kelwyn relates.

Come now, Syr Ethnographer, don't protest your innocence! Kelwyn's nostrils tell him when your skepticism overwhelms you. Irritating, isn't it? One cannot lie to him, ever. I know, I've tried, but the nose-twitching sod always sees through me.

Now, where do you want me to start? The journey from Amkabraig to the Floating Mere—ah, yes, unpleasant, to say the least. More than once I regretted that we had not taken the shorter route down the Kilgair Spill, but the cost, when I had inquired in the city, was way above what we could afford out of our card-cheating gains.

It wasn't that the way was long (though it was), it wasn't that it rained a lot (though it did), it wasn't that we were all tired of the humidity and heat (though we were); what made the trip unpleasant was Flame's behavior and our growing conviction, Ruarth's and mine, that something was deeply wrong with her. The rest we'd had in Amkabraig had restored much of her physical strength; that was no longer the problem. The trouble seemed to be more in her head. She was moody. She could swing between being her old self, and being downright nasty. At times she seemed insanely jealous, castigating Ruarth or both of us in language that was more than just crude; it was perturbing in its illogicality, frightening in its virulence.

What do you think is wrong with her? Ruarth asked, several times a day.

"Something to do with the dunmagic subversion," I would mutter. "Just a lingering effect that will wear off . . ." Hope dies hard.

It's getting worse, not better, he pointed out. He didn't mention that Seeker, who had once thought nothing of licking her face and otherwise being around her, now seemed to avoid her, treating her with the same caution he gave to the odd snake we saw along the roadside.

The truth was, I didn't know what was wrong, and I sure as the Great Trench is deep didn't know how to fix it.

Poor Dek, he had thought he was going off to fight evil in the company of a group of unsullied heroes. Instead, he found himself sharing his fate with an unpredictable, unstable, often foul-mouthed woman; a bird who was petulant and sick with worry; a dog that didn't seem to know much except how to make a nuisance of himself; and a swordswoman who had as much idea of what was going on as a decapitated lobster. (Dek still managed to make me laugh sometimes, though, with his romantic view of the world: "But, Syr-aware Blaze, you *have* to have a banner with your emblem on it when you ride into battle! Otherwise how is your enemy gunna know who is attackin' him?")

In the privacy of my own thoughts, I missed Tor. I missed his advice, his sanity, his quick mind and his ability to see the larger picture. I missed the way he looked at me. I missed his hands on my body. And yet, in my heart, I still sensed that I had done the right thing, and if I'd had to leave him all over again, I would have.

More immediately, I sharply regretted that Kelwyn Gilfeather had not come with us. We needed him. *I* needed him. I needed to know whether Flame's problem was a medical one.

I needed his sense of smell. I needed his fresh way of looking at things. Somehow, when Gilfeather was around, I seemed to be able to see new paths, new aspects, even though the scenery may have been old. At times, he could be grouchy—Dek called it "having the mulligrubs"—but even when he was at his grumpiest, there was always a twinkle lurking in those dark, red-flecked Plainsman eyes of his. I liked his skepticism, his inquiring mind, his need to understand the world around him. I appreciated the kindness of his heart. I admired his courage: he'd known exactly what he was doing when he'd killed Jastriá, and he'd accepted that he would have to live with it. He made no excuses for himself. He'd destroyed part of what he had believed in to save her pain: it had cost him even more than he'd expected, but he'd accepted that with, for the most part, dignity. There was also something immensely appealing about him: a boyishness that was matched by a wildly unruly head of red hair and freckles; a childlike sense of wonder that he never seemed to lose, even in his darkest moments. He was clumsy, his nose twitched at the end, he blushed like a lovelorn adolescent, but when he was around, I felt that the world was a better place.

The only damn problem was that he wasn't around, the stubborn, overly hirsute, grass-eating *fool* of a medicineman. *Confound* all dove-cooing peacemongers! And I *hated* being read like the open page of a book, just because I apparently exuded as many smells as the scent glands of a civet cat.

Halfway to the Floating Mere, I told Ruarth I thought we ought to turn around and go back to Amkabraig. Flame, I said, was just too unpredictable. We would never have any success against the sly intelligence of Morthred with her like this. Ruarth concurred, but when we tried to persuade Flame, she refused outright to go. When she was at her most irrational, she castigated us angrily and accused us of not wanting her to have her revenge, of wanting the glory of killing Morthred ourselves, without her. When I tried, in her more rational periods, to discuss the matter with her, she didn't seem to be aware of the problem. She turned those innocent blue eyes to me in puzzlement and protested that she was fine—what in all the wide seas were we fussing about? Were our teeth beginning to chatter? Morthred was still out there, and every moment we delayed was another moment during which a sylv could be subverted, a child enslaved, a woman raped . . . is that what we wanted?

Of course not. But I didn't want to carry a liability into this confrontation with Morthred and a liability was what I felt Flame to be.

We have to go on, Ruarth signed when Flame wasn't looking. *Maybe if Morthred dies, she will be all right again, once and for all . . .*

That was the crux of it, of course. We had to do this for Flame. And if we didn't try, we'd never know.

So in the end we continued.

As we traveled, I gathered as much information as I could from the villages we passed, and from travelers along the road. Even so, my first sight of the Floating Mere took me by surprise. I had expected a lake, swampy perhaps, but still I anticipated an expanse of water. But when we topped a rise and saw the Mere below us, there was hardly any water visible at all. It was there, all right, but it was covered by plants. Floating plants.

"That's pandana," Dek said.

"How do you know?"

"Oh, people say it grows on the Mere," he said, and added unnecessarily, "It floats."

And now we have to find out exactly where the dunmagickers are, Ruarth said. *That's a big lake.*

He was right. We were at one end, and it was three or four miles wide, but it stretched out as far as I could see to the north.

"Maybe there are Dustel birds to ask in the village down there," Flame suggested. She sounded her normal self.

"If not, we can ask the ordinary villagers if there is anything odd going on anywhere," I said, confident that we'd get an answer to that question.

Or I can fly around until I see a hint of dunmagic color, Ruarth said.

In the end it was my suggestion that gave us the information we needed. The villagers were only too willing to talk about what was bothering them, but the tale was muddled. There was something very strange indeed on the island in the middle of the lake, we were told. There used to be a settlement there, pandana collectors and their families. Now though, for some strange reason, no one could get near the place.

When I questioned them about that, they shuffled their feet and looked embarrassed. They just couldn't get there anymore, that's all. No one wanted to go out collecting pandana anymore either, because you couldn't be certain that you would come back. People disappeared. Lake spirits, maybe. But there was that girl from a neighboring village. She'd been taken by strangers, or so she'd said afterward.

They didn't know anything about dunmagic, they were all God-fearing Menod here, they told us indignantly, but there were whispers. They were frightened. There had been strangers coming, and they took boats without asking, without paying. And if you objected, you got sick and died. It was better not to be around when people like that came. You just slunk away and let them take what they liked. The village headman had been brave enough to send word to the Havenlord, but Mekatéhaven was a long way away, and the governor of Porth in Amkabraig was a niggling little mouse who wouldn't so much as squeak until he had heard from the Havenlord . . .

The pandana collectors were only too willing to rent us a boat, for an outrageously high price, but refused absolutely to pole it for us.

"You want to stir the muck up with your pole," one of them said, "that's your business. But don't expect us to help you prod the monster there into wakefulness." The others gathered around nodded solemnly. I didn't know whether he was being metaphorical or not.

I took a look at the boat. It was flat-bottomed and broad, constructed to carry heaps of pandana leaves rather than people. It would be a bitch to maneuver. Seeker hopped in and gave it the once-over, apparently to his satisfaction, because he made himself comfortable and beat his tail thunderously against the boards.

"Which way is this island?" I asked.

"Due north," the boat-owner said, and pointed.

"You're mad, Scedriss," one of the others told him. "You'll never get your boat back."

He shrugged. "What if I don't? 'Tis no use at the moment, with us all too scared to go out on the lake. I need the money to feed my family."

I promised to do my level best to bring the boat back and we haggled for a bit. We didn't get anywhere at first because he was asking a small fortune, but when I threw in the donkey, he had a grin on his face, and we had a boat. I guessed that at that price he wasn't too worried about not seeing his craft again.

"You're not thinking to go *now,* are you?" Scedriss asked in astonishment as we began to stow our bags.

I nodded. "Why not?"

"Because it's only an hour to sundown."

"And how long will it take to reach the island?"

"About two hours. More if you get lost. And you will be in the dark. Come to think on it, you'd get lost in the daytime too."

"Yes," I said in answer to his question, "we are indeed going now." I didn't worry about becoming lost, not when I had my Awareness. If Morthred was there, I'd see his dun.

Scedriss shrugged and handed me the pole. "There are a few deep channels where the pole won't touch bottom. Use the paddles then. The water flows from south to north, but at no great pace except where the Kilgair Spill enters over there," he pointed to the left, "and where the Kilgair Slug leaves, way up to the north."

"Slug?" Dek asked, interested.

"Yes, lad. But it's only a slug if you compare it to the Spill. In fact, you can coast all the way to the sea on the Slug, if you like, as long as you have a flat-bottomed boat like this, and you'd have trouble getting back because of the flow. We used to float the pandana out that way on bamboo rafts, all the way to Port Rattéspie."

Reckon you can manage this thing? Ruarth asked, from his perch on the prow. *It looks more like a punt than a boat.*

I nodded as I stowed the last of our things. "We'll manage."

"I can pole it," Dek said.

I was about to veto that, when I realized it wasn't just a boy's boasting; he had spent much of his life maneuvering a skiff around the shallows of the Kitamu Bays. I handed the pole to him. "Knew I brought you along for a reason," I said.

He grinned and, with the help of the pandana gatherers, pushed us away from the shore.

Flame and I helped keep the cumbersome craft straight with the paddles and we headed across a stretch of open water toward the pandana.

"Which way?" Dek asked. He had a point. At first glance, there seemed to be a solid wall of plant growth in front of us, a boatman's nightmare. They grew in clumps, each about the height of a man. We later found they could grow four times as high. Each clump had a barrel-like central core that sprouted stems on which long narrow leaves grew in spirals. Each yellow leaf was thick and solid, edged with a rim of green that sported nasty hooked spines, and each could be three or four paces in length. About three-quarters of the way up each leaf, the leaf-spike folded over and drooped downward as if it couldn't support its own considerable weight. "Creepy," Dek muttered. "They look like green and yellow spider legs."

Big spiders, Ruarth said, awed.

As our craft made ripples on the water, the clumps stirred. When I looked down into the blackness of the tannin-stained water, I could see their thick roots spreading out, tangling with one another, forming rafts, catching their own dead leaves to use as self-cannibalistic nourishment. Fortunately for us, not all the clumps joined. They were floating islands, rafts varying from three or four plants across, to sizable platforms that stretched for several hundred paces. You wouldn't have wanted to step on any of them, though: the leaves sprouted out in all directions, each one lethal with its arsenal of spines.

"That way," I said to Dek, and pointed to a narrow waterway between two islands. "Flame and I can use the paddles to push us off if we get too close. Ruarth can fly up every so often and check that we are heading generally north."

Once it is dark? Ruarth asked doubtfully.

"I suspect that we will see the red of dunmagic as a glow in the sky."

No one said anything to that.

Under different circumstances, I might have found the Floating Mere beautiful. In the occasional clearing in the pandana, the blackness of the open water reflected the plants and sky with mirror-like clarity. The plants floated with a deceptive serenity considering their weaponry, and the waterways twisted and slithered blackly between them, like forest paths heading into the depths of some primordial jungle. Sometimes the plants met overhead and the paths became tunnels that undulated gently as we passed through. It seemed as if it were all one living creature, observing us neutrally as we slipped by. Occasionally we had to turn back because we had entered a dead end, but we were able to avoid this happening too often thanks to Ruarth's exploratory flights ahead of the boat.

I wasn't sure that the place was entirely benign, though. Occasionally we heard strange sounds, eerie song notes that seemed to have no pattern or even discernible origin. They would whisper through the pandana and then die away as mysteriously as they had started. Perhaps unconnected, every now and then something would rise up through the water to break the surface, and I would have a momentary impression that I was being watched. When I turned my head, I'd have the briefest glimpse of something large and of an indeterminate color, before it slipped beneath the surface, gone in a swill of ripples. Dek swore he got a good look at one and that it was one of the merfolk.

I was uneasy. I hated things I couldn't explain, and I couldn't help feeling that we were being followed. Followed, or hunted? I tried to tell myself that anything that was so skittish was not going to be much of a threat to us, but still I didn't feel comfortable. I refrained from telling Dek that merfolk didn't exist. The lad obviously found the idea harmlessly exciting; perhaps it was better to have him believe in them than have his imagination run wild with the idea of monsters. In the meantime, wielding the pole with skill, he enjoyed proving that he was a useful member of the team.

Flame, on the other hand, seemed morose. She managed the paddle clumsily with only one arm, but she did her best. She spoke little, and barely uttered a sound when she was scratched on the neck by a low-hanging leaf. I thought back, trying to remember just how long it was since we had indulged in any lighthearted banter, and decided, in shock, that it had been while we were still in Amkabraig. The gall of worry lodged in my chest seemed to grow at the thought. I desperately wanted to talk to her about just how we were going to tackle Morthred and Domino when we found them, but every time I brought it up, every time I suggested that we plan, she turned her head away. Ruarth, of course, was more than ready to talk, and we prepared for a number of different scenarios. Unfortunately, most of them entailed having Flame use her sylvpower to blur our arrival, and illusions to confuse our entry into their enclave; now neither of us was sure how reliable she was going to be when the moment came.

When the last of the light had gone from the sky, we lit the lantern and hung it on a paddle that we wedged to project in front of the prow. If extra illumination was needed to pinpoint the best waterway to take, Flame obliged with a sylv ball. And above it all, we were guided, as I expected to be, by the foul red glow of dunmagic in the sky. We couldn't always see it from the boat, but when we needed to know where it was, Ruarth would fly up and take a look.

The large creatures under the water became bolder now, coming almost up to the boat, then sliding silently by into the darkness. I could never quite make out what they were, but was encouraged by the fact that Seeker didn't seem to be fazed by them. In fact, when we tied the boat up to one of the pandana plants so that we could rest and eat an evening meal, he chose to plunge into the lake.

"He dived," Dek said. "Did y'see that? He dived right down, like a porpoise!"

We stared into the blackness of the water but couldn't see him. After what seemed to be a long time, he popped up behind us, a fish in his mouth. I tried to take it from him, but he was having none of that, and we had to haul him back in the boat, fish and all. Of course, he then shook himself, before settling down to eat his catch—alive.

"Disgusting animal," Flame remarked, but she said it amiably enough. I acknowledged uneasily to myself how tense I was; every time she opened her mouth, I dreaded what she might say.

We poled on. When Dek was weary, I took over the job for a while. The strange song notes continued to resonate out of the blackness around us, sad and beautiful and spine-tingling.

About two and a half hours after we had set off from the village, Ruarth came flying back to the boat after a long time away. *Bad news,* he said. *They've warded every single passage of open water around the island. He's blocked every way in.*

"You flew all the way around the island?" I asked.

No. That would have taken too long. But I did go both right and left. I couldn't find an unblocked opening anywhere, and I think I would have if there'd been one. There's enough dunmagic out there to light up a whole town. Blaze, he's a lot stronger than we thought he'd be by now.

I considered. Dek and Ruarth and I weren't going to be affected by the wards. Flame could destroy wards, but only if they were made by a dunmagicker who had weaker powers than she did. If this ward was made by a dunmaster, backed by other dunmagickers—

I sighed. He'd been clever; he was using less power by also relying on the pandana to protect him, and concentrating only on the open water between.

"We can't go over the pandana islands. We'd be cut up like we was walking on barnacles with bare feet. Are we gunna have to give up?" Dek asked, his face a picture of disappointment.

"Whoever mentioned giving up?" I asked. "If Flame can't go through, then she's just going to have to go under. Better not to try to break the ward anyway; Morthred would know."

She looked at me, horrified. "*Under?* Under the water? Are you saltwater mad? Have you forgotten I can't swim?"

"I'm not asking you to swim," I pointed out. "In fact, I want you to sink. *Under* the ward."

She still looked utterly appalled, and muttered something about halfbreeds with half a brain missing. Even Dek looked dubious. We all remembered the shapes in the water.

"I'll go with you, Flame," I said, sounding a lot more cheerful than I felt. "And so will Seeker. Ruarth, show us the way to the ward."

He took us down a dark undulating tunnel, where the pandana wove itself into a low, curving roof overhead. Flame winced as the spines brushed along the sides of the boat. At the end of the tunnel, I could see the dun-red color of the ward. I stopped the boat just short of it.

"Are we there?" Flame asked.

I nodded. I could see it, even if she couldn't. "Dek, you take the boat through and wait for us on the other side."

He looked at the shimmering red curtain dubiously. "Will it hurt?" he asked.

"Not at all. To us Aware, it's no more than mist."

"What about those . . . those things in the water?" he asked.

We could have done without the reminder. I didn't reply, but heartlessly tossed Seeker overboard. I stripped off my boots and most of my clothes and followed him. I clung to the gunwale and tilted my head at Flame. "I'm going to take a look first. Can you send that sylv light into the water about two paces ahead of the boat? I want to see how deep down the ward goes."

She nodded, but her face looked strained.

The light slipped into the depths without the slightest flicker, and continued to burn brightly. I followed it as she dropped it deeper. The ward sparkled back at me all the way to the bottom. I popped back up to the surface. "Can you send the light under the pandana, a little to the left?"

Wordlessly she did as I asked. This time I dived down under the pandana, and Seeker followed me, his eyes wide open, his nostrils closed. It was as I thought it would be: there was no ward under the floating island. All we would have to do was dive deep enough to dodge the tangle of pandana roots.

I came back up. "It's easy," I said brightly, trying to exude a confidence I didn't feel. I couldn't forget those gray shapes. "Leave the light down there, Flame."

She grunted.

I grinned at her. "You can keep your eyes closed."

"You keep hold of me, or I'll put an illusion on you that will stick with you for the rest of your life!"

I didn't ask what sort of an illusion—with her sense of humor, it would probably have been a wart on the end of my nose, or something similar.

She entered the water reluctantly and I took hold of her before she went under. "I'll count," I said. "On three, you take a deep breath and then we go down."

She nodded miserably, and I started to count.

CHAPTER 17

NARRATOR : BLAZE

TWO PILLARS OF PULSATING LIGHT, LIKE gate posts to an unknown realm, held in place the filigree curtain that was the substance of the ward. The dun-red filigree stretched across the gap of water and extended upward into the blackness of the night sky before fading into nothing somewhere above. Dek, with Ruarth perched on his shoulder, took a deep breath and pushed the punt forward with his pole. He flinched as he moved through the barrier, but emerged on the other side none of the worse for his first experience with dunmagic warding.

Flame yanked a fistful of my hair and just about tore it off my scalp as I dived down toward the glow of the sylv light with her on my back. Then, just when we were at the deepest point of the dive, I saw several gray shapes in the water ahead of me. And that was when the sylv light went out. Flame, stricken at the thought of being underwater, had lost her hold on her magic. With her eyes closed, she had no idea she had plunged us into the red murk of a dun-lit netherworld.

I swore. I could no longer see the gray shapes in the gloom, and had no idea where they were. Peering upward, I could see, faintly, the light of the lamp on the boat. I had no choice. I aimed at the lamp and shot toward the surface, dragging Flame with me. Seeker followed in my wake, as at home in the water as he was on land. Something scraped along my arm, scratching me. Pandana? Something butted into us, pushing us both sideways. And then our heads were out of the water.

"Crabdamn it, Flame! Leave some hair on my head, will you?" I growled.

Dek grinned at me. "Wow," he said, "is that what dun-magic is? That was gawp-makin' goin' through that! But, lordy, it pongs like a rotten fish. Are you all right? You nearly came up into that bunch of pandana there."

"I noticed," I replied, with some asperity. "Someone let the damn light go out."

I felt as if I had lost a handful of hair, and my arm was bleeding and still stuck with broken off pandana spines. I scrambled over the stern and pulled Flame, then Seeker up after me. Seeker promptly shook himself, sending a shower of water over Dek.

Flame slowed her breathing and calmed. "Sorry about the hair. But it doesn't matter, surely; you have plenty more."

"I was unaware you coveted it *quite* so strongly," I said, rubbing my scalp. In truth, I was relieved that she could still try for humor, however weak.

"If you had let go of me, you'd have been bald in a second. Do you think the bastard has more wards on the island?"

"I doubt it. Too draining," I said. I looked anxiously over my shoulder, only to see a large shape skimming the under-side of the surface nearby. Even with the reflected red light from the ward, I still couldn't make out what it was, but it seemed to have the effortless streamlined movement of some-thing seal-like, rather than fish-shaped. It approached us and then veered off, only to halt, motionless, a few paces away. I could just make out a pair of eyes, glinting in the glow, watch-ing us. *Intelligent* eyes.

"Dek," I said softly, not taking my eyes of the shape, "get us out of here. And do it quietly and softly. We can't be far from the island now. Ruarth, can you take a look?"

Dek took up the pole and started easing us forward. The gray shape slipped astern and disappeared.

It was cold now that we were wet. Flame and I rummaged in our packs for some dry clothes and changed then and there. "Are you all right?" I asked as she pulled on a dry tunic. I pushed Seeker away as he came to curl up next to me, still damp.

"Bruised," she said. "Something banged into us, hard. What was it?" There was a new edge to her voice, an angry intensity that was uncharacteristic. Or had been so once.

"I don't know." And I didn't, but I couldn't help thinking that it had been alive and that its collision had been deliberate. I shuddered. Maybe it was the dun in the air. Maybe it was the way Flame looked at me just then, as though I were a stranger. I told myself not to be fanciful. "Could you make a sylv light here? I want to pick the thorns out of my arm."

She obliged, but with a lack of interest in my injuries that was chilling. *This wasn't the Flame I knew.*

Dek interrupted my train of thought. "Cor, this is where it gets excitin', right?" His eyes shone in the lamplight.

I sighed. I was saltwater mad. Why had I ever embarked on this adventure in the first place? Even Gilfeather had more brains than to get involved in dunmagic. Not only would I have to keep an eye on Flame, but I'd have to make sure that Dek didn't go plunging into trouble, thinking he was being a hero. I gave him a short lecture on obeying orders, and wished Tor was here. He was so much better at that sort of thing than I was.

Ruarth was gone about ten minutes. When he returned, he perched on the gunwale. *Dead ahead,* he said in his usual mix of movement and sound, *about two hundred paces or so. There are no buildings nearby. No lights, anyway. The worst of the dunmagic is a mile or two further on, on the lake edge to the right. I suspect that's where the village is.*

"We'll go straight in," I decided, "then sleep for a while. At first light, we'll take a look. Dek, extinguish the lantern, will you? We'll go the rest of the way on Flame's sylv light alone."

"They can't see that?" he asked.

I shook my head. "The only people who see a particular piece of magic are the Aware and the person who initiated the magic in the first place. Others can see the effects of magic without the magic itself. It's hard to miss a dun sore, for example. From now on, though, lad, I think we had better not talk, or at least not above a whisper. There may be guards around. Flame, send that sylv light a bit further ahead of the boat so that I can see better. Ruarth, guide us in to some safe spot."

The island was largely denuded of forest vegetation, as far as I could tell by Flame's sylv light. There was some sort of crop planted where we had landed, but I couldn't see any buildings. Dek and I pulled the boat up, and we made a makeshift camp in its lee.

"Fishguts 'n pox," Dek muttered. "This place *stinks*. Will we set up guards? I don't mind taking first watch."

I just stopped myself from laughing at his enthusiasm. "I don't think that will be necessary. We have Seeker, and Flame can erect a simple illusion and a ward that can be maintained even when she's asleep."

"If someone blunders into the ward, they'll make enough noise to wake us in plenty of time," Flame said in reassurance. She seemed to be back to her normal self. "It wouldn't bother Morthred, of course, but I would know if he broke it. I'll put it a couple of hundred paces away so we'll have sufficient warning. My illusion will make us almost impossible to see anyway. Don't worry, Dek, I'm a very good warder and my illusions are good enough to fool Morthred himself—I know that, because I've done it before."

"Oh." He seemed both disappointed and impressed. He watched as she walked away and erected the wards at a distance from us, simply by an act of pure, focused concentration. "Why are they that funny color?" he asked. "Sylv wards are s'posed to be silver-blue! That's what Flame told me back in Amkabraig."

I glanced over at them. The ward pillars were a kind of purple color and the filigree was a mix of silver and pink and mauve. "They are usually," I agreed uneasily. "Every damn thing on this island is tainted with dun, it seems."

Dek looked troubled. "What happens tomorrow? I got no sword," he added as he unrolled his bedding by the glow of the sylv light. "I only got my fish-guttin' knife."

"No one's going to ask you to fight anyone," I said. "Dek, there are only three of us, plus Ruarth; it would be an act of colossal stupidity to take on a whole enclave of dunmagickers. We have to find out what is going on first. Think of what we're going to do tomorrow as . . . as information gathering."

He brightened. "Spyin'?"

"If you like."

"And what if they nab us? At least you got a sword!"

"You have an even better weapon than a sword," I told him. "You have your Awareness. And we have something better than Awareness. We have Flame's sylvpower. Tomorrow morning, early, we will investigate the village while Flame blurs us with illusion. If we can, we will kill Morthred under the cover of that illusion. If the opportunity doesn't arise, then we will simply find out all we can and retreat to make plans."

He began to look excited again. "You've done this sorta thing before, haven't you? You and a sylv, snuck in and attacked, and then snuck out again . . ."

"Yes, I have." Arnado and I. Too many times. An Aware to identify the dun, a sylv to creat the illusion, two swords to kill. "One thing, Dek, if you are ever caught by a dunmagicker, the first thing he—or she—will do is lay a coercive spell on you. He will tell you that you are in his power, and you must do whatever he says. Being Aware, you, of course, wouldn't feel a thing. But you play along; pretend you have to do whatever he says. Then, as soon as you get the chance, you escape."

"You make it sound easy." He looked at me dubiously, excited, but wise enough to know that things were rarely so simple.

"Sometimes . . . sometimes the dunmagicker is clever enough to test you, to find out if you are Aware. And what they ask you to do to prove yourself may not be easy. Hurt someone else, for example."

He thought that over, then turned troubled eyes to meet mine. "What'll I do then?"

"Then you have to make a choice. It's a choice only you can make. You weigh all the advantages, decide, and move on. Whatever choice you make, you never look back." You never think about what you sometimes do to other people. What you sometimes have to do. To people like Niamor . . . Or you *try* not to think about it.

He considered that too, and looked even more disturbed.

Flame came back with Ruarth. "Don't forget the lakeside," I told her. "We don't want anyone to come at us from the water."

She nodded, and sat down at the water's edge to link up her wards in that direction.

"Dek," I said quietly as he lay down and rolled himself into his blanket, "if you are going to make a life for yourself fighting dunmagic, you have to know that it's not a heroic tale. It's real and dirty and sad. People die who shouldn't. They suffer. *You* will suffer. The best thing you can do is remember that you are not a hero when you are dead. You are just dead. You usually achieve much more by being a coward and staying alive, than by being a hero and dying in the process." He frowned at that, and I knew I hadn't convinced him. He still dreamed of banners and swords and noble fights between heroes and villains. In Dek's world, there were no dead innocents, and no dying heroes trying to stuff their guts back in their abdomens as the villain walked away unscathed.

I said, more sympathetically, "You can wait for us here, if you like. You are still young. You can decide these sorts of things when you are older, when you have more experience to make good judgments. You can always change your mind. Always."

He didn't need to think about that one at all. He shook his head. "No, I'm going with you. I just wish I had a sword, that's all."

"I'll get you one soon, I promise you. And I'll see you know how to use it."

He grinned, and I suppressed a sigh.

Flame came back to join us. She seemed somber, which didn't surprise me. Tomorrow, one way or another, she could well face the man who had raped and abused her. "Are you all right?" I asked her as Dek dropped off to sleep.

She nodded and took my hand. "You worry too much. I'm fine, really." She smiled at me, a loving smile just for me. There was no thought of betrayal there, I swear. She was just Flame, as she had always been: brave, determined, wry. "A little tense, but relieved too. Relieved it will all be over soon. He's here, Blaze, somewhere, I feel sure of it."

I agreed with her. There was something about the dunmagic that reeked of Morthred.

I squeezed her hand. "We *will* stop him," I said.

Oddly enough, I didn't have any trouble falling asleep, and I must have slept well, because I never heard a thing when Flame left the camp in the middle of the night. I didn't wake till an hour before dawn, when someone kicked me hard in the ribs.

CHAPTER 18

NARRATOR : KELWYN

TOR RYDER AND I DID NOT REALLY SPEAK
until the middle of the next day, when the raft stopped again.
That morning we had been roused early, and we didn't have
another private moment until we stopped for a midday meal:
eels baked in slow-burning moss. I ate some more cheese.

Ryder came and sat beside me, bringing his plate, away
from the other rafters and their crews. "You don't like the
food?" he asked.

"Sky Plains people dinna eat flesh that's slaughtered."

"Ah. That must be difficult."

"Not on the Sky Plains."

He smiled. "No, I guess not. Jakan tells me your name is
Kelwyn Gilfeather, and I know you must be from the Roof of
Mekaté. I want to know how you came to meet Blaze. Would
you mind telling me?" Outwardly he seemed calm and controlled; inscrutable even. But he couldn't hide what was inside
from me.

I shrugged. "Why not? I imagine that Blaze would want ye
to know that she is safe, if she could have guessed that our

paths would cross. She had nary an idea ye would come after her, y'know. I assume that is what ye are doing?"

He nodded. "Sort of." He said that in a way that made me suspect that he had a marked reluctance to lie.

"We, er, came across each other in Mekatéhaven. She and Flame arrived there after riding a sea-pony from Gorthan Spit to Cape Kan."

To my surprise, he paled. "They *what*? Why would they want to do something as dangerous and . . . and as *stupid* as that?" Even knowing that she must have survived the journey, he was still upset.

I backtracked a bit, and told him the story as far as I knew it: how she had rescued Flame from Duthrick, and how they had eventually ended up playing cards in an inn in Mekatéhaven. I then gave him the bare outline of the tale up until we had parted company in Amkabraig. I skimmed over my personal story, saying merely that I had been in Mekatéhaven on matters pertaining to the death of my wife. A euphemism, if ever there was one. I wondered if I'd ever be able to say calmly, "Oh, that was when I killed my wife. To save her from pain, you know."

"So," he asked, "how is it that you are now following them to the Floating Mere, if you were so adamant about not getting involved?"

I shrugged, trying to be offhand, and probably failing miserably. "I realized that dunmagic should be stopped. I saw its . . . evil . . . firsthand. In a girl raped by a dunmagicker, or dunmagickers, and subverted to dun."

His brow wrinkled. "And?"

"It was also pointed out to me that I have verra little left in this world except friends, and Blaze and Flame have become friends to me."

"It sounded more as if they did you a major disservice. You are exiled because of them."

"They need me," I said simply.

He looked politely disbelieving, obviously unable to conceive what I could do to help.

"Flame is . . . not well," I said. "I believe that her dun infection wasn't entirely cleaned from her system. It flares up from time to time. I'm a physician. I may be able to help."

"*If* dunmagic is an illness."

"As ye say."

"You know what that woman went through before?"

I nodded. "Blaze told me. So did Ruarth. And Flame too, in part. No one should have to suffer that way."

We looked at each other and I think we both felt obscurely ashamed, as though it was our fault. "I should never have left them," he said.

"Nor should I," I acceded. "Why *did* ye leave anyway?"

"I thought I had a duty to attend to Alain Jentel's affairs in the Spatts. He was a priest killed by the Keeper's cannonguns in Creed. In the end, through, I didn't go to the Spatts at all. I changed my mind and went straight to the High Patriarch on Tenkor Island, because I realized there were things that he should know urgently about the guns, about Morthred and the subversion of sylvs, about Castlemaid Lyssal. I intended to go to the Spatts afterward."

"But he sent ye here instead."

"Yes. To find Flame and Morthred."

"Ye're an agent of the Menod?"

"Yes. In the same way that Duthrick is an agent of the Keeper Council, I have been working for the Patriarch Council." He laid his plate aside with much of the food still uneaten. "And now I'm actually the newest *member* of the Council." He gave a wry smile. "Not something I ever wanted to be, because the duties include attending a great many boring meetings concerning things like whether we have enough believers in Upper Scuttlebutt to warrant funding a new house of worship, or pedantic discussions on the nature of sin. Fortunately, the first thing they sent me to do this time was find Flame, protect her if necessary, and to help Blaze get rid of Morthred and his ilk."

"How did ye know where to look?"

"I didn't. I followed Morthred's trail, not Flame's. Followed him the same way that Blaze would have, by asking around. Although I didn't think to go to the ghemphs. I went to the Menod. Gilfeather, I have heard that Plainsmen physicians are truly skilled. Will you be able to help Flame?"

"I don't know."

He said, almost to himself, "When things like this happen,

my faith wavers most. Sometimes . . . sometimes it is hard to believe in a *just* God."

I didn't know what to say to that, so I changed the subject. "And will your Council return her to her father? And an unwanted marriage?"

He blinked, surprised. "You know who she is? There's not much you *don't* know, is there?"

"Very little. Blaze told me the whole story: why she went to Gorthan Spit, and what happened there. And aye, I know Flame is the Castlemaid."

He stared at me, then said with a shake of his head, "Blaze must think a great deal of you."

"Blaze owes me a great deal."

He nodded, digesting that, and then returned to my original question. "No, of course we won't send Flame back to Cirkase and that marriage. It was a nasty bargain, concocted between the Breth Bastionlord and the Keepers. The Bastionlord wanted the Keepers to officially sanction his inter-island marriage to Flame, in return for something they wanted."

"The ingredient in the black power the Keepers use in their cannon-guns."

"Yes. A mineral, mined on Breth. Something called saltpeter, which I gather is found in the caves of the Two Paps. I wouldn't have known that much, except that I had a piece of luck. On my way back from the Spit, on board ship, I met a Breth Islander who trades in the stuff. He told me that for some time the Keepers have been buying saltpeter in small quantities, but word now has it that they want large amounts, and the Bastionlord is digging his heels in. He doesn't need money, but he hankers after an heir, and apparently the Castlemaid is the only woman he fancies. His taste more normally runs to boys not even old enough to wear trousers."

"Blaze said that this black power is more powerful than any dunmagic. It could level whole towns in minutes. Whoever controls it, will control the whole of the Isles of Glory."

"I'm afraid she's right. As if the Keeper Isles doesn't have enough power already! I saw things on the Spit that were . . . unpleasant to say the least. And one of the worst was seeing sylvs using their healing powers as bargaining stakes. Even before that, what they have been doing in the name of their

Liberty, Equality and Right motto has been despicable. As they become more greedy, they are raping nations of their wealth with their trading tricks and money-lending skills. They grasp power by any means possible and they cover their sordid trails with illusion. As their power grows, so their justification for it becomes more obfuscatory, until they no longer recognize the darkness of their own souls. I don't know which is worse: a dunmaster who knows he is evil and delights in it, or a sylv who does evil and doesn't even recognize it as such." The look in his eyes was more distressed than hard, but he *was* angry.

"Are the Keepers still going after Flame?"

"Oh, I would think so. Flame is one of the few people who can make a difference to the future of the Isles of Glory, because she is the Castleheir of Cirkase. For a start, there are other ingredients needed in their damn black powder, besides saltpeter. Ransom—did she tell you about Ransom? He's the Bethany Holdheir. Silly young fellow who fell in love with Flame. Anyway, he was on board the *Keeper Fair* and he mentioned the smell of sulfur to me. I do know that the Keepers have also been buying unusual amounts of sulfur from Cirkase. I wouldn't have been suspicious, except that they have been trying to keep the sales quiet. There have been whispers about that for some time; silly stuff—people saying they use it in their magic. If Flame is kept safe until she becomes the Castlelord, as is her eventual right, she can stand between the Keepers and the sulfur they need. On the other hand, if she ends up under the thumb of the Breth Bastionlord, then not only do the Keepers get their sulfur, but they can buy their saltpeter from Breth."

"So the Menod sent ye to keep her safe?"

"Yes. And to offer her sanctuary on Tenkor, for as long as she needs it."

"In my opinion, it is almost impossible to get birds back into the cage once ye've opened the door. And I'm not talking about Flame. Ryder, the weapons are a fact. Blaze told me of that attack on Creed, in graphic detail. D'ye think the Keepers will calmly give them up simply because they can't find Flame?"

"Well, we *can* make it difficult for them to get the ingredients. Unfortunately, what will probably happen in the end is that every other islandom will be scrambling to get cannon-guns for themselves. Maybe that might even be better than only one islandom having them. Although, God knows, the idea that everyone would have filthy weapons like that at their disposal is horrific."

I hadn't thought of that, but I knew in my heart he was right. Other Islandlords would be hearing about cannon-guns after what happened on the Spit, and either their fear or their greed for power would have them hunting for the secret.

Just then Mackie came up to tell us it was time to get back on the water for the final stage of our journey, so we didn't pursue the conversation any further. As I sat on the raft that afternoon, I wondered why Ryder had told me so much, and decided that it was because he had faith in Blaze's judgment. If someone as wordly-wise as Blaze wanted me along, then I had to be a man who could be trusted. There was something, though, that told me it wasn't the whole story. My sense of smell indicated that the patriarch was a man in turmoil, for all that calm exterior and his careful thought. At the time, I could not explain it.

I did not know, for example, that the old High Patriarch, a pragmatic and far-sighted man, was grooming Ryder to take over his position of titular and spiritual head of the Menod, and Tor Ryder was astute enough to know that he had come to a crossroads in his life. He had to make a choice. If he accepted a life in the lesser post he now occupied, he would never make a difference, not really. If he accepted power, and used it wisely, he might have a chance to change things for the better. The catch was, it would not be the kind of life he personally wanted to lead.

It was not an easy decision. He was not an ambitious man; by nature he was, in fact, a man of action, rather than negotiation and compromise. He enjoyed his work as a Patriarch Council agent. He disliked meetings, doctrinaire discussions and dealing with the politics of the Patriarchy. One part of him wanted to walk away from what was being thrust at him. The problem, however, was that, above all else, he also wanted to rid the Isles of magic and Keeper tyranny.

Simply put, Tor Ryder wanted to change the world.

* * *

WE ARRIVED AT THE VILLAGE OF KAL-
garry, at the mouth of the Kilgair Spill, in the late afternoon. I
asked where the road around the Kilgair Massif ran and was
told that it came down into another village, Gillsie, some
miles away to the east—too far for me to identify by smell if
Blaze and Flame were there. No one in Kalgarry could tell us
if Blaze and Flame had arrived at the Floating Mere, let alone
where they were, but Gillsie was the place to ask. Ryder inquired about the island the Mekaté ghemphs had mentioned,
and was rewarded with an avalanche of stories about Keepers,
abductions, magical barriers and vengeful lake spirits.

No one wanted to take us to the island; no one would rent
us a boat. The best Ryder could do, even using his considerable charm, was to buy Jakan and Mackie's raft. Apparently,
before walking back up the road to Amkabraig, the brothers
and other rafters usually sold their craft to the pandana cut-
ters, who then used them to drift their harvest down to the
coast along the Kilgair Slug. Now, however, no one was cutting the pandana, because they were too frightened to venture
onto the lake, so no one wanted to deal with the brothers.

Ryder bargained with a skill I couldn't help but admire and
we split the cost of the raft. We never actually discussed joining forces; somewhere along the line it was just assumed by
both of us that whatever we were going to do, we were doing
it together. I can't say I trusted him entirely. On the surface he
continued to be that calm, thoughtful man, given to introspec-
tion, but my nose was beginning to tell me a different story.
He was a man of strong passions, with an anger bordering on
violence that was a constant element lying just beneath that
unruffled surface. "Have you any idea," he asked me once,
much later, "how hard I have to struggle sometimes to contain
a desire to send certain members of the human race to perdi-
tion?" I wasn't sure whether I should admire him for his rigid
control over his baser emotions, or be afraid of him because
those same emotions could break through and make him an
aggressive man. It certainly made me regard him with caution. A few weeks earlier I would not have understood him at
all. I had lived my whole life up to then without ever feeling

the kind of rage he carried with him. But since then I had faced Exemplar Dih Pellidree across his desk at the Fellih Bureau of Religious and Legal Affairs. Since then I'd held in my hand the stone that had taken Jastriá's life. Since then, I'd come to know Flame, and I'd found out about dunmagickers. I knew now what I was capable of, given the right circumstances. And if I could perform an act of violence, then so certainly could Ryder.

To add to my wariness, before we arrived in the village he extracted a huge sword from his belongings. He now wore it in a back harness, just as Blaze did. When he handled it later that night to oil it, he did so with the same easy familiarity and elegance as Blaze handled hers, and I turned away, disturbed. And then I thought of his compassion for the child with the skin complaint, of his love for Blaze that caused him so much hurt, and wondered if he was really so dangerous. Having the ability to scent human emotions so well was not always an advantage; it could just add to one's confusion.

We never did seriously discuss leaving Kalgarry that night. By the time we had haggled over the raft, bought an extra store of food, and questioned the villagers as much as seemed wise, it was already long after dark and it seemed foolish to risk a journey through the lake to a place we did not know. I think if I had explained to Tor the true extent of my olfactory abilities, he would have insisted that we leave there and then, but I didn't tell him. My mistake, but I had no way of knowing that we were so close behind Blaze and Flame, that they'd left Gillsie for the island that very afternoon. Perhaps, too, I lacked experience with dunmagickers, and that made me less driven than Ryder, less aware that every moment could make the difference between life and death, between sanity and madness.

CHAPTER 19

NARRATOR : KELWYN

RYDER WOKE ME LONG BEFORE DAWN THE next morning. Light was only just fingering the sky, but he made no apology for the early start.

We had slept on the raft and we left silently after a hurried breakfast of bread. It was the work of moments to push the raft into the water and start across the lake, apparently the only living things yet awake. Ryder poled, with a graceful efficiency that left me wondering grumpily if there was anything at all that the man *didn't* do well. I had charge of the paddle and was supposed to help keep us away from the pandana plants and their array of spines. I knew before long that I did a poor job. We didn't have any rivers on the Roof of Mekaté that were large enough for even a coracle, let alone a craft like this. I felt clumsy and graceless. Ryder, of course, was far too polite to comment.

We had decided to visit Gillsie first, where the road ended. We wanted to know if Blaze and the others had arrived; it seemed a logical beginning. As we were approaching the place, I found myself with an immediate problem: whether to tell Ryder about my nasal skills. It was a difficult thing to say, just as it had been difficult to tell Blaze and Flame. We Sky Plainsfolk have so few weapons and generations of our people had decreed that to give away information on the one that we did have would be folly. It did not sit well with me to speak of it, and yet here I was contemplating telling yet another person.

I said, "There's something I need to tell ye, although I'd appreciate it if ye kept it to yourself."

He tilted his head at me, questioning. "I'm a priest, Gilfeather. We are used to keeping secrets."

"I, er, I smell with unusual intensity."

He was perplexed. One of his eyebrows quirked. "You do? I hadn't noticed."

I flushed. Bright red, as usual, from the tips of my ears, across my face and round to the back of my neck. I took a deep breath. "I mean that I can smell aromas—people, anything—with unusual, er, acuity. I can tell that Blaze and the others were in the village last night, but they left before nightfall, heading out into the Mere."

He didn't say a word, but the look he gave me was peculiar. And he continued to guide the craft into the village, which spoke volumes. The sun had not yet risen, but the village was already stirring; I could see chimney smoke.

I said defensively, "It can be a verra useful ability to have."

"I'm sure," he agreed. He was picking up my mild antipathy to him, I could tell, and it puzzled him. Come to that, it puzzled me too. He had done nothing to earn my suspicion or dislike.

Later, as he punted away from Gillsie after having spoken to the villagers, he was silent for a while. Then he asked, "How did you know all that—about the time they left?"

"From the strength of the traces they left behind. I guess ye could say I have the experience to judge. The strongest aroma was down at the water's edge, so I guessed they'd taken a boat of some kind."

"Can you, er, smell them now?"

"Sufficiently well to know that they were here. But the trail is not clear enough to follow precisely." We were heading north merely because that was the direction the villagers had mentioned. "Water doesna hold smell the same way the earth does. It moves, and the smell goes with it. And this lake has a strong aroma of its own."

We were facing a wall of pandana islands with a number of small waterways separating them. I pointed. "That way." He obeyed, but his expression questioned, so I said, "I can smell the open water on the other side of that tunnel for a start; and that's the direction of the island. I can smell the dun stink from here."

He was startled, but said nothing. I guessed that the smell was not yet obvious to him. I had one more piece of news he wasn't going to like either. "Flame is going to betray Blaze and Dek," I said quietly.

"How can you possibly know that?" he asked.

"I can smell her intention."

He had trouble accepting the truth of that.

"Betrayal of your closest friend is a very base action," I explained. "It leaves a stink."

"You think she's already subverted? Again?"

"Not again. I think this is the same subversion, it just wasna wholly cured last time," I reminded him.

"Impossible," he said flatly. "Duthrick and the sylvs would have known. Besides, I was there, remember? So was Blaze. And Ruarth. Three of the Awarefolk. We would have *seen* any traces left behind after the sylvs cured her. There was nothing, I swear it."

"I think my nose is more . . . sensitive than normal Awareness. I could smell Flame's latest problem before Blaze could. And Blaze didn't mention seeing any dun color. Whatever it is, it's getting worse."

He wasn't convinced, but he didn't contradict me any further. We chatted in a desultory fashion as he poled on. I told him all I had learned about magic from Garrowyn's papers in Amkabraig, and he told me all he knew about dunmagic, but none of that really explained what was happening to Flame, so we let the subject drop, and spoke instead of other things.

He wanted to know about the Roof of Mekaté. Although he had never been there, I found he already knew more than any other downscarper I'd ever met. In fact, he seemed an extraordinarily well-informed man. When I asked why that was, he said, "Well, I started off as a scribe, you know. I traveled a lot, and read whatever I could. It was my love of learning that made me interested in the Menod in the first place. Only the Menod have public libraries and scholar-teachers. Only the Menod, outside of ruling Keepers, had the kind of information that gave me answers to all my questions. In my experience, Keepers withhold their knowledge, not disseminate it, whereas the Menod try to educate. Now I see that I shall have to visit the Roof of Mekaté too, if, as you say, every family has documents and texts about their professions. That must be such a wealth of knowledge. Do you think that it would be possible for Menod scribes to visit the tharns of the Plainsfolk and take copies of such texts?"

I thought about that. "I dinna think my people would fret over it. The one thing that we need to keep to ourselves is our selvers, because wool is the only commodity we have to exchange for things we need from the outside world. But our knowledge? I dinna think ye can put a price on things like that. It should be freely available. Ask my Uncle Garrowyn. I'm sure he'd help."

"Garrowyn Gilfeather is your uncle?"

I nodded.

"An interesting man. He saved Flame's life, in all probability, with his herbs and medicines. The only 'chirurgeon' we had to amputate her arm was a butcher who had murdered his wife."

"He's very knowledgeable. The sight of fresh blood makes him sick, though, so ye were lucky he helped out. He has a lot of medical books from his travels, y'know. I think ours are better, though. We Plainsfolk have a long history of the study of disease and its causation, treatment and such like. On the Roof of Mekaté, the deceased are always dissected before burial, and all treatments and deaths are recorded in detail. We have records going back a thousand years."

He seemed thoughtful, and asked a great many more questions about our medicines and surgeries. Like Blaze, he explained his interest by reminding me that he was Aware and impervious to sylv healing. "So are many of my fellow patriarchs," he added. "Anything that offers cures, or remedies that work, is of interest to us."

His explanation made perfect sense. If I had not had my sense of smell, I would have accepted it as the truth, and thought it logical. Instead, I knew he was lying or, at the very best, not telling me the whole truth. What I couldn't work out was *why*. Tor Ryder had his own motives, his own plans, and I would do well to remember that.

As we pushed on through the pandana, I was several times aware that there was something following us through the water. When I looked behind, there would be a swirl and a glimpse of a gray body. Whatever it was, it never stayed long enough for me to see it properly. I couldn't even be sure if there were a number of the creatures, or just the same one deliberately following us. I might have decided it was the place that was making me fanciful, except for one thing: *I couldn't smell the creature.* Water may sweep smells away with its movements, but it couldn't hide something that was right under my nose. And this . . . these . . . things were sliding under the raft. A lack of aroma was worse than too much. I felt as if I was blind and I didn't like it one little bit.

There was more that was eerie about this floating world: sometimes we poled through tunnels for half an hour or more, twisting pathways of black water lit only by sunlight shattered to splinters by the thick network of barbed leaves. Sometimes the tunnels split into branches, then rejoined, rather like a network of arteries and veins and capillaries. Even more disconcerting, sometimes a tunnel would close up behind us, as if the floating plants were trying to block our retreat. A silly notion, I know; the islands moved only because we stirred the stillness of the water with our passing. Probably the feeling was aggravated by the strange noises of the place: dissonant whistles that seemed to seep out of the water on every side at odd intervals, akin to the music a wind may make playing around the corners of a building. I might have dismissed it as nothing, except that there was no wind, and occasionally the notes seemed more . . . deliberate. Like language. Only who—or what—was speaking? And to whom? I shivered.

It took us about two hours to reach the island and we arrived about an hour after dawn. Just before we did, we came to an area where the stink of dun was as thick as spring honey, and a great deal less sweet. Nauseating, in fact. Ryder said it was a dun ward, but I couldn't see it and we passed through it without problem, unless you count me throwing up over the side.

"We're close," I whispered when we poled on another few hundred paces. I pointed. "There's someone close by. Two people in a boat. And another two further away in that direction. Strong stench of dun."

"Guards maybe," he whispered back. "Can you get us to the island without them seeing?"

I nodded. Using my sense of smell I found it easy enough to decide which channels to avoid.

I paddled on and shortly afterward the raft emerged from the archway of pandana into light. There were several more pandana islands floating serenely in front of us, and beyond that a settlement. Ryder stopped the forward movement of the raft with a deft prod of the pole. Fortunately our arrival was blocked from the view of the people in the village by the screen of the floating islands.

"Well," he said softly, "I owe you an apology, Gilfeather. I thought you were exaggerating your olfactory skills." He looked around, assessing. "I think we will watch for a while, unseen, from over there." He indicated a place on the edge of the water where a low line of pandana, less than waist height, grew up to the shoreline. It was thick enough to screen us, yet sparse enough for us to be able to watch the houses. Once there, the raft grounded in the shallows and we knelt and watched the village through the leaves.

The closest of the houses was twenty paces away. The largest building was a shed of some kind with a pair of tall doors. They were closed and there was no way we could see what was inside. Something must have been going on in there, because there were several armed people outside apparently on guard. There were other people as well, but they seemed to be going about their normal chores. A flock of waders poked along the shoreline in front of the shed, and there were several boats pulled up. The stink was appalling.

"Do you have a weapon on you?" Ryder asked, surveying me critically, as if he wanted to assess how much use I was going to be to him when he hit trouble.

I flushed. Again. "Only a dirk. And a chirurgeon's knife in my bag."

"Would you use your dirk?"

"Ye mean use it to—? I don't know," I said frankly.

He nodded, accepting the information. I untied the bag and extracted the dagger. It was sharp enough to cut a selver whisker endways. He rummaged in his pack at the same time, to pull out his bow string. As he strung this bow, bending it with deceptive ease, he asked, "What can you smell?"

He was still skeptical, so there was a good slice of "I'll show him" in what I said next. "Mostly dunmagic. It masks just about everything. But I'd say there are, er"—I paused to count— "forty-five or forty-six people around here. That's not counting the four out on the lake." I kept my voice to a whisper. "They're scattered in the buildings. Twenty or so are ordinary folk. Of the remaining, there's Blaze and Flame and Dek, another who must be your dunmaster—"

"Are you sure? How can you be sure it's him?"

"Well, put it this way, there's one man who stinks worse than the others. A lot worse. And there are two others who must also be dunmagickers. The rest are—" I hesitated. "I think they must be what ye call subverted sylvs. They have a trace of the same aroma that Flame has, but it's only a trace. The rest is . . . putrid." And that didn't even *begin* to describe the foulness. "Nineteen of them. Those three outside that first building there, the shed, for a start. There are five of them outside the village too, scattered all around. Quite a ways back. On guard duty, at a guess, like the ones on the lake. Blaze and Flame and Dek are all close by. In the shed, I think, but it's hard to say positively. The dun smell is so—so *obliterating*."

"Can you tell if they are alone?"

"They are together with the dunmaster and one ordinary man and about twelve of the ex-sylvs. And the dunmagickers. I canna smell Ruarth at all, but that might be because he's verra small and there's just too much of the dun stench."

The wrinkles at the corners of his eyes tightened, but that was the only external evidence of the pain he felt right then. "How in God's name," he said softly, more to himself than to me, "did that idiot woman manage to get herself in another pickle barrel of dunmagic so soon? Has she *no* sense?" He could have been talking about either of them, but I knew he referred to Blaze. "I had not expected so many subverted sylvs," he continued evenly, this time for me. "I thought this would be just a small group, but he has obviously had this place prepared as a second hideaway for some time. The dunmagickers, I might be able to deal with; too used to using their magic to survive, they might not have any skill with the sword. But ex-sylvs? Many of them will be Keeper trained. Swordsmen and women."

I nodded unhappily. "There were eight Keeper sylvs on the *Keeper Liberty,* or so Blaze told me. They could all be here."

"And Morthred's been subverting Keepers for some time. He'd want the best. So, tell me, Plainsman, how do we—with one sword between us and no magic—get these two reckless females and the boy out of this fix?"

I had no idea.

CHAPTER 20

A KICK IN THE RIBS IS NOT A GOOD WAY to wake up. You know the moment the boot connects that you are in the worst kind of trouble. I was groping for my sword even as I opened my eyes; it was not where it should have been, at my side.

The sky was lit with a predawn glow, and a number of sylv lights hung suspended around our campsite. Sylv lights . . . but they all gave an unhealthy reddish glow. The first person I saw was Morthred.

After the kick, he'd stepped away and was now looking down on me from a cautious pace or two away, a lantern raised in his hand. "Hello, Blaze," he purred. "We meet again." He was backed by a phalanx of subverted sylvs, every single one of them a Keeper, each carrying a drawn sword except for one who had a quarrel cranked up on a crossbow. Behind the sylvs were two dunmagickers.

One wrong move, and I was dead. Of course, no move and I was dead as well, probably a lot more painfully. Dek stirred in the blankets next to me and poked his head out. Then he gurgled in surprise, like a sea-cucumber squashed underfoot. "Keep still, lad," I warned.

Morthred nodded. "Good advice."

I stared, but I scarcely knew him. There was nothing of the twisted man he had been as Janko, the waiter from The Drunken Plaice in Gorthan Docks, nothing of the deformed man he had been when he had lost the battle of Creed. He was beautiful. A blue-eyed Southerman, tall, straight, with a charming smile that did not touch the cruelty of his eyes, or the pleasure in his tone. As he saw my shock, he added, "I do so like surprises, don't you?"

All I could think of was, how had *Janko* come to *this*?

"Mind if I stand up?" I asked politely. "I feel at a distinct disadvantage lying down like this."

For a split second he just stared; then he laughed. "Always the smart comment, eh, Blaze? One of these days—quite soon—I will stop that mouth of yours."

He took another step back and indicated that I could get up. I did so, with exaggerated care, my hands held where they could all see them. Dek followed my lead. I used the time to take a quick look around. To assess just how bad the situation was.

Flame's wards were gone, of course. She knelt at the back of the group, her arm around Seeker with her hand clamped around his snout. He was whining, worried, but not frantic. Flame, after all, was supposed to be a friend. She looked at me blankly. There was no trace of sylv around her; nor was there animation.

Ruarth was over in some tall grass nearby, perched on top of a stalk. He was calling out nonstop, mostly, as far as I could tell, to Flame. He was trying to get her to look at him so that she could understand him properly, but she didn't seem to be listening. No one else seemed to take any notice either, which was good—it meant that they didn't know about him.

My mind was racing like a minnow fleeing a wrasse; I had to work out what had happened, and fast. The wards had come down, and Seeker had been neutralized, and there was only one way that both those things could have happened: Flame had betrayed us. She'd risen in the middle of the night and gone to alert Morthred in the village. Deliberately thrown Dek and me to the dunmaster. *But not Ruarth.*

Morthred signaled to one of the sylvs to search us both, which he did although he seemed wary. Perhaps my reputation had preceded me. I gave him a toothy grin; I'm a great believer in persuading others that one's reputation is warranted, even if it's not. There was nothing to find; they had already removed my sword, and the rest of my weaponry was out of reach. Seeker growled sharply, teeth bared, hackles rising. He wasn't happy, and he had long since been uneasy with Flame anyway. I should have listened to him.

Well, I *had* listened to him, in a way. Just as I had listened to Gilfeather. Just as I had listened to my own misgivings. But nothing, and no one, had told me that she was on the verge of betraying us. That she would indeed do so at the first opportunity. Even so, I had kept a watch on her and compared what I sensed to what she had been like when she was infected with dun on Gorthan Spit, and there was no similarity. This time the whiff of dun contamination had been mild and occasional. Her temper had been worse, it was true; worse, and nastier. It was still hard for me to believe that what had happened to her was just the return of the contamination she had been infected with back on the Spit. Subverted sylvs didn't look like Flame did now. They had that trapped look in their eyes. They had the haunted expression of a decent person struggling, in vain, to escape what he or she had become. They were healthy, strong people *driven* to do what they didn't want to do, helpless in the face of a greater magic.

Flame had just looked ill. Listless. And, occasionally, enraged.

I was missing something. We all were. Something important.

"You've changed," I told Morthred. My mind was still racing, assessing, absorbing every detail, no matter how insignificant. You never knew what might be valuable later. If there was a later. Flame released Seeker and stood behind the sylvs, staring dull-eyed at nothing.

Morthred was glowing, not with crimson, but with a sort of purple color. He was taller than I remembered; I supposed because he was now able to stand straight. His eyes seemed clearer, less . . . what? Angry? No, that wasn't it. And the madness was still there too, not so much subdued, as under strong control. Control, that was it. He was in control in a way that he had not been before. My heart sank. There was no way that this man would fall for the same sort of ploy I had used to trick him on Creed.

"You look well," I said calmly. "And very . . ." I looked him up and down appreciatively, "handsome. What have you done to yourself?" I took special care to make sure there wasn't a trace of mockery in my tone.

Dek, as wide-eyed as an octopus, stared at me as if he couldn't believe his ears. Morthred smiled, still charming. "It took me almost a hundred years, but I finally discovered the cure to my little, er, problem." He waved a hand, indicating that I was to walk next to him, away from our camp.

"Do you mind if I put on my boots first?" I asked, as if that were a perfectly reasonable request to which he would, of course, accede.

With a gesture that was supposed to indicate his magnanimity, he waved a hand at my footwear. I sat down and pulled them on without emptying them out first, not always a good idea when camping in the open. This time there didn't seem to be anything lurking inside. I stood up again. Dek jammed his feet into his own shoes without waiting for permission.

We left our packs and everything in them behind on the ground. I noted, however, that the sylv who had my sword kept hold of it. One of these days, I thought sourly, I am going to lose that damn Calment steel for good. A loss that would be quite deserved too, at the rate I was going.

As we walked in the direction of the village, Morthred kept well off to my left, and his underlings ranged themselves around me. I was horribly aware that a fidgeting, nervous ex-sylv kept the crossbow pointed at my back. The sylv lights bobbed along with us at shoulder height, a sickly red remnant of once pure sylvtalents.

"Sylv healing," Morthred said.

"Pardon?" I asked politely.

"The cure to my problem."

"*Sylvs* healed you?" I was incredulous.

"*My* sylvs," he amended, indicating the people around him.

"Subverted sylvs? You can't expect me to believe that.

They lose their sylvtalent once they are subverted, surely,
even if they could be, er . . . persuaded." But the sylv lights
told me I was wrong, at least partially, even as I spoke.

His smile was smug. Everything about him spoke of a man
who felt himself to be both triumphant and invincible.

When it was clear that he wasn't going to reply, I said,
"Those reinforcements that came to join Duthrick in Gorthan
Spit came in handy, I take it."

"Indeed." The smile stayed. I heard Dek draw in a sharp
breath, and I knew why. There was savagery in the glitter of
Morthred's eyes as he relived a memory.

I clapped my hands together, twice. "My congratulations.
Your looks now are a great improvement on those of Janko the
waiter." Seeker slunk obediently away, with one hurt look
over his shoulder.

My mind continued to race, trying to find a way out of this.
Morthred hadn't killed me already; that was his first mistake.
But the only real hope I could see was that Flame had not told
him about Ruarth, and perhaps had not told him that Dek was
Aware. I glanced at her. She was walking off to one side and
she looked broken to the point of indifference. My heart
lurched sickeningly, and whatever anger I'd felt toward her
dissipated. Who was I to even *begin* to judge what she had
been going through?

Half an hour later we topped a bit of a rise, and were looking
down on a few houses surrounded by some kitchen gardens.
There was one building that was larger than all the others. It
didn't seem to have any windows, but it had large double doors
facing the water and latticework at the top of the walls. Some
sort of warehouse, I guessed. Maybe that was where the villagers stored the pandana they collected. A number of punts
similar to the one we had used were pulled up on a beach
nearby; a few fishing nets were hanging out to dry on a bamboo
rack. The whole place flickered with crimson; there were flames
of it skittering across the ground, licking at all the buildings.

It was still early; the sun had not yet risen although the sky
was lightening. Smoke oozed out of the chimneys of several
houses into the cool, damp air. As we walked on down, the sun
came up, and the village seemed to shake itself awake all at
once. People emerged: some to fetch water, some to wash

clothes at the water's edge; a lad to feed the flock of domesticated waders, another to pluck some bananas. It could have been an ordinary waterside village just about anywhere in the Mekaté Isles, except that there was a play of red over everything and everybody. Someone had worked magic here on a scale that spoke to me of a dunmagickers' enclave. Another Creed.

These people did not seem to have been enslaved for as long as the people of Creed had been; they weren't as thin. Yet. There were other signs of enslavement, though: no one spoke; there were no cheery greetings, no gossip as the women washed the clothes, no laughter from anyone. And there were no young children to be seen; they would have been the first to die when the dunmagickers moved in. Children were a nuisance to be disposed of immediately.

The first person to greet us when we walked into the village was Domino. He hadn't changed, not an iota. The look he gave me was a mix of vitriolic hatred and intense, focused pleasure. I found I loathed him just as much now as I had back on Gorthan Spit, when he'd tortured me and delighted in it.

"Hello, Halfbreed," he said, and smiled.

"Hello, Domino. Still as short as ever, I see."

He hissed his rage and came close to punching me, but a frown from Morthred was all it took to stop him. I sighed inwardly. When would I learn to keep my mouth shut? Domino was going to make me regret that remark.

They took us straight to the large building. It proved to be some kind of drying shed for the pandana leaves. It was empty now, except for the drying racks and the raked-out hearth in the center of the floor, for the fire.

Morthred turned to his sylvs. "Guard them. If the woman says one word or makes one move, kill the boy. Domino, Lyssal, you two come with me."

Dek went pale and shot me a terrified look as the dunmaster left. I made the Dustel gestures for "stay still" and "keep quiet," hoping he would recognize them—but even that minimal movement made one of the men raise his crossbow threateningly. I decided I wouldn't try that again.

Time passed slowly. No one spoke. I remained alert, but so did our captors, and there were ten of them. They stood in a circle around us, far enough away to ensure that any lunge of mine would be futile. Every time I so much as shifted weight, fingers tightened on crossbow triggers or sword hilts and all eyes went to Dek. Poor Dek, he was fast discovering what it was really like to be a hero.

After half an hour or so, Ruarth entered through the latticework at the top of the wall. He came and sat on a cross beam where I could see him.

Flame, he said, *is all right. Morthred told her he is taking her back to his ship. He's leaving soon. He keeps telling her that he is not going to harm you.*

I gave the faintest of nods, but didn't risk answering him further, so after a while he flew out again.

I almost felt relieved when Morthred finally returned with Flame and Domino, two dunmagickers and several more subverted sylvs.

They had evidently already decided what they were going to do with me, because what happened next occurred without any extraneous conversation. One of the sylvs tossed a rope over the cross beam above our heads. Another two grabbed me by the arms. One end of the rope was looped with a slip knot and the man who held it approached me.

They were going to hang me.

I started to struggle then, frantically. Out of the corner of my eye, I saw Dek take advantage of the diversion to make a dash for the door.

I banged my heel behind the knee of one of the men who held me, then trod on his stomach when he collapsed. I went down on one knee, dragging the second man with me. As he staggered off balance, I punched him in the nose with my free hand, as hard as I could, and heard the satisfying crunch of bone. I grabbed the first man's sword and brought it around in a wide two-handed sweep. More by luck than anything, I slit open the arm of a Keeper sylv, and then plunged the tip deep into the side of a dunmagicker. A sliver of a second later I was hit in the back by what felt like an enraged walrus. I went down flat, six or seven people scrabbled to hold me there, and the noose was slipped over my head. The whole fight had lasted less than a minute.

The man I'd punched prodded at his broken nose, yelped in pain, looked at the blood on his hand and then prepared to kick me hard in the face. As I was still on the floor, held down by any number of willing hands, there was nothing much I could do about it. I turned my head away as far as I could, and collected his boot in my ear. Everything went black for a moment. When I was capable of thought once more, I was standing upright with my hands tied behind my back and everyone was stepping away from me. I staggered, and was brought up short by the rope around my neck.

I choked. I straightened and the pressure on my throat lessened enough for me to breathe. Just. I couldn't hear anything from my right ear except a loud continuous buzzing. Carefully, I risked a glance around. The door to the shed was pulled shut. Dek was standing by the wall, held tight by a Keeper sylv. He had a bruise on his cheek. The man with the broken nose was doing his best to breathe through all the blood. Flame was staring at him dispassionately. Domino, standing next to her, had his hands clenched so tight he must have been hurting himself. The man who had taken a sword in his side was now lying on the floor, and the blade was still lodged in him. The results of my wild stroke looked messy and smelled worse; I doubted the ex-sylvs would be able to cure that. My own sword was lying on the floor where someone had dropped it in the melee.

And I wondered why I was still alive.

Morthred came and stood directly in front of me. "That was stupid," he said.

"No, it wasn't," I replied, still breathing heavily. "You are going to hang me. I wouldn't be able to live with myself if I died without a fight."

There was a moment's silence, then he laughed out loud. "Trench take you, Blaze Halfbreed! There aren't too many people who still have the power to amuse me." He shook his head in mock sorrow. "A pity you are who you are. I would go further than I ever dreamed possible if I had you behind me." There was no sexual intention behind his words; Morthred had never found me attractive. He meant that I would have made a good henchman.

"It's never too late," I said, trying to sound amiable. It's remarkable what incentive a noose around the neck will give you.

Dek gave an indignant squawk as if he couldn't believe I'd said that. I ignored him.

"Ah, no," Morthred said. "We both know you would be utterly untrustworthy. Anyway, you are laboring under a misconception: I am not going to hang you, as much as I would like to. I am not even going to have you tortured to death, as much as Domino would like to do that. I have struck a bargain with Lyssal here which entails leaving you and the boy alive, you will be glad to hear."

I wasn't glad at all. I didn't believe a word of it.

He turned to Flame. "Do you want to tell Blaze anything before we leave, my dear?"

She took a few hesitant steps toward me. I looked at my sword on the floor a few paces away from my feet, and then back at her face. "Domino is going to kill Dek and me both," I said flatly, "the moment your back is turned."

"If he did that, I wouldn't cooperate," she said listlessly. Faint tendrils of dun curled up over her body and along her arms. "Morthred knows that."

"He's lying to you, Flame; he'll kill us without you ever knowing we died," I pointed out. "Insist that we come with you."

The dun around her blossomed into scarlet, bright and stench-laden. Morthred smiled at me, just in case I didn't realize the magic was his.

"But I don't *want* you along," she said, sounding petulant. Then she added with a childlike lack of logic, "We have made a pact. You aren't to die, and I'm to do what he wants. There's a part of me that wants you dead, you know. If you came along, I might just . . ." She trailed off as if she had lost the thread of what she was saying. Which was probably just as well. It sounded as if she had been going to say that she might kill me herself.

"You see?" Morthred said gently to her. "Blaze is fine. Now go get into the boat, my dear. We will leave shortly."

I took another desperate look at my sword, although I'm not sure what I expected her to do about it, but Flame turned and walked out past Morthred into the sunlight. I ground my teeth in helpless frustration.

Morthred lingered a moment. "Poor girl, she is torn between wanting to watch you tortured, and saving your hide; her struggle amuses me so. Sylv and dun. The eternal battle. I love to watch her pain. Physical torture does not interest me, except for the fear engendered by its anticipation, or for the horror of its legacy. But the pain of the mind—aah." He licked his lips with the tip of his tongue, a gesture as deliberately provocative as his words. Still staring at me but gesturing to the sylvs, he said, "Leave us, and take the boy with you."

"Who, me?" I asked. "Gladly, if you'd just loosen the rope a bit."

Domino looked as if he wanted to protest Morthred's order, but one glance from the dunmaster stopped that conversation short. He glared at me instead, and I shrugged as if to say I didn't know what it was all about either. The sylvs left without a word, taking the wounded men with them. Dek was hauled out, protesting at the top of his voice. Brave perhaps, but not very sensible, as it earned him another clip over the head. The only good thing was that my sword still lay on the floor.

Morthred kept his distance. I thought he overestimated my abilities; I was barely a finger's breadth away from choking. There was no way I was going to launch any attack on anyone. Domino hadn't left either. He stood with folded arms by the door, even further away.

I twisted slightly and glanced behind to note that the other end of the rope was tied to a wall stanchion. The whole setup was diabolical. If I stood upright I was comfortable enough; I could even turn my head. But I had no leeway to bend down. I couldn't even slump. I fiddled with the cord that tied my hands, but it had been knotted by someone who knew what they were doing. There was no slack to play with, no knots that slipped. My fingers twiddled uselessly. I knew that there was no way I was ever going to get out of this one alone, and it was too much to expect that Ruarth or Dek would be able to help, or that Flame wanted to . . .

Sod it, I thought. Not *again*. How the shoal-laden *hells* did I manage to get myself into fixes like this? What was it about me that I couldn't lead a *normal* life?

I turned back to face Morthred and tried to sound philosophical—difficult, seeing as it was far from the way I felt. "Now what?" I asked. "I'm surprised you haven't hanged me already. You know from past experience that it's not wise to leave me to your underlings. I'm a resourceful lady—ask Domino the

Dumb, over there. Best just to get on with it, don't you think?"
There, I thought, bet that has you wondering what I'm up to.

He frowned slightly and turned to Domino. "Lyssal and I
will leave in a moment, as soon as Aiklin finishes the packing
and brings the bags down to the boat. Kill this one the moment we are gone. The boy too. But not until we are out of
sight and sound. I don't want Lyssal to hear any screaming; is
that clear? She has to think I am acceding to her request to just
imprison Blaze here until we abandon the island for good."

Domino frowned. "Is she going to believe *that*?"

"She's so muddled by dunmagic she believes anything I
tell her at the moment, as long as there is no direct evidence to
the contrary. So no screams until after we are out of earshot.
In a minute, when we are outside, I am going to give you orders about how to treat Blaze nicely after I am gone. That will
be for Lyssal's benefit, of course. You understand?"

"Yes, Syr-master."

"I don't want any mistakes this time. No being smart. You
are not to untie Blaze. She dies where she is, tied as she is.
Just how you do it is up to you."

Domino grinned at me. "Whipped to death with pandana
fronds . . . I *hate* quick deaths."

Morthred snorted. "Domino, you don't even *begin* to know
the true meaning of torture." He looked across at me. "Blaze
and I understand that it's all in the mind, don't we, Blaze? Try
whipping the boy to death in front of her first." He didn't wait
for my reaction. He walked to the door and pushed Domino
out ahead of him. Then, in the doorway, he turned back.

My heartbeat a little faster. I didn't know exactly what
was coming, but I knew it would be hell. He said conversa-
tionally, "Amputating Lyssal's arm to rid her of my contamination was a clever idea. It worked too, you know. Together
with the sylv healing, it did rid her of all the infection. But
there was something you *didn't* know. And you still don't
know, do you? Now that amuses me. In fact, you haven't the
slightest idea of why she betrayed you, have you? Let alone
the greater implications of that. I've half a mind to tell you,
because I know you'd die enraged, spitting your despair because you couldn't do anything about it . . . but I won't. Because I know true torture lies not in the big things, but the

little ones. You are going to die not knowing why Lyssal betrayed you, or what is wrong with her. You are going to die not knowing what I am planning and not knowing what I have planned for her. You'll die wondering . . . and that, to me, is exquisite."

He smiled, pure poison. "That will be the true despair of your death, Blaze. Moreover, you will leave nothing behind you that is worth anything, because you will have failed. My legacy, on the other hand, the hell I will eventually leave behind me, will span the archipelago. And there is nothing, nothing at all, you can do about it. Think on that, my dear."

The bastard. He was still smiling as he turned to go.

"Morthred—"

He turned back, eyebrow arched in question.

"Who are you?"

"What do you mean?"

"Just that: who are you? You sank the Dustel Isles. You didn't do that without a reason. Did that missing earlobe of yours once carry the tattoo of a Dustel Islander?"

He looked at me, intrigued. "Why in all the Isles should I bother to tell you that?"

"Wouldn't it be nice to have someone . . . understand the irony?"

He hesitated and then smiled in amused appreciation. For a moment he was almost benign. "You know, don't you?"

I nodded. "I think you are Gethelred. Which probably makes you the legitimate Islandlord of the Dustels. And that has to be the ultimate irony, seeing as you are the one who sank the whole island chain under the ocean and ended up with nothing to rule."

If I was right, Gethelred's father had been Willrin, the Rampartheir to the Dustel Islands, until he was murdered by his brother, Vincen. Willrin and Vincen's father had been the last Rampartlord. After Willrin's murder, Gethelred had sailed on a Menod ship to surrender himself to his grandfather in exchange for the lives of his mother, his sisters, and his twin brother. He had arrived too late.

It had been Alain Jentel who had told Tor and me the whole story of a brother's treachery, a treachery that had started the savage civil war which had devastated the country in the months leading up to the inundation of the islands.

Morthred came closer. "How did you know?" He was genuinely interested.

"I don't know, really," I said, honest to the last. "I'm just guessing. You have the coloring of a Southerman. The accent of a Dustel Islander. Then there's the way you made yourself that throne back in Creed. Something about the way you hold yourself now. You reek of Islandlord nobility. And something made you angry enough to drown a whole string of islands . . . The last Rampartlord slaughtered Gethelred's father, then his mother, twin brother and two little sisters. He nailed their bodies to the castle ramparts. They were the first thing Gethelred saw when he sailed into the harbor on a Menod ship to surrender himself. You were, what? Twelve years old then?"

A flash of dun color played across his forehead, then sparked into scarlet through his hair and over his shoulders. "I was thirteen."

"But Gethelred can hardly have been a dunmagicker, surely."

"No, of course not. He—*I* was born a sylv."

"So what happened?"

"Ask the Menod," he said. "Ask the Menod Aware scum."

"I'm not likely to have the chance, am I?"

He laughed. "No, you aren't at that. Very well, I'll tell— because it amuses me to do so. There is so much that is amusing today, isn't there? It amuses me because it will tell you more of what I am, and therefore what I can become . . . and your imagination will torment you till the instant of your death. You know the story, but do you know *why* I was late arriving in Dustelrampart to surrender myself, Blaze? It was because those puling priests insisted on tending to the wounded first. They wanted to heal nobodies, like my father's guard. And so we didn't get to the city before the deadline. My grandfather's men raped my mother and my little sisters before they killed them. And all because I was a day late. When I arrived, they were just meat hung on the city wall, like offal in a butcher's shop. Their eyes were pecked out by gulls.

"And so the Menod turned tail and took me to their monastery in Skodart. I told them my sodding grandfather would come and kill us all, but they wouldn't take any notice. I was just a whingeing child to them."

Scarlet flared from him, and it was all I could do not to flinch away, even though I knew it couldn't hurt me. He went on, "The Menod had a dunmaster there, imprisoned in one of their cells, buried beneath the ground. They wouldn't kill him, because the Menod don't like to kill, cowards that they are, so they'd kept him there for years. They thought he was safely imprisoned, unable to blast his way out because the cell was buried. They allowed only the Aware to tend him, so he couldn't magick anyone." He laughed, a laugh of genuine amusement. "I heard about him, of course."

I saw where his story was going. The inevitability of the path he had chosen was as clear as moonlight on a still sea. I said, "So you used illusion to gain access to him. And then you sold the dunmagicker his freedom, in return for the kind of power you wanted." My breath caught at even the thought of it.

"It's a pleasure to talk to you, Blaze," he said, but the curl of his mouth was all nastiness, not pleasure. "I like people who understand. Who get the point."

"You *deliberately* asked to be subverted."

"You can't kill anyone with sylvpower," he said softly, "and there were a lot of people I wanted to kill."

It was a moment before I could speak. "The fellow couldn't have been much of a dunmaster: he didn't tell you how to avoid the backlash of power use."

He didn't answer that. Instead he said, "I was no subverted sylv, you understand. Why do you think I am so powerful? Because I *welcomed* the union of opposites. It wasn't subversion, but conversion. I gloried in it, accepted it and made it grow. Ah, Blaze, to feel that power within. The *strength* of it. Even now, I really don't understand why the sylvs I subvert struggle against subversion. Their resistance keeps them weak. Often it makes them confused and capable only of obedience, not initiative. I suppose I should be glad of that—none of them will ever threaten me. It was my conversion which gave me the idea of sylv subversion in the first place, of course. I just wasn't able to implement it until recently when my powers started to return."

"You didn't really intend to sink the islands, did you?" I blurted that intriguing idea out without even knowing how I knew.

"No, of course not. Or only part of them. I wanted to *rule* them." He shrugged. "I was just more powerful than I thought I was going to be, and very inexperienced." He smiled faintly. "Dear Grandfather sent forces after me, of course, led by Uncle Vincen. The whole of Skodart and the surrounding islands rose up against them. If you know your history, you will know about that bloody war. I was just biding my time, waiting till I learned how to control my magic. The Menod, of course, abandoned my cause the moment they smelled the dun on me." He shrugged again. "It didn't matter. I had an army of my own by then. I thought to sink the city of Dustelrampart, along with my grandfather's palace and his men; instead, I submerged a whole islandom. It was . . . very spectacular. I think I would do it all over again, were I to be in that same position."

"And the birds?" I asked. "Why birds?" I was trying not to show him my sick fear. The *power* this man must have once had . . . more than any dunmaster before or since. Would he be able to do that sort of thing again? Could he do it *now?*

"When I saw what was happening, I didn't want everyone to die," he explained. "What would be the punishment in that? Better to have them live a little longer, knowing what I had done to them, knowing what I had done to their land. Small, nondescript, powerless little birds that a man could crush in his hand, or keep in a cage . . . but what terrible memories they had." He smiled.

If he had thought to shock me, he was successful. The callous indifference to what he had done, his total lack of remorse, was perhaps to be expected, but still it was shocking, given the scale of his crime.

He saw my reaction and savored it, saying, "It was *worth* it, Blaze. It was worth the backlash to my body. It was worth all those years of weakness where I could hardly cast a spell. It was worth all those years of recovery." His smile mocked. "Sinking the Dustel Isles was to me the greatest orgasm the world has ever seen, or is ever likely to see again."

On that line, he opened the door and went to leave the shed. He relished that exit, I could tell, so I had to spoil it for him. I asked, "What were the names of your little sisters, Gethelred?"

Outlined in the doorway, he went rigid.

I may not have had Gilfeather's nose, but I can sniff out weak spots any time. I knew when I said the words that it wouldn't do my situation any good, but it didn't matter. It made a difference to me to see him hurt.

Well, I never said I was *nice,* did I?

A letter from Researcher (Special Class) S. iso Fabold, National Department of Exploration, Federal Ministry of Trade, Kells, to Masterman M. iso Kipswon, President of the National Society for the Scientific, Anthropological and Ethnographical Study of non-Kellish Peoples.

Dated this day 59/2nd Darkmoon/1793

Dear Uncle,
I am delighted that the committee has approved my new paper on religious practices in the Glory Isles. I shall ask my assistants to design the magic lantern slides.

In the meantime, arrangements for the next trip are proceeding apace. I find that having missionary backing has certain advantages: there is a great deal of pressure applied on the various ministries involved, and things do move quickly as a consequence. I believe His Excellency the Protector is taking an interest as well. Unfortunately, H.E.'s interest seems to be motivated primarily by Her Excellency: she is pressing for women to be included in the expedition. Can you imagine? Has our royal lady taken leave of her senses? Sometimes I wonder why, when we deposed our kings and queens during the revolution, we did not rid Kells of all royalty—why have this vestige clinging on to the State making nuisances of themselves? They should confine themselves to opening exhibitions and closing the Houses of Debate for the summer recess, which is their true job.

Anyara, of course, is in full agreement with the Protectoress!

By the way, Anyara did some lovely sketches for me based on Glorian material. She is extraordinarily talented. I shall use them to illustrate a book of my travels one day, if ever I have the time to write one. Her line drawings are simply perfection. Aunt will be glad to hear that I have broached the matter of formalizing our relationship. However, Anyara is reluctant to make a commitment. I do not hold this against her: as I have said before, a field ethnographer makes a poor husband, and we are both cognizant of the fact that were we to marry, she would too often be alone.

Please extend my fondest love to Aunt Rosris, and tell her I am reading the novel she sent.

Your obedient nephew,
Shor iso Fabold

CHAPTER 21

ONE THING FOR CERTAIN, I WAS GLAD RY-
der was there, because I didn't have any ideas. We were two
against more than forty. They couldn't hurt us with magic or
whatever it was that smelled so terrible, but they didn't need
to. They carried an arsenal of swords and knives and probably
bows as well.

I dithered, feeling useless. From the perspective of safety, I
thought we were far too close to the first of the houses. Close
enough to have eavesdropped if there had been anyone there.
But Ryder seemed oblivious to danger; in fact, the tang of his
excitement, rather like the faint reek of fermenting apples,
was an undercurrent to all the other aromas wafting into my
nostrils. Confound it, I thought, can't the man just be scared
stiff like any sensible human being? I myself felt as vulnerable as a meadow flower surrounded by a flock of grazing
selvers.

He asked calmly, "Have you any idea if Blaze is all right?
Or Flame?"

I was about to answer when something large surfaced alongside the stern of the raft. I jumped, almost upending us all. Ryder

moved faster than a grass-lion racing a Plains hare. One moment he was kneeling back on his heels, peering out between the pandana leaves to our left, the next he was half-crouched with his sword already drawn, facing the creature that had surfaced.

I laid a hand on his arm, trying to still my pounding heart. "Wait a wee bit," I whispered. "That's only Seeker."

The dog whined and pawed at the end of the raft, his tail slicing the water with enthusiasm. I grabbed him by the scruff of the neck and heaved him aboard; anything to stop the splashing. He had a makeshift collar and a leash made out of string trailed behind him.

Ryder lowered his weapon and ducked to avoid a shower of water from the animal. "*What* is that?" he asked.

"Seeker. Blaze's dog."

"That's no dog." He turned back to look at the village once more. "That's a Fen lurger. Look at its webbed feet. Where did she pick that up?"

"Back in Gorthan Docks, I believe." I was surprised. I would have thought he knew about Seeker.

I was hit by a whole heap of his emotions: hurt, jealousy, grief. And then wry amusement. The man was laughing at himself for being envious of my relationship with Blaze. Before I had time to mull over that, he was saying, "Look out, there's something happening there."

Flame came out of the shed. She was alone. She did not look left or right—she simply walked past the guards, marched straight across the sands of the beach and sat in one of the boats pulled up at the water's edge.

"She's not guarded," Ryder said. I smelled his sorrow. "You were right. She betrayed them. What does your nose tell you about her now?"

"Hard to say. There's too much dun around . . ."

He sat quietly, thinking. Before he made any decision, some more people came out of the shed. "The boy is Dek," I said, "the lad I told you about. I don't know the others, but the two dunmagickers are among them." Dek looked scared out of his wits, and I can't say I blamed him. He wasn't tied, but one of the men had a firm hold of his arm.

"Morthred's not there," Ryder added. "Nor is Domino." Nor was Blaze. There were three people who were wounded, though: one had a bloodied nose, another a slashed arm and a third was carried out. Ryder smothered a laugh. "It doesn't pay to turn your back on that woman," he said.

We continued to watch, but nothing much seemed to be happening. Everyone just stood around, most of them silent and still. Beside me, Ryder was becoming increasingly anxious, although you wouldn't have known it by looking at him. He hardly moved a muscle.

Just when I felt sure he was going to do something, another man strutted out of the shed. He was short, and overdressed in brightly colored clothes.

"That's Domino," Ryder said.

Domino stopped to speak to some of the sylvs, who were gathered around the wounded. He pointed down to the lake shore where Flame still sat in the boat. We could hear him, but not clearly enough to make out the gist of the conversation.

"The dunmaster is still inside the shed," I whispered. "I'm certain."

"With Blaze?"

I nodded.

"I can't see Ruarth."

"I canna sense him either."

"Damn. I would have thought he wouldn't be far from Flame. He could probably tell us what is going on if only we could get hold of him. And if we could understand him."

"I can, some."

"You can? Good. And Blaze—she . . . she's still all right?"

"So far." I tried to pick up a trace of her that would tell me more: there was nothing. The woman was too darn good at keeping herself closed; besides, the dun stench was overwhelming. Beads of sweat trickled down my face from my forehead. My stomach heaved. I had to keep my fists clenched to stop my hands from shaking. Selverspit, I thought, this is poisoning me.

Ryder bowed his head. For a moment I couldn't think what he was doing. Then I realized, he was praying. After all, there wasn't much else we could do. There were only two of us.

Flame sat still in the boat, apparently unmoved by anything that was going on around her, and making no attempt to escape. Dek was a slightly built lad, and the sylv holding him had no trouble keeping him still. Domino gave some more orders to several of the sylvs, and they walked away down the beach toward a clump of pandana that floated there. Inexplicably, they started to cut long leaves of pandana and pile them up on the beach.

Every now and then Seeker gave a low growl in the back of his throat.

You and me both, I thought. It's an awful stench, isn't it?

The fetid stink was overpowering, so intensely unpleasant it was hard to breathe, hard to *think*. I'd already thrown up all I'd had to eat earlier that day and now I sat miserably in the raft, one part of me wishing that I could just curl up and die. It was worse than being seasick.

A tall man came out of the shed. He was alone.

"Ryder," I said, "that's him. The dunmaster."

Ryder shook his head. "No, that's not Morthred."

"Well, put it this way: that's the man with all the power."

"Morthred's crippled. Sort of squashed-looking. He actually didn't have all that much power left when we saw him last. He had been too profligate with it."

"Look at him! You must see that power—the smell is poisonous!"

Ryder looked again. "There's certainly a lot of dun," he conceded. Then he drew in a sharp breath. "God in heaven! It *is* him! He's been *healed*."

"He must have repaired his powers as well. There's nothing weak about that man's abilities." Even then I couldn't help but want to find out more. To know what this stuff called dunmagic was. To know *why*.

"We thought his powers would be *reduced*. How the crabdamn did he get to look like that?"

"Ruarth," I interrupted. "Ruarth's here somewhere. I can smell him." We scanned the village, and finally spotted the bird flying across to land on the ridgepole of the shed.

"We've got to get him here," Ryder said.

It seemed impossible. How could we attract Ruarth's attention without also alerting everyone else on the beach? We watched helplessly while Ruarth flew across to the house next to the shed. At least he was a little closer to us than he had been.

"I'm going out there," Ryder said. I opened my mouth to voice my reservations, but he had already made up his mind. He crawled off the raft straight into the village garden. There were tapioca and banana plants and a selection of spices: ginger, galangal, turmeric, lemongrass, chillies, pepper vines; fortunately enough of them to give him some cover. Heart in mouth, I watched. Beside me, Seeker continued to growl until I clamped a hand around his snout.

Somehow Ryder made it to the first of the houses unobserved. Once there, he stood up and walked openly. He didn't have his sword in his hand—it was still in the harness on his back—and he hadn't taken his bow. At the doorway, he picked up a wooden bucket and was about to walk on when someone stepped out of the house. Ryder snapped at him, "Go inside and stay there!"

The man reeked strongly of fear, dun stink and a sourish odor that was the same as that of a dog when it grovels in subservience. He did as he was told. Ryder grinned at me.

Blue skies above, I thought, he's *enjoying* this!

He was out in the open where he could be seen from the beach now, but no one took the slightest notice of him. To them, he was just a slave with a bucket. I continued to watch; he was close to the house where Ruarth perched. Once there, he called to the bird by name, softly. I didn't hear him, but Ruarth apparently did, because he came down to the guttering and had a look.

Morthred went to the boat to speak with Flame. She didn't say much; he seemed to be doing all the talking.

Ryder switched his sword harness to his front where it wouldn't be seen so easily from behind, and started to walk back toward the raft. He was still carrying the bucket. I wondered if I would have had the nerve to turn my back to my enemies and calmly walk away. I relaxed only once he was back on the raft, apparently unremarked by anyone. Reaction had started me trembling and I had to clench my hands so Ryder wouldn't notice.

Ruarth flew to join us. He was in a terrible state. I expected him to say something about the fact that Ryder and I were there at all, but he just said, *She won't speak to me.* His grief and despair blotted out every other emotion.

When I translated, Ryder said harshly, "We will talk about her condition later, Ruarth. Right now we need to know what is happening. Where's Blaze? What's happening there? Have you been inside the shed? Oh, hells. Gilfeather, what's he saying?"

In truth, I had trouble following what he said next, his chirps and flutterings were so fast.

Domino: he's going to kill Blaze and Dek. Morthred's taking Flame away. Kel, what can you do? Tor? You know what she went through—you know what she's going through now . . .

I wanted to use a variation on my usual mantra: I'm a physician, not a fighter. I don't know *how* to fight!

"What's he saying?" Ryder repeated, his frustration clear.

I translated.

Ryder looked back at what was happening on the beach. "Discounting the slaves, there are some twenty men and women out there who'd rather run a sword through us than talk to us. We need more time to plan, Ruarth. How long do we have before . . . How long before Blaze dies?"

As soon as Morthred and Flame leave. Any time now, he said.

I translated.

Ryder looked at me bleakly and made a decision. Once again he didn't bother to ask my opinion. "Gilfeather: you've got to go after Flame. You and Ruarth. You are her one chance. Take this raft and follow. Find out what's the matter with her, if you can. Help her."

"*Me?* Ye want me to rescue her?"

"She's not a prisoner. You may find an opportunity to speak to her. Or something. The first chance you get, go to a Menod patriarch or matriarch. Tell them I sent you. Tell them it is a Menod duty, imposed by the High Patriarch, to bring her to safety on Tenkor. You will need help. The Menod will provide it.

"I will come after you as soon as I can, if I can. With Blaze and the boy, I hope. Leave messages with the patriarchs along the way so I know where to find you. Just remember that you can't trust her. She might betray you both . . . she can't help herself. You must never forget that for a moment."

I wondered if he had any idea of what he was so matter-of-factly asking me to do. We wouldn't just be following Flame; we'd be following Morthred. I licked lips that were unnaturally dry. "And ye?" I asked hoarsely. But I already knew. I could smell his intention.

"I can't let her die alone," he whispered. "I can't just walk away. I *can't*." He wasn't talking about Flame.

"She wouldn't want your death, Ryder. It would devastate her." He intended to fight his way to Blaze's side, but there was no way he could succeed in her rescue. "More than twenty of them," I reminded him. "Most right here in the village, all crowded around the shed and the beach. Not to mention the slaves who could be commanded to help."

Kel's right, Ruarth said.

"Ruarth agrees with me," I added. "And ye were sent to look after Flame, not Blaze." Tor had told me that much himself. It was a cruel thing to say, and I knew it. It was also one of the hardest things I'd ever had to say to anyone, because the truth was that I wanted him to try, no matter how useless it was. The idea of just leaving Blaze there to die, without any one of us at least *trying* to save her . . .

I swallowed, and tasted bile.

He stared at us, thinking, his aroma reflecting his contempt for my words. "Morthred will take some of the sylvs with him," he said finally. "I may have a fighting chance. That's all I need. Just a chance." He held my gaze. "You don't understand."

Oh, but I did. I knew *exactly* how he felt. It was the way *I* felt that shocked me to the core . . .

I had to make the offer, even though my fear made me ill. "Ye'd have more of a chance if I helped."

"If you came with me, and we failed, Flame would be doomed, as well as you. My way, at least we can be sure that you and Ruarth will come out of this alive, and maybe Flame as well."

"Right," I said with a snort. "After I've killed the most powerful dunmaster the Isles has ever known, and presumably the sylvs with him, and forced Flame to Tenkor, where she will probably not want to go. I'm a *physician,* Ryder, remember?" I took a breath. "The only thing I know about swords is which end is the sharper. I'd never been in a serious scrap in my life till I met Blaze. I'd have more of a chance if ye were with me, and you know it." I added in a whisper, because that was all I could manage, "Going after Blaze is suicide." I knew he agreed with me: his resolution was mixed in with an acceptance of death that smothered his fear of dying.

"She would do it for me," he said simply.

Voices floated back to us from the beach. Ryder and I peeked over the leaves to see what was happening. Several men were putting bundles into Flame's boat and another alongside it.

Ryder was agitated, but he still disguised it well. "I hope to the skies above that Flame hasn't told Morthred about Ruarth," he said. "I'm guessing not yet. But don't doubt it, Gilfeather: she will. It's as inevitable as the tide. As soon as she is fully infected."

The thought was sickening. What sort of thing was it that could force someone to betray all that they had ever loved most?

"Ruarth, how is Domino going to kill Blaze?" Ryder asked.

She and Dek are both going to be whipped to death with the pandana fronds. If Blaze struggles against the whipping, she'll hang herself on the noose they have around her neck. Flame thinks Morthred will allow them to live. I tried to tell her, but she wouldn't listen.

Involuntarily I glanced at the plants in front of us. The long narrow leaves were edged with a lacing of thorns, brutal hooked things that would rip flesh to shreds.

Ryder nodded when I translated. His rage was all the more terrible for being tightly leashed. "And in the meantime?" He picked up his bow and tested the tension in the string.

In the meantime she is to be kept tied up just as she is, in the shed, Ruarth said.

Ryder slung his quiver over his shoulder. "Follow Flame and Morthred, Gilfeather. And I'll make you a twofold promise. Before I die, I will do my level best to tell Blaze that you will see Flame safe, and I will see her dead by my own hand before I will allow her to be whipped to death." He raised his eyes to meet mine. "But having said that, I'm not going there to die if I can help it, I promise you. And I have God on my side. Ruarth, tell me about Blaze. How is she confined? Where is her sword? What does the shed look like inside?"

While Ruarth explained and I translated, Morthred climbed into the same boat as Flame, along with several sylvs. Others piled onto a second boat. All told: five sylvs and Morthred. Six less for Tor to kill. Those remaining behind began to push the boats into the water. Four of the sylvs entered the shed, obviously on Morthred's orders.

"Right, that's it," Ryder said. "We're running out of time. You are Flame's hope, Gilfeather. Poison the bastard if you have to. Anything." He scrambled off the raft and was gone, crawling at first, just as he had before.

For a moment I couldn't move. He did not know it, but he had left his emotions behind him in his aroma: his fear, his sadness, his acceptance of death, his determination. I was mired with the weight of another man's courage and grief. I thought of Jastriá. Of the possibility of failure. Most of all I thought of Blaze. And Dek. Of how the boy's death would devastate her.

Just then another Keeper sylv entered the shed, dragging pandana leaves behind him. I nodded to myself and finally accepted the inevitable. I bent to untie the string from around Seeker's neck. "He may be of some use," I said to Ruarth. My fingers fumbled, trembling, making a poor job of it, but eventually Seeker was free and I pushed him off the raft after Ryder. At the very least he might be able to offer some kind of diversion. I was darn sure he wouldn't stand meekly around while Blaze was whipped to death. I knew I was probably sending him to be killed too, but I did it nonetheless.

"Ruarth," I said, "I want ye to get in to Blaze if ye can do it safely. I want ye to tell her that Ryder is coming. The more prepared she is, the more chance she has. In the meantime, I'll set off after Flame. Ye can catch me up."

He nodded. Briefly, we stared at each other: a bird and a man, and I had my first intimation of Ruarth as he would be if he was a man. In that moment, I could almost see him through the scent of him: a younger man than I was, and tenacious. A complex person who battled the limitations of his body every day and never submitted to forces that would have crushed a lesser man.

"We will pull Flame through this," I said quietly, but they were only words. In my heart I didn't really believe it.

He nodded and then he picked up the length of hempen string that had been Seeker's leash, and flew away.

I watched. No one saw him, not even as he trailed the string behind him. I couldn't imagine what he wanted it for, and it was heavy enough to have him laboring by the time he reached the shed. He was still carrying it as he slipped past two men guarding the door and then inside. Ryder retreated behind the first house where he could not be seen from the beach, and then ran on to the next, still out of sight. Seeker sidled after him.

I pushed the raft away from the shallows and began poling it back toward the floating islands. Fortunately I had taken a turn with the pole earlier in the day, but I was still clumsy. When I passed a gap between islands and was able to look back at the beach, I saw Domino still standing there with his phalanx of sylvs and dunmagickers, looking in the direction Morthred had taken. The dunmaster's boat was about to enter a tunnel of pandana plants; the other boat had already disappeared. Any moment, Domino would turn and go to the shed . . .

I stopped poling, unable to go on. Fortunately no one was looking my way.

Behind Domino, near the door to the shed, a sylv toppled to the ground. His companion looked at him, baffled, then moved to help. As he stooped, he too crumpled. I looked to the right of the shed where Ryder was notching another arrow. He took aim and I glanced back at Domino. He was about to turn, about to see what was happening behind him.

I didn't even think. I gave the pole one last hard push and let the raft sail out into the open water in front of the beach. A glance to my left confirmed what I had hoped: Morthred and his party were out of sight, already lost in the tunnels between the islands.

"Hey, Shortie!" I bellowed with my hands cupped around my mouth. "Domino! Remember me?" Of course, there was no question of him remembering a red-haired physician from Mekaté; we'd never met.

Behind him a third man fell, still unnoticed. A fourth sunk to his knees with an arrow in his back. He screamed, alerting

others. Five or six more arrows followed, some of them finding their mark. Then Ryder was running, sword in hand, aim-
ing for the shed door.

"Squib!" I yelled. "What's the matter, you stump-legged
tosspot? Who shrank you? Ye're the size of a docked duck,
Domino!"

Domino shouted something to his men, and I didn't need
to hear the words to know he was furious. A dunmagicker
launched something at me. Creation knows what, as I couldn't
see anything. I could smell it, though, and would probably
have emptied my stomach over the side yet again if I hadn't
been hanging on for dear life. Whatever it was hit the raft like
a boulder from a crag top. The front part splintered into bamboo needles, several of which pierced my arm.

I winced and picked myself up. "Are ye man or barnacle?"
I asked at the top of my lungs. "Bearded barnacle maybe?"
I'm not much of a man for vulgarities, but Flame had taught
me that one and it seemed an appropriate time to use it. "Ye
couldna manage a lady the size of a butter-churn, ye pygmy
pee-pot, let alone Blaze Halfbreed!"

When they saw that I was unaffected by the dun, several
sylvs ran for one of the remaining boats. One fitted a quarrel
to the crossbow he carried, but at least I had bought Ryder the
precious moments of distraction he needed.

The Stragglerman had reached the door of the shed. He'd
been seen by then, of course, and another man died on his
sword there after an exchange of blows. On the beach, Dek
had broken free from the man who was holding him.
Domino's men divided, some coming after me, while others
hurried up the sand to tackle Ryder. Everyone was shouting,
and to add to the confusion, Seeker had plunged into the fray
around the Stragglerman. The dog clamped his jaws around
someone's arm and tugged him out of the way.

An arrow thudded into the bamboo at my feet. I dug the
pole into the water and gave another push; if I wasn't out of
there soon, I would be the next victim. I ducked down and
started to use the paddle instead of the pole; it seemed wiser.

I was still nowhere near the nearest passage or tunnel that
would offer some protection, when something broke through
the water ahead of me. A gray head. Behind me, long clawed

hands with an impossible number of digits curled themselves around the bamboo and the raft tipped alarmingly as something tried to climb in. I turned to face this new danger, and altered my grip on the paddle to use it as a cudgel. A clawed leg snatched it out of my hands. I fell sideways, squawking my terror, and had a momentary glimpse of the lake between me and the shore. The water was boiling with activity as gray heads and bodies churned up the surface.

I think I screamed then.

But there was no one to heed.

CHAPTER 22

NARRATOR : BLAZE

WHEN I LOOK BACK ON THAT DAY, IT STILL frightens me how well Morthred knew me. How often he must have watched me when he was serving in the taproom of The Drunken Plaice; how often he must have talked to Flame about me, extracting my personality from her perception of me.

Because he was right: the not knowing, the not understanding—it *was* torture.

He'd sketched a few verbal lines that were as succinctly suggestive as a scrimshaw carving, yet I couldn't fill in the whole picture. He'd given me a clue, he must have done surely, but where? *What I am, and therefore what I can become . . . the hell I will leave behind me . . . my legacy will span the archipelago.* Why did Flame betray me if she wasn't subverted? Or was Morthred lying to me?

Domino. Dek. *Try whipping the boy to death in front of her first . . .*

Immediately after the dunmaster had left, I had trouble breathing, and it had nothing to do with the rope around my neck. I closed my eyes. Ruarth was screaming overhead somewhere, but I couldn't look at him, not then.

Everything that we had done to Flame, we had done for nothing; she was in his hands again. She was ill. All her suffering had been doomed to be repeated. She would be compelled to live within her corrupted mind, to struggle—in vain—with her corrupted personality for the rest of her days. I was speechless with rage.

Saltwater hells, I thought. Gilfeather, why didn't you come with us? You might have seen what was coming . . . you might have saved us.

I *had* to get out of there. I was tired from having to stand so straight with my neck held high; I felt like a marlin hanging on a hook outside the fishmonger's. And trussed up like that, there wasn't a blessed thing I could do about anything. The only good thing was that the ringing in my ears was gradually clearing. *Think,* woman, *think!* I opened my eyes and looked upward. Ruarth was on one of the cross beams. He was crouched down on his stomach with his wing tips touching the beam; a posture that indicated extreme distress.

"Ruarth, I have to get my sword. It's on the floor over there."

It's too heavy for me to lift, he said, stating the obvious.

"Yes, of course. You have to find Seeker and get him in here. Or Dek. Or get a piece of string long enough to stretch from the hilt to me. Quick, now go!"

He went without a murmur.

I also had a flexible knife tucked in the lining of my boot, and a pick-lock in the heel—an old habit I had reestablished after being imprisoned in Mekatéhaven. Trouble was, I didn't know how to get at them while I was trussed up like this. I looked up at the beam and over to the stanchion where the rope was tied. The rope was taut, but the stanchion was at a slight angle . . . not much, but enough to make a difference. If I edged sideways, directly under the beam, and could coax the rope to move along the beam with me, then I would shorten the distance between myself and the stanchion. And that would mean that the rope would have a little slack . . .

I stood up on the balls of my feet and jerked my head sideways, against the rope. Fortunately, the knot was at the side of my neck, not at the back, and that made it a shade easier. Even so, it was a painfully slow business. The rope continually caught on the rough edges of the beam. When I lost my balance, I almost hanged myself. Inch by painful inch, I edged closer to the stanchion. Finally I was directly opposite and the rope was no longer taut. I took a step away, which pulled the rope forward across the beam, and I had the slack I needed. It wasn't much, but at least I didn't have to stand tall just to breathe; I could turn my body, I could bend my head to look behind. I could now maneuver enough to take my boot off, surely. I bent my right leg up behind me, and caught hold of my foot with my fingers. I would have to undo the laces before I was going to be able to pull the boot off; difficult when my wrists were bound together.

I set to work.

As I fiddled with the knots, I tried to make sense of all that had happened. Flame must be holding on to something of her decency, even yet. She obviously hadn't told Morthred about Ruarth. And Morthred said he needed her cooperation. If she was entirely subverted, then he would already have had that. She would just do what he said without question. She'd *want* to do what he suggested. So she must have managed to keep a small part of herself inviolate. In order to control that part, Morthred needed to have leverage. So he'd lied. He'd said he would keep Dek and me alive in exchange for her cooperation, but why did he need her openly compliant in the first place? He could coerce her if he needed, couldn't he?

Or did he need her to do something of her own free will? What?

And if she wasn't subverted, then what was the matter with her that had made her betray us? There was plenty of dun color enveloping her, but it was impossible to say how much was hers, how much Morthred's.

And *what* was going to span the archipelago? And why the hell was I thinking about this now anyway? I needed to get out of here!

My fingers were beginning to feel numb: my wrists were tied far too tightly. They fumbled with the knots. I wasn't having much success. I still hadn't removed the boot when four sylvs entered the shed, on Morthred's orders, I assumed, their job evidently to guard me. I put my foot back on the floor. They came in without speaking, swords drawn, and stood one in each corner. There was no way that the two in the corners behind me would not notice me extract a knife from my boot, but I stood on one leg again nonetheless and resumed my fumbling with the laces. It didn't seem to worry any of them. One, a woman, I knew: she had gone to the same elite girls' school in The Hub that I had attended for a while at Duthrick's insistence. She had been a year or two older, but she should have known me. If she did, though, she gave no sign of it. I called her by name, Selmarian, and there was a momentary flicker in her eyes, but that was all. I tried to talk to her, to remind her about her past; she ignored me. So did the others. They just stood where they had been told, their haunted eyes dulled, not even speaking among themselves. I've always had mixed feelings about Keeper sylvs, especially Council-employed sylvs, swinging between admiration of their skills and talents, and dislike of their air of superiority and snobbishness, but right then I could feel nothing but compassion. That those proud people should come to this pitiful end, subservients of a dunmaster, ready to do anything he asked: it was horrible.

A while later another sylv came in and dropped some pandana leaves on the floor. Listlessly, he said to me, "I was told to tell you that these are to be used on you. You and the boy." He left without even bothering to look at me.

I gazed at the leaves with their clawed edging.

And I remembered another boy, another time. Tunn, his lonely, tragic death, all because I had involved him in my affairs. How could I possibly watch while another lad died? Dek didn't deserve to suffer in such a fashion, not Dek, not at his age, not with his hero worship and his crazy ideas of chivalrous behavior and bravery. My fury rose, at myself, at Morthred, at Domino, at Duthrick and his sylvs, at Tor for washing his hands of the problem, at Gilfeather for refusing to join us.

Trench *damn* it, how could I have got myself into such a stupid position as this? Tor would be furious with me when he found out. *If* he ever found out. Which he probably wouldn't. I pushed that thought away: it upset me too much. Only trouble was, I started thinking of Flame instead, and that was even more upsetting. I had made a solemn promise to her. I had sworn that I would never let her live if she was subverted; it hurt to think I had failed her.

For some reason or other I then thought of Gilfeather. And my thoughts weren't particularly nice. I wanted to throttle the selver-herding shrimp-brain, with his idealism and his pacifism and his disbelief. If he'd only acknowledged the truth about magic, if he'd only been prepared to admit that dunmagic was a danger to the world, not a case of some scrofulous skin disease or body odor or whatever he thought it was, maybe he would have come with us. And maybe he would have been able to prevent me falling gormlessly headlong into this ridiculous predicament.

And that was when Ruarth flew back in and landed at my feet. He was trailing a piece of doubled-up string behind him like a streamer. I glanced around at the sylvs. Evidently a small dark bird hardly registered on their consciousness, because none of them gave any sign that they had noticed.

He spat the string out on the floor and started making conversation. I tried to follow, but I wasn't sure what he was saying. He was trying to tell me something about Tor and Gilfeather, and to be prepared, but I couldn't make any sense of it. I glared at him and nodded at the sword. The sylvs maintained their expressionless watch.

Ruarth ruffled his feathers in exasperation and shut up. I didn't have to tell him what I had in mind; he picked up one end of the string in his beak, looped it over the hilt and then tied a knot. I had thought a bird would find that appallingly difficult, but it didn't seem to bother him at all. Then I remembered that birds fashion nests far more complicated than I could manage with two hands.

Still pulling at my boot laces, I looked out the door, trying to see what was going on out there. My view was limited, but it was obvious that Flame and Morthred had gone and so had two of the boats. Domino was standing on the beach looking out at the lake. Dek was still being held by a sylv. Most of the others I couldn't see. Inside the shed, the sylv guards stood silent, apparently oblivious to Ruarth and indifferent to what I was trying to achieve.

Where was Morthred going? Why did he need Flame's cooperation?

Power, he wanted power . . . and Flame was the Cirkase

Castlemaid, heir to her father's islandom. Was Morthred going to send her home? And wait for her to come into her inheritance, when he would . . . what? Marry her? Be the power behind the Castlelord? No, there was something wrong with that scenario. Morthred had waited in the background long enough; he wanted power now.

To span the archipelago . . .

Breth. Breth Island was to the west, Cirkase to the east, bracketing the Keeper Isles. The Breth Bastionlord wanted to marry Lyssal. He would marry her immediately if he had the chance. Trench *damn* him, Morthred was going to take Flame to the Bastionlord. I shivered, suddenly cold. I was convinced I was right, but I still didn't understand his full intent. He wanted Flame to marry the Bastionlord, but where was the benefit in that for him?

Ruarth had the string tied to the hilt of the sword to his satisfaction. None of the sylvs had noticed anything. I was grateful for the dimness of the light in the shed; both the string and Ruarth blended into the background of an earth-packed floor. He picked up the far end of the string and walked across the floor to my feet.

And the string wasn't long enough.

There was no way that Ruarth was going to be able to fly it up to my hands. Cautiously I stretched out my foot and probed at it. It was several inches out of reach. When I tried harder, I started to choke. I stared at it in frustration.

I'm sorry, Ruarth said. *But Tor will be here soon anyway.*

Which was ridiculous. I'd obviously misinterpreted what he'd said; Tor was an entire ocean away. But I didn't want to ask Ruarth to repeat it, for fear the guards would take an interest in him. I jerked my head toward the door, willing him to go and get more string. Or find Seeker. Or *something*.

Obediently, he flew off.

And I thought again of Flame. And Morthred. And a plan for hell in two islandoms. What was it Morthred had meant about his legacy? If Flame was married to the Breth Bastionlord, where did that leave the dunmaster? Nowhere . . . unless, unless . . .

Unless the Bastionlord was doomed. If he was murdered,

Flame would be free to marry again. Free to marry Morthred. No, I still wasn't getting it. That wouldn't help Morthred. Flame would lose any power in Breth once her husband died.

Not, it occurred to me with breathtaking clarity, if she had given birth to the Breth Bastionheir in the meantime. Then she would be the Lady Mother. She might even be able to have herself declared regent for her son; not so impossible, considering her own royal lineage. Besides, she could use coercive magic.

Eventually she would rule Cirkase as well. And if Morthred dominated her as he seemed to now, then he would rule through her. His power would in fact span the archipelago . . .

The cold deepened, reaching far into my bones, as I remembered something Flame had told me while we shared the back of that sea-pony, something she had learned from Duthrick. Breth had saltpeter. Cirkase had sulfur. Together with charcoal, these were the main components of the black powder of cannon-guns. And Morthred had seen what cannon-guns could do.

Breth and Cirkase were just the beginning. Morthred was going to rule the Isles of Glory, and he was going to use cannon-guns to do it.

Yes, it was just possible. But it presupposed much. That Flame had a child by the Breth Bastionlord, for a start. That the child was male, as the islandom did not recognize female primogeniture. That Flame was either totally subordinated to Morthred, or totally cooperative. That Breth had no Awarefolk at court to tell the Bastionlord his intended bride was a dunmagicker.

Something didn't quite add up. I was still missing something. Something important. Something that had made Morthred as smug as a hermit crab with a new shell. And I just couldn't see it.

I attacked the shoelace with renewed vigor until finally I felt it loosen. I started to ease the boot off my foot.

Just then, one of the men who had apparently been on guard outside the shed dropped across the doorway, with an arrow sticking out of the side of his neck. It had torn away his throat and he died silently. My mouth fell open like a stranded cod. At the crucial moment, I lost my grip on the boot and dropped it, knife and all. *I knew that arrow.* It was fletched, not with feathers, but with the backbones of tumblefish, which made the arrow spin and added to its lethal accuracy and speed. There was only one person I knew who made such arrows: the man once known as the Lance of Calment. Tor Ryder.

Tor *was* here?

Oh, hells. Rescued by Tor, yet again. He was going to be *furious* with me. The second, no *third,* time he'd had to kill to save my hide.

I glanced at the four guards. Not one of them was in a position to see the doorway without turning their head, and not one of them seemed to show the slightest interest in what was happening outside, or in the fact that I had removed a boot. I could be grateful for that; still, it was frustrating in the extreme to stand there and not be able to do a damn thing. I felt around with my toes to see if I could extract the knife from the boot lining.

Confound it, I thought. Tor would *never* let me forget this.

And then everything outside seemed to shatter into noise and movement and death. I thought I heard Gilfeather shouting. *Gilfeather?* I looked out at the lake and saw him standing on a raft offshore, and wondered if I was going mad—yet his unruly red hair and the appealing winsomeness of his expression (now marred by the scruffy beginnings of a new beard), were unmistakable. Tor *and* Gilfeather?

The Plainsman seemed to be calling Domino a stumplegged tosspot, or something equally tactful. Domino, predictably, was furious and had the dunmagickers throw some destructive magic at him. It couldn't hurt Kelwyn, or I didn't *think* it would, but what it could do to the raft would be another matter. Oh, charnels, I thought. Gilfeather, you fireheaded cretin, *get out of there!*

By this time, of course, the noise had alerted those guarding me that there was some kind of trouble outside. They looked at one another doubtfully, obviously wondering if they should abandon their guard posts to see what was going on. Then one of them saw the dead man lying in the doorway and started forward.

"Great," I told him, and grinned ferociously. "That's what I

like to see. Leave me alone in here, why don't you, and see if
I'm still here when you come back." Anything to stop them
joining the fray outside.

The man halted and looked back uncertainly at the others.

Dek chose that moment to hurtle into the shed. He was
coming out of the glaring sun into the dark, and he belted
straight into the sylv and sent him flying.

I yelled, "Quick, Dek, my sword—right in front of your
nose."

Dek, bless him, grabbed the sword. The sylv grabbed his
arm. Dek did the only thing he could think of: he tossed the
weapon to me, but he had forgotten that I had my arms tied
behind my back. The sword whacked me on the thigh and fell
to the ground. It had not done any damage, but it remained at
my feet, useless. The other sylvs came forward to pin Dek
down. At least they weren't going outside to give Tor still
more opposition. If it was Tor. I hadn't actually *seen* him, but I
could hear the clash of sword blades outside now. And
screaming. Someone was wounded and he wasn't taking it
well. A blast of dunmagic hit the shed wall; boards shuddered
and cracked.

While all this was happening, I felt around the floor for the
string attached to the sword, and blessed the fact that I now
had one bare foot. Meantime, Dek went on struggling, which
was good, because it kept the sylvs occupied and no one noticed my acrobatics. More dunmagic whizzed, into the shed
this time, to blossom out on the back wall like a bunch of full-
blown red roses. Part of the wall gave way and wisps of smoke
played around the hole. The sylvs took no notice; they were
busy pummeling Dek. Dek yelled.

I curled my toes around the string and passed it up to my
fingers. I gathered it in, pulling up the sword so that I could lift
it into my hands. As I did so, I saw what was happening outside and it didn't seem to make sense. The expanse of water
that was clear of floating pandana was full of swimming gray
shapes churning up the lake. Many of them were already in the
shallows. *Monsters?* But I didn't have time to consider that.

I now gripped the sword by the hilt. But I still couldn't cut
the rope that tied my hands . . . In the end I swung the sword
so that it was pointing at the roof, and let the blade slide, very

carefully, through my fingers until the hilt was on the floor and I had hold of the blade near the tip. I took a small step forward as far as the noose would allow, and I was able to slip the tip between my wrists. Then I pushed down, sliding the rope along the blade. I jabbed one wrist with the sword tip, and slashed the other with the sword edge, but the rope parted. The weapon fell to the floor again, but I still held the attached string. It was the work of a moment to get the hilt into my hand again.

At that exact moment, Domino came charging in, bypassing the fighting outside. He didn't carry a sword; he was used to being protected by others. But he did have a knife. Perhaps his idea was to make sure I died, no matter what. Perhaps his intention was to use me as a hostage to stop Tor's rampage outside. That was still going on, I could tell: I could hear the clash of blades, and someone gasping. He was quite a fighter, Tor. I knew that from my Calment days, not to mention from a certain fray in the taproom of The Drunken Plaice back in Gorthan Docks.

The smell of dunmagic was suffocating and the red glow of it filtered into the shed. Domino lunged toward me just as I swung my sword up. I managed to point it in the right direction, and that was all. In the dimness of the shed, I don't think he even saw it until it was too late. To the surprise of us both, he ran onto the blade like meat onto a skewer. The expression on his face was worth a lot to me. Unfortunately, the force of his onrush sent me reeling back. The rope around my neck tightened and I choked. I lowered the sword and Domino collapsed, sliding away from the blade. For a moment he knelt, looking up at me in disbelief. Then horror. His hands went to his stomach to feel the gush of blood there, and then he crumpled at my feet, screaming. I raised the sword, spraying his blood across my face and neck, and slashed the rope above my head.

I eased the slip knot even as I ran to Dek. Somehow or other he had managed to keep three sylvs fully occupied with his struggles, but he had been badly beaten with their fists. For some reason, they had not used their swords on the boy, perhaps because they knew Domino had him marked for another kind of death. I came up behind the first man and cut his throat from behind before he even knew what happened. He already had a stab wound in the chest. I pulled Selmarian off and plunged my sword into the other man. Dek was a mess, but he sat up, groping for his knife. The woman then came at me without giving sufficient thought to what was happening, and I slashed off her hand. I noted with surprise that the fourth sylv—the one Dek had sent flying when he entered the shed— was still lying against the wall, doubled up but trying to get back on his feet. It was then that I realized that not much time had passed from when Dek had come to rescue me. It had just *felt* like an age.

When the winded man finally uncurled enough to stand, I kicked him, hard, in the stomach. He collapsed yet again. Selmarian started to wail but I ignored her.

"Dek," I said, "take care of this lot, will you? And be careful, lad." I ran for the door.

I didn't understand much of what I saw when I got there. It was like a scene from your worst nightmare: fighting, blood, screaming, dunmagic, and a clawing mass of gray creatures. Kelwyn Gilfeather was pounding up the beach toward me. His raft was pushed up onto the sand, although I felt that was inexplicable. How had he managed to get ashore so quickly? But I had no time to think about that. I looked around for Tor. He was to the left of the shed door, and he was just going down under a mass of people. I waded in, sure he was being stabbed to death in front of my eyes. I slashed downward with my blade, I flung people away bodily. For a while I seemed to go berserk, wielding my sword and roaring my anger. I was close to panic, not thinking too well, and putting myself in danger by turning my back on those behind me. I didn't care. Vaguely I was aware that there was someone helping me. Then several people. And someone was speaking in my ear, saying things that soothed, that seemed to make sense.

In far too short a time to be possible, everything seemed to be over. Tor was on the ground, lying on his back, looking up at me, and we were in a cleared circle. My sword was dripping blood, and there seemed to be dead sylvs everywhere. I certainly had not killed that many people—had I? Besides, some seemed to have had their throats torn out and others were badly clawed. Several slaves lay on the ground unmarked, as if they had just been knocked unconscious. Seeker pawed at me, wagging his tail and dripping blood from his jaws. Oh, sea-slugs, *he* hadn't chewed up all those people, had he?

"Easy, Blaze," someone said in my ear. "Dinna fret, lass. It's over now." Kelwyn Gilfeather. There was something extraordinarily calming in being called a "lass." But what in all the soulless hells was he doing here anyway?

I looked up, taking everything in, but without understanding. We were surrounded, not by people, but by ghemphs. *Ghemphs*. Naked ghemphs at that, which is why I had not at first recognized them for what they were. Nothing made sense. I gave up trying to understand, dropped my sword, and knelt at Tor's side. He was alive. I took his hand and he squeezed it, but he didn't seem able to speak.

Kelwyn knelt on the other side and started to examine him. Without looking up he said, "Someone get my physician's bag from the raft." His voice radiated the confidence of a man used to being obeyed. I blinked. *Gilfeather?* Here?

Tor spoke then, in a hoarse whisper. "Fetching necklace, m'dear. What did you do first, hang yourself or slit your wrists?"

I looked down. I was still wearing the noose around my neck. I ripped it off and flung it away. Right then I wasn't too bothered about the wrists; they were still bleeding, but not badly.

Tor switched his attention to Kelwyn. "You were supposed to go after Flame."

Limpets and lobsters, I thought, the two of them came here *together*. I couldn't even begin to think of an explanation for that.

The Plainsman said, rather absently I thought, "I will, dinna fret. Ruarth's tracking her at the moment." Right then he was far more worried about Tor, I could see. "Don't move and don't chat." He looked up at the ghemphs and pointed at those closest to us. "You three: get some water boiled. And I want some alcohol and a clean scalded basin or bucket or something. I want the table in one of the kitchens in those houses scrubbed spotless and scalded. Some of you others, check on the lad in the shed. And get those five sylvs who were guarding the village up there somewhere and the four

who are out on the lake, but *dinna,* for pity's sake, kill them.
We may have need of them."

His bag appeared, brought by a ghemph, and in a remarkably short time and with an economy of words, he seemed to
have organized a whole beachful of ghemphs into doing
things: burying the bodies, tending to the unconscious slaves,
helping those who were recovering, rounding up the sylvs
who had not been killed. And all the while that he was dis-
pensing advice and giving orders, he was also attending to
Tor. The patriarch had been slashed and stabbed, several
times. He had lost a lot of blood and was drifting in and out of
consciousness.

I was superfluous. Gilfeather, in his element for once, had
everything under control. I couldn't bear to watch. I stumbled
to my feet and went to the shed to see if Dek was all right.

The double doors had been pushed wide open to flood the
place with sunlight. Dek was sitting up with his back to the
wall and one of the ghemphs was dabbing at his face with a
wet cloth. He looked awful: both eyes were swollen; his lip
was split; one of his front teeth was chipped and loose in his
mouth; his nose was broken and by the way he winced when
he moved I suspected several of his ribs were cracked as well.
I looked around to find that all the sylvs, including Selmarian
and the man I had kicked, appeared to be dead. Domino
groaned, rolling around as he clutched his stomach. Stomach
wounds are, I'm told, excruciatingly painful. The ghemphs
were already carting away the bodies, but none of them took
any notice of Domino.

Dek's face lit up when he saw me, which was no mean feat,
seeing he was so battered. "Oh, y'are all ri'! They said
y'were, but I couldn't belief it! Wh'about Kel?" He touched
his split lip cautiously and spat some blood out of his mouth.

"He's fine. Unhurt. What happened in here? Did you kill
the two I left alive?"

"The man, well, yeah, I did. Y'don't mind, d'you? At first,
I tried just throwin' th'weapons out th'door. You wanna'd me
to take care of things, but 'twas sorta hard t'kill them like
tha'—ouch, tha' hurts!" He pulled a face at the ghemph, who
just smiled and went on treating his wounds. "Then, when he
tried to whup me wi' th'pandana, I stabbed 'im." Some of his

enthusiasm ebbed away. "I don't thin' I like killin' people very mu', even when they d'serve it. But if I'm gunna be a dunhunter, then I will've to learn to—t'cope, won't I?"

I nodded. "I'll let you in on a secret, Dek. I don't much like killing people either, not even when they are trying to kill me. And especially not when they were once sylvs." I smiled at him. "I'm glad you don't like it much. People who enjoy it are usually not much different to dunmagickers at heart. What happened to the sylv woman?"

The ghemph—he had wrinkles which made him old enough to be male, so I thought of him that way—answered that one. He said, "She's dead too. We did that."

"I thought, um . . . I thought ghemphs weren't supposed to harm humans."

"We of Eylsa's pod will tolerate dunmagickers no longer. We do not feel that dunmagickers are human, or in fact worthy of life. They are a sickness, a scourge." He nodded at Domino. "I'll get to him in a minute too. I thought you might want to question him first.

I shook my head. "You knew Eylsa?" I asked.

He nodded. "She was my pod-sister. All of us here were pod-siblings." He sat back on his heels and smiled once more at Dek. "That tooth of yours needs fixing. And you had better see the physician later. Your ribs need binding." He turned to me. "Could I—may I see the bouget Eylsa made for you?"

I showed him my palm.

He ran his finger over the gold, tracing the curly M shape. "Do you know what it means?" he asked.

"Eylsa said it was the mark of your people."

"In a way. It is the mark of our pod. It means that you are to be treated as one of us. The line through it: that means that one of us died for you. But in our culture that alone has a strong meaning. It says that if we allow you to die before your time, then we are scorning her death, belittling it. To make *her* death meaningful, we must preserve *your* life."

Dek said, "Tha's gawp-makin'!"

I looked at the ghemph, half appalled, half in wonderment. "You mean, you mean—you are all here because of *me*?"

He laughed—at least I think it was a laugh—as if any other notion was absurd. "Of course!"

I absorbed that, humbled. Finally I said, "You saved our lives. All of us—we would have died without help. Where did you all come from?"

"Well, from all over Mekaté. Our pod is scattered, and the others couldn't get here in time. So our pod-sister, Emiliassa, the one you met in Mekatéhaven, she just called those of us who were closest."

"Called?" I was thoroughly confused by now.

He nodded. "Called through the sea. Our songs carry."

I thought about that. The webbed feet. The eerie whistled sounds we'd heard in the Mere. The gray shapes in the water. The thing that had bumped against Flame and me . . . it had been trying to save us from cutting ourselves to pieces on the pandana.

Because we always saw ghemphs dressed and behaving like humans, we never thought of them as creatures of the water. "You swim," I said inanely. "But we never see you swimming . . ."

"We always live by the sea or a river. We swim in the dark when we cannot be seen. Come morning, you will find us home in our beds."

"Emiliassa: what did her song say?"

"That we should follow you. To keep you safe. For you had become our pod-sister, and you were hunting the dunmaster who killed our kind."

"Emiliassa's here?"

"Yes, indeed. I myself come from Ezun Island. We knew you were heading here, and that it was here that you might require our help. So we swam to the south, and came up the Kilgair Slug from Port Rattéspie, to await you in the Floating Mere."

"Crabdamn," I muttered. "I don't know what to say."

"Learn from us. When you have nothing to say, say nothing."

He leaned across to Dek, who had been listening openmouthed. "Lad, you will not speak of what you have heard from me this day. Nor will you tell of what happened here, at least not about the part my people played."

Dek's eyes shone. "No, won't, I swear. On m'honor, truly."

The ghemph made a noise that may have been a laugh. "I'll gift you something to remind you to keep that promise. Close your eyes and open your mouth."

Dek, overawed, did as he was told. The ghemph lifted his leg and placed a claw against Dek's broken tooth. The lad winced and then was still. Something liquid poured down the hollow groove of the claw. When the ghemph withdrew his foot, Dek had a gleaming gold-colored tooth. Gingerly he ran his tongue over it.

"Blaze?"

I looked up. Gilfeather was standing in the doorway. "I've had Tor taken to one of the houses."

I stood, shocked to realize how weak I felt. "Can you save him?" I asked, and dreaded to hear the reply.

He was silent.

"Please," I said, begging. "There must be a way. There must."

His face looked ravaged as he turned away, and he ran a hand through his rumpled hair. "It would take this magic ye speak of," he said. "Sylv healing. I've done all I can, and it's not enough, lass."

I stared at him dumbly. Then I walked over to Domino where he still lay on the floor, groaning. He looked up at me, terrified, and was silenced by what he saw in my face. I placed the tip of my blade against his eye and drove it in as hard and as far as I could.

Tor was Aware, and the Aware were impervious to magic. All magic, including sylv healing.

CHAPTER 23

NARRATOR: KELWYN

WHEN THE GHEMPH HEAVED ITSELF UP onto the raft, I died a thousand deaths before I knew it for what it was. My fear—for Blaze, for Tor, as much as for myself—had already stretched my hold on reality to the breaking point. My guilt at leaving them all was hammering at my senses with the ferocity of a tropical midday sun; my integrity, my very core, felt naked, exposed, ripe for destruction. In that state, my overactive imagination turned the ghemph into half a dozen things: all of them some kind of monster that lurked deep in lakes, a deserved nemesis for my faithless hide . . .

And then, once I recognized them for what they were, and realized that there must have been fifty or more of the creatures around, I found trouble believing it, just as I found it hard to believe that I might have a future after all.

"Is Blaze in trouble?" the ghemph asked politely, as a shower of arrows bypassed us to land in the water behind. If visible emotion was a guide, then we could have been sitting in some cozy eating house, sharing a jug of mead and some idle conversation. I smelled nothing of him.

I huddled on the floor of the raft and blinked, tried to reduce my fear down to something I could handle. For a brief moment I did consider asking questions like: Why do you ask? But knew I was being absurd. Whatever the reason, they were not here to hurt Blaze. I swallowed and said, pointing back at the beach, "Aye, she's in trouble. She's in that shed. The big building." Hope lurched and I hurriedly added more information, just in case they were going to help. "The man in black is trying to save her. And there's a boy in trouble too. A lad of about fourteen or so."

Two arrows hit the raft, one of them so close it tore the shoulder of my tunic in passing. I flattened myself still further, like a frightened puppy trying to pretend it wasn't there.

The ghemph dropped back into the water and out of sight. And then I heard that eerie sort of whistled tune again, only this time it was close enough to make me rub the back of my neck as the hairs rose up. Sweet Creation, I thought, that's how they communicate underwater. They *sing* to one another. And the scientist in me was shocked once again at how little we knew about these creatures with whom we shared our islandoms and whose skills we used so thoughtlessly to enforce our stupidities.

Within seconds there was an upsurge in the sound, a vibration that rippled the surface of the lake, coming from all directions. Just as I had decided I would be safer in the water, the raft started moving, fast. It was being pushed, almost lifted so that it skimmed toward the shore, far quicker than I could ever have paddled it. Cautiously I raised my head. The dunmagickers who had been throwing their so-called magic at me, the subverted sylvs who had wanted to follow me by boat, those who had shot the arrows—they were all standing on the beach, open mouthed in their consternation. Then, one by one, they retreated up the sand. I sat up, a little braver after that. I was still shaking with reaction, though, wondering if I was going to live through this. If any of us would.

Just before the raft hit the beach, Ruarth flew up. We were traveling so fast he had trouble landing. "Ghemphs," I croaked unnecessarily. "I think they've come to help. Ruarth, ye've got to go after Flame. I'll follow. As soon as I can, I promise."

He stared at me, head cocked, his blue eye accusing. And

then, without a word, he lifted off and was gone. The raft hit the shore and I sprawled flat again.

I tumbled out and looked about me. The sand between the water's edge and the shed was a chaotic mass of fighting bodies. There were ghemphs everywhere and their mode of attack was brutal, if effective. They banded into groups of two or three, jumped their targeted sylv and brought him to the ground. Once there, several of them held their victim down while another ripped the sylv's throat out with the claws on his feet. Red stains appeared on the sand, uniting from single splotches into spreading streams. I didn't know what was worse: seeing people die like that, or knowing that it was ghemphs, normally such gentle, kindly creatures, who did it. We had been brought up to believe that ghemphs never hurt anyone, and this systematic slaughter was like having a bevy of field mice tear down a pride of grass-lions.

I hesitated briefly, scanning the scene for Blaze. When I saw her emerge from the shed, apparently in one piece, I felt some of the tension across my shoulders ease. And then I saw Tor. He was being attacked by the four or five sylvs still alive, and some slaves as well. So focused were they on bringing the Stragglerman down, that none of them seemed to have noticed the slaughter behind them on the beach. I pounded up toward him, even though I was unarmed and had not even thought to bring the paddle with me. By the time I arrived, though, Blaze had swept into the group, and then through it, with all the immediate effectiveness of a burning brand thrust in straw. It was frightening to watch; she was caught up in a fighting frenzy, ready to take on anyone, kill anything. She was in danger of beheading the ghemphs who had come to her aid, not to mention me and anyone else who unwisely came within range.

I approached cautiously. "Blaze," I said softly, "easy now. Put your blade down . . . It's me, Gilfeather—y'know, the red-headed, cabbage-munching peacemonger . . ." I risked putting a hand on her shoulder and she turned to look at me. "Easy, Blaze. Dinna fret, lass. It's over now." The horrible killing light faded from her eyes and her shoulders slumped. When my nose told me she was all right, I dropped to Tor's side and began looking at his wounds, sniffing out the damage. He was still alive and conscious, but right then that was about the only good thing that could be said about his condition. I pushed away thoughts of all else and, even though I smelled death in him, began to do all I must to give him a chance.

By this time, one of the ghemphs had brought me my physician's bag, and I was able to stop the worst of his bleeding. Then I happened to catch sight of Blaze's face as she knelt on the other side of Ryder. If I had needed confirmation that he was the man she'd once cared for, I had it then. Her feelings were raw and undisguised. She stood up and walked away, her pain contained once more.

When I had stabilized Ryder as best I could, I asked the ghemphs to help me carry him to one of the houses, where we laid him on a kitchen table. There, I put a straw into his forearm vein and started to drip in selver ichor, after heating it slightly in warm water. I gave him some painmask, then cleaned and stitched some of the wounds, spreading them with a Plains concoction that stopped infection. The worst, I left till last. He had been stabbed in the abdomen, and the thrust had pierced his intestines. I could smell it, and knew what it portended. It was just possible—not likely, but possible—that had we been back on the Sky Plains, with my father and brother assisting, with Garrowyn's pharmacopoeia and a major operation, we might have been able to save him. As it was, there was only me. I had few of the necessary instruments, none of the help and none of the medications I needed. I left the wound as it was, and went to find Blaze.

She asked me, of course, if he would live. When I told her it would take sylv healing, the aroma that came from her was heartbreaking enough to stop words in my throat. And my own reaction shamed me; I had no right to feel the way I did then. She nodded, and then walked over to Domino and killed him with a sword thrust into his brain through the eye. Without any outward display of emotion, she drew the blade out and wiped it clean, I watched, shocked by the cold in her. Then she turned to me, asking where Tor was.

"He's not going to die any time soon," I said. "And ye won't help him if your cuts are infected. Let me take a look at your wrists."

Under protest she let me bandage them, then she helped me strap up Dek's broken ribs. "He was brave," she told me as we worked. "He saved my life. If it hadn't been for Dek, Domino would have killed me while I stood there absolutely helpless." She smiled at the lad. "Rushing in here the way you did, throwing me my sword—that was one of the bravest things I've ever seen anyone do. Thank you, Dekan Grinpindillie!" The boy swelled with pride, and I wondered at her ability to ignore her own despair and praise the boy. I laughed and teased him, and then we left him there to rest while I took Blaze to see Tor.

"And you," she said as we walked across that blood-soaked ground to the houses. "If you didn't want to be disappointed in me, then you shouldn't have made me into what I am not."

I turned toward her, startled. "What are ye talking about?"

"The expression on your face when I killed Domino. I'm a swordswoman, Gilfeather. I kill people."

"Domino was not threatening ye."

"Not this time," she said grimly. "But he tortured me once, remember? And he tried to castrate Tor and rip his tongue out. He was going to whip me and Dek to death."

I said slowly, "It wasna that ye *killed* him. It was that ye did it with—with so little emotion."

"Trench damn it, Kel, I save my emotions for people who matter. Would you like me any better if I'd done it with *joy*? That'd make me a monster!"

I was silent.

"Tell me, what made you follow us here? You are supposed to be a Sky Plains peacemonger, remember?"

"I had naught better to do."

She raised a scathing eyebrow. She could do more with one eyebrow than most people could do with a whole gamut of facial expressions.

"I started to worry about . . . all of you. And about the threat of dunmagic. I couldn't—I couldn't bear the thought of it."

"You're a damn fool, Gilfeather. Standing out there on the lake, a target for arrows and dunmagic, shouting rude things at Domino. Are you mad, you bushy-chinned bonesetter? Have you stuffed your head with selver wool? Did I *really* hear you call him a bearded barnacle?"

I blushed. She laughed. But there was tragedy there, in that laugh, and the humor did not reach her eyes. Just as we were about to enter the kitchen where Tor was, she laid her hand on my arm. "Thanks, Kelwyn. If you hadn't done what you did, I would be dead, and so would Dek and Tor. You gave us the time we needed. For a peacemonger, you didn't do too badly at all."

Tongue-tied, I waved her wordlessly into the kitchen ahead of me.

The ghemphs, who had gathered there to keep an eye on Tor while I was gone, retreated to the next room. I peeled back the sheet I had placed over him, and showed her his wounds. "This is the only one I canna mend," I said, indicating the abdominal cut. "A blade went in here and, although it has not severed any major blood vessels, it has pierced the intestines in several places."

"You can tell that?"

I nodded.

"Your nose?"

I nodded again.

"What does all that *mean*?"

"It means his body is contaminated by the contents of his gut. There will be a septic reaction, and he will die. Painfully. Although I will do my best to control that. The pain, I mean."

She took Tor's hand in her own, but he didn't respond. "He's unconscious?"

"It may be the painmask. I gave him a hefty dose."

She looked across his body at me. "He came back for me."

I shook my head. "I dinna think that's true. He was sent back."

She digested that. "By the Menod . . . because of Flame."

"And Morthred, aye."

She was wryly disappointed, but not surprised. "Damn you, Gilfeather," she said, "you enjoyed telling me that, didn't you?"

"Ye deserved it," I said, "trying to make his wounds all your fault." I indicated his abdomen. "Could sylvmagic heal this kind of wound?"

She nodded. "Probably, on an ordinary person. Especially if there were several sylvs, and if they wanted to. But Tor's not ordinary. He's Aware."

"Dek and Flame said something once about sylvs healing one of the Awarefolk."

"A tale, Kel. Good theater for an itinerant storyteller."

"Maybe. But it fits with a theory I have."

"A *theory*? Confound it, Gilfeather, are you still pounding this idea of yours that magic doesn't exist? What will it *take* to convince you? A hundred Morthreds shooting scarlet from Cirkase to Porth and withering every leaf in the forests between?"

I winced and blundered on. "I know it exists. I just think it is a disease. And that the Aware have immunity, just as a person gets immunity from the six-day fever if they had fish-spot fever as a child."

She folded her arms. "And all the dun that got thrown about out there during the fight—dun that almost demolished your raft and the shed, I might add—that's a disease?"

I was silent. I had no answer to that.

"Well?"

"I don't understand everything yet . . . but I still think it's a disease."

Her scorn now mingled with the tangy aroma of reluctant interest. "So how does that change anything?"

"Sometimes immunity can be overcome by the sheer . . . *weight* of the disease. By the amount of infection a person is exposed to. Just like that Syr-aware fellow on the Cirkasian island that Dek spoke of. Similar to the way that Flame's sylv-magic was not enough to withstand Morthred's dun."

"You mean, if we expose Tor to every sylv healer we can find, he may be cured?"

It sounded silly when she put it like that. I glanced at Tor, rather than meet her eyes. "It's possible," I mumbled. "If ye are right in the first place that there is such a thing as sylv healing." I indicated his abdomen. "We could concentrate it all on this one area."

"Even if it was true, we don't have any sylvs. This is a Menod area, and people don't believe in using sylvpower even if they have it."

Mackie had used it, but I didn't pursue that thought. Instead I said, "We have twelve subverted sylvs still alive. Three mildly wounded ones, five who were guarding the settlement on the other side, and four who were guarding the lake in boats. They were all Keeper sylvs, some of them worked for the Keeper Council, so they at least must have been strong sylvs once. Blaze . . ." I took a deep breath, and risked her scorn on the basis of little evidence. "It's my belief that sylv and dunmagic is the same disease; it's just that one has progressed further than the other along a continuum . . . which would explain what you told me once about the color of that sylv woman's placenta. A concentration of sylv begins to look like dun." I paused, then added, "We could try to get these ex-sylvs to heal him."

"They are dunmagickers now, not sylvs." She sounded like a teacher trying to be patient with a particularly stupid child.

"Aye, but what if they could still heal?"

"Dunmagickers can't heal." Then she hesitated. "Although, Morthred did seem to hint that Duthrick's sylvs had healed him. I assumed that was before they were fully subverted."

"My theory is even more . . . startling. I believe that full-scale dunmagickers, even ones who were never sylvs, can probably heal. After all, they do heal themselves, do they not? Even Morthred was gradually healing himself of the backlash from the Dustel Islands sinking, or so ye once told me."

She nodded, obviously mentally kicking herself for never having thought of the implications of that.

"Blaze, dunmagickers dinna normally heal others because they dinna *want* to heal others, not because they *can't*. They dinna use sylv to do it either, of course. They use dun."

She stared at me, hope and disbelief warring. "Are you *sure* you know what you are talking about?" Blaze, as blunt as ever.

"No. It's only a theory, and I could be wrong."

"Do you even *believe* in sylv healing? You're thinking of it as a disease!"

"I dinna think I am certain of anything anymore. One thing, though, the human mind is remarkable. And sometimes, well, even up on the Sky Plains, without a sylv in sight, I have seen people come back from Creation's pathway because they had the determination to do so. The Menod would call such recoveries miracles, I suppose, born of God's will. I am a physician. I say it's something more prosaic and yet just as miraculous: the human will. Maybe the mind of a sylv or dun-magicker has a power I know naught about." I had seen what they had done to my raft with the power of their minds. I hesitated. "Ryder has naught to lose." And I pushed the other thought away: *but others might . . .* "Normally one of the Aware would automatically resist a dun attack, by using their own immunity to do so. But Ryder will be unconscious. That will probably make it easier too."

"How can we persuade dunmagickers to heal when they don't want to?"

"We have to give them something they desperately want in return."

"Which is?"

"Life. They are prisoners of the ghemphs. They have seen what the ghemphs wrought here, I made sure of that. They now know that their magic has no effect on ghemphs. They know they canna escape and they know they will die with their throats torn out. It is only my request that is holding the ghemphs back."

"We could promise they would go free after healing Ryder, but they wouldn't believe it."

"They would if the ghemphs promised it. Ghemphs never break a promise."

"The ghemphs wouldn't promise that! They seem to have taken a stand against dunmagickers. Because of Eylsa."

"They would do it if Blaze Halfbreed asked it of them."

She stood there, looking at me, holding my gaze. Between us, Tor lay breathing raggedly, his muscled body a reminder of all that was beautiful in Creation. "You would let *twelve* dunmagickers loose on the world to save one man?" she asked in little more than a whisper. "A man you can scarcely know? Do you *really* understand the damage that such evil corruptions of humanity can do to the world?"

"Aye. At least I can guess now, after today. Dinna forget, I can smell them. And evil has its own reek." I remembered Ginna. "Aye, I understand."

"Letting such people free to kill and corrupt is not the mark of a good physician. Or a good—a good anything."

"*Ye* would do it," I said.

"I would do it for him," she agreed. "But I have loved him. And I'm not a fine upstanding citizen of an islandom, with hefty slices of honor chiseled into me by my early upbringing.

You, on the other hand, are a physician who won't even kill animals to eat! Why would you let loose such a scourge on the world?"

She genuinely didn't know. I could scent her puzzlement, her desire to understand. I hesitated to tell her, not wanting to change anything between us. I looked away, ashamed, knowing my weakness, knowing what I was about to do was morally wrong. Men like these ex-sylvs should never be able to walk the earth to bring their brand of hell to others. "Just let's say that I have my reasons. Tor Ryder is a fine man who will do much good in his life, if he is allowed to live it." A rationalization, that: such that men make when they commit great wrongs for good reasons.

In my heart, I didn't even know if my reason was a good one, or an unselfish one. I did know, and I know it to this day, that it was wrong. And we all paid for it. I with my conscience, Blaze with the loss of a friend, and Tor—well, Tor lost the most of us all. He lost his integrity. He lost himself.

I HAD SPOKEN CONFIDENTLY ENOUGH TO Blaze, but within my thoughts, I was not nearly as sanguine about my plan's chances of success. Perhaps I was wrong about the possibility of dunmagickers healing others in the first place. Perhaps the subverted sylvs might prefer to die than save one of the Menod. Perhaps they may not trust the ghemphs anymore; after all, the creatures had just killed as many ex-sylvs as they could put their claws into, rather nastily ripping their throats out. Not, I suppose, that there are too many nice ways to die in a battle.

But the twelve sylvs, like us all, had been brought up believing in ghemphic honesty and the concept that ghemphs could not lie, so they were prepared to believe in their integrity now. I suppose the fact that dunmagic robbed subverted sylvs of so much of their sharpness and critical faculties may also have had something to do with their acceptance of the proposal. The agreement was that they were to try to heal Tor, with Blaze and me watching to make sure that they didn't also seed him with a dunmagic sore. Blaze thought she'd be able to tell the difference between their healing power and their killing power: I hoped she was right. After that, as part of the bargain—and only if they had managed to heal the Stragglerman—Blaze, Dek, Tor and I were to leave the island. Ghemphs would escort us down the Kilgair Slug to the coast, which would give the ex-sylvs a chance to escape and go where they would.

We already knew that Morthred had gone that way too; the subverted sylvs made no secret of his destination. He had a ship in Port Rattéspie, which was the town at the mouth of the Slug.

It was hard to be in the same room with these twelve subverted sylvs. I had never had anything to do with ordinary sylvs, with the exception of Flame. I'd certainly never met a subverted one until I was called in to treat Ginna back in Amkabraig. The dun in Ginna had taken its physical toll on me, but this was much, much worse. Blaze had told me often enough that the Aware could smell dunmagic, and that it had a foul odor, but I don't think she had any understanding of what dunmagic stank like to me. The reek was so strong I kept wanting to gag, to run from the room. My hands shook, so I kept them clasped behind my back. I could scarcely think straight, my head pounded, my heart raced.

It wasn't that they smelled like a long-dead selver baking in the sun, or a leaking latrine in Lekenbraig; it was more than that. It was more akin to the smell of a lethal tumor, or a wasting lung disease—not the toll those illnesses take on the body, but the disease itself. It was just plain . . . wrong. It should never have been.

And I was acquiescing in the release of these walking cesspits of disease, knowing that they would spread their contagion. I was supposed to be a physician who healed, but there was something within me that told me I should have killed these men and women, just as I should cut out a tumor or kill an infection with medication.

One of them grinned at my open revulsion. "How does it feel, herder?" he said softly in my ear as we were about to begin. "How does it feel to make bargains with those you despise? Whatever happens here, you lose—and we win." He smiled at me, a malicious expression of his enjoyment of the situation.

I knew he was right, and I felt besmirched.

They stayed with Tor for five hours. At first it seemed they were uncertain that they could heal him, although they all admitted that they could heal themselves. They each laid a finger on his abdomen, encircling his wound, while they appeared to do no more than concentrate. Most of the time he was unconscious, although occasionally he moaned and thrashed about on the kitchen table. The dun smell was everywhere.

There were no problems, but none of it sat easily with me; ironic, considering it was my idea in the first place. It was hard to believe that something good could come out of evil. Ironic, too, that I—the careful scientist—should be recommending a treatment that appeared to have no basis in reality. My mind felt as confused and sick as my body. Was I mist-mad?

For the first hour, none of us was sure that anything was happening, but then we all noticed the beginnings of a difference. Tor's color improved. The smell of a perforated gut diminished, and then finally vanished. I could smell no taint of it remaining, not even deep inside him. The stomach wound no longer looked fresh; it had more the appearance of a cut that was several days old and on the way to healing. It all smelled of dun, of course. I hoped that would wear off in time, or I wouldn't want to be spending my days with the patriarch.

By the time it was all over, it was nightfall, and I was so weak I could scarcely stand. The ghemphs took the sylvs away and closeted them under close guard in one of the other houses. I asked the slaves to prepare us a meal. The bread I'd had that morning in the raft was only a memory and, freed from the proximity of dun, I ate hungrily. There was nothing on my plate that was overtly flesh-related, so for once I didn't even ask what it was I was eating. I simply didn't care.

We had promised the ex-sylvs that we would leave that evening, but I wanted to give Tor as much time as possible to recover. He was awake now, but weak. The abdominal injury smelled fine, except for a lingering whiff of dun, and, better still, even the other wounds seemed to have been improved by the spillover of power. Faced with that evidence, it was hard to remain skeptical.

"What do you think?" Blaze asked me quietly. She had

been sitting at his side, holding his hand, but she followed me out when I left the room.

I shrugged. "I don't know. Ye have more experience than I with sylv healing. I dinna even believe in it, remember?"

She grunted. "You're a fine man, Gilfeather, but you think too much."

I waved a hand at the room we had just left. "So does he."

She cocked her head and regarded me thoughtfully. "You are trying to tell me something: spit it out."

"He will not forgive ye if ye tell him what bargain we made to save him. He's a verra upright man, Blaze. He would never countenance buying his own life with the granting of freedom to twelve new dunmagickers." Tor had not always been honest with me, but I could sense that much about him.

"He was willing enough to turn his back on dunmagickers and go to Tenkor from the Spit. How is this any different?"

"It's *personal.* Believe me, he won't like it. Dinna tell him."

She threw up her hands. "Great Trench below, but you sanctimonious bastards are hard to deal with! All right, so I won't tell him." She turned to go back into the room, then changed her mind and came back to me. She took hold of my shirt in both hands, pulled me toward her and kissed me gently on the cheek. "I don't really think you are sanctimonious. Or a bastard. Thank you, Kel. I know how much this has cost you."

But she didn't, not really. She didn't have the slightest idea.

CHAPTER 24

NARRATOR: KELWYN

WE STARTED ACROSS THE FLOATING MERE at about midnight. Both moons were just slivers of light, but fortunately the constellation we call Pitaird's Armada was at its brightest. By the sheen of starlight, we had made Tor as comfortable as possible in one boat with me to keep an eye on him; Dek and Blaze and Seeker were in another one, the craft they had bought in Gillsie. The ghemphs took over then, telling us they would get us to where we wanted to go, which was to Port Rattéspie. When I demurred, trying to be polite, and said we could manage the poling ourselves, the oldest of them replied that, as they had to accompany us to fulfill their pledge to the subverted sylvs, they may as well make themselves useful by getting us there. In truth, I was delighted. I had rarely felt as tired as I did that day. Or as sick.

The old ghemph clung to the side of the boat for a minute as the others began pulling on the painter to move us through the water. "You have done something this day that shames you," he said gently. "So have we."

"Then why did ye lend yourselves to this?" I asked wearily. I was surprised at his comment. At various times during the course of the day, I had spoken to the ghemphs, but I had found it always ended up being a one-way conversation. They listened; then they either did what I suggested, or they didn't. There was never any discussion, nothing that could be called a chat. The only person any of them seemed to want to talk to was Blaze. They treated her with an odd sort of reverence, almost sad, as if by spending time in her company they could bring back the one they had lost. And yet now, here was one of their number showing an inclination to have a philosophical discussion with me.

He seemed almost as tired as I was. I invited him into the boat, but he shook his head, saying he preferred to hitch a ride on the side. "We like the water," he said. "It is our world." Then he answered my original question. "Sometimes you have to take risks. We ghemphs see life differently. We see patterns and make projections. We see troubles ahead for our kind, and so we seek to minimize them. Having this man alive," he indicated Tor "might help us, for he has a generous spirit and much potential. So we made a choice, just as you did. Just as we have chosen to aid Blaze."

"My motives were more—personal," I admitted, all too aware of my guilt. "Less altruistic. And people will die because we chose that he should live."

He nodded soberly. "Yes, I fear you are right. And it won't just be because there are dunmagickers loose in the world. In retrospect, I have the feeling that we did more evil than we knew tonight, Gilfeather. And you will have to learn to live with that. Just as you have learned to live with killing your wife."

I stared at him. "Ye knew about that?" Neither Blaze nor Flame, surely, had told any ghemph the full story of why we'd had to flee Mekatéhaven.

"That you killed your wife? Knowledge is our . . . passion, Plainsman. There is no citizen we do not touch with our claws when we engrave their citizenship tattoo. And what one ghemph knows, we all know in the end. We have touched your blood, and heard you named, Kel Gilfeather of Wyn, and we do not forget."

It wasn't an explanation that really answered my question.

I stared at him and shivered. "Humans underestimate you all, don't they?".

"Indeed," he said. "But we do not endanger humanity. Unless we have good reason, we do not involve ourselves in the affairs of men, and we do not kill lightly." He regarded me with sad gray eyes. "Worse times are coming, I fear, for some men have become too powerful, and others are restless within the confines of their far distant shores. There will be changes. I feel for you, Kelwyn, for you are a good man, and it is in times like these that good men suffer."

With that cheering thought, he released his hold on the boat and vanished into the blackness of the water.

I turned away to look at Tor and found him staring at me.

"Ye heard that?" I asked.

He nodded.

We both stayed silent for what seemed like a long time. I wasn't sure how much he had heard until he asked, "You killed your wife?" He sounded as if he found that hard to believe.

"Aye, I did. If ye want to hear that story, ask Blaze. She was there, more or less."

"Ah." He stirred uneasily, trying to get comfortable. "Are we going after Flame? Where *is* Blaze?"

"Aye, we are, and Blaze is in another boat, just behind us."

With that he seemed to be content. He closed his eyes and drifted off again.

I PEERED OUT OVER THE PROW. FOUR ghemphs swam there, pulling effortlessly on the painter. In the darkness, with their large webbed feet and naked streamlined bodies, they were creatures of the sea or rivers, not landdwelling tattooists. And for a moment I was again appalled at our human ignorance. How could we have lived so long with another race of beings and come to know them so little? We had thought them meek and gentle and rather stupid, but they were none of those things. And they knew so much—they even knew, somehow, that you Kells were coming. You tell us you don't know about them; you even think they don't exist, that they are part of our mythology. Well, they knew about

you. That old ghemph, he even warned me. You were getting
restless within the confines of your shores, he said.

You may not meet a ghemph here in the Glory Isles anymore, but one day, somewhere, you will. For I believe they are
out there still, watching us all. Next time, perhaps, we will be
wiser, and we will learn from them.

I SAT IN THE BOAT THAT NIGHT, AND
wondered how Blaze had managed to establish such a rapport
with Eylsa in the first place—that's me; always wanting to
know why—and decided it was probably because she genuinely lacked prejudice. Having suffered so much during her
own life from the preconceived ideas of others, having been
often dismissed by authority as worthless or dishonest simply
because she was a halfbreed, she did not judge others by ex-
ternals.

As the two boats were maneuvered through the floating islands of the Mere toward the Kilgair Slug, she talked quietly
with several of the ghemphs that swam beside her boat. Dek,
in spite of his broken ribs, slept curled up in the prow like a
contended selver kid. He had proved himself that day, and he
knew it. He had been bursting with pride and excitement after
the fighting was over, but it had taken its toll; now he had
dropped into an exhausted sleep, aided by a sedative I had
slipped into his drink.

For the first hour or so, I sat next to Tor, keeping an eye on
his condition. He napped easily enough, still drugged by the
medications I had given him. When the first bladder of ichor
finished, I replaced it with a second—the only other one I had
brought from Wyn—and the steady drip into his vein continued. After I had rigged up the second bladder, I fell asleep myself, and I did not wake till morning.

WE WERE IN THE RIVER BY FIRST LIGHT.
When I sat up, I saw the banks slipping past only a couple of
arm lengths away. We were sheltered by an overhang of trees,
each so laden with its burden of other plant life, we could
scarcely see the sky. For a Plainsman, used to the open spaces

and vistas of the Roof of Mekaté, it was both beautiful—and claustrophobic.

Ryder was awake. I checked his pulse; he seemed fine. I looked back: the other boat was still behind us.

"How do ye feel?" I asked.

"Better. But—strange."

He went to sit up, but I pressed him back. "Wait till I check your injuries." I peeled back the outer bandages, and gingerly wiped away the poultice from the first of the shallow chest wounds. I almost gaped. Apart from an ugly scar that still looked new and scabbed, it appeared to be healed. I touched it, and then pressed harder. "Does that hurt?" I asked.

He shook his head. "It's itchy, though." He raised himself to take a look. "I was stabbed there," he said. "I remember. A sword blade thrust . . . how come it's so well healed? How long was I unconscious?"

I hedged. "Not long."

I took a look at all the wounds, including the intestinal one. They were all more or less at the same stage of healing.

"I feel fearfully weak," he complained. "What's this stuck into my arm?"

"Well, ye lost a lot of blood. It is a drip of liquid extracted from the blood of selvers and then distilled. We find it efficacious in the treatment of blood loss."

He managed to look both interested and revolted at one and the same time. "Trying to convince me you aren't a hill-country bumpkin by using long words?" he asked.

"Something like that."

"Is the other boat still with us?"

I nodded.

He suddenly realized that we were moving rather faster than the current warranted. He looked over the side and came face to face with a ghemph who was just rising up to the surface to breathe. He sat down again, bemused. "I rather think a lot has happened since I was hurt. But that was only yesterday, wasn't it? Would you mind telling me how it is I have healed so well? Did the ghemphs do this?"

"In a way." I wasn't in the habit of lying, and it was surprisingly difficult to utter the words and look him in the eye. I found myself flushing. I changed the subject in a hurry. "I think it would be better if ye dinna eat solids today. I will give you honey and water."

He stared at me shrewdly, but didn't comment. Suddenly feeling weak, he lay back down again. "You'll have to tell me some time soon why you don't like me, Plainsman."

"Ye're imagining things. I scarcely know you; certainly not well enough to dislike you. In fact, your courage yesterday merits my admiration."

"Is that why you talk to me like a scientific treatise was stuffed up your butt?" he asked amiably.

I flushed still brighter. "Oh shut up, Ryder," I said.

"That's better," he remarked, closing his eyes. Within minutes he was asleep again.

THE COASTAL PORT OF RATTÉSPIE WAS, we were told, usually a bustling place, full of traders. It had auction houses by the dozen, and all the businesses normally associated with a thriving sea trade: chandlers, ropemakers, sailmakers, coopers, shipwrights, carpenters, ratcatchers, oakum pickers, pitch-pot boys, hoopers, brothels, breweries. The auction houses sold the two main products of the Floating Mere, the pandana and the reeds, to dealers from all over the Glory Isles. Pandana ended up as sails for the local Porthian vessels, as well as Xolchastic ships, because flax and hemp for canvas was scarce in those islands. But it was sold much more widely than that because it was also used for matting or for the woven bottoms and backs of chairs (then the latest fashion in The Hub). The reeds, on the other hand, were all exported to Xolchas, which had no trees of any kind, to be made into baskets and paper, or to Breth, where they were used as high-quality thatching.

All this had to be explained to me, because when we arrived in Rattéspie the place was almost deserted of ships and had the appearance of a town that had wearied of commerce to the point of its abolition. There simply appeared to be none: no buying, no selling, no bartering. The reason for all this stagnation, townsfolk later told us, was that the supply of reeds and pandana coming down the Slug had been reduced to almost nothing for the past eight months. Those swamp-brained Mere people, they said, had suddenly become frightened of lake monsters, and were refusing to cut anything that didn't grow within sight of their villages, and that was mostly poor-quality stuff. It wasn't worth sailing a ship all the way from Xolchasbarbican to Rattéspie for rubbish like that. The townsfolk were disgusted with the Floating Mere folk, so much so that a few of their more hot-headed young men had gone up the Slug to cut pandana themselves. They were due back any time.

We hadn't seen them, had we? Four of them. In fact, they were actually rather overdue . . .

BUT I AM GETTING AHEAD OF MYSELF. When we arrived, we were directed to a small jetty some way before the river mouth, just outside of the town. Even before we tied up, all the ghemphs had vanished as if they had never been.

"Where did they go?" I asked Blaze as I secured the painter.

She shrugged, watching Ryder as he clambered gingerly onto the jetty. "Who knows? We won't see them again unless I get into more trouble. Which I assure you, I have no intention of doing. Should you be walking around?" This last was addressed to Ryder.

He grunted in disbelief. "You are constitutionally incapable of keeping *out* of trouble."

"Middens. Left on my own, I am the epitome of sane, rational, skin-saving behavior. It's only when I start mixing with Keepers and Cirkasians, not to mention the Menod, that trouble seems to find me whether I want it or not." He gave a sound that was suspiciously like a snort, which prompted her to add, "And what about your own risk-taking? You are a fine one to talk!"

He ignored that and asked, "And will the ghemphs turn up, miraculously, once you are in trouble again? Just like that?"

"Well, they have told me how to let them know, using this thing on my hand. I have to rub it underwater, in the sea or in a river. Eventually they will come. How long it takes will depend on how far away I am from members of their pod."

"What is this pod stuff?" Dek asked.

"I don't know exactly," Blaze admitted. "Sort of like an extended family, I think. Pod members are all related in some way. Dek, I want you to stay here and watch our boats and our gear. I'll leave Seeker with you. Can you do that?"

"I'd do a better job if I had a sword," he grumbled.

"Not with your ribs broken," I told him. "Your knife will do nicely."

"And try not to stick anyone with it. We aren't seeking trouble," Blaze added, looking him over critically. He had two black eyes and his nose was the size of a melon. "Although your face looks such a fright, I imagine most villains would take one look and run anyway."

Her banter was just a cover, of course. I could smell her worry, she reeked of it, and that was unusual in Blaze. She normally kept herself a lot better contained than that. "Tor, you had better stay with Dek—"

"I'm fine," he said. "A little weak, but I can walk." He sounded snappish, as if he resented her asking.

For a moment I thought she would protest, but in the end she just looked across at me and said quietly, "You can't smell her, can you?"

"I—I'm not sure. I think she was here. Perhaps she still is. It's just that—she doesna smell the way she did." It was hard to tell her, hard to acknowledge even to myself, but Flame was smelling more and more like a dunmagicker as time went by, the change occurring much faster than I had anticipated.

"And Ruarth?"

I shook my head. "Impossible to say. I can't get anything more than the faintest of traces. I dinna think he's here any more."

When we'd left the Mere, I'd thought that there was a good chance we would find Flame without too much trouble. We weren't that far behind, and we'd had ghemphic help to speed us along. And a Cirkasian beauty traveling with a man as imposing as Morthred was hardly going to be hard to find. But we were also aware that there was a ship waiting for Morthred, probably already provisioned and ready to sail. Whether we found Flame or not might depend on something as insignificant as the tides in the port that day.

We left the jetty and walked into the town. The first person we asked, a cooper who was sitting outside his workshop with a bleak expression on his face, burdened us with the woes of the Rattéspie economy before he answered us and pointed out to sea. "Sure, I know the couple you're talking about. They set sail not three hours back. That's their ship out there."

We swung around to look: all we could see were white sails against a blue sky on the horizon. "What ship was it?" Blaze asked. I scarcely recognized her voice, it was so charged with emotion.

"Oh, that fellow, Gethelred of Skodart, he called himself: it was his. He came in on it a couple of weeks back, and then he went on up the Slug. The ship's crew waited for him. Funny lot that, Keepers most of them, but can't say I've ever met Keepers quite like that mob. People were scared silly of them, you know? And the town whores had a real hard time, or so I'm told. Sodding pilchards."

"What was the name of the ship?" Ryder asked.

"*Amiable.* A ketch. Little beauty, that one. Fast too, I'll warrant."

"That's not the one he stole back in Gorthan Docks," Blaze said to Tor.

"I heard that was found burned on a beach near Amkabraig," I told her.

"Probably pirated this one first," Tor said.

"Very likely." Blaze looked across at me. "Well, selver-herder, what do we do now? We've lost her, and we've lost the dunmaster too."

She had tears in her eyes, and the air around her was redolent with her emotions, a mixture of grief and despair. For the life of me, I couldn't help myself. I found myself saying, "Well, we go after them, of course. What else?"

CHAPTER 25

NARRATOR : KELWYN

THE PEOPLE OF RATTÉSPIE WERE ONLY TOO glad to tell us everything they knew about the *Amiable,* its crew and its supposed owner. There were no Awarefolk in town, so they had not known that they'd been dealing with dunmagic, and Gethelred-Morthred and those on board had apparently been careful not to make any overt use of magic while they were there. They had been a nasty lot, nonetheless. They hadn't actually killed anyone, or raped anyone, or even stolen from anyone, but they had intimidated and frightened and bullied. Gethelred himself had been honey-smooth, and several people seemed to have been charmed by him; others were more suspicious. Flame didn't appear to have spoken to anyone at all.

The ketch, the harbormaster informed us, was a small ship with too many people on board. It didn't carry enough water for a long trip, not with that many people. They wouldn't be going far. They had mentioned Brethbastion, but that city was on the far side of Breth Island. The *Amiable* would have to replenish supplies along the way. Probably they would go to Xolchasbarbican, the capital of Xolchas Stacks. It wasn't a hard guess: the

Barbican was the closest port and the logical landfall between Porth and Breth. And Blaze was convinced that Morthred was taking Flame to Breth to marry the Islandlord.

"And how can we get to the Stacks?" Blaze asked the harbormaster. She swept a glance over the port. It was hardly a bustling scene of marine activity. "Is there a packet? A trader leaving any time soon? Anything at all?"

The harbormaster regarded her morosely, and wiped his dripping nose with a kerchief he wore at his neck. "Packets don't run here anymore. Not for months. And the traders don't come."

Ryder waved a hand at a shabby two-masted ship that was tied up to the wharf. "Who owns the schooner?"

"That's a local trader, that is. Belongs to Scurrey. He used to run reeds over to Xolchas every few weeks, and bring guano back for our vegetable gardens and crops. Hasn't left the dock for weeks now."

"Is it seaworthy?"

"Yes, of course. It's just that there have been no cargos, and Scurrey can't afford to pay the crew or for the victualling if he has no cargo outta here."

"Would he sail it to Xolchas for us?"

The harbormaster stood a little straighter. "You would charter a whole ship?"

"If the price was right."

He dabbed at his nose. "Weed fever," he said miserably. "Always get it at this time of the year. I'll speak to Scurrey for you. Reckon he'd be delighted."

Blaze interrupted. "We would have to leave on the next tide."

The harbormaster opened his mouth to protest the impossibility of this, and then thought better of it. "I'll tell him." He hustled away, sneezing as he went.

Blaze cocked her head in Ryder's direction. "Charter a schooner? Just for us? Menod patriarchs must earn a whole lot more money than I thought."

"I have enough for victualling. To arrange payment for the rest, I'll write a draft on the Menod treasury for the local patriarch here so that I have some cash."

His tone was coldly distant, which puzzled her, I could see. She didn't reply, but I knew what she was thinking. What Ryder had said was evidence that he'd not come back for her. He had been sent by the Menod—for Flame.

IT WAS A CLOSE CALL, BUT WE MADE IT, slipping out on the tide with just minutes to spare. We would never have managed it if the whole of Rattéspie had not taken it as a challenge. This was the first local ship to set sail for weeks; it meant money in the townsfolk's coffers and they weren't about to waste the opportunity. Chandlers bustled, farmers appeared out of nowhere with fresh produce, sailors signed up, longshoremen came looking for work loading the ship, shipwrights recaulked part of the deck where timbers had dried out and shrunk.

While all this was going on, Ryder went to look for the local patriarch with Scurrey, the schooner's owner and captain. Dek scouted around to see if he could sell the two boats we had used to get to Rattéspie. Blaze dropped by the blacksmith's, carrying both her sword and Ryder's, to have them sharpened. I went to the medicine and herbalist shop to see what was available to restock my supplies. On my way back to the ship, I passed the blacksmith's and was surprised to see Blaze putting the final touches to the blades herself.

Seeing my surprise, she laughed, saying, "You didn't think I would allow anyone else to sharpen a Calmenter sword, did you? Did you get the things you wanted?"

"Some of them. And some others I didna expect to find. The herbalist is quite a competent fellow." I glanced at the weapon she had just finished honing. "Why are the sides of the blade so sharp? Most swords aren't like that."

"Calmenter steel holds an edge, and a well-honed edge makes for a more effective weapon. Another blade would just be weakened and there'd soon be nicks along it. Anyway, I've finished now. Let's go back to the ship." She dug into her purse and paid the blacksmith for the use of his grinding wheel, whetstone and oils. As we headed back to the wharves she changed the subject. "Kel, I really want to know what made you follow us." She grinned at me. "That question can hardly be a surprise."

Considering that back in Amkabraig I had been adamant

that I wasn't getting involved in her affairs, it was no surprise at all. I smiled back rather ruefully, and sketched out what had happened to me back in Amkabraig, and how it made me feel. Unfortunately I didn't tell her any of the details, either about Ginna, or about what I had read. I sometimes wonder: would it have made a difference if I had? Perhaps not. Perhaps we would still not have found the opportunity to mend what had already happened.

At her request, I then went on to relate the circumstances of my meeting with Tor Ryder. She listened intently, without interrupting or asking questions, until I finished by describing my decision to yell at Domino so that Ryder would have a chance.

"That was mad," she said. "You should have gone after Flame."

"It was just as well I didn't. The ghemphs didn't know how much trouble ye were in until I started yelling. It was only then they realized ye probably needed help, only then that they popped up and asked me."

"Oh. But why did you come into the beach then? You could have been killed."

"Er, actually the ghemphs didn't give me a choice," I admitted sheepishly. "They more or less picked the boat up and whisked it onshore. And then I saw Ryder go down, and I felt I couldna just leave. He would have bled to death right there on the sand."

She sighed. "The right decision for him, the wrong one for Flame. Trench below, Kel, why is nothing ever simple in this world?" Her despair filtered into the air. "It's too late for Flame, isn't it? By the time we catch up, she will be too deeply subverted, beyond help. Not even the sylv healers can bring a sylv back once the subversion has fully corrupted."

"We can try."

"You really care for her, don't you?" She frowned slightly, then added, "Flame is a wonderful friend: she's kind and caring and generous and brave. Or she was. But she . . . she uses men, and then walks away. It's because of the way she feels about Ruarth. Even if she recovers, there will never be anyone but Ruarth for her, never."

I blinked, taken aback. She didn't think I cared for Flame,

did she? I put an arm around her shoulder as we walked past the rows of chandlers and out onto the wharves. "Blaze, I know. Ye forget my nose."

She made a noise of disgust at herself. "Yeah, I do. Which is probably just as well. It is disconcerting to know that you can read my smell like—like I was a bunch of roses. Or maybe a donkey turd."

I laughed. "Hardly. In fact, ye are the most enigmatic of non-Skyfolk that I know. Ye remind me of my own people— they keep their emotions muted. So do you."

"Not to be wondered at, I suppose, considering how I was raised. If a brat showed her feelings, she was vulnerable. Simple as that. Much better to keep a tight hold on how you felt, never to let anyone see." She changed the subject before I could comment. "And Tor? How is he?"

"He's all right, I think. Weak still, though. He'll be tired for a while."

"Has he spoken to you about the way he was healed?"

"He thinks the ghemphs did it."

"You—you know how I feel about him, don't you?"

"I know ye have a cheek to tell me to be careful about *my* romantic life."

She gave me a long hard stare. "That nose of yours must be a handy appendage to have, Gilfeather, if it tells you that much."

"It isn't my nose that tells me that the two of you are not suited. That I would know all by myself, noseless."

She sighed. "Yes, I suppose so. We are aware of—of our incompatibility. And we had decided to part."

"Had?"

"Still have. Nothing has changed, and I don't suppose it ever will. His faith is part of him, and it is something I could never share." She withdrew from me, seeking some inner strength, or solace. I let my arm slip from around her shoulders. "What about Dek?" she asked. "He looks awful."

"People usually do after they have been beaten. His nose and ribs and lip will heal. The bruises will fade. He's sore, but he's trying to be brave about it."

She smiled fondly. "I noticed."

The wharf looked chaotic when we returned, but I suppose

it was an ordered chaos. Scurrey, a portly bearded man whose name didn't suit him, directed things from the deck, mostly by shouting. There was a flow of longshoremen and sailors up and down the gangplanks. Dek was there, bubbling over with pride: he had managed to sell both the boats for what he considered a huge sum. Neither of us disabused him, and I suppose he hadn't done too badly in a town that was facing commercial disaster.

"Can I use the money to buy a sword?" he asked hopefully.

"It wouldn't be enough," Blaze told him. "However, I did buy this for you." She reached over her back, pulled something from the long package she had tied to her harness and handed it to him. It was a sword, of sorts.

"But it's made of wood!" he said, trying to hide his disappointment.

"Come now, you don't think that any apprentice swordsman starts with a real weapon, do you?" she asked. "I am sure the Havenlord's troops trained with practice swords."

"Yeah, I suppose so."

"We shall start your lessons as soon as you are healed," she promised. "I bought two of them."

He tried to look suitably grateful.

She relented then. "Oh, and I almost forgot: I bought this for you as well." She pulled out a knife, complete with belt and holder. "I think you will find this better than your fish gutter."

He beamed like a meadow daisy hit by sunlight, momentarily speechless.

She pulled his earlobe, which was about as affectionate as she ever became with him. "You'll get your sword when you show me you can handle the wooden one. In the meantime, treat that knife with care. And that means using it only when there is no other way to save your own worthless hide, understand?"

He grinned and nodded, still wordless.

"Blaze," I said suddenly, "I can smell Dustels." I spotted them first, a small flock that came and sat on the rigging of the schooner. I gestured at them and one flew down to sit on a bollard close to us. Seeker, at a word from Blaze, lay down obediently at her feet, and ignored the bird.

Are you Kelwyn Gilfeather? it asked, laboriously spelling out my name.

I squatted down next to the bollard and spoke softly. No point in having the whole wharf wondering why I talked to a bird. "I'm Gilfeather. Ye have a message for me? From Ruarth?"

Yes. He went on the ship that sailed this morning, with the Cirkasian and the dunmaster.

"The *Amiable*?"

It nodded. *The message was that he would continue to follow Flame, and that they were heading for Xolchasbarbican, and then Brethbastion. He said to tell you that he would leave messages with the Dustels wherever he went. And that Flame was worse, much worse. She is hostile toward him—swatting him whenever he comes near. He said you must hurry.*

"Thank you," I said. "We are leaving as soon as we can."

"Did he tell you who the dunmaster is?" Blaze asked.

The bird nodded again. *The Dustels live in hope,* it said. *And we honor you all for what you are attempting to do.* His smell was at variance with his words: the aroma of an overwhelming sadness clung to him like an aura. I wondered about that, but only idly. It didn't seem likely that it was any of my business.

I said, "We'll do our best."

The bird inclined its head.

Blaze did the same. It should have seemed rather theatrical or silly. Instead, I found myself moved. And sometimes I wonder, even now, about what happened to that bird, and all the others who dreamed of the Dustel Islands and, perhaps, never made it back.

ABOUT MIDNIGHT WE CLEARED THE mouth of the Kilgair Slug, and I started feeling ill. It was odious down below: this was no packet boat with neat little cabins; this was a ship that usually carried cargo, not passengers. The space below deck was airless, dark and still smelled—vilely—of guano. We shared what I supposed was a hold: they had strung hammocks for us, and that was all.

The ship heaved and so did my stomach.

Without saying a word to anyone, and in a desperate hurry, I went topside.

I felt a little better once I had disposed of dinner over the side, so I crawled to a more sheltered area near the foremast, and hunkered down out of the wind. At least the air was fresh. All around me the ship groaned and timbers creaked like an old man aching in every joint; above me the wind sang in the sails and rigging.

I must have dozed, because I woke some time later to the sound of voices. I was instantly aware that I still felt ill and debated whether to crawl back to the railing, or whether I could convince my stomach it really didn't need to do this. On the Floating Mere I had thought the close proximity of dunmagickers was worse than seasickness: I was beginning to revise that opinion.

My misery can be my only excuse for what happened next. I was so intent on quelling my stomach, so focused on my own nausea, that I did not think to declare my presence there on the deck to the speakers. At first, I wasn't even aware of the actual conversation, and by the time I was, it was too late, and I was too embarrassed to stand up and let them know I was there.

It was Blaze and Ryder, and he was saying, "Gilfeather implied it was ghemphs, but it wasn't, was it?"

There was a pause. Then, "What makes you think that?"

"No games, please, Blaze. Gilfeather couldn't lie his way out of a lobster trap. Anyway, I overheard part of a conversation between him and a ghemph. There was mention of . . . evil. Of people dying because I lived."

"Leave it, Tor. What's done is done."

"Don't patronize me! Do you think I can't sense that there is something wrong? I have something inside me which should not be there!"

"What—what do you mean?"

"It was Morthred's subverted Keepers who did this to me, wasn't it? Somehow you got them to heal me, impossible as we've always thought that was. Why did you do it, Blaze? *I have dun in me!* Did you know me so little?" He smelled of hurt and sadness and pain, and worse still, of an intense fury.

Blaze was more opaque and whatever she felt, she hid well. "You would have died, Tor."

"And don't you think I would have *preferred* that? Have you any idea of what you have done to me?"

There was a short silence. And then, "I guess not."

"They transferred some of their dun to me. It's there inside of me, a constant whispering of evil. I hear it all the time. It affects even my prayers . . . I know it's not possible, but I feel that—that I am cut off from God."

She could not have failed to hear the horror in his voice. I heard her sharp intake of breath, then: "Oh, middens, I'm sorry. I didn't know . . ."

"How could you not know? They were *dunmagickers*! What else were they going to do except try to contaminate me as best they could?"

In her distress, she was silent.

"Tell me, were you thinking of yourself, or me, when you concocted such a diabolical scheme to save me?"

"That's unfair."

"Is it?" He gave a bark of cynical laughter. "Maybe you're right at that. It's probably the dun talking. Its nastiness swamps me sometimes, until I can't control the way I think. Oh, don't look so worried. I will battle it, and with God's grace, I will win. This is no subversion; it's just a taint they left behind to taunt me. Or maybe because they could not help it. What I want to know from you is what you had to give them for them to heal me."

She was a long time answering. "Their lives," she said at last.

"And . . . ?"

"Their freedom."

"How many of them?"

"Twelve. We needed as many as possible to make it work . . . because you are one of the Aware."

It was his turn to gasp. "*Twelve?* Dear God, you set twelve dunmagickers free *just to cure me*? So that *I* could live? Sweet heaven, Blaze, have you any idea how many sylvs they will subvert, how many women they will rape, how many families they will enslave as they rampage from one islandom to another? Have you any idea how many folk will *die* as a result of this?"

"Don't preach to me, Tor Ryder," she snapped in a fury. "You are the man who sailed away from Gorthan Spit, leaving

Flame and me to track down Morthred and the Floating Mere enclave. You didn't seem to care too much about battling dunmagickers then, did you?"

"I was not a free man; I serve the Patriarchy and I must do their bidding. I had to return to Tenkor."

"Oh, don't give me that twaddle. You could have come with us, and you know it. You have no right to preach to me—and you know that too."

There was a long silence, during which neither of them seemed to move. Then he said, "Maybe there's some truth in that. But it's not the same. You exchanged my life for theirs in a bargain I would never have countenanced, had I been conscious and rational. You had no right, none, to assume that I would want to buy my life at such a price. It wasn't *right*, Blaze. You have loaded my future with guilt and it is almost too much to bear."

"Don't be ridiculous! If there is any guilt here, it's mine, not yours. Mine and Gilfeather's. You were hardly in a position to make decisions, after all. You were unconscious! Or are you trying to say that it is our love that is to blame for this?"

He was silent.

"Trench below, you are saying that, aren't you?"

"I don't want to quarrel with you."

"Well, you are doing a damn good job of it nonetheless! I suppose I shall have to blame the dun taint inside you, because you certainly aren't being sensible about this."

The ship dipped its prow into a wave and I buried my head in my arms and desperately tried to keep my stomach still.

Blaze sighed. "I am sorry, Tor. Sorry for everything. Sorry I can't be the kind of woman you need. Sorry I loved you enough to save you, no matter what the cost. Sorry I've given you a burden of guilt as a consequence. I'm sorry, but y'know, I'd do it all over again. I wanted you alive." The ship shuddered under the onslaught of another wave and Blaze waited till the deck was steady again. I thought: Go to her, you knuckled-headed priest—can't you see how much she needs you? But he did nothing, and eventually she said, "We were right to part, Tor. We never see the same patch of ocean the same way, you and I."

Another silence. Then, from him, "No, that's true. And I'm sorrier than I can say, too."

"Stupid, isn't it?" she said lightly, but her pain was intense. "I shouldn't have been angry like that just then. You did what you thought was right."

"But you don't believe it was . . ." She sighed. "We can't undo anything, can we? So maybe we had better just . . . let it go."

"Yes. I think that would be best," he agreed.

He turned to go, but she spoke again. "Wait. I—I want to thank you for what you did back on the Floating Mere. I'd be dead but for you. You took a terrible risk, Tor. I'll never forget that, ever. I'll never stop being grateful. I'll never lose my sense of—of astonishment, that anyone would do that for me."

He tried to say something, but couldn't find the right words.

There was another short silence, then she added gently, "Go below to your prayers. I want to be alone for a while."

He walked away without another word, and his angry pain came to me in waves. I wondered if she knew, if she felt it the way I did. And then she said, "Damn. Damn, damn, *damn*! Gilfeather, why did you have to be *right*?"

I thought she had seen me. I stood up, embarrassed beyond measure, feeling ill and guilty. And she jumped back, startled into groping for her sword, only to swear when she realized she wasn't wearing it, and then swear even more eloquently when she realized it was only me. "Gilfeather! What in the seven seas are you doing spying on us like that?" She had her hands on her hips, demanding an explanation.

"I was sick," I mumbled. "Sorry."

She stared, started to speak, changed her mind, then threw her hands up in the air in surrender. "Oh, it doesn't matter. Forget it. You would have smelled out that argument tomorrow anyway, I suppose. Right down to the last nuance," she added bitterly.

I felt an idiot, but the way she stood there, looking at me, shook me. She looked defeated, and I wasn't used to seeing her that way. "Nay, lass," I said, "that's blatherwump and moonbabble, ye ken."

She stared. "It's *what*?"

"Blatherwump and moonbabble. Nonsense."

"You made that up."

"Nay, never. It's Plains talk."

She smiled weakly. I put my arms around her and gave her a hug. "I'm too old for comforting," she said.

"Nonsense. One's never too old."

She said softly, laying her head on my shoulder, "You were right, Kel. This was one thing he will never quite be able to forgive."

"He loves ye still."

"Does he? Perhaps that's what makes it so awful." She paused. "No, that's not what makes it so awful. It's the dun that does that. He's right, Kel. There's something inside of him that wasn't there before. He had the right of it—he's tainted." I smelled her horror. "What have we done? Dear heaven, Kel, *what did we do to him?*"

I wanted to deny that we had done anything, but it wouldn't have been true. We had changed a man into something he had never wanted to be.

I stroked her hair and tried very hard not to throw up down her back.

CHAPTER 26

IF YOU HAVE BEEN TO XOLCHAS STACKS, you will know how amazing the first sight of it is.

It was early morning when we arrived, and the slanting light of the rising sun transfixed the stacks with gold and sent their shadows racing out over the water like fingers pointing to some far off invisible destination. Each stack towered out of a crashing sea, each had a gathering of rocks around its foot like children playing at the skirts of the giant that had birthed them. Each stack was a rugged pillar of crannies; and birds— thousands upon thousands of seabirds—wheeled and screamed as they launched themselves from the cliff sides to plummet seaward or soar skyward on unseen air currents.

People lived at the top of each stack, housed in buildings of stone that sometimes perched precariously close to cliff edges, their windows staring down on an ocean that crawled far, far below. There were, Blaze told me, about one hundred stacks. Ten of them were large enough to have towns, the others had hamlets surrounded by meadows and fields where they grazed their sheep and grew their crops.

The largest stack of all was Xolchasbarbican, where the

Barbicanlord lived. The town covered the entire top of the stack from cliff to cliff, with the Lord's House in the center. The name barbican came from the fortification built at the top of the zigzag path that wound its way up from Xolchasport.

Dek, standing beside me while our ship hove to and we waited for the pilot, pounded Blaze and Ryder with questions. He'd had days of frustration cooped up on board: there had been no rigging-climbs this time because of his broken ribs, and the sword lessons had not progressed far either for the same reason. He'd spent most of his waking hours with Blaze up on deck, while Ryder interrogated me—there's no other word for it—about medical practices among the Sky Plains-folk. His intense interest was genuine, and therefore flattering, but I never lost sight of the fact that he had a motive. He still had not been honest with me over that. A patriarch, in the normal course of his work, could hardly have needed to know what percentage of Sky Plains births resulted in the death of the mother, or whether we could cure the six-day fever or fix a broken back. Now, of course, I know that Ryder was already planning a future when the Patriarchy did indeed need to know things like that.

In addition, he wanted to know all my theories—even unproven as they were—about dunmagic and its contamination and subversion of sylvs. Given his concern for Flame, this was not surprising, and I'll admit I enjoyed the hours we spent discussing my theory that magic was an illness. He didn't think it was quite so simple and, to be honest, my own ideas had also been shaken.

How could this theory explain things I had seen with my own eyes: the healing of Ryder's wounds by sheer concentration when he himself was unconscious, for example? Or the physical damage to the raft I was on when the dunmagickers had thrown their dun at me? Or how Flame could control the way others viewed the hallucinations she gave them? These were mysteries I would dearly have loved to investigate. They fascinated my thirst for medical knowledge, for the joy of *knowing*.

Ryder was both amused and exasperated by my determination to prove that magic was just natural phenomena for which we had not yet found explanations. "How can ye, a rational man, believe in magic?" I asked him once, frustrated in turn by his ability to accept so unquestioningly the concept that sylvtalent and dunpower had a magic base.

"You forget," he said, smiling slightly, "I believe in the power of God. It's not much of a step from that belief, to a belief in an opposing power of evil, and of dunmagic. Not much of a step to believe that God may have planted the seeds of sylvpower or Awareness to give us a chance to fight back. Magic, to me, is just a name for forces that are supernatural in the same way that God is supernatural. Believe in God, Gilfeather, and it won't be long before you accept the existence of magic as an unknowable power."

I sighed. There was no way I could counter that sort of statement, because we didn't use the same basis for argument. I needed proof, or at the very least a measure of probability; all he needed was faith.

In truth, I must admit I developed a sneaking admiration for the man, even though I didn't *like* him much. I could not but respect the way he battled his demons. He was a man whose natural reaction was to fight, but whose intellect told him there was a better way, so he curbed his urge to hit back when he was threatened. Unfortunately Blaze and I had unwittingly nurtured that violence when we had let the power of the subverted sylvs into his body. And we had burdened him with a new guilt: the price we had paid for his life. He confronted both those new demons on our way across the ocean, spending hours locked in silent prayer to a God whose compassion he could no longer feel. I wondered if it helped: his rage continued to simmer, only just within his control. I don't think Blaze understood the full extent of his struggle, but I did. I smelled the faint contamination of dun, I sensed his guilt, and his torment at what he thought to be his unworthiness of the price paid for his life. To me, the veneer of calm he showed to the world was just that: a surface covering. Underneath, a turmoil of emotion raged, a simmering stew of fury at the world and resentment at the two of us for doing this to him, all of it fed by the dun.

And yet, in his daily contact with us, he tried to maintain a facade of courtesy. It must have taken intense effort and control. He failed from time to time, and his bitterness would seep through in pointed jibes or just a cold demeanor. Perhaps his love for Blaze was the factor that gave him some equilibrium; I glimpsed it sometimes in the longing in his eyes. And yet he had to fight that love too, because it had no future. The one thing he could not reject, his faith, was the very thing that split them apart.

And so it was we came to Xolchas: three people all seething beneath with our numerous personal demons, all of us coping with one general guilt: our failure to protect Flame and our inability, up till now, to save her. All of us were haunted by the horror of her present situation, knowing she was being twisted into the antithesis of herself, subject to constant degradation and pain, fearing she was destined to be the wife first of the Breth Bastionlord, a perverted lump of lard who tortured boys as a pastime, and perhaps then of a dunmaster who thrived on the pain of others. It was unthinkable. And yet she was suffering, even now, as we waited for the pilot to come out from Xolchasbarbican's port.

Only Dek was free of those demons of ours. "Do all the stacks have paths going to the top?" he asked. "What's all that white stuff on the cliffs? Is that stack *joined* to the one behind it? Do the stacks ever fall over? What happens if they do?" At least, I thought, Dek is uncomplicated. Not for him our mass of guilts and tangled emotions: all he wanted to do was learn how to use a sword and fight dunmagickers. One day, perhaps he, too, would start to realize that life wasn't that simple, but he hadn't come to that stage yet.

"The white stuff is guano. Bird shit," Blaze told him. "That's the only thing they export from Xolchas."

Dek looked at her as if she was teasing him.

"It's used as fertilizer to make farm soils more productive. Honest!" As Ryder came up from below to join us, she added, "Tor's brought up his spyglass so you can better see the suspension bridges that join the stacks."

We all had a look through the brass instrument, and sure enough we could see that two adjacent stacks were joined by a rope bridge. It swayed far above the sea, linking the pillars in a way that seemed to have all the fragility of the strands of a spider's web.

"Please dinna tell me we'll have to walk any of those," I said as I closed up the spyglass and handed it back.

"No head for heights, Gilfeather?" Ryder asked. Once that would have been just banter, said with a smile; now there was an edge to it.

"Heights dinna fret me," I said morosely, and it was true enough, "but I'm as clumsy as a selver going downstairs backward. I'd be bound to slip and fall through the gaps."

None of us mentioned just what was going to happen when we did land in Xolchas Stacks, because none of us knew. What we did know was daunting: the *Amiable* was manned by a crew of at least eight, who were probably all enslaved. The people of Rattéspie had mentioned another twenty-one people on board: Flame; Gethelred; seventeen Keepers, most of whom had been wearing chasubles; and two other men. We suspected that these last two were probably genuine dunmagickers, perhaps even dunmasters. The chasubles told us that the Keepers were Council trained. Most, perhaps all, would know how to handle weapons. It was a formidable force. And we were three adults, only two of whom knew the first thing about swordplay, a lad with several broken ribs, and a mongrel Fen lurger. It was hardly fair odds.

The pilot came eventually, pulling alongside in a boat that the others told me was called a pinnace. He climbed on board and took the wheel, although Scurrey assured us he himself knew the way into the breakwatered harbor through the shoals and rocks heaped around the skirts of the stack, just like a shearwater knew its way home to its burrow on the cliffs. However, the Stacks' authorities would not allow the berthing of any ship without a pilot: it was one of the many ways they had of collecting money from visitors. We would soon realize, he added darkly, that Xolchasmen knew everything there was to know about scamming money out of respectable traders and calling it legitimate taxation.

As we came into the wharves, we saw the ketch tied up there, with several sailors leaning over the rail, watching our arrival. In spite of the strong smell of guano all over the wharf area, I could smell the dunmagic from the *Amiable*.

"Is Flame on board?" Blaze asked me.

I shook my head. "I dinna think so. In fact, I think Morthred and most of the sylvs and dunmagickers have gone too. There's probably no more than two subverted sylvs on board, plus all the crew."

"When the time comes, perhaps we can start with those two," Ryder said quietly. "Kill them first." Blaze blanched. I wondered why, then realized that she was not used to Ryder displaying cold-blooded ruthlessness. I shivered slightly, and wondered if he would dispose of Flame as readily, should we be unable to help her. He'd probably have the blessing of the Menod, I reflected; they would not tolerate a dunmagicker married to the Breth Bastionlord, let alone one who was also in line for the throne of Cirkase, any more than the Keepers would.

"Can I help?" Dek asked, eyes shining.

"You can go below and get my sword and scabbard," Blaze said.

Ryder smiled at her after Dek disappeared down the companionway. "You hold an octopus by just one tentacle there, Blaze."

She sighed. "I know, but what the squirming hells am I to do with that lad? He doesn't seem to have a drop of fear in him."

"Or any reservations about slaughtering people, that I can see."

"Well, not if they are dunmagickers," she amended.

"What are ye going to do?" I asked, and I wasn't referring to the question of Dek. "Just march up and kill every subverted sylv we meet? Starting with the two on the *Amiable?*"

Ryder raised an eyebrow. "Are you thinking that we should have a polite conversation with the dunmagickers first, Gilfeather?"

Blaze intervened hastily. "We'll leave them be for the moment. Firstly, I wouldn't want to hurt the coerced, if I could help it. Secondly, Xolchas takes a dim view of murder. They are a disciplined, law-abiding people." She pointed up at the cliffs that towered above the port and into a sky that was whirling with birds. The whole cliff face was covered in a network of ropes. "The ropes are for use by the guano collectors," she said. "Every family on the stack has a stake in a certain section of cliff. There's enormous potential for legal wrangles and theft and argument, but it doesn't happen. Families don't even guard their territory, because the stealing of even a single dropping is unthinkable. It simply does not occur. As I say, they are law-abiding."

"So we won't murder anyone openly," Ryder said. "We'll do it quietly instead." He was only half joking.

Blaze shot him a worried glance. "We'll try legal methods first. We'll go to the Barbicanlord and ask her to intervene. Or if she will give us permission to intervene."

"You can't sense Flame anywhere?" Ryder asked me.

I shook my head. "But then, I wouldn't, if she has gone to the town on top. I canna smell anything from way up there; it's too windy for a start, and then there's all that guano stench."

"We noticed," Blaze said dryly as Dek came back with the sword. She strapped it on, just as the ship came into the wharf and the last of the sails came rattling down.

"The first thing we do anyway," I said, contradicting them both, "is find the Dustels."

AS IT TURNED OUT, THEY FOUND US, EVEN before we left the ship. They had evidently been watching for me. Ruarth, I thought, had a lot of faith that I, at the very least, would turn up.

The leader of the flock who came and sat on the railing and asked for me was an elderly, pompous fellow. For once I had no problem discerning both the sex and age of a Dustel. *Young man,* he began, *are you the one called Gilfeather?*

"Aye," I said, and introduced the others. Dek and Blaze he completely ignored, Ryder he looked up and down before saying, if I understood him correctly, that he had no time for religious fanatics, and why was it that the Menod did not minister to the Dustel birds anyway? (An illogical question, I thought, seeing as the birds mostly kept their sentience secret.) Without waiting for an answer he informed me that he had no idea what right I had to be called Gilfeather, or in fact anything-feather, as I most definitely was not and never had been a Dustel, or even a bird. Feathers, he said, were the prerogative of those of avian disposition, and I shouldn't forget it. His name, he added, was Comarth.

I finally managed to shut him up, and ask him what Ruarth wanted us to know. It turned out that he had more than just a message from Ruarth; he knew where Flame was and, thanks to a network of Dustels who were flying up and down the cliffs between Ruarth and himself, his information was up to the minute.

It seemed that Morthred-Gethelred had decided that, as Flame was actually Lyssal, the Castlemaid and heir of Cirkase, and about to become the wife of the Bastionlord, it was fitting that she be introduced to the Barbicanlord. He had taken her upcliff.

Blaze took no pleasure from being right about Morthred's intentions toward Flame. "Trench below," she muttered, "that sodding dunmaster must be confident that there are no Awarefolk here to unmask them."

The only Awarefolk here are us, Comarth said. *And the Xolchasfolk don't have the wit to know us for what we are, shit-grubbing island-hoppers that they are.*

"So where are they now?" I asked. "Flame and Ruarth and Morthred?"

Being feted by the Barbicanlord. Honored guests, they are, housed in the best guestrooms of the Lord's House.

"For how long?" Blaze asked.

Another day or two. Tomorrow the Barbicanlord is formally announcing her own engagement to the scion of a noble Stacks family, so Gethelred and the others will stay for the celebrations.

"That's a piece of luck," Ryder said thoughtfully. "A lot can happen during celebrations. Blaze, am I right in thinking that you have met the Barbicanlord?"

"Yes, when she was just the Barbicanheir. I did some work for her father. He had called on the Keepers to identify and kill a dunmagicker that was causing trouble, and Duthrick sent me. A simple job. But the old lord was impressed and asked me to stay a while and spend some time with his daughter, to give her what he called 'some Hub polish.'" She snorted. "Amazing, isn't it, what a difference being a Keeper agent can make? When I was thirteen I was hounded out of this very islandom because I was citizenless."

We all stared at her. Ryder said carefully, "The Barbicanlord asked you to give his daughter some 'polish?'"

"That's right."

Neither Ryder nor I said another word. Blaze smiled blandly. "We got along famously. She taught me how to sneak out of the Lord's House and climb down the cliff ropes at night. I taught her how to bet at cards and drink sailor's rum. She taught me to rappel; I taught her how to fight unarmed."

The Dustel gave an avian version of a snort.

"I'll bet that wasn't quite what the Barbicanlord had in mind," Ryder remarked dryly. "But it sounds as if we might have friends in high places."

"Well, I'm not so sure about that," she said. "We were young in those days and I am no longer a Keeper agent. I've heard that she settled down and has become quite a stickler for protocol and such now. Lords tend to do that once they are sitting on the throne."

That's true, Comarth said. *She was renowned for her heedless, rash behavior, but once she inherited, she turned her back on all her old companions and her behavior has been impeccable. As is proper.*

"We'll try to wangle an audience," Ryder said. "I'll go and see the Menod House here. Maybe they have some influence."

"First," I said to the Dustel, "can ye send someone to Ruarth and tell him we are here? We need to speak to him. As soon as we have completed the port formalities, we'll start up to the town. He can meet us along the way, if that is possible."

"I still want to know what happens if a stack falls over," Dek said, craning his neck as he looked up at the path that zigzagged, impossibly steep and narrow, to the top. We could see the barbican gate, but nothing more of the town. "What a colossal splash it would make! D'y'think, if it did fall, that the top of it would crash into that other stack there?"

Without warning, my heart started hammering in my chest, and it had nothing to do with falling stacks. Morthred was just a climb away, and this time, he would die, or we would.

CHAPTER 27

NARRATOR : BLAZE

I HAD LIKED XETIANA WHEN SHE WAS THE Barbicanheir, and I was a Keeper agent. She was about the same age as I was, and far, far crazier. Her father had despaired of ever governing her, and his request for me to stay a while and take her under my wing was an act of desperation. Of course, if he was really wanting Hub polish, I was hardly the right person for the job, but it had been fun while it lasted. My aim had become not to put an end to her escapades, but to show her how to assess a danger, or a person, or a situation. To recognize the difference between a man who liked her and one who liked what she could give him, be it prestige or power. And maybe, somewhere along the line, I did manage to encourage her native caution. I had stayed four months in Xolchas Stacks, with Duthrick—as irate as a crab with its claws tied—demanding all the while that I return.

Three years later Xetiana's father had died in a stack fall. Many Xolchasfolk did, in fact, die that way. Dek's question about falling stacks was not so ridiculous: it was a perennial problem, a fate that hung over the whole islandom. Sooner or later every stack would fall, a victim of the ocean's relentless battering. Every few years or so, one of the smaller, narrower stacks would tumble, taking its inhabitants with it. Or sometimes part of one of the bigger stacks would simply slip down into the ocean, leaving a sheer cliff face behind at the mercy of the ocean's pounding and the burrowing seabirds.

The consequence of this uncertainty was to be found in the character of the Xolchasfolk: they were phlegmatic to a fault. They rarely planned for the future, being generally satisfied to surround themselves with their families, happy just to catch enough fish or herd enough sheep or collect enough seaweed to live on, and to harvest enough guano to buy a few luxuries from other islandoms. They lived lives of quiet contentment, blocking from thought the possibility that their stack or their piece of guano-rich cliff could be the next piece to fall.

When a stack or a farm or a cliff face did vanish into the sea, it was never spoken of again. The missing stack was erased from maps, the victims were mourned only minimally, at least in public, and the manner of their deaths was never mentioned. In a fit of irritation, I had once told Xetiana that Xolchasfolk were like a school of stupper flounder, hiding under the sand waiting for prey. These flat fish were so complacent in their camouflage, that fishermen could walk along the shallow sandbars and collect them by hand, one after another, and not one of them would ever think to swim away.

Xetiana had then said quietly, "But, Blaze, where would we go? When you have no escape, is it not better to enjoy whatever is left, rather than panic and blunder this way and that?"

Perhaps she was right.

SCURREY WAS DEFINITELY RIGHT ABOUT the taxes. I found it was one thing to arrive in Xolchas Stacks as the requested emissary from the Keeper Council; it was quite another to be just a halfbreed nobody. It was three setus for me just to set foot on the wharf, and they intended to enforce the usual islandom three-day limit on my stay. Seeker was banned altogether on the grounds that he might disturb the birds, but I had to pay another two setus just to keep him on the boat.

Tor was granted free entry as a Menod priest, but Kel had to pay a physician's tax, just in case he treated anyone while he was on the island. Dek, because he was traveling without an adult relative, had to have one of us sign a paper assuming responsibility, and it was another setu for the paper. Then there were wharf charges, a daily rate while our schooner was tied up (we had asked Scurrey to wait for us), and if the crew were to be allowed into the port, it was a twentieth part of a setu every time they left the ship. And for us to use the track to the Upper Town, as they called the city, it was a tenth of a setu, for purposes of "road maintenance." Only paid, of course, by foreigners. They had taxation down to a fine art on Xolchas Stacks.

Tor paid it all with coins from his purse, and waved away Kel's offer of a contribution. It seemed he had access to a limitless expense account, and that worried me. I knew why it niggled: it was proof of his trusted position in the Menod hierarchy. And it meant that the Menod Council was happy to spend a small fortune on the rescue of the Castlemaid. What I couldn't decide was whether that was to keep her out of the hands of the dunmagickers, or whether it was because they wanted her to be returned to her proper place, just as they had returned Ransom Holswood, the runaway Bethany Holdheir, to his. I was beginning to wonder if the choice for a Flame cured of dunmagic could ever include freedom.

Perhaps there was little difference between being born heir to an islandom and being born an unwanted halfbreed: we had both ended up prisoners of what was ours at birth.

THE PATH UP TO THE BARBICAN WAS SO narrow it had to have passing places where those going down could maneuver around those going up. The only thing between us and a fall hundreds of feet into the port was a flimsy rope railing. The climb itself was so steep it was more like climbing a rock face than a casual hike. Dek wouldn't take a step without holding on to the rock wall, so we made slow progress. It must have been rather traumatic for a boy who had never seen anything but mudflats and mangroves until he was thirteen or fourteen.

We were less than halfway up when we met Ruarth coming down.

He looked awful. His maroon breast band was dulled, the sheen his feathers usually carried seemed lifeless. He was missing several tail feathers. His initial greeting was a snappish twitter at Kel, which I didn't understand, but Kel obviously did, because he blushed.

"I'm sorry, Ruarth," he said. "I was delayed. But we are all here now, and we have a ship at our disposal. How is she?"

How do you expect her to be? She's being poisoned! Ruarth replied.

What happened next was awful. He sat there on the rope railing, and shook all over. Not the way a bird fluffs itself to tidy up its feathers, but the way a bird would shake if it cried. We all exchanged looks, helpless.

It's too late, he said when he had finally recovered himself. *There is no way she will ever rid herself of the subversion now . . .*

We were all at a loss, I think. It was hard for me to accept that I might have lost the only female friend I'd ever had and in such a way; Tor admired her, I knew—he had watched her fight the subversion once before and win, after her amputation; Dek adored her; and Gilfeather, well, I thought he was attracted to her and hiding it because he knew she loved Ruarth. I was surprised, therefore, when he was the only one of us who seemed to retain composure. And the only one of us who seemed to have thought things through.

"There's no need to despair yet, Ruarth," he said gently. "Who knows what will happen to Flame when Morthred dies? And we are just beginning to find out things about healing that we never knew before. Perhaps if we can get enough sylv healers together—"

That would mean taking her to the Keepers, Ruarth protested. *The Keeper Isles is the only place that has abundant sylvs.*

I translated that for Tor, who then said snappishly to Gilfeather, "Flame would think death was preferable. Believe me."

Gilfeather frowned. "And that from a priest who intends to return her to Cirkase?"

"That's not the same thing as returning her to her father.

The Menod would *never* countenance her being put in a position where she would be forced into a distasteful marriage."

I stepped in hastily, before the argument developed further. "We have to free her first. Let's concentrate on that."

"Aye," Gilfeather agreed. "Sorry." He turned back to Ruarth. "Does she not talk to ye at all?"

Ruarth shook his head.

"Does she threaten ye? Has she betrayed ye to Gethelred?"

He shook his head again.

"Then there is hope. She has retained *something* of herself. Ruarth, we will get her to the ship, somehow. And we will try to cure her. There has to be a chance . . ."

Ruarth looked at Kel, eyes glittering harshly. *First,* he said, *you will have to part her from Gethelred and the subverted sylvs who surround her. How are you going to do that?*

Tor looked at me. "Ghemphs?" he asked.

I shook my head. "The ghemphs made it quite clear: they do not want to have the people of the islandoms suddenly become aware that they can kill humans. It was one thing to come to our aid in the middle of the Floating Mere, observed only by a few subverted sylvs and enslaved villagers; it's quite another in a place like this. They will help if I am in danger, and they may consider helping you, Tor, but not in some full-scale public battle. And they don't particularly care about Flame one way or another."

Dek looked disappointed. "I thought they were our champions," he said. "Like the cave-dragons are in all those old tales—"

I quelled him with an exasperated glance.

"Let's go on," Kel said. "We will talk to the Barbicanlord." He looked back at Ruarth. "Would you like to ride on me?"

The Dustel did not answer, but he flew to Kel's shoulder and they started up the path.

Tor and I exchanged glances. "We can't lose her, Tor. We *can't,*" I whispered.

He didn't answer, and the sadness in his gaze almost overwhelmed me. He turned away and began to follow Kel. I trailed after him, my spirits as dark as the Trench. Tor thought Flame was beyond help. And from that, it was just a step to accepting that she had to die. *Blaze, don't let me live like this,* she'd said. *Promise me.* I'd managed to save her that time, by cutting off her arm, but I had made that promise. And she had trusted me.

THERE WAS ANOTHER TAX TO PAY AT THE barbican gate. A tenth of a setu each. And then we were in the town.

It was built all of stone, with flat stone roofs, one building sharing a wall with the next. The only parts that weren't built over were the innumerable paved streets, hardly more than winding aisles between houses, where the wind raced through like a bore tide. There were no plants, no open spaces, nothing but the city buildings and streets stretching from one side of the stack to the other. Windows were glassless, tiny, and always high up on the walls, offering no hint of interiors or views of the street from the inside.

Gilfeather looked stunned. Put him in a closed city environment, and he ended up in a state of shock, at least until he managed to adjust his senses to the olfactory assault. He didn't complain, but I knew the signs by now. Dek was only marginally better: he may have grown used to Lekenbraig, but he had never seen anything as claustrophobic as Xolchasbarbican.

We went first to the Menod House, where Tor's letter of introduction gained him an immediate interview with the local head patriarch, who in turn arranged a meeting with the Barbicanlord's chamberlain. Chamberlain Asorcha remembered me, perhaps not that fondly, but as soon as we mentioned that we had reason to believe there were dunmagickers in the city, she sent a message to the Barbicanlord.

Asorcha was a woman of about sixty. Like most Xolchasfolk, she was tall and spare, with sandy-colored hair—now graying—and brown eyes. When I had last been in Xolchas Stacks, she had been Xetiana's Maid of Administration, a post that had entailed trying to restrain the Barbicanheir's more outrageous escapades. Xetiana had been loud in her complaints of the woman's spying ways, so it was surprising to find that Asorcha now occupied the islandom's chief administrative post.

"Lord Xetiana will be with her dressmaker," she told us,

after sending off the message. "There are festivities tomorrow, you know; she is to be formally betrothed to the Master of Stabbing Stack—that's one of our outer islands—and we are holding a stack race followed by a formal dinner and ball to commemorate." She turned her attention to me. "I believe, Syr-aware, that you are familiar with the stack race." She said it blandly enough, but it was a pointed comment, nonetheless, indicating that she remembered me very well indeed.

A stack race, held usually once a year, was open to any who cared to register, and pay the entry fee, of course. It lasted the better part of a day, and started and finished in the forecourt of the Lord's House, right in the center of town. Just about the whole of Xolchas came to view the race, taking up their favorite viewpoints on the stacks involved. In Xolchasbarbican, they lined up on the roofs to get a good view of the commencement and the finish. To see the closing stages of the race, they lined the western cliff edges and watched the contestants race across the stacks along the narrow straits called the Skinny Neck.

Women started the race first, an hour earlier than men, which was supposed to even up the disadvantage most women had of being less muscular than the average male. The number of women who had ever won the race, however, was minuscule—but Xetiana was one. Thanks, in part, to me, who had undertaken her training in secret.

Make no mistake about it, the race was dangerous; on average, at least one participant died or was badly injured every year. Far too dangerous for the female heir to the throne to be allowed to enter, but a little thing like that had not daunted Xetiana. She had enlisted my help, and we had registered her as a foreign woman from The Hub. She'd dressed herself as a Keeper woman would, and kept a scarf wrapped around her face at the start, saying she had toothache. Once the race was underway, she'd abandoned the scarf and the word had swept through the spectators that the heir was participating, but by then it was too late to stop her. Her father could not risk the unpopularity that would have engendered.

I'd gone with her, just to keep an eye on her, but she had one advantage over me: she, like all Xolchasfolk, could swim far better than I could. On each swimming leg of the race she had left me further behind. Afterward, her father was so enraged that I had helped her, he'd had me put on the next boat out of Xolchasport. Worse still, he'd sent a note of protest to Duthrick. Councillor Duthrick had then refused to pay me for my work in Xolchas, citing this complaint as his justification. Duthrick did things like that.

Now, as we waited for a message to come back from Xetiana, I found the injustice of that still rankled, even all those years later.

Asorcha personally ushered us in to see Xetiana. The dressmaker was not in evidence, but the Securia, the man in charge of the islandom's security and specifically the safety of the Barbicanlord, was there. I knew him too. His name was Shavel and he'd nearly lost his job because his charge had entered the stack race, so it wasn't likely that he would regard me with any kindness. Not a good beginning.

The first thing he did was stop us at the door and make us leave all our weapons behind. That wasn't unexpected; no sensible Islandlord was going to let armed people into their audience room.

In keeping with protocol, we advanced halfway to the foot of the steps that led up to the throne where Xetiana sat. I knelt, eyes on the floor, and the others followed my lead. At one time Xetiana would have given me a hug and a grin and invited me to have a beer, but things had changed. She gave us leave to rise, which was also permission to lift our eyes. She sat, unsmiling, while Asorcha came and stood on her right and Securia Shavel on the left. She was wearing a gown and jewelry, whereas I had been more accustomed to seeing her striding about in knee-length trousers with her hair roughly tied back with a leather thong. That change summed up a lot of what had happened in the intervening years.

"Blaze," she said. "It is good to see you again. Although Asorcha says that what you have to tell me is not good news." Her fingers were tapping on the arm of the throne, a nervous gesture that worried me. I would have done a lot right then to know what Kel was smelling. "So, tell me what you have to say."

I did so, but was careful to address her as "my Lord" and to utter all the required fancy phrases protocol demanded. Xetiana and I may have been friendly once, but I had never made the mistake of thinking that she regarded us as equals. Both

Tor and Gilfeather were impressed by my behavior, I could tell. Punctilious observation of protocol was a side of me they had never seen, but I'd had a good teacher. There wasn't much that Syr-sylv Arnado had not known about the correct procedure to be followed at the different courts, and I'd had hours of patient coaching.

Xetiana fixed me with a disconcertingly direct gaze. "So, you say that some of my honored guests are actually dunmagickers. And that the one who says he is the heir to the Dustel royal house is in fact a dunmaster. What about the Castlemaid who is in his company? Are you about to tell me that she, too, is a dunmagicking monster? Perhaps you would like to give me one good reason why I should believe you, a halfbreed renegade?"

"Renegade?" I asked, blurting out the word in my surprise.

She made a slight gesture and Shavel stepped forward. He looked as if he was going to enjoy what he was about to say. "We have had word from the Keeper Council. You are wanted for complicity in the kidnapping of the Castlemaid and for threatening the life of Councillor Syr-sylv Ansor Duthrick on Gorthan Spit. All islandoms have been asked to apprehend you, should you be found, and to return you to The Hub for questioning and trial." He smiled at me. "I understand that threats to the life of a Keeper Councillor carry the penalty of death by drowning."

CHAPTER 28

IT STARTED TO RAIN AS WE ARRIVED AT the Lord's House and were admitted to see Asorcha, the Chamberlain. While we waited for the Barbicanlord, Dek fidgeted, Ruarth preened, Blaze paced, and Ryder sat silently with his head bowed. Praying, I guessed. I leaned against the wall, sensing the rainwater gurgling its way through a network of drainpipes and guttering into some kind of underground cisterns. I suspected it rained a lot in Xolchas Stacks; it was certainly windy enough. We had been battered as we climbed the cliff face to the city; Dek had even been petrified that he'd be hurled to his death. At the top, the streets—hardly wide enough to let three people walk abreast—funneled the wind into solid blasts of air that would have whisked away anything not tied down. I hated the closed-in feeling, although the air itself was fresh and clean. Too clean, in a way. It smelled of sea and salt and guano, not of dunmagic, or Flame. I had no idea where she was.

Xetiana impressed, right from the start. She sat tall and proud on an ornate stone throne, and her face gave away no secrets, none. Her smell did, though. She was in turmoil, torn between excitement and distrust. I hoped that the excitement was at seeing an old friend, although of course I had no way of knowing. I smelled emotions, not the cause of them.

Asorcha was remarkably neutral, although it was clear she loved the Barbicanlord. Shavel the Securia was another matter; he didn't like Blaze one little bit. When his gaze settled on Dek, then me, then Ryder, I decided he didn't much like anyone. He certainly trusted on one. Ruarth, of course, he didn't see, although the Dustel was still with us. I spotted him sitting on a wall bracket and quickly looked away.

And then Shavel announced that Blaze was wanted by the Keeper Isles. She was shocked; I felt her emotion as waves of astonishment and indignation. She really had not thought that Duthrick would go to such lengths.

It was Ryder who stepped forward to speak while Blaze was still trying to accustom herself to the idea that she was being hunted throughout the Glory Isles. With polite deference, but never wavering in his own sense of worth, he introduced himself as a member of the Menod Council of Patriarchs—which Blaze had not known he was, if her surprise was anything to go by.

"The Council sent me to aid Blaze and Kel Gilfeather of Wyn in their efforts to rescue the Castlemaid," he explained to Xetiana. "The dunmagicker Gethelred may indeed be the rightful heir to the Dustel throne, but he is also a subverted sylv who is now a dunmaster. He seeks to subvert the Castlemaid in turn. And the Keeper Council, sadly, is mistaken about what happened when Blaze rescued Lyssal of Cirkase. With your leave, my lord, I would tell you the whole story. It makes for interesting listening." He smiled at her, radiating charm. Fog-damn and mist-wraiths, I thought, the man is *flirting* with her.

She settled back on her throne. "Very well," she said. "I am always willing to listen to a good tale. Proceed, Syr-patriarch."

It took Ryder about an hour, during which we stood where we were and tried not to fidget. Dek found that almost impossible, and Blaze ended up gripping him in a deceptively casual hold by the back of the neck. Ryder's tale was not quite the same one I knew; he glossed over a few salient points like the fact that Blaze had seized Flame from Duthrick's Keeper ship and rendered the Councillor unconscious in the process. His

tale blithely made me Aware, to avoid explaining about selver-
herders and their abilities. He didn't mention that he believed
Gethelred was actually over a hundred years old, and had
sunk the Dustel Islands some ninety or so years earlier.
Ghemphs didn't figure in his story at all. Neither did Dustel
birds or Ruarth.

He did spend a great deal of time describing the horrors of
the dunmagic enclave at Creed, on Gorthan Spit, and he de-
tailed the Keeper attack there, when they had flattened the village with their cannon-guns. He was quite graphic when it
came to the death of Alain Jentel, cut in two by a cannonball.
He said Flame had been infected by dunmagic, but that I, a famous physician and chirurgeon from Mekaté, hoped to be
able to cure her illness and return her to her former sylv status. *If* we had access to her in time.

He ended with an eloquent outline of what would happen
to Breth's nearest neighbor, Xolchas Stacks, if a dunmagicker,
in the form of Castlemaid Lyssal, married the Breth Bastionlord, murdered him once she had borne an heir, and then married a dunmaster called Gethelred. For good measure he
tossed in the idea of a grossly powerful Keeper oligarchy who
controlled weapons as vicious as the cannon-gun. I remembered then that Blaze had once made some remark about how
the Keeper Isles had seized economic control of Xolchas's
guano exports in a trade war, and I guessed that the patriarch
was sneakily playing to the Barbicanlord's justifiable fears of
Keeper domination.

Skies, he was clever. Never once did he allow his gaze to
stray to the two more experienced statesmen in the room, Asorcha and Shavel: his whole attention was focused on Xetiana. He
sounded so rational, so palpably honest and upright, even when
he bent the truth. He scattered his account with seemingly in-
genuous comments that implied that, of *course,* only an intelligent listener such as the Barbicanlord would understand what he
was getting at. He charmed and flattered, but so subtly and so
sincerely, it was impossible to fault him. He genuinely did seem
to admire Xetiana's acuity. Never, at any time, did he talk down
to her or patronize her for her youth or her gender or her inexpe-
rience. He managed to treat her as both a desirable woman and
a wise head of state, at one and the same time.

Tarnation, I thought. There really was nothing the man did not do well.

When he finished he bowed his head once and stepped back a pace. None of us moved.

Xetiana raised a finger on her left hand. It was obviously a signal to Shavel, calling for his comment, because he cleared his throat and took a step closer to her. "My lord," he began, "there is no way we can check this tale. We have no other people who are of the Aware on the Stacks at the moment, that I know of anyway. The only facts we can be certain of are these: the halfbreed is Aware; she did work for the Keeper Council; there was a fight against dunmagickers on Gorthan Spit, and it was won by the Keepers. Recent Keeper dispatches have told us that a dunmaster is believed to have escaped, and he did steal a ship. It was called the *Keeper Liberty,* and it was a brigantine, not a ketch called *Amiable*. The name of the dunmaster was Janko, or Morthred, not Gethelred. We know nothing about a dunmagic enclave anywhere on Mekaté. We do know that the Keepers have asked all islandoms to report dunmagicker activity to them, and that they have promised to help any islandom with a dunmagicker problem."

He paused for a moment to allow all that to sink in, then added, "This man here before us does possess what appear to be genuine papers of a patriarch called Tor Ryder, but we have no proof that he *is* Ryder. We have no proof that the Castlemaid is a subverted sylv. None of our guests from the *Amiable* have used magic while here, at least that we know of. Their behavior has been impeccable. And it is hard to imagine that a man of Syr-sylv Gethelred's charm is a dunmaster. He has told us he is a sylv."

Xetiana inclined her head. "It is also hard to imagine that a man of Syr-aware Ryder's charm could be lying, is that not also right?"

The faintest of pauses this time, then, "As you say, my lord."

"Let us assume for a moment that he is indeed lying. Can you think of any reason?"

"I know of none, my lord. That does not mean that such a reason does not exist." He waved a hand at us. "These people may have a personal vendetta against the Castlemaid or against Syr-sylv Gethelred. They may have reasons to want to cause a rift between Cirkase and Breth on the one hand, and Xolchas on the other, so that we are forced even further into Keeper pockets. There is even a possibility that this is all some diabolical machination of the Keeper Council. Blaze may still be working for them, for all that she says she is not."

"That is a lot of 'maybes,' Shavel. Asorcha, your thoughts?"

"Syr-patriarch Lancom of the Menod House here does not doubt Ryder's credentials, or his identity. And he said in his recommendation of Ryder that he had recently heard of the Syr-aware Patriarch's promotion to the Menod Council, a fact which would not yet be widely known. I remember Blaze well, from when she was here last; she was brazen, outspoken and self-serving. But one thing I do know: she hated dunmagic. As do all the Aware, or so I understand. If we can prove that even one of these people we harbor is a dunmagicker, then I think we can be reasonably certain the rest of the patriarch's story is true."

"Hmm." Xetiana turned back to Shavel. "What can you tell me about these people of Gethelred's?"

"There are five women, all Keeper sylvs. Or so they say. They do not leave the Castlemaid's side. The rest are men. They accompany Gethelred everywhere. He calls them his bodyguard, and says that those among them who are of Keeper citizenship have been appointed as such by the Keeper Council. There is also a Calmenter and a Stragglerman, if I remember correctly."

"Seeing that Gethelred claims to be of Dustel Island descent, it is odd that there are no Dustelfolk among his entourage, is it not?" Xetiana said. "It is my understanding that there are many Dustel Islanders still living scattered in the Souther Isles. I would have thought that such people would look to a man of Gethelred's charm, wealth and lineage for leadership." She paused for a moment in frowning thought, then continued, "Shavel, single out one of these Keeper sylvs. Tell Gethelred we intend to honor his men by making this particular man a marshal in the race tomorrow. Separate that man from his friends and his weapons under some pretext to do with . . . oh, I don't know, measuring him for a uniform or something, and then have one of your men attack him with a sword. If he defends himself with dunmagic, then we will know what he is, won't we? Of course, you must have someone hidden nearby with a crossbow so he does not escape back to Gethelred."

Ryder was the first one of us to understand what she meant. He stiffened and his face went red. "My lord, Shavel's man will die!"

"So you say. And that will be sufficient proof for me that your story is true."

"My lord, as one of the Menod, I cannot countenance deliberately sending a man to his death—"

She snapped, "I am not of your faith, Syr-patriarch. My family worships the God of the Winds. And any armsman who gives his life for the ruling house of Xolchas is honored by the god after death. Such a man is blessed."

The arrogance of it took my breath away, but to her it made perfect sense. Skies, I thought, life is cheap when you think you know the mind of a god. It must be darn handy for a ruler to be able to use that kind of rational when they send young men into a fight . . .

Shavel was already leaving the room. Blaze, Ryder and I exchanged glances.

Xetiana relaxed a little once he had departed. "So, Blaze, tell me this. There are twenty-one dunmagickers here, by your count, if you include the Castlemaid. And three of you. Just how do you intend to win this one? Surely the odds are a little steep, even for Blaze Halfbreed."

"There are four of us, actually," Blaze said. "Dek is Aware too. And quite versatile with a knife."

Xetiana looked at Dek, unimpressed. "Oh." Her gaze slid on to me. "And you, physician? What was your name again?"

"Gilfeather."

"Gilfeather. You don't even have a sword."

"I dinna fight. And I dinna understand. Why can't your guards help us arrest these dunmagickers and be done with it? Why can't we just separate Flame from them and take her with us?" I was naive, I suppose. I hadn't seen enough destructive dunmagic to be otherwise.

Xetiana's surprise was genuine. She looked at Blaze. "Where did you get this fellow? I thought the priest said he was Aware?"

Blaze sighed. "He not only can't be hurt by dunmagic, he can't see it either. So he doesn't quite believe in it."

The Barbicanlord began to laugh. "Oh, this is too rich. A versatile lad with a knife, a priest who doesn't like killings, Blaze Halfbreed, and an Aware physician who is so unaware he doesn't even know what dunmagic is!" She stood up and came across to me, taking me by the arm. "You poor man . . . You don't *arrest* dunmagickers. You kill them. Come, let us all adjourn to the inner rooms where we can sit and be more comfortable while we wait. That damn throne is as hard as it looks. Asorcha, have some refreshments brought."

Seated once more, in a much smaller room, and without the combined watchful presence of Asorcha and Shavel, she seemed less the imperious monarch, and more just a woman who found us amusing. She leaned forward, fixing her gaze on my face. "Are you really so naive?"

"I suppose so. I'm from the Roof of Mekaté. We dinna see many dunmagickers up there. Or sylvs. Or anyone else, for that matter. I'm a selver-herder and a physician, not a man of action."

"Then let me tell you what you face when you take on dunmagic. There is no way an ordinary person can deal with a dunmagicker unless he takes them by surprise with an arrow. If one of my guardsmen were to approach one of them with a drawn sword, he'd get a bolt of magic through his belly and he'd burn from the inside out as though someone had set his guts on fire. Of course, that's the *quick* way to die. Dunmagickers actually prefer it slow, like a dun sore that can take days to kill you. A dunmagicker could, however, kill ten or twenty or thirty people in a row before he ran out of power and had to rest for a few days.

"And let's say we knock one out, and throw him in our jail. How long do you think we could keep him there before his magic burned a hole in the wall and he walked free? Normally, of course, we don't even know someone is a dunmagicker to start with, because there are no Awarefolk born on the Stacks. And no sylvs either.

"I remember the incident that brought Blaze here in the first place, years back. Someone was entering our houses, raping the women, then killing the occupants with dunmagic and stealing their wealth. If anyone saw him, they died too. He killed a friend of mine. I saw the body, I saw what he had done to her before he'd pulled out her heart. He'd burned her throat with magic first so she couldn't scream while he did those things to her. We'd never had to worry too much about such evil before that; we've never been rich enough to attract dunmagickers, and we don't seem to breed them.

"We sent a ship for Keeper help, and they sent Blaze. Eventually. A hundred and two more people had died in the meantime, and we still didn't even know who he was. She found him within a matter of hours and killed him for us. He was just eighteen years old, not particularly bright, a lone dunmagicker trying to carve out his own territory."

I suddenly felt chilled. She was speaking of horrors that were beyond my ken. It was hard to accept that one man could murder so many, hard to accept that Blaze's job had once been to kill for the Keepers. I wrapped my taigard a little tighter.

Xetiana sat back in her chair as a spread of food was brought in on trays and laid on the low stone tables. For a while the conversation continued along more socially normal lines: "Do try this pastry; it is a speciality from the Claw . . ." and so on. After that, Xetiana, Blaze and Ryder had a long conversation about the growing power of the Keeper Isles, and what Xetiana and Xolchas Stacks could, or couldn't, do to stop them.

It was the Barbicanlord who brought the subject back to dunmagickers. "So," she said at last, "I repeat, Blaze: if you are telling the truth, how are you going to tackle twenty or so dunmagickers led by a dunmaster? Especially when they cluster around Gethelred or Lyssal like flies on a couple of dead fish?"

"Perhaps Gilfeather can poison them for us."

I dropped my cup with a clatter, spilling the liquid it contained. If my sudden queasiness was any indication, my heart had plunged somewhere to the level of my stomach.

Surprisingly, Ryder seemed to think that was a good idea. "An overdose of sleeping draft: what better way to die than to fall asleep and just never wake up? Or you could just put them to sleep and Blaze and I will kill them in their beds."

Dek's jaw dropped. "That's . . . that's . . . not . . . not *nice*."

Blaze just stopped herself from sighing. "Killing is never *nice*, Dek," she reminded him.

I intervened hastily before that idea went any further. "It's out of the question. I know naught of poisons and I don't have much sleeping draft, even if I knew how to administer it." And even if I could bring myself to kill someone using my physician's skills.

Blaze glanced momentarily at Ryder, then back at the Barbicanlord. "Then we have to think of some way to separate them, one from the other. Kill as many as we can with arrows before the others know it. With your guardsmen spearheading that attack, my lord. Then we—Ryder, Gilfeather, Dek and I—we'll tackle the rest."

A voice interrupted from behind us. "There's one problem with that, Syr-aware. Xolchas Stacks is a windy place. We don't use bows and arrows here much. Even crossbows and quarrels have only limited effectiveness. And if we mount a surprise attack inside a building . . ." Shavel stood there, looking grim. "Difficult. Rooms are small. Doorways are narrow. We could never tackle them all at once." He crossed the room and nodded to the Barbicanlord. "My man died on the spot, my lord. The blast of dun threw him across the room with a hole burned in him big enough to stick my fist into."

"And the Keeper dunmagicker?"

"Dead with a quarrel through his heart before he even had time to think. We have disposed of the body."

Xetiana nodded soberly. "So you are right, Blaze. We have dunmagickers in our midst." She was tapping her fingers angrily on the arm of her chair as though she blamed us for this incursion. "So, how do we separate these . . . abominations one from another?"

"You can't carry a sword on the stack race," Blaze said slowly, "and if you race to win, you get separated, strung out . . . why don't we get them to enter the race?"

My heart thumped down still further. I didn't know what a stack race was, but I had a good idea that it was something I wasn't going to enjoy.

CHAPTER 29

NARRATOR : KELWYN

XETIANA QUARTERED US IN HER PER-
sonal apartments, so there would be no chance that we'd
bump into Flame or any of the dunmagickers. They were in
the guest quarters, which had a separate entrance. Blaze was
next door to Dek and me, and the guarded entrance to Xetiana's suites was just down the corridor. I had never seen a
room like the one Dek and I were given that night. The whole
building may have been built of stone, but little of it was in
evidence in our room. The walls were covered in woven
woolen hangings, the floors thick with woolen rugs.

"What is this stuff?" Dek asked, burying his toes deep into
the pile.

"Sheep's wool," I said. I knew that much, courtesy of Garrowyn and the tales of his voyages. I even knew what sheep
looked like; I'd seen wood cuts and engravings in books.
"This particular stack may have only a city on top of it, but the
others are mostly farms, and they run sheep. Animals that
look a bit like goats."

"You may not know any *useful* things," Dek said disparag-
ingly, "but you know all sorts of other stuff, don't you? You

haven't been lots of places like the Syr-patriarch and Blaze,
but you still know things. How is that?"

As Dek's idea of useful things included sword fighting,
fletching an arrow or beating an opponent into insensibility
with one's fists, I wasn't too shattered by that part of his assessment. I said, "I listen well, and I read a lot."

"I can't read much," he admitted. "Nor write. My ma did
try to teach me. She used to write the letters on the floor-
boards with a piece of charcoal, till my da beat her for it. So
then she did it with a finger dipped in water when he wasn't
around, so he wouldn't know. But we never had anything to
read . . ."

"Then ye will have to learn, my lad. I'd be glad to teach ye.
And I imagine that Ryder would too, if either of us get a spot
of peace and quiet to do it in."

"What's gunna happen tomorrow?" he asked. "I could
scarce tell what they was talkin' about earlier."

I shook my head helplessly. I knew how he felt. Xetiana,
Blaze, Ryder and Shavel had pored over maps and diagrams
and planned and discussed and argued. Xetiana, now that she
had overcome her initial suspicion, thrust herself into the
preparation for slaughter with enthusiasm. Her one proviso appeared to be that none of the ordinary race participants was to
be harmed, a concern that struck me as surprising, seeing as she
had not cared one iota for the unfortunate guard who had died
just to prove that Gethelred's bodyguards were dunmagickers.

The rest of the day had passed in a blur, of which I understood little. Not only had I never been to the Stacks before, but
I didn't know what a stack race was, had only a limited idea of
what a dunmagicker or a dunmaster could do to one of the
non-Aware, and wouldn't have known the range of a crossbow
if my life depended on it. Dek was not much better off, so in
the end, we'd retreated to our sumptuous room and taken a
bath instead.

This was a new experience for Dek, whose only encounter
with bathing had been an obligatory quick wash every morning under a pump in the guardhouse yard back in Lekenbraig,
and similar ablutions at the inn in Amkabraig. Perfumed hot
water, luxurious towels and scented soaps were a whole new
experience, and one which he had initially regarded with a

strong dose of skepticism. In the end, however, I had to haul him out of the water.

As the Barbicanlord had sent someone to fetch our things from the ship, I told Dek to put on his nightgown, which he did before demolishing the bowl of imported nuts that was in the room, followed by a plate of roast mutton a servant brought for both of us. Then, as we sat about and waited to see if Blaze or Ryder were going to come and tell us what was happening, he began to yawn. Ten minutes later he was sound asleep.

Much later, perhaps around eleven o'clock, there was a knock at the door. It was Blaze. "Can I come in?" she asked.

I stepped back and waved her in. As I closed the door, she took one look at Dek and grinned. "Ah. I guess it has been quite a day. Maybe then we'd better go to my room. I need to talk to you, to tell you about what we have decided."

"All right," I said. "Just let me get one of my tagairds. I'm feeling cold." I dug one out from my bag, and wrapped it around me.

"Dashing," she said. "Did anyone ever tell you how attractive that piece of cloth can be? At least, it is the way you Sky Plainsmen wear it."

"I wouldna know," I said. "Though Jastriá did expend considerable energy trying to get me out of it, y'know."

She was laughing as she opened the door, but her amusement died when she stepped out. It was easy to see why. At the end of the passage, Ryder was standing with his back to us, outside the doors to Xetiana's apartments. One of the guards had evidently just knocked on her door, because the Islandlord opened it. She was dressed in something as flimsy as it was alluring, and as we watched she reached out and drew Ryder inside. The guards resumed their position at the doorway, without a flicker of emotion. Neither Xetiana nor Ryder had noticed the two of us.

Wordlessly Blaze led the way to her room. As I entered and she closed the door, she said, "Don't you *dare* feel sorry for me, Gilfeather."

"I wouldna dream of it," I said flatly.

"There is nothing between Tor and me anymore. We both know it wouldn't work. And he has every right to seek what he wants elsewhere."

"Aye," I agreed.

"Which is not easy, or often, when you are an unmarried patriarch and therefore supposedly celibate."

"Aye, there is that."

"And you don't say no to an Islandlord with impunity either."

"No, I suppose not."

She gave an exasperated growl. "Oh, shut up, you selver-herding heathen, you." She flung a cushion at me with surprising force. And Seeker followed it, jumping from her bed to greet me with tail wags and slobbering enthusiasm.

"Where in all the skies did he come from?" I asked, happy to change the subject.

"Oh, I asked for him. I told Xetiana that he doesn't chase birds. Sit down, Kel, and let me tell you what is going to happen tomorrow. And what you will have to do."

I did as she asked, but I hurt for her, nonetheless.

THE STACK RACE, AS I LEARNED, WAS AN annual affair, and each stack entered their best athletes. The course covered Xolchasbarbican and nine or ten of the Inner Stacks that were clustered around it. Each one had to be crossed over the top, and in a certain order. There were race marshals to make sure those rules were followed. There wasn't that much choice about how you got from one stack to another: no boats or sea-ponies were allowed. Some stacks were linked by rope bridges suspended high above the water; others were freestanding, or not linked to the next stack in the race—then you had to swim. You could either take the path down to the ocean, or you could use the rope netting erected by the guano collectors, which was usually faster, but much more dangerous. If you really knew what you were doing, you climbed part of the way down and then jumped or dived into the sea. If you misjudged the height, then you could knock yourself unconscious on the surface of the water and drown. If you misjudged where you were going to land, then you could hit one of the numerous rocks around the foot of each stack.

For an indifferent swimmer such as myself, it sounded like a sure way to commit suicide, and I told Blaze so as we sat and ate the late supper she had a servant bring to the room.

"No one is asking you to enter," she said with a grin. "I can imagine that the average citizen of the Roof of Mekaté swims about as well as a tailless lobster."

"Something like that," I agreed. The streams up on the Sky Plains were rarely more than knee-deep, and the water was cold.

She sketched a plan of the stacks for me in chalk on a piece of slate. (Those rooms of Xetiana's were supplied with just about every item you could possibly ever want.) "Look, the first leg of the journey is a swim from Xolchasbarbican Stack to the stack known as the Beak. Then there's a climb up to the top of the Beak. By this time, competitors are already going to be strung out. They cross the stack to the bridge that gets them to the Tooth, cross that, bridge to the Molar. There are checkpoints all along the way, of course, to make sure no one cheats. Then you cross the Molar, climb down to the sea, swim to the Claw, climb up. Cross the top, jump across to some basalt columns called the Peppers. Jump from one to another, ten all told, then back to the Claw. Cross the Claw again, climb down the cliffs and swim to the Talon . . ."

"Ye're mad," I said.

"Me? Why?"

"Because ye once did this."

She shrugged. "It was quite fun, to tell you the truth. The only disappointment was that I came in fifteenth, and didn't win any money. Now listen carefully. Xetiana has already told Gethelred-Morthred and Flame that she expects all their bodyguards to enter, and she has sweetened the attraction of it with a substantial prize for whichever one of them does best."

"Which she won't have to pay out if they are all dead. But why on earth would Morthred go along with this plan? He must realize that it is going to leave himself and Flame without any guards for the better part of a day."

"Why should he be worried? He doesn't feel himself in any danger here."

"Maybe not, but all it would take would be for one of the Awarefolk to turn up, and he's in trouble."

"Xetiana can be very persuasive." She looked at me, daring me to comment. I said nothing. She said, "She appealed to his sense of pride. She suggested it to him, then quickly changed her mind, implying that it was a foolish idea because his guards might get hurt, and it was unlikely they would be good enough to complete the course anyway. When he objected to that, she made him a bet he couldn't resist." Blaze grinned at me. "Xetiana relished relaying the whole conversation to me afterward; believe me, it was masterful."

"What was the bet?"

"If any of his guards came in among the first twenty to finish the race, Gethelred's firstborn child could marry one of her children."

"And he *believed* that?"

She nodded.

"And it never occurred to him that she might murder any guard of his who looked like succeeding?"

"Apparently not. Remember, she's supposed to believe he is of royal Dustel blood. He arrived here dressed for the part, wearing a lord's ransom in jewelry and fine silks, in the company of the Castlemaid, and laden with presents he's no doubt looted over the past couple of years, ever since his power started to return. He's arrogant enough to think all that might count with the royal house of Xolchas. Xolchas Stacks is hardly of importance in the Isles of Glory pecking order, you know; it's too small and too poor. He was right: Xetiana *was* flattered. It's not beyond the realm of possibility that she would look to the idea of allying her islandom with the royalty of another, vanished as it might be. She's ruthless enough to jilt her present betrothed without a qualm."

"And the laws regarding inter-island marriage?"

"That's the beauty of it. The Dustels don't officially exist anymore. Oh, their human citizenry are tattooed, what remains of them, but no island laws apply to them. Most of them live on the Stragglers, but they can live where they like, marry whom they like and have their children be citizens, go where they like. That was something that was agreed upon by all Islandlords when the Dustel Isles vanished. A humanitarian gesture to a devastated people."

"Morthred has a tattoo?"

"No, it was cut off. He told Xetiana he did that himself, while he was still a boy, out of disgust at the last Dustel Islandlord's actions in murdering his forebears. Might even be true. Anyway, let's get back to what is going to happen tomorrow. Two of the subverted Keeper sylv women can't enter because they can't swim well enough. There's a good chance those two will remain on board the *Amiable* to keep an eye on their coerced slaves. We will deal with them later. Neither Morthred nor Flame will be entering, of course; they will be entertained by Xetiana and her betrothed, Yethrad, respectively, while the race is on. One man is already dead, thanks to Shavel's orders.

"Each of the other sixteen will be wearing a red sash so that they are easily distinguishable from the local race entrants. Xetiana's guards will be stationed all along the route as race marshals. Many more of her armsmen will be entrants. Unbeknownst to Morthred, Xetiana has drastically reduced the number of ordinary entrants. As this is not the annual race, but a special race for her betrothal, she can do that. She wants to diminish the chance that ordinary people will get hurt.

"Her armsmen are going to eliminate as many of the dunmagickers as they can as the race progresses. But they can only deal with them one at a time. If one sees another attacked, then there will be a dunmagicker on a rampaging slaughter, and believe me, you don't ever want to see that."

She stood up and began pacing to and fro. I had come to recognize this as a Blaze phenomenon: she could not keep still while she planned action. "Tor and I will station ourselves on the stack called the Talon. If we can, we will get rid of any dunmagickers still alive at that point, before they go any further along the race course; after that, the race is watched by spectators lined up on the roofs of the western cliffs of Xolchasbarbican—they can see what is happening across on the last group of stacks because the straits there are narrow. Morthred will be among the watchers, and we don't dare arouse his suspicions."

"Why not deal with him first, and the others later?"

She gave a slight laugh. "Because we may fail when we tackle Morthred. He's strong, Kel. Stronger than we bargained for. And he knows Tor and me. We can't sneak up on him. So we get rid of as many of his subverted friends as we can first;

then at least we will have achieved something before we die."
She sounded so matter-of-fact, it was hard to believe she was
talking about her own possible death, hers and Ryder's.

I asked, "Is there no way the Xolchas guards can take care
of him? With arrows?"

"Not impossible, but it would be risky. He is never parted
from his subverted sylvs and those two dunmagickers he has,
not for a moment, so getting crossbowmen anywhere near before the race would be difficult. And think of the carnage if
just one of those in his entourage escapes the arrows. Gilfeather, I know you have problems believing this, but please
don't take what I say lightly. In a few seconds, a dunmaster of
power like Morthred could level this palace and everyone in it.
Even these subverted sylvs have enough raw power to kill
everyone around them. They can kill us too, you know, by . . .
by collapsing a wall on us, for example.

"The best chance for us to act is during the race when his
guards are gone. One problem then is this: we can't trust
Flame not to use her power against us if we attack Morthred.
So we have to separate her from Morthred. The second problem is that during the race Morthred is going to be in the company of either Xetiana, or her betrothed, Yethrad. All he would
need is a few seconds—*seconds*—between being warned and
dying and he could kill everyone around him. You're a doctor,
you should know that if you get a crossbow bolt in the heart, it
can take more than a few seconds to die. Death has to be instantaneous. And Xetiana must not be anywhere near. We are
still discussing the details of how to set this up. Xetiana would
be loath to lose her betrothed, too, it seems, so we have to
make sure we can do this without anyone getting hurt except
Morthred."

"So what do Dek and I do?"

"The Talon has a bridge across to Xolchasbarbican. I want
Dek to guard that just to make sure that no dunmagicker aban-
dons the race and tries to get back to Morthred, for whatever
reason. Dek's job would be to make sure they don't make it."

"Ye are asking a lad to kill, just like that? And what's more,
to kill grown men ye believe are hellishly dangerous?"

She met my gaze. "He's Aware. It's his job. Anyway, we

don't expect any of them to reach the Talon alive. And if they
do, well, Dek'll be in less danger than the Xolchas armsmen
who will be there with him. Dunmagic can kill *them*. And
none of the dunmagickers will be carrying a sword. You can't
swim with a sword weighing you down, you know. Anyway, I
will not be asking him to tackle a grown man head on. Lately,
I have been trying to impress on him that it is not dishonorable
to kill a dunmagicker with a booby trap . . ."

She must have seen my distaste, because she said, "If you
have any reservations, Gilfeather, go and talk to Ruarth, as I
have done today." She had stopped pacing and now stood over
me, with her hands on her hips. She could be intimidating
when she put her mind to it. "You want to hear this? Maybe
you had better hear it, no matter how much it hurts, just so you
understand what we are up against. I've had it in graphic detail from Ruarth. Flame struggles against her subversion. The
real Flame is there, trapped inside, and occasionally, just occasionally, the pain that she feels is there, in her eyes, begging
Ruarth for help. So far, the sylv part of her has managed to
keep him a secret from Morthred, but how long she will be
able to maintain her loyalty to the Dustel is uncertain. She no
longer talks to him. She hardly looks at him. He talks to her,
whenever he can, whispering his words of encouragement and
love . . . and she slaps him away.

"Morthred seduces her every night. At first she struggles,
but then the dunmagic inside her takes over, and she enjoys it,
even when he deliberately hurts her. Then, just to make sure
that she doesn't enjoy it *too* much, he gives her to one of the
others, and they all watch. They dream up new ways to rape
her each night. A sort of competition to see who is the most
original. And if she objects too much, you know what they
do? Or at least what they did when they were on board the
ship? They would bring up one of the slaves and force her to
torture the poor sod. Oh, she doesn't struggle too much, you
understand; in fact, part of her actually enjoys doing it. Although I am not sure how much she enjoyed it the night they
made her cut—"

I jumped to my feet and closed both ears with my hands as
if I could shut out the horror. *"Stop it,"* I screamed at her.

"Stop it, *stop* it! How *dare* ye say things like that about her! That's *foul*!"

And then I stood there, aghast, staring at her. "Oh *Creation*, Blaze." She looked at me, unshed tears lurking behind her intense pain. I pulled her into my arms, and we stood there, rocking each other, while both of us wept. I cried for Flame, for Ruarth, for Blaze. I cried for myself, for the absolute end of my shredded innocence.

I LEFT HER ALONE SOME TIME LATER, after we had talked about the part I had to play in the next day's events. It didn't come as any surprise to me, the role they had chosen. There could only be one part for someone with my olfactory talents: I had to stand watch over Morthred, to warn everyone if he became suspicious. For the whole of the day, I was to be an honorary member of the Barbicanlord's personal guard. If the dunmaster decided to turn his dunpower against Xetiana and her islandom, if I scented anything alarming, it would be up to me to give the signal.

It sounded simple. Of course, it wasn't: for a start, Flame would be there and she knew who I was. And then there was that small problem of killing someone in less than a second or two.

Letter from Researcher (Special Class) S. iso Fabold, National Department of Exploration, Federal Ministry of Trade, Kells, to Masterman M. iso Kipswon, President of the National Society for the Scientific, Anthropological and Ethnographical Study of non-Kellish Peoples.

Dated this day 12/1st Single/1794

Dear Uncle,
Here we are into a new year again, and what an exciting year it promises to be for me! I can scarcely believe that in less than two months the RV Seadrift *will set sail again, as the heart of a fleet of five ships, and I shall be on board. Our intended sailing date is the 20th of 1st Doublemoon.*

Glad to hear that my Glorian tales continue to interest you and delight Aunt Rosris. I understand perfectly why you prefer to relate them to her, rather than let her read them! Blaze in particular is sorely lacking in feminine niceties and I would not like to expose a lady to her blunt crudity. Nor would I want a well-bred lady to know of Flame's woeful lack of moral character. Anyara and I had a long discourse on just this subject the other evening. She maintains that sometimes Kellish sensibilities border on hypocrisy, but I feel it can never be amiss for ladies to maintain their feminine character. We should shield them from the worst of the world; they have not the constitution nor the moral strength to face all that a man must. I am sure Anyara saw the strength of that argument, because she did not pursue the topic.

Women . . . ! They are so impressionable. Anyara maintains that Gilfeather and Blaze must be telling the truth, and that therefore the Glory Isles were once full of alien creatures and wicked magicians . . . Nothing I say seems to be able to persuade her that we are dealing with a culture riddled with superstitious nonsense, in which anything that they couldn't explain was called magic. It is my belief that once the Glorians were faced with the very first Kellish traders—that is, true "aliens" in their landscape—they dropped the idea of mythical ones. They wrote the ghemphs and the magicians out of their folklore, in effect, and stopped wasting their energies on the problems of citizenship so as to have the unity and focus to cope with the dilemmas of the new world they faced. And our Kellish advent did indeed bring them a new world, believe me.

Thank you for your invitation to hunt on your Emmorland estate. I have wonderful memories of the stags there, and will do my best to escape the city for a week to join you all.

Your fond nephew,
Shor iso Fabold

CHAPTER 30

I SPENT MOST OF THE DAY FEELING ILL. I wasn't sure whether it was because I was in the presence of a dunmaster or simply because I was, as the Sky People put it, scared woolly.

I thought it was probably the latter. I was frightened not so much that I was going to die, but that I might have to make a decision at some stage during the day that could mean life or death to those around me. If I misinterpreted what my nose told me about Morthred, I could even be the cause of the death of an Islandlord. It would have been easy enough to do, make a mistake, because Morthred smelled so strongly of dun it tended to mask the subtleties.

I had done everything I could think of to minimize my chances of drawing attention to myself. I had dyed my hair again, a nondescript brown, and shaved off my beard. I was wearing the uniform of Xetiana's personal guard, which included a hat with a brim, and I had, at Blaze's instigation, toned down my freckles with a liberal application of ladies' face powder (I then had to restrain the urge to touch my face and look at my fingertips). I was grateful that custom dictated that no guard, with the exception of the Securia and the Captain of the Guard, carried a weapon in the immediate presence of their Islandlord; I would not have known what to do with a sword, and probably would have made a fool of myself by getting it caught between my legs and falling flat on my face. I did, however, secrete my dirk in my boot, a fact which was known to the Securia, the Captain, and the Islandlord herself.

As I positioned myself behind Xetiana, Morthred and Flame at breakfast that morning, I kept glancing at Flame, as inconspicuously as I could. She did not look my way, and I doubted that she saw me. I was, after all, just a man in a uniform, one of several, but it was more than that. She seemed remote, withdrawn. She spoke when spoken to, courteously and sensibly, but she never volunteered a remark. Her expression seemed both haunted and distant. She reminded me of patients of mine who had suffered a loss beyond imagining; the death of a young child, for example. Skies, I wondered, will she ever be able to recover from this, from whatever it is they have done to her?

I wanted to do something to attract her attention, knock something over perhaps, just to make her look at me, see who I was. To tell her wordlessly that she was not alone. I quelled the urge. It would have been foolhardy to take that risk.

I could now smell the dun around her like gangrene. Other subverted sylvs all had a similarity to their aromas; hers was different. More patchy . . . and something else. I tried to put my finger on it. And then I had it: everyone else smelled much like Morthred. She didn't. It was foul and stinking and *wrong,* but it wasn't a Morthred smell. I tried to make sense of that, without much success. Blaze and Ryder had both continued to maintain that there was something odd about Flame's subversion, that it couldn't be a flare-up of her first contamination on Gorthan Spit, but we hadn't solved that puzzle. Perhaps, I thought as I stood there, we never would.

The sweetness of sylv was there within her too, which I took as a good sign. Part of her was fighting back. The sylv was losing, but she hadn't stopped trying. When I thought back to what Blaze had told me the night before, I was overwhelmed by the courage of her battle, by the strength of her drive to preserve her integrity. She must have known the odds of her survival as a sylv were nil, but still she would not surrender.

When I gazed at Morthred-Gethelred, it was hard to keep my fury in check. The dunmaster could sit there next to the woman he had repeatedly raped, telling droll stories and spreading his charm to include all Xetiana's ladies. He could sit there flattering the Islandlord, while the foulness was spreading through Flame's body, fundamentally changing her into a creature she did not want to be. Dun contagion: a diabolical form of murder. The worst kind, because it left the victim alive, perpetually aware of the death of their true self.

When Blaze and Ryder had taken me aside early that morning and run through the final plan, and my part in it, I had not protested. After what Blaze had told me the night before, I wanted Morthred dead so badly that any reservations I had about participating in his death had vanished. To tell the truth, I had been so sickened by Blaze's account of Flame's suffering, I felt I could have torn Morthred's throat out with my bare fingers given the chance.

No one, however, envisaged Gilfeather the physician from the Sky Plains as the avenging nemesis of Morthred the dunmaster. If things went well, my role was to be marginal. Or so we all hoped. Nervously, I fingered the one thing I was able to carry openly, just in case. It was Xetiana's spyglass, a heavy brass tube almost as long as my arm, wrapped in soft felt cloth. The Barbicanlord herself had been the one to suggest it as a possible weapon, after I mentioned that one way to ensure the dunmaster could not attack anyone with dunmagic was to knock him out first, then kill him. Now that I had the spyglass, however, I was afraid I would end up dropping it, or something equally clumsy.

Immediately after breakfast, the royal party was augmented by a few of the more important island dignitaries, including Xetiana's betrothed, Yethrad, who was the Master of Stabbing Stack, and everyone adjourned to the balcony overlooking the palace forecourt. I followed, together with the other Xolchas guards. The Securia, Shavel, raised a questioning eyebrow at me; I shook my head. I had detected not the slightest unease in Morthred. As far as I could tell, the man was oozing only a smug smell of triumph. After all his years as a deformed, powerless man living in poverty outside the power structure of the Isles, he was enjoying being feted as a handsome nobleman. He enjoyed Xetiana's courtesy. He enjoyed the coy glances of the court ladies. He enjoyed both the subtle deference and the overt flattery. I had to subdue a desire to kill the man then and there.

The first participants in the race, all women, were milling around in the courtyard beneath the balcony. The sylvs wore red sashes, otherwise everyone was dressed much the same way: trousers that ended above the knee, snugly fitted long-sleeved tops. I sensed a surge of sexual interest from Morthred, but surprisingly little from anyone else. The people of Xolchas Stacks were used to women who swam and such outfits were commonplace.

As a mark of honor, Xetiana invited Gethelred to start the women's section of the race, which was done by beating a huge brass gong hanging on a wooden stand on the balcony. The watching crowd fell silent as the man stepped up to the instrument, the padded drumming stick in his hand. On the third stroke, cheering erupted and the crowd of women competitors surged along the street.

Xetiana turned to Gethelred, smiling. "My lord," she said, "it is now customary for us to go up to the rooftops and walk to a viewpoint where we can see some of the cliff descent." She offered him her arm. "Perhaps you would be good enough to escort me?" She smiled, ducking her head just a little, and looking up at him from under her lashes.

Skies, I thought as I followed the two of them, two or three paces behind, she has courage, this Islandlord!

It took twenty minutes or more for us all to arrive at the place where it was possible to obtain a clear view across a bay to the cliffs on the opposite side. There was a viewing platform here for the most important guests, with padded armchairs and a railing to stop anyone toppling over the cliff. The race participants were already climbing down the opposing cliffs when we arrived, the three subverted sylv women, easily identifiable in their sashes, among them.

"Ah," Xetiana said to Gethelred, delighted, "your sylvs have chosen to climb the cliffs too! I thought they may have taken the track down."

"They are Keeper Council trained," he said urbanely. "Descending a cliff is no hardship to them."

I wasn't so sure about that. The three Keeper women were slower than the Xolchas competitors and they were more visibly disconcerted by the aggression of the seabirds. The Xolchas women moved smoothly and rapidly downward, gripping the ropes where needed, or finding handholds and footholds in the rocks with ease. They ignored the angry cries of the birds and the diving attacks they made when their nests were approached. I thought I would have found it unnerving: some of the birds were huge, with a wingspan that matched the height of a man. As the first women came closer to the surface of the ocean, they began to drop from the cliff, either jumping or diving into the water. The watching crowd, most of whom had seen this often enough, even perhaps participated themselves, still gasped and applauded the higher dives or riskier jumps. The Keeper women wisely climbed down almost to the water level before letting go of the ropes.

And yet they were not the last. There was another trio who entered the water even later. This was planned, I knew; they were all women from Xetiana's guard.

Xetiana turned to Gethelred once more, with yet another smile. "Your ladies performed well, my lord. Now it is time for us to return. I must start the men's race." Even as she spoke she glanced over the dunmaster's shoulder to where I stood. I knew that her questioning eyebrow was for me, and I gave a faint shake of my head. I could still scent nothing that told me Morthred was suspicious.

The dunmaster had his back to me and missed the exchange. Flame, however, stared and I sensed her bewilderment. I stood still, sure she would say something, sure that my masquerade was about to be uncovered, but she turned away, and to my surprise I sensed nothing more from her except a vague neutrality. It was as if she simply refused to think about anything at all that aroused any emotion. I had no idea of whether she had recognized me or not.

Selverspit, I thought. Has that bastard destroyed her mind already?

I smelled my own rage.

CHAPTER 31

NARRATOR : BLAZE

A LOT OF WHAT HAPPENED THAT DAY I only pieced together afterward. Xetiana and Chamberlain Asorcha told me bits, Gilfeather and Dek and Tor did too, of course. Chania, one of Xetiana's guards, filled in some of the gaps. And then there were the Dustels, who acted as our eyes and ears. They flew to and fro the whole day long, telling us what was happening to the others, describing the progress of the race. Without them, we would never have had a chance.

Tor and I were already on the stack called the Talon when one of their fliers brought us the first news of the women's race. Three Xolchas women guards were involved, all strong swimmers who were unfazed by ocean swells. Xetiana had hand picked them herself; their leader, Chania, I knew quite well. She had competed in the same stack race as I had, all those years ago. They were competent women, but unfortunately they did not understand the true nature of dunmagic. They lagged behind on the climb down from the Upper Town and deliberately entered the water behind the three sylvs. They thought to drown the last of the Keeper women, not realizing that she would lash out with magic even as they pushed her under and tried to hold her there.

The magic boiled the water, stirring it into a maelstrom. One guard, hit by the worst of the bolt, died immediately, her stomach torn out. The second was driven downward with such force that her lungs burst. Their bodies had to be fished out of the water by the rescue boats before the men's race started. Chania was luckier. She was thrown upward out of the water in the same explosion of dunmagic, only to fall back, terrified but unharmed. Realizing at last that they had made a major error of judgment, she expected to die; instead, she discovered that the Keeper woman, a poor swimmer, was herself drowning in the very turbulence her power had created. Chania, sickeningly aware that her two companions were nowhere to be seen, felt for her knife. With one swift move, she seized the dying sylv by the hair and drew the knife across her throat. This time there was no explosion of magic. She left the body for a guard mounted on a sea-pony, who had arrived too late to help.

In fury, Chania swam after the next of the Keeper women, who was apparently unaware of what had happened behind her. The Xolchas woman caught up just as the Keeper reached the foot of the cliffs of the stack called the Beak. She grabbed the woman from behind, and broke her neck with a savage sideways twist. Then she hauled herself out of the water and began the long climb up the cliff behind the third and last of the Keeper sylvs.

She was, however, denied the pleasure of killing her as well. The sylv was well ahead, and climbing steadily upward. She reached the top just ahead of Chania, but as she began to haul herself up over the lip of the cliff, she was hit in the eye by a crossbow bolt. For a moment she teetered on the edge, then toppled back and fell, tumbling, in silence to the sea. Panting, Chania pulled herself up onto the grass at the top of the stack. The yeoman guard there lowered his crossbow. "Was that the last of the women?" he asked. He walked to the edge and looked over. Below, the birds wheeled and screamed, but there was no one climbing the cliff. Down in the water several guards on sea-ponies were hauling another body out of the water. "Where are your companions?"

"They are not coming," Chania whispered. "May the winds cradle them into eternity." Wearily she stood up, feeling more despair than triumph. "I think, yeoman, that we have seriously underestimated the difficulties."

The Dustel who had been watching and listening flew back to Xolchasbarbican to spread the word.

ON THE TALON, WHICH CONNECTED DI-rectly to Xolchasbarbican via a bridge, Tor and I established ourselves at the Temple of the Winds. The temple occupied the top of a hill, the highest point of all Xolchas Stacks. It was paved with marble and roofed with enormous slabs of stone but, apart from one inner sanctum which was buried under the floor, the whole building was open to the wind. The stone columns that held up the roof were carved with strangely shaped holes, and it was not long before we discovered there was a reason for this. They made the wind sing, giving rise to unearthly musical sounds that hummed and glissaded all over the stack. Xolchasfolk believed that it was the voice of the Wind God, and it was the task of the priests to interpret the songs. For a fee, of course.

Initially, many of the island's inhabitants had crowded around the temple to witness the race, but Xetiana's guards had sent them back to their homes, under stern orders to stay there till the race was over. They had complained, but they had obeyed; by this time there were abundant rumors circulating across the Stacks and many people must have been aware that there was something wrong.

Just below the temple was a race checkpoint, so race officials, who were all men from Xetiana's yeomen reserve guard, waited with us. They were farmers who had been armsmen in their youth, and they handled their weapons with the easy competence of experienced soldiers. Their conversation while they waited did not touch on the fight that was to come, or the possibility of death, but on the state of this year's sorghum crop (poor), and this season's wool clip (excellent). When the first of the Xolchas competitors appeared, they hid their weapons and melted into the role of officials with unflurried ease.

Comarth, the elderly Dustel bird, brought news of the men's race to me a few minutes later. When two of Xetiana's armsmen, posing as competitors, approached one of the two dunmagickers on the first swimming leg of the men's race, the dunmagicker had ripped open the leg of one armsman, using dunpower to lacerate his artery so that he would bleed to death, and had then pushed a flow of water into the face of the other, drowning him before he even understood he was under attack.

The dunmagicker swam on, Comarth said, his chest swelling with indignation as he gestured this tale to us. *As if nothing had happened! Doubtless he was confident that the two deaths would be ascribed to accidents, not magic. But I saw.* The Dustel could hardly contain himself. *That—that—spawned* monster *of a blackguard. And do you know what was the worst thing, Syr-aware? His violence was prompted only by his desire to do harm, the wretch. He could not have known that he himself was a target, because the armsmen had not yet attacked him!*

"Is he still alive?" I asked, after translating this much for Tor.

As far as I know, the Dustel replied and then sketched in the rest of what had been happening. Two of the male sylvs died on the Beak. One death was accidental: a Keeper had slipped and fallen as he climbed. The second was killed by a crossbow as he skirted a farmhouse on the top of the stack. His body was quickly dragged out of sight before the next of the racers appeared, but no other opportunity to kill had presented itself to the guards who had shot him.

On the bridge across to the Tooth, another sylv had died, tipped through the rope railing by a fellow competitor, a Xolchas guard, of course. The terrain of this stack was rugged, with crags erupting out of the farmland like towering sculptures of wind-worn stone: perfect cover for crossbowmen. Another two sylvs died here in a hail of quarrels, but not before one of them, only wounded in the initial attack, had cut a swathe through the armsmen with his magic that had cost the lives of six men.

That's eight dunmagickers dead, including the women, Comarth said. *Nine more to go.*

"Not counting the two not in the race," Tor murmured

when I filled him in after the old Dustel had flown off. "And Morthred. And Flame."

I looked across at him. "We *will* win this one."

"There's too much that can go wrong. The whole plan is too complicated."

"It's a complicated situation, demanding a complex solution."

He grunted. "Well, it's certainly that."

I sighed. Nothing had gone right between the two of us since he had been dun healed. Most of the time he simply turned his back on me, walked away, left the room when I entered it. Anything to avoid me. "Tor," I asked, "how long is this going to go on between us? And don't pretend you don't know what I mean."

He looked straight at me then. "I find I can't forgive you, Blaze. I *understand,* but I just can't forgive. You should have known me better. I know that as a Menod I should forgive, and it haunts me that I can't. And you know what the other irony is in all this? It's the dun within me that sabotages my forgiveness, that accentuates my bitterness."

"You hate me."

"No, nothing could turn what I felt to hate. What I felt was—profound. Which made your betrayal of all I stand for the more hurtful. Did you know me so little?"

"I loved you too much to let you die."

"Was it love to condemn me to a life of guilt? To make me live with an evil inside me that is none of my making?"

"Is it . . . is it so very bad?" I asked in a whisper.

It was a long time before he answered. Then he said, and his voice was filled with sadness, "I am not the person I was. I thought I could fight it, and return to being myself, but now I know that will never be possible. This Tor Ryder speaking to you now, you don't know him at all."

We stood there, looking at each other, the musical wind making eerie, unearthly music around us, and I felt the further dying of something that had once been beautiful.

SOME TIME LATER ANOTHER DUSTEL FLEW in with more news. On the Molar, Xolchas yeomen had set up a detour. Two subverted sylvs were directed along a narrow path between some rock outcrops. Both died when they fell into a sink hole that had been loosely covered with straw. Another had been killed by a well-placed quarrel on the Claw. A fourth had misjudged his jump to the Peppers: he'd hit the rocks below. A fifth, one of the slowest of the competitors, was attacked by three uniformed armsmen and fell to his death on the basalt rocks. His last action was to direct a fire of dun away from himself as he fell, killing all his attackers. Later still, on the long exhausting swim to the Talon from the Claw, a sylv drowned when he was battered on the rocks at the foot of the cliff because he didn't understand the nature of the waves there.

Later still, the next messenger brought worse news concerning the two dunmagickers. The older of them, a Stragglerman, lacked the athletic prowess of a Keeper-trained sylv, so he had ordered the other, a younger man from Calment called Jaze, to stay with him. Fearing the Stragglerman's superior dunpowers, Jaze had obeyed. Because they stayed together, they had unwittingly avoided attack. They were now both climbing up the cliff to the top of the Talon, and they were still together. Ruarth had been keeping an eye on them, and it was he who passed on the bad news to us through another Dustel. Jaze chanced to look over his shoulder and had seen what had happened when yet another subverted sylv was attacked on the cliff wall of the Claw behind them. He alerted his companion and they both watched while the sylv died. They were apparently not strong enough or close enough to send their own powers across the expanse of ocean to help, but they were close enough to know that the sylv was murdered, deliberately, by men wearing the uniform of Xetiana's royal guard. "What the red hells is happening?" Jaze shouted.

"That was planned," the other said. "The bitch of an Islandlord must have found out we are not as harmless as we pretended to be. Rot it, Jaze, those two armsmen who came up to me in the swim to the Beak, they were trying to kill me, not help me!" He gave a bark of laughter. "And I thought I was just killing them for the sheer pleasure of their pain. It looks as though that bitch of a lord will do anything to win a bet!"

"So what do we do now?"

"Take off that sash, for a start. That's how they know us . . . Damn them to a godless eternity! Have you seen *any* of the other sylvs lately?"

Jaze ripped off his sash in disgust. "There was one just ahead of us a moment ago. But apart from him . . . no."

"They've been picking them off, one by one, like tuna from fish hooks! We must get to Lord Gethelred as soon as we can. Get moving—fast."

The younger man nodded and both of them resumed their climb. This time they were watchful of all that happened around them, not just how they placed their hands and feet. Still, neither of them saw the small blackish bird that flew off in a flurry of feathers, taking advantage of the updraft of air along the cliff face, even though he really wasn't built for soaring.

At the top of the cliff, Ruath stopped for a minute or two to ask one of the other Dustels to take the news to Tor and me; then he himself flew back to warn Gilfeather.

THE TALON HAD THREE EXITS: A BRIDGE TO Xolchasbarbican, another to the Tooth, and a rope slide to the Fang. The two bridges were deliberately not marked on the maps that had been given to Morthred's people, and the ground route, marked with flags, went nowhere near either of them. "But it shouldn't matter anyway," I said, after the Dustel had explained what had happened. "These dunmagickers aren't going to get off this stack now, not if we can help it. Not even if they have learned about the bridges." I glanced at Tor. "Let's go intercept them before they get to the temple."

He nodded and we started off down the path at a run, heading for the cliffs opposite the Claw. "This reminds me of something," I said. "Calment. Only this time we are on the same side."

He grimaced. "Hell's teeth, Blaze, I'm too old for this sort of thing now. I'm out of practice."

"You still shoot a mean arrow and I seem to remember you lopping off a few heads and limbs with that sword of yours quite recently."

"Maybe, but look what happened to *me*!" He was trying to keep the mood light, but I heard his pain anyway.

We had not gone far before we saw a man coming up the path to the temple toward us. It was the last of the subverted sylvs. "On the run," Ryder said with a laconic lack of emotion. "You take the left, and go high. I'll go in right side, low."

"Almost too easy."

We ran on, only drawing our swords at the last moment. Too late the man realized our intention, and flung a bolt of dun at us. We ignored it and swung our blades.

"As I said, too easy," I remarked as I wiped the blood from my weapon onto the man's wet shirt.

Tor looked down at the body. "I hate killing these subverted sylvs," he said. "It seems too much like murder of an innocent."

There was something that did not quite ring true in what he said, and I gave him a sharp look. And saw something lurking there in his eyes; something I had never thought to see in him: a feral celebration of a kill.

It was only then that I truly understood what Gilfeather and I had done to Tor Ryder. It was only then that I feared, with reason, for his future. For a moment we stood looking at each other, caught up in the tragedy of what had happened to us. He said softly, "You will take care, won't you?"

He didn't wait for a reply, but started running down the track again. Somewhere ahead, two dunmagickers were climbing up the cliff toward us.

CHAPTER 32

NARRATOR: KELWYN

"MY LORD GETHELRED," XETIANA SAID, dabbing at her lips with her napkin as she finished her luncheon, "it's time for us to go and see some more of the race. The first competitors should be somewhere on the last four or five stacks by now, and we have a good view of those from the westerly cliffs of Xolchasbarbican. They will be close enough for us to be able to identify some of the racers."

The dunmaster rose from the banqueting table and held out his hand. "Then let us proceed, lady." He glanced over at Xetiana's betrothed. "You do not mind my escorting your lovely bride-to-be, do you Syr Yethrad? You, after all, will have her by your side for a lifetime. I, alas, have but a day or two."

"Not at all," the Stackmaster replied. "I shall be only too happy to escort the Lady Lyssal instead."

Yethrad's underlying calm had already told me that he had no idea that he was addressing a dunmaster. His easy acceptance of the obviously predatory looks that Morthred was giving the Islandlord also told me his affections for his intended bride were negligible. Xetiana's scent likewise showed she had little affection for Yethrad, and wasn't particularly concerned for his safety. She was not intending to embark on a marriage of equals: she was going to rule, and if that meant withholding information from the man who would be her husband, then she would do it. If anything happened to him that afternoon, she would regret it, but for political reasons, not ones of the heart.

The more I found out about the Islandlord, the less I liked her. I suspected she deliberately alternated between charming informality and imperiously applied protocol in order to keep her courtiers off balance. Yethrad, with his lazy indifference, was probably the only man who could be prevailed upon to put up with the uncertainty and the subordinate position in exchange for the obvious advantages of being the consort of an Islandlord and the father of the next heir.

They mounted the stairs once more, their entourage straggling behind them, me included, and then headed across the flat roofs of the town toward the cliff top, this time on the western edge of the stack. The wind was strong, carrying with it the sound and smell of seabirds and the tang of salt spray. The ladies squealed and giggled as they held down their overskirts and gripped their bonnets; even I—grateful that the breeze whisked away the worst of the dun smell—found myself jamming my uniform hat on tighter. Every now and then we would cross a footbridge, and it was clear that the rooftop ways were less frequented than the alleys below; they were thronged with people. When I asked a guard why, I was told that the roofs were only for people above a certain rank. Artisans, shopkeepers, farmers or laborers never used roofways; people of rank never used the alleys. It all seemed rather silly to me, but right then I was glad of it. It meant there were fewer people around, and therefore fewer strong odors for me to filter out. I could concentrate on those that mattered.

The view from the cliff-edge platform on this side of the city was spectacular. We were looking out over a narrow strip of water called Skinny Neck, now crowded with small boats, all full of wealthy patrons well primed with food and drink. Most had anchored to watch the progress of the race, others scudded to and fro; to us, far above them, they looked like water beetles skimming a stream in erratic dance. On the other side of the Neck, the last five stacks of the race were a giant's staircase, diminishing in size from the Talon, the tallest of them all, at the north end, to the Crumble at the southern. The Talon was too far away for us observers on the viewing platform to be able to make out much except the tall columns of the Temple of the Winds. People there were no more than smudges of color.

By now I knew that the connection from the Talon to the next stack, the Fang, was a sloping rope called the Slide. Anyone who wanted to go from the higher stack to the lower hooked themselves on to this and simply slid all the way down. Going back up was trickier, but possible with the use of pulleys and counterweights. Apparently it was thought that the place was not suitable for a suspension bridge, although just why a rope was considered better, I had no idea. As much as I strained, I could not see the Slide: it was lost against a background of sea and rock.

The route of the race was along the eastern cliff edge of the Fang, where the racers would become more clearly visible to us on Xolchasbarbican. The next stack, the Milktooth, was lower and nearer still. Next, so close to its two neighbors that they were all almost touching, was the Fin, and then the lowest of all, the Crumble, little more than an uninhabited pile of rocks that did indeed crumble down to the sea. All these last four stacks were normally connected by wooden bridges, more after the style of sloping gangplanks, but for the purposes of the race these had been removed. Contestants were expected to jump across the gaps between the stacks. If they missed, the fall was enough to kill. The gaps were hardly more than the length of a man, an easy jump for an active person. If, of course, he had no fear of heights. Still, my mouth went dry just looking at them.

When the royal party arrived at the viewing platform, the first contestants were already racing across the Talon toward the rope of the Slide. It was important to be there first, because only one person at a time was allowed to cross, and a wait could mean the loss of precious seconds. Excitement in the watchers was now rising in pungent waves around me. Several of the nobles had spyglasses and they were able to identify the leading race contenders, and a number of new bets were being laid. Xetiana, of course, did not ask for her spyglass. She gave a good imitation of a woman who had no worries on her mind, and clapped her hands like an excited schoolgirl on being informed that the person lying third was a woman. I was not foolish enough to be deceived. Xetiana was intensely focused, her emotions taut.

I glanced around, trying to see the hidden archers. There were several close at hand, and others concealed further away, but I could not spot them, even after the Captain of the Guard told me where they were. The platform and the rooftops were thick with bunting and decorative banners; a couple of men would not have found it hard to secrete themselves away. It would have been hard for them to get a clear shot at the dun-master though; there were too many people milling around. Xetiana's ladies seemed to be much more interested in parading up and down than in the race, while some of the men preferred to stand along the railing rather than sit.

They all strained to see as the Slide was completed by the race leader, who then loped across the meadows of the Fang, scattering the sheep as he went, and was lost from sight. "We'll see him again in a few minutes," Xetiana explained to Gethelred, "once he has skirted the curve of the bay."

By the time the man appeared again, several others had caught up with him. None of them wore red sashes, and to Xetiana's disappointment, the woman had dropped behind. The first contestant to reach the southern edge of the Fang did not hesitate. He launched himself across the gap to the Milktooth, scrabbled a moment to regain his balance, and was off running again. I smelled his exhaustion on a gust of wind.

The second man took a moment to catch his breath before he, too, jumped. The third, the one who had been the first to cross the Slide, was laboring when he reached the edge. Desperate to catch up, he took the gap at a running leap, but landed badly and fell, right on the edge of the Milktooth. The watchers gasped in a mixture of horror and knife-edged excitement that made me wince.

The man slid backward as he clawed unsuccessfully for purchase. Tired and disoriented, he seemed unable to stop his inexorable descent over the cliff edge. Then, at the last moment, several of the race officials who had been on duty at the narrowest point grabbed his arms and hauled him back to safety. A hiss of disapproval mingled with relief rippled over the royal watchers. "Poor man," Xetiana said to Morthred, but her tone was amused. "He will have to live with the ignominy of having to be rescued during the course of a race. He will *never* live that down, not unless he actually enters again and wins some time."

A few minutes later we saw the two race leaders make the jump to the Fin, a small stack that was the domain of a single farming family. They crossed that at a run, and then jumped down to the Crumble. At this point Xetiana rose, saying, "Syrsylv, my ladies and I must leave you now and return to the Lord's House. We have to change before the end of the race, so that we may greet the winner suitably attired for the presentation ceremony and the celebratory dinner and ball that follow. However, I am sure that you and Yethrad would prefer to see more of the race here, so I suggest you stay. You will want to see the progress of your men and women."

Gethelred stood and bowed. The smile on his face was a little fixed. I sensed his brewing anger and took a step closer. The dunmaster was no fool; he knew that Xetiana was subtly mocking the apparent failure of his guards to do well. Smiling, he conquered the emotion. "Of course," he said.

I shivered at the menace I smelled behind the curve of his smile.

Xetiana turned to Flame. "Lady Lyssal, would you like to accompany me? Yethrad will bring Lord Gethelred back to the House in time to see the end of the race—won't you, beloved?"

Yethrad bowed in turn, still neutral; Xetiana and her ladies and Flame—together with several guards, including the Securia, and some of the other men of her court—swept off. Flame seemed almost ethereal; haunted, aloof from us all.

As Xetiana passed she gave me a meaningful look. I knew what it meant: she had given me my orders in no uncertain terms earlier that morning. Gethelred was not to leave the viewing platform alive.

The arrangement was for Tor, coming direct from the bridge that connected the Talon to Xolchasbarbican, to arrive in time to take care of the dunmaster. Tor had been chosen over Blaze, because he would be less instantly recognizable by the dunmaster. The plan was for him to don the garb of a

Temple of the Winds priest, a robe that was sufficiently volu-
minous to disguise his Souther origins and his sword. If something went wrong with that plan, then Blaze would step in. If
they were both delayed, then it was up to me to signal the
archers at an opportune moment. Quite frankly, though, now
that I had seen what the weather was like, I didn't have much
faith in the success of crossbows. The wind around the viewing platform was building up into a gale. Bunting whip-
cracked and frayed in the gusts. The seabirds sailed by on
majestic wings, whining and screaming defiance as they
banked, but even they were sometimes swept past their intended cliff-top perches as the fickleness of updrafts and
downwinds tumbled them. A crossbow bolt would more likely
go astray than hit its target.

I fiddled nervously with the spyglass, and prayed that I
wouldn't have to use it. It was unlikely, surely, for even if Tor,
Blaze and the archers failed, there was still the Securia.
Shavel had accompanied Xetiana back to the Lord's House,
but he had every intention of returning immediately, once the
Barbicanlord was safe inside her apartments. Earlier that
morning he had looked me up and down and informed me that
he was quite sure he could murder any sod of a dunmagicker
with a single blow before the sodding bastard had time to use
his powers. I hoped he was right. Although I desperately
wanted to see Morthred dead, I wasn't sure that I had the
nerve to do it myself.

I scented the air. A few more participants were now straggling along the cliff top of the Fang and the Milktooth.
Morthred was still angry, presumably because his guards had
not performed as well as he had thought they would, but he
was not yet suspicious. It would not be long, surely, before he
began to wonder why *none* of his sylvs or dun colleagues
were anywhere to be seen.

Tor, I thought, you'd better hurry up. I'm not sure I can do
this.

Edgily I looked around, and caught Ruarth's scent. The
Dustel, buffeted by the wind, flew down to land on the viewing platform, not far from my feet. On the pretext of doing up
my shoe, I knelt and fiddled with my laces while I watched
and listened as the Dustel brought me up to date.

Where's Flame? he asked when he had finished.

"The women went back to the Lord's House to change," I replied in a whisper.

I'll go and check on her. He hesitated, glancing across at the dunmaster. *Kel, with both dunmagickers being together like that, it means Tor and Blaze will have to fight them together . . .*

I nodded, appalled. Ruarth was wondering if either Blaze or Tor was going to get to us in time.

Do what you have to, Kelwyn. If I could, I would do it myself . . . remember that, no matter what happens. And don't ever look back. With that cryptic statement, he launched himself up into the wind and was gone. Much, much later I would understand what he'd meant. He was deliberately leaving his words behind to heal a wound which had not yet even been inflicted.

CHAPTER 33

NARRATOR : BLAZE

TOR AND I WERE TOO LATE TO INTERCEPT
the dunmagickers as they came over the lip of the cliff. The
two men were already crossing the meadow when we first saw
them, and if the bands of dun color that played across them
were any indication, they were in the mood to use their powers. We automatically dived down into the grass before we
were seen, and I reflected that it was nice to be working with
someone who didn't need to be told what to do.

"The sheep," Tor said, nodding toward the flock that was
grazing the meadow between us and the dunmagickers. Together we wriggled and crawled our way down into the flock.
As we neared the first of the animals, they edged together for
protection, which gave us more cover, especially useful as the
grass was shorter where the sheep had been grazing. Tor took
a moment to take his crossbow from his pack and crank a
quarrel into place. I took a brief peek over the backs of the animals to judge the distance between us and the approaching
dunmagickers.

"Not quite," I whispered, my voice almost drowned out by

the unearthly wind-song from the temple. "It's windy. You'll have to wait till they are almost on us."

Tor nodded calmly, and slipped a spare quarrel into the clip on the handle of the bow. It was unlikely he would have time to use more than two; the crossbow took too long to reload. He either had to get in two killing shots, or we would be sword fighting.

"Now," I hissed.

He stood up and fired. The wind gusted and the quarrel was edged off target. It scored the older Stragglerman along the top of the shoulder, ripping both clothes and flesh, but not doing any fatal harm. The younger dunmagicker, Jaze, was ready for the second shot: a blast of magic disintegrated the quarrel in midair. By then I was already running, scattering the panicked sheep. Tor leaped after me.

We had both thought the two dunmagickers would fight, that they would realize too late they were dealing with Aware-folk who were both accomplished sword fighters. Instead, the older Stragglerman snapped an order to the other, and Jaze turned and ran. I hesitated between the two men.

"After him," Tor said. "I'll manage here."

"Kel—?"

"I'll deal with it—go!"

I didn't wait any longer. I sheathed my sword and tore after the younger man, leaping rocks and grass tussocks as we both headed for the Slide.

The man was a Calmenter, born to a landscape of mountains and steep hill paths. The slopes of the Talon were probably nothing to him, and I soon found that I was hard put just to keep up. It didn't help that I was carrying my sword on my back. It was large enough, and heavy enough, to be a nuisance.

When one of the yeomen, whose job it was to direct race contestants to the temple, tried to point out the correct path to the dunmagicker, he was blasted with dun and died on the spot. Jaze, I decided, must have studied the race map; he knew he had to bypass the temple to take the quickest route to the Slide, and that was where he was heading. I knew there were several men concealed around the rocks, each ready to kill, but I also knew that their orders were to eliminate anyone alone who wore a red sash. The Calmenter had thrown his sash away. I could expect no help.

Worse, when he arrived at the Slide, the group of Xolchasmen on duty there assumed he was an ordinary contestant: he killed them all with one blast of dun before they realized who he was. By the time I pulled up, the dunmagicker was almost to the other side. I raised my sword to slash the rope, then realized he wasn't far enough out from the Fang for me to be certain he would be killed. And if I severed the rope, I was going to be cut off from the Fang. There was another sling already hooked on and ready to use, so I ignored the regulation about one person on the Slide at a time. I stepped over the body of an attendant, seated myself in the sling and pushed away from the mounting block.

The mechanism was simple: if you squeezed the iron clip that attached the sling to the rope, you slowed down. If you didn't touch it, you went as fast as momentum carried you. And I wanted to go as fast as was humanly possible. I leaned back and gripped the sling so that I was almost parallel to the rope. I traveled dangerously fast, and I risked falling out of the sling altogether, but I also knew that if I lagged too far behind the dunmagicker, he would have time to destroy the rope, and me along with it.

When the dunmagicker was about to arrive on the other side, he let go another blast of magic and killed the two race officials and the Slide attendant on duty on the Fang side. Hurriedly, he extricated himself from the sling and looked back. The sight of me rushing directly at him, feet first, at enormous speed, unnerved him completely. He threw a dun bolt at me, and then was momentarily nonplussed to see that it didn't have any effect. It did scorch my tunic a little, but that was all. Awareness, fortunately, cast an aura that was usually enough to protect clothing from too much damage.

By the time he had worked out that I must be Aware, it was too late for him to do much. I was coming at him far too fast. He made an attempt to burn the Slide rope with dun and missed. I hurtled straight at him and he was forced to fling himself backward. I barrelled into the bale of straw that was strategically placed for emergency stops. By the time I had untangled myself from the sling and the straw, Jaze had gone.

I started off after him once more, cursing the fact that of all the dunmagickers in the world I seemed to have encountered the one who could run faster than a sand crab heading for its burrow.

BACK ON THE TALON, TOR WAS HAVING his own problems. I imagine that Tor was aware of the irony: the man he had to kill was a fellow Stragglerman. It made a distasteful task that little bit more distasteful. And to do it to the accompaniment of sweetly sighing notes filling the air around them probably seemed sacrilegious. Tor, however, never did tell me too much about how he felt during that fight; just what happened.

When I ran after Jaze, Tor dropped his crossbow and pulled out his sword. As he closed in on the man, Tor recognized him: the fellow had been at Creed when Tor had been a prisoner there. Tor and I both remembered Creed far too well. The half-starved people. The torture room. The cruelty of the enslavement.

Physically, it should have been easy: Tor had a Calmenter blade, the dunmagicker had only a small knife he had pulled out of a sheath tied to his calf. But Tor underestimated how inventive the dunmagicker would become after the man realized that his opponent was one of the Aware. When Tor approached, the man directed his dunpower down into the earth at Tor's feet, to shower him with dirt and grass. Tor could ignore the dunmagic, but he couldn't ignore being pelted with earth and rock. He couldn't ignore holes opening up at his feet. He ducked, holding an arm up over his head as he scrambled away. The wind blew dirt into his face, choking him, and the dunmagicker took advantage, leaping at him with the knife upraised for a downward stroke. It was the mark of an amateur and Tor dodged sideways, then fell into a forward roll. It was a move designed to disconcert, and he came up behind the dunmagicker, forcing his opponent to turn to face him. The wind was now coming from behind Tor, so the next explosion of turf raised a cloud of dirt that was blown straight back into the dunmagicker's face.

Tor didn't miss the opportunity. He slid his blade in low,

angling it so that it slipped easily under the rib cage and up into the lungs. As the man fell, Tor twisted the blade just to make sure it pierced the heart as well. "That," he said quietly, "is how you make a killing stroke." Dunmagic erupted in gaudy fountains of color as the man began to die. With one last desperate act, the dunmagicker shifted the stones under Tor's feet. Tor, unable to keep his footing, fell backward and his head slammed into a rock.

When he did not immediately get up, several Dustel birds that had been watching came forward. One of them perched on his shoulder, and twittered in his ear.

Tor did not move.

CHAPTER 34

NARRATOR : KELWYN

I STILL FIDGETED UNHAPPILY WITH THE
spyglass. My father's dirk, hidden away in my boot, seemed
horribly inaccessible. Where in all Creation was Shavel? He
should have been back by now. It didn't take that long to walk
to the Lord's House and back again, even allowing for time to
escort Xetiana right to the door of her apartments, if that was
what he felt he had to do. So what was taking him so long? I
wanted desperately to signal the archers to kill Morthred and
be done with it, but the wind was becoming stronger by the
minute. No quarrel could possibly find its target in this, or so
it seemed to me. And if they missed, I would be the one who
had to deal with the consequences. There was no sign of Tor,
or Blaze. What could have gone wrong? And Ruarth hadn't
come back either. Surely he had intended to . . .

My thoughts centered around the same doubt that had
plagued me all day: would I have the courage, the savagery, to
kill again? I glanced at Morthred: maybe I should do it now,
while the dunmaster is unsuspecting, and not wait till he becomes suspicious. Morthred chatted with Yethrad, both as
much at ease as tharn neighbors exchanging pleasantries.

They laughed and watched the contestants who were making their way across the stacks opposite.

"I'm sure your men must be among them," Yethrad was saying. "They have simply jettisoned their red sashes as a nuisance, so we can't tell them apart anymore."

And if I failed, who was going to back me up? The Captain of the Guard and his men could not contend with dunmagic.

Where in all the mists of a moonless night was Shavel?

Please, I thought, let Blaze or Ryder come in time to deal with this . . .

CHAPTER 35

NARRATOR : BLAZE

THE TOP OF THE FANG WAS SWAY-BACKED in the center. As I tore down the slope of the dip, I could see the dunmagicker struggling up the opposite slope toward the edge that faced the Milktooth. I gritted my teeth and plunged on, my breath coming in ragged gasps. I had actually passed several of the race contestants, just as Jaze had before me. At least he had not killed them.

Probably didn't want to waste his energy, I thought. All that blasting of people back at the Slide must have depleted his strength. Just as lugging a Calmenter sword on my back was depleting mine.

Still, I had my second wind now, and gained as I panted up the slope after him. By the time he reached the gap that separated the Fang and the Milktooth, I was a bare twenty paces behind. He hesitated on the edge for a few seconds, took one look over his shoulder at me, then backed up a couple of paces and made a running jump.

When I was close enough to the edge to see, he was already up and running again. I glanced down at the sea where the white lines of waves rucked up through the blue far below, and then leaped. The Milktooth was lower than the Fang and I felt a moment's fear as I fell. It seemed a long way down. The soil was soft and spongy, however, and I landed well away from the edge. I rolled and came up already moving. Jaze raced passed the officials at the checkpoint, and so did I. The officials, presumably all guards, dithered, but did nothing, because neither I nor Jaze wore a red sash.

Vaguely I was aware that there were people lining up on the roofs of Xolchasbarbican opposite, waving and, I guessed, shouting. I could not hear them over the sound of the wind and the cries of the birds. I did spare one glance as I ran, but I could not make out individuals in the crowds, and I had no idea which exactly was the royal viewing platform. I assured myself that there was no way that Morthred would be able to identify me, not at this distance. After all, he had no idea I was anywhere near; as far as he was concerned, I was dead in the shed on the island in the Floating Mere.

I ran on.

The Milktooth was a small stack; the Fin was even smaller. Jaze leaped the gap between the two with ease, and I followed seconds later. The Fin sloped downward toward the Crumble, and at times I felt I had lost control of my headlong rush across the top. As fast as I ran, I never seemed to be able to quite catch up with the dunmagicker, not until the very end of the Fin. There, just as Jaze launched himself into the air to make the final jump to the Crumble, I stretched out a hand to grab him. My fingers only grazed his jacket. Without waiting to see what happened to him, I leaped across. I landed feet first, right behind him. He stumbled forward and half turned, off balance, throwing dun at me in a desperate attempt to confuse and give himself a chance to escape.

Even as I landed, I was groping over my back for my sword. Jaze had fallen heavily onto his backside. He pushed himself along the ground facing me. In his terror, he tried to envelop me in wave after wave of dun, but I took no notice. I kicked him hard under the chin with my booted foot. He fell back with a grunt, hardly conscious. I killed him as efficiently as I knew how, with a twisting thrust up into the heart.

Quickly I looked over at the opposite side of the Skinny

Neck, to where the crowds watched. Had they realized what I had done? If anyone had been using a spyglass just then . . .

Charnels, I thought, I hope someone has killed Morthred by now.

Wearily I leaned on my sword and looked around me. I would have to clamber down to the ocean and swim back to Xolchasbarbican. I drew in a deep, calming breath.

My moment of peace was all too transitory. One moment I was letting the tension and fear drain out of me, the next, appalled, I watched a wall of dunmagic surge across the water from Xolchasbarbican like a rain squall. *Oh, middenshit,* I thought. Oh, damn the selver-herding, peacemongering idiot, I'm going to *die*!

This, I thought with knife-edged clarity, is what the people of the Awarefolk of the Dustel Islands must have seen in the last moments of the islandom. The billowing purple, a mountain of it roiling across the sea, the smell overpowering as the cloud of magic came onward . . .

I knew there was no way I could dodge its power. It may not have been able to hurt me directly, but its potency was enough to destroy the stack I stood upon, enough to turn it to dust or sink it beneath the waves. To destroy it just as the Dustel Islands had been destroyed.

Gilfeather, I thought. Oh, Kelwyn. I wish you hadn't been such a *good* man . . .

Without a shadow of a doubt in my mind, I knew I was about to take my last breath.

CHAPTER 36

SHAVEL HADN'T RETURNED, BUT A DUSTEL
had arrived. At first I thought it might have been Ruarth, but
the moment the bird started talking to me I realized it was
someone else, a female, I guessed, although I am not sure
why. She told me that Shavel was not coming back because
Flame had disappeared and he was concerned that she was a
danger to the Barbicanlord. Shavel, it seemed, was not leaving
his Islandlord's side, and he was directing the search for the
missing dunmagicker himself. It gave me a shock to hear
Flame described as a dunmagicker, and still another jolt to
know that she was being regarded as a menace to Xetiana.
"What do you mean, disappeared?" I mouthed, close to panic.

She went back to the Lord's House with the others, the bird
said, *but the maid that Xetiana had appointed to keep an eye
on her could not find her. They are scouring the buildings and
the whole Upper Town right now . . .*

"Ruarth?"

He can't find her either. He's looking.

Illusion, I thought. She has used illusion. They may think
of her as a dunmagicker, but she still has a hold on her

sylvpower . . . But where would she go, and *why*? "Ruarth is Aware," I muttered out of the corner of my mouth. "Maybe he will find her." He at least could see through her illusions. "What about the others? Tor and Blaze? Where are they?"

But the Dustel didn't know anything about what was happening elsewhere.

I turned my attention back to Morthred in an agony of indecision. The Dustel flew off.

"Who *is* that?" Morthred was asking Yethrad. He was pointing in the direction of the gap between the Fin and the Crumble.

"I don't know," Yethrad said, without really looking. "Which one do you mean?"

"The woman running behind the man."

Yethrad squinted at the racers. "I don't know. One of your sylv women, perhaps?"

"Can I borrow your spyglass?"

"Of course." Yethrad held out the brass instrument. "It works best if you rest it on something. I use the railing."

As I stood behind the two men, I looked to see which contestant they were talking about. And froze in shock. *It was Blaze.* I didn't need a spyglass to recognize her. She was racing after a man who was about to make the jump to the Crumble. I drew in a breath, tasting it for the dunmaster's emotions; it was all there: suspicion, a surge of suppressed hatred, and anger as cold as midnight rain.

Disdaining Yethrad's advice about the railing, Morthred had raised the spyglass to his eye. "The *bitch*!" He spat out the words in a seething outpouring of hate. "How did she survive yet *again*?"

Yethrad stared at him in astonishment.

A gust of wind spun my cap from my head and out across the cliff edge. In that slivered second I knew it was useless to ask the archers to do anything. I unwrapped the Islandlord's spyglass and lifted it by its narrower end to slam the heavier end down, as hard as I knew how, on the back of the dunmaster's head. In that same splinter of time, a surge of dunmagic raced outward, as huge as the swell of storm surf. I could not see it, but I could smell it. My blow had come too late to stop his rage of magic.

The dunmaster crashed forward, falling onto the railing. I thought I'd hit him hard enough to kill, but I did not smell his death. And the world around me seemed to go mad. Men jumped out of their seats, trying to avoid the lash of dun that radiated outward from Morthred. Seats went flying, whipped through the air as if they were made of paper. The railing broke and decorative bunting disintegrated, licked by flame that seemed to have no logical origin. The Captain of the Guard was sent sprawling across the platform, flattened by an unseen force of dun. He slid across the paving, gathering speed as he went, until he slipped under the railing and disappeared into the air over the Skinny Neck. I lost sight of him, but his scream echoed in my head for much longer.

Yethrad had leaped to his feet the moment he saw me strike the blow, a horrified expression on his face. In its caprice, the dun had passed him by, and it was me who riveted his attention, not the damage done by the magic. I was desperate to save Blaze. I went to hit Morthred again, but Yethrad grabbed my arm and wrenched the spyglass from me. "What are you *doing*?" he asked, totally incredulous. I shoved him away, and groped for my dirk. People were screaming, scrambling to escape, not smelling or seeing the magic, but being buffeted by unpredictable dunpower as if it were a tangible thing. Yethrad gaped at me in appalled incomprehension. "What the windhells! *Guards!*" Using the spyglass as a cudgel, he slammed it down on my wrist. My dirk went flying.

There was no one to answer his call. The guards had been flung in all directions. I saw several sent through the railings; others were simply blown back to the rooftop street, tumbling like thistledown before a wind. Then Yethrad himself was hit by a bubble of dun and was repelled to the back of the viewing platform as if he were weightless. A glance around told me that there was no one left standing. Creation, I thought in horror, the bastard's *killed* everybody!

I whirled around looking for my dirk, and spared a glance at Blaze. She stood there on the Crumble, her hair whipped free from its ties in the wind. The man she had been chasing lay at her feet, and she held her sword, point down. It should have been impossible for me to have scented her in that wind, and yet I was somehow aware of how her weariness vanished into horror. A fraction later the neighboring stack, the Fin, shuddered as if it had been hit by a gigantic wave. At the base, on the side facing the Crumble, the rock seemed to have been pulverized, undermining the cliff above. On the meadows at the top, several race contestants fell as the ground under their feet shook.

Blaze had turned her head toward the Fin. *And the stack began to tilt.* Slowly, inevitably, the Fin leaned toward the Crumble. Blaze dropped her sword and flung away her back harness. Then she leaped away, her huge strides eating up the ground as she fled down the blocks of the Crumble toward the ocean. She took risks, almost sailing through the air as she descended from one block to another, to land heavily but still upright. Heart in mouth, I watched. I expected her to fall, to break a leg as she landed, to slip and plunge into one of the numerous gullies and rifts that scored the stack. To slip into the sea from far too high . . .

Horrified beyond rational thought, I could only watch as the entire stack of the Fin fell sideways against the Crumble, like an old forest tree that has lost its rooting. Birds rose from the cliffs in black and white patterns of anger, screaming endlessly as they were tumbled on the savage eddies of air. As the top of the Fin tilted, there was one absurd moment when a farmhouse, complete with orchard and outhouses, seemed to hang in the air as if it were a ghostly creation of the clouds of rock dust that surrounded it. A flock of sheep went tumbling across the meadow like marbles on a slope and shot out into space. Their fall to the sea seemed slow, endless. I could see people as well, clinging hopelessly to the grass as if they could save themselves by holding on to a land that no longer had any solid base. The top of the Fin hit the edge of the Crumble and the pieces began to avalanche downward, following Blaze with relentless, terrifying speed. Inexorably the people on the Fin disappeared into a pall of dust and spray as the rest of the stack plunged into the ocean or crashed into the cliffs at the northern edge of the Crumble. Chunks bludgeoned transitory craters in the sea. Gouts of water shot up in fountains and fell back in sheets. The ocean's surface heaved, and swelling waves and deep troughs radiated outward, scattering or sinking boats.

At my feet, Morthred moaned and stirred. Dun was ripping from him in aimless streams of foulness, the stench so intense it was hard for me to breathe. I rolled him over onto his back and found my dirk. As I bent to kill him, his eyes opened and stared into mine. I faltered, momentarily unable to kill a man who was meeting my gaze. "Who *are* you?" he asked. He'd never seen me before in his life; he'd probably never seen *any* Plainsman before and he was genuinely puzzled.

A tide of dun, directed dun this time, spilled its stench into my face. I felt its passing, grateful that the wind whipped the nauseous reek away. His eyes narrowed in chagrin at my lack of reaction, then he erupted from the floor, springing at me with surprising strength and energy. I tried to fling myself away, and lost my dirk in the process. His hands clamped around my throat.

"You dirty Aware-born freak! I'll kill you for this!" he hissed, shaking me. He was strong, stronger than I'd expected, and I hadn't been in a fight since Jaim and I rough-housed on the hill slopes of the Sky Plains when we were boys. Harking back to those boyhood memories, I hooked a foot behind his knee and flung my weight at him. We fell over together, but I was on top. His head was bleeding and he should have had the grandmother of all headaches, but he seemed unaffected. Dun healing, I thought. *Scab* it.

Somehow he kept his hands around my throat and continued to squeeze. I twisted his nose, hard, then jammed a thumb in his eye. He screamed then, and let go of my neck. What was left of a wooden chair burst into flames near us. He rolled us over toward it and tried to thrust me into the fire. It took all my strength to resist. He grabbed my hair and banged my head against the floor. I rammed the heel of my hand into his nose, breaking it. He let go and jumped to his feet, swearing. Globules of blood poured from his nostrils, and he gagged, half choking. The blood stopped running, far too quickly to be natural, and he took a deep breath. He grabbed one of the broken bunting poles from where it had been resting against the remains of the railing. The tattered flag at the end started to burn, and he thrust it at me, using the pole like a lance. I tripped, and for one panic-filled moment I was enveloped in flames and smoke as the bulk of the burning material settled across my body. Frantic, I pulled it off, scorching my hands, and tumbled away.

When I looked up, Morthred had gone.

I spun around wildly, but couldn't see him anywhere. The people I had thought were dead were stirring, groaning, vomiting. A fresh squad of guards was pounding in along the roofway to help.

I turned around to look for Blaze. The fight had seemed endless to me, so I was astonished to see she still fled the chaos that threatened to overwhelm her from behind. She threw herself between the rock columns with reckless desperation. Just when I feared she had been overtaken by the avalanche, I would glimpse her again, still leaping, still doing the seemingly impossible. One final bound took her to the top of a thin column of rock, perhaps just five strides wide, at the ocean's edge, still far above the water. Only then did she turn and look behind her.

The rock slide tumbled on, pouring into the sea at the base of the column she occupied. She staggered to her knees as the stone beneath her was battered and shuddered in response. Gradually the noise faded, leaving only the wail of seabirds. Miraculously the column still stood. She crawled to the edge and looked over. A succession of waves, separated by churning troughs, surged out of the Skinny Neck, to slam into the foot of her tower, one after the other. The column swayed.

Appalled, I realized that there was no way it was going to survive the onslaught. Evidently Blaze recognized that too, because she scrambled to her feet and took three running strides to sail out over the ocean, a tiny figure against the background of a vast blue wave that engulfed the place she had stood upon. When the water receded, the column of rock had been obliterated as if it had never been.

Only then did I become aware that both Tor Ryder and Dek were standing beside me, gripping what was left of the railing with the same white-knuckled emotion that filled me. Ryder had suffered some kind of head wound; dried blood matted his hair. He turned his head to look at me, and I knew that my own face reflected the same shock that I read on his. And for the same reasons.

"Damn you, Gilfeather, if you have killed her," he said quietly.

I stood silent, unable to answer. Unable even to think.

He conquered his vengeful dun and added, offering comfort, "She has more lives than an octopus has tentacles. And she can swim."

I was the first to turn away, to look behind.

Yethrad was arguing vehemently with Shavel, gesturing at me, demanding the arrest of Gethelred's attacker. Other courtiers stood around in various stages of shock which manifested itself in everything from excited talk to uncontrolled sobbing or vomiting.

"Where's Morthred?" Ryder demanded.

"I don't know," I said. "He—he disappeared."

He stared in disbelief. *"You let him get away?"*

I winced, shame-faced. "He—vanished. We were fighting, he flung a burning flag at me. I was tangled up—and then when I was free, he wasna there anymore. There were people coming. He must have realized his charade here had ended, and he fled."

"In what direction?"

I forced myself to think, to reason. Dek and Ryder had come up the roofway from the center of town and no amount of illusion would have hidden Morthred from them. And he hadn't passed me, I felt sure. I pointed along the bluff to a narrow ribbon of land that edged the first house walls of the city. "He must have gone that way." The bunting on the buildings along there would have blocked my view of him.

Ryder didn't wait for me to finish. He called to Shavel, and moments later he, Dek, the Securia and the guards left the platform to follow the cliff-top track that squeezed between the house walls and a dizzying fall to the sea.

I should have gone with them. My sense of smell for dun was better than either Ryder's or Dek's; I could have been of use. But they ignored me and I was exhausted, an exhaustion that was as much emotional as physical. Even now that my part appeared to be over, I was sick with worry about what had happened to Blaze. Had I been too late for her, as I had been for the folk on the Fin? People had died because I had hesitated. My hands started to shake.

Yethrad, having been abandoned by Shavel and the guards, gave me an angry look and stalked away toward the roofways, along with other battered courtiers. In the meantime, townsfolk rigged makeshift stretchers out of broken chairs and railings to carry the more severely injured away. Wearily I leaned against the remains of the railing and looked out at where the Fin had once stood. Part of it was still visible above the waves: white remnants of cliff and rock, a broken, jagged tooth in a heaving sea. Above, birds screamed their incomprehension. In the Skinny Neck, what was left of the flotilla of pleasure boats circled like headless beetles as they searched the wreckage for survivors. Perhaps one of them would find Blaze . . .

I leaned out as far as I dared, to see if there was anyone sailing in the area where she'd disappeared, and was relieved to see how many boats and sea-ponies there still were all the way along the narrow waterway.

And then I saw him: directly below me. Morthred. He hadn't fled along the bluff; he'd climbed over the lip and down the cliff face. Doubtless he intended to use his powers of illusion and coercion to entice a boat in to rescue him once he reached sea level, but in the meanwhile he had to get there and he had not, in fact, gone far. His descent down the web of ropes used by the guano collectors was slow, his movements studied, a parody of a spider stalking prey along silken strands.

Dun smell and fear odor drifted up in wisps.

It took a moment for me to understand.

He was scared. No, more than that. He was *terrified*. I didn't need to smell him to know. The slowness of his descent, the cautious way he felt for the ropes, the rigidity of his refusal to look down to find a foothold, the long pauses between each move, the flinch he gave every time a seabird sailed by screaming its defiance at the intruder . . . Morthred, who had terrorized and murdered without compunction on his route to power, who had deliberately chosen to be what he had become, was scared of heights. Paradoxically, I could almost admire the dogged way he continued down; to undertake such a descent took courage when you suffered from vertigo.

I looked behind me to find my dirk where it lay on the platform, and then swung myself over the cliff edge. There were many things that frightened me, Morthred being one, but heights was not on the list. Even so, the calm I felt seemed almost unnatural. I had decided I would win this one, or I would die, and, having acknowledged that, I lost all fear of the dunmaster. I climbed down quickly, using the ropes and the ledges and the nest holes with an assurance that was not normal for someone as clumsy as I was. The birds I ignored, although the sight of a creature with a wingspan as long as I was tall barrelling through the air inches from my head should have been unnerving.

It didn't take long to reach Morthred.

He looked up and saw me. His arrogance and charm had all vanished, leaving only his fear of falling and a burning rage—not just at me but at his whole changed situation. He must have read the determination in my eyes, but he had a hard time taking it seriously. He already knew I lacked the edge of a true killer.

I smelled the dun he used, but didn't know where it went until I saw the ropes above my head burning. Strands parted, the web loosened and jerked. I grabbed for the cliff face and hauled myself away from the ropes and onto a narrow ledge just level with the top of his head. Several of the larger fledglings standing outside their nest holes hissed at me in righteous indignation, and vomited up the foulsmelling contents of their stomachs to signal their annoyance.

I crouched there, fingers hooked into the rock crannies. He threw dun at the cliff above me and stone crumbled. I flattened myself against the rock face to avoid the worst of the cascade of rock. Much of it rained down on him. "People in grass huts shouldna light fires," I told him. His section of the web was already less stable; ropes sagged and when he moved he swung out from the cliff and back again. I wondered just how long I had before he decided he was going to die and he may as well take me with him.

He spat rock dust from his mouth. *"Who are you?"* The words burned in my mind. That's coercion, I thought. But instead of being forced to answer, I was amused by his insistence; bemused by the idea that it was important to him to know who his tormentor was, puzzled that he was even trying coercion when he already knew I was impervious to it.

I pulled out my dirk. "Nobody. Just an ordinary man, like all the hundreds of ordinary folk ye have tortured and killed over the span of your wretched life, Morthred. What makes me different is that I am the one who is going to kill you." I wasn't even listening to what I was saying; my mind was racing, wondering how to tackle him. Looking for the best way to bring this to an end.

"I can offer you anything you want, riches beyond your most naked dreams . . ."

"There is naught ye have that I want."

He must have heard the truth in that, because something flickered in his eyes: uncertainty. "Power," he said. "You and I, we could go far. You are Aware and I have magic." He had one arm hooked through the web of rope. The other hand was clutching at a small knob of rock just below my ledge. I stood up and, in one swift movement, ground my boot down on his fingers, hard, and had the satisfaction of scenting the breaking of his finger bones. "For Lyssal," I said. It was a lie; I just needed to justify the cruelty to myself.

He screamed and my boot began to smoke, but the magic somehow could not gain a hold. I lifted my foot and he snatched his hand away. I had effectively crippled him. His other hand, still gripping the ropes, had several missing fingers. Blaze had done that, back on Gorthan Spit.

He risked a look down. The waves on the sea were hardly more than scribbled lines below. There was no way anyone would survive a fall from that height. I wondered whether he had enough power left in him to flatten Xolchasbarbican, to kill us all.

"Come and get me, you freckled tomatl-head—" he screamed at me but, for all his anger, he could not hide his fear.

And I wasn't that foolish. "Cornered grass-lions scratch the deepest" was a well-known saying on the Roof of Mekaté. I looked around me. A stone that his power had dislodged from above had fallen onto the ledge beside me. With both hands, I picked it up. It was the size of a Plains pumpkin, and much, much heavier. I lifted it directly over his head. He looked up. "Anything," he said, and the steadiness of his voice did not reflect the fear I smelled in his sweat. "I'll give you anything. You name it. What is it you want, Mekatéman? Wealth? Power? Women at your beck and call?"

And something in me rejoiced. In that moment, he was reduced to nothing. This was no longer a mighty dunmaster who had sunk the Dustel Isles, this was no longer a fearsome sorcerer who had subverted Keeper Council sylvs, this was no longer a powerful man who had raped and tortured his way across the Isles. He could have used his last magic to tear away the cliff and send us both plummeting to our deaths, but fear of dying rendered him powerless. An ordinary, frightened man at the end of his life, no different from the rest of us, bargaining for salvation in his last moments. In that second of time, I could almost feel compassion. Almost.

I dropped the stone.

And yet it wasn't so simple, not even then. He hit the stone with a bolt of dun and it splintered into a thousand pieces. I was peppered with shards, the skin of my face and hands abraded raw from the blast. The dust and pebbled rock fell back onto him and he raised his damaged hand against the shower. In that moment, I had my chance. I flung myself flat on the ledge, grabbed him by the hair and, in one fluid movement, drew the dirk across his throat. Desperate to stop me, he let go of the rope with his good hand and grabbed my wrist. Then he started to fall, pulling me with him.

I dropped the dirk as his weight yanked me from the ledge. I snatched at the rope webbing with my free hand. For a terror-filled minute, that one-handed hold was all that kept the two of us from plunging into the sea. With extraordinary clarity, I realized it was going to be a matter of which one of us could hold on the longer . . . or if the webbing itself held. So much of the rope directly above had already been shredded or burned away.

Blood oozed from the slit in his throat. In dismay I realized I had not severed the carotid artery. He was not going to bleed to death, not yet anyway. He looked at me, scorching me with his hatred. And still he asked, still he had to know, even though the words he framed carried no sound anymore. *Who are you?* His grip was powerful, in spite of his missing fingers. *Who—?* I felt I was being torn in two. He reached out with his other arm, wanting to hook it into what was left of the webbing. I knew I had to stop him. I could not afford to give him time; he would kill me somehow or another, or he would kill us all. And so I kicked him in the throat, driving the toe of my boot into the gaping wound with a vicious savagery that would once have shamed me. His head slammed back into the cliffside even as his throat tore and arterial blood spurted. His hand lost its grip and slid across my wrist. Then his body fell free and I clung to the rope, alone and panting.

My gaze followed his fall as he cartwheeled silently through the air. It seemed to take a long while. I knew the moment when it came, as surely as I would have done had I been listening to his heartbeat: I knew the smell of death. The splash when his body hit the water a second later was small and insignificant, hardly the kind of ending for a man who had destroyed a nation.

I thought I'd had enough horror for the day, enough of everything. But even as I looked up to start the climb back, a naked man came hurtling through the air past me. He was screaming, appalling sounds of animal extremity. He bounced off a ledge with a sickening sound I never want to hear again, and then fell silently, tumbling without any semblance of life, till he hit the sea.

I didn't understand. It didn't make sense. His lack of clothes made nonsense of every explanation that flitted through my mind. I climbed up, my thoughts incoherent, concentrating on nothing except getting myself back to the city. When I reached the top, it was Dek and Ryder who helped me up over the edge.

"We saw you fighting from along the bluff," Ryder said quietly, "so we came back. That *was* Morthred? He is dead?" He seemed strangely subdued. His smell spoke of a tight control over his shock.

I nodded.

"Are you *sure*?"

"I smelled his dying."

At the back of the viewing platform, the body of another naked man lay on the flagstones, his face smashed, his limbs at unnatural angles.

"Who—who's that?" I asked without comprehension.

And who was the man who had plummeted past me into the sea?

From all around came unearthly, inhuman cries of anguish, as though in my brief absence there had been a catastrophe that had consumed part of the life of the city. I began to shake, uncontrollable shudders.

"I don't know," Ryder said.

I scented the patriarch's reluctance to give voice to his thoughts. There was grief there, and rage, and most of all shock; a mixture of emotion revealed in his stance as well as his aroma. I turned to face him again, questioning, yet knowing I didn't want to hear the answer.

He said, "I think it—he might be Ruarth."

I struggled with that, trying to understand what was not said.

"The man fell out of the sky as we came back," Ryder explained. "Out of nowhere."

"There are a c-c-couple of others back there too," Dek added, shaken. "Naked p-p-people. Men, women. A lad of about my age. All sort of—*squished* when they fell." His eyes were wide, his pupils dilated. He had wanted action; now that he'd seen it, he did not know how to handle it.

For a moment I still didn't understand. I looked back at all that was left of the Fin and the Crumble, then at the sea where somewhere Blaze may or may not be alive, then at the naked body on the platform floor. And then in a blinding moment of realization my world changed forever.

I sank to my knees.

I had been so blind. So convinced that magic didn't really exist. So sure I was right. So certain that the people of the Dustels hadn't *really* been magicked by Morthred the Mad, Gethelred of Skodart.

"Sweet skies above," I whispered, *"what have I done?"*

CHAPTER 37

NARRATOR: KELWYN

I REMEMBER ONE THING FROM MY WALK back to the center of the Upper Town. There was a crowd at one place along the roofway, all looking down at a ledge over a window. A girl sat there on the narrow projection of stone. She was naked, aged about three, I suppose. She was crying in terror. A palace guard attempted to reach down to her and pluck her to safety, but she was so frightened of him that she tried to escape the only way she knew how. She spread out her arms and launched herself from the ledge . . .

I went straight to my room and picked up my physician's kit, then asked a maid the way to the nearest Upper Town hospice.

I don't remember much about the rest of that day, or the night. There was a succession of people, most of them with broken bones and internal injuries, and there were too few physicians and no sylv healers. And so many of the victims were so young . . . After a while they blurred into one another. Another crushed body. More broken limbs. Or were they the same ones, over and over? I no longer knew.

When they finally stopped bringing in new patients late the

next day, I left and returned to the Lord's House. On the way out of the hospice, I saw the room where they were stacking the dead for identification. Most of them were naked.

I REMEMBER SITTING IN MY ROOM IN THE dark for a long time. I don't know that I thought about anything much. The truth was too large, too terrible, too much to accept, let alone contemplate in detail. So I just sat there.

I was vaguely aware that Dek came in, complaining that it wasn't fair, everyone else had had all the excitement the day before, while all he'd been doing was standing by a bridge that no one had used till Tor had come racing through and collected him on the way. And even when they'd reached the viewing platform, there had not been anything useful for them to do.

When he realized there was no response from me, he went away again.

A few minutes later Seeker padded in through the open door. He laid his chin on my knee and whined. He, too, had been left out of things the day before: he could be dunmagicked, so Blaze had locked him in her room. When he didn't get any response either, he left as well.

A terrible lethargy seemed to have crept over me, where it was too much trouble to speak, or even to pat a dog on the head.

Blaze came next. I wasn't surprised to see her; someone, I couldn't remember who, had already told me she was alive. One of the boats had fished her out of the ocean, battered, exhausted, but unharmed. She shut the door behind her, but she didn't say anything. She went into the bathroom and turned on the spigot to fill the tub with steaming hot water. Then she came back and knelt at my feet and unlaced my boots. She still hadn't said a word. I was aware of her, but in a vague, far off sort of way, as if I were watching all this happen to someone else, and through a fog, what's more.

She untied my bloodstained shirt and, listless, I let her take it off. One part of me was aware of all the blood, of the horrible redolence of it, but I didn't seem able to move of my own volition. She pulled me up so that I stood, still unresisting. She slid my trousers and underdrawers to the floor and propelled me to the bath. It was a mark of my befuddlement that I was not embarrassed. I wasn't *anything*.

I suppose she must have washed me, but I don't recall that. She might even have helped me dress afterward, because the next thing I remember with any clarity was sitting on the edge of my bed fully clothed in a clean outfit. And she was sitting in front of me on a chair, her knees touching mine. She had her hands cupping my face so that I was forced to look at her. To meet her eyes.

"I'm right sorry I was irate with ye," I said, referring to the last time we'd spoken privately. "About Flame." It seemed to be important to say that. I had shouted at her in terrible anger, and when I'd thought she was going to die, I'd been ashamed of that anger.

She said, "I know you are. And I'm sorry I said what I did, in the way that I did." She touched my cheek gently, as if I were a child. "Kel, we don't know for certain that was Ruarth's body. It could have been any of the Dustels." She repeated it twice, until I really heard and made sense of what she was saying.

"I know it wasn't him," I said, finally forcing my mind to think of something far too terrible to ever accept. "The smell was not Ruarth's. But does it matter? If he hasna turned up, we both know that he's dead."

She dropped her hands from my face to clasp them around my own hands, to hold them tight. "Kel—"

I interrupted. "Every single Dustel who was flying, Blaze, all over the Isles. Think about it for a moment. A mother, perhaps, bringing food to her young. Or a youngster taking his first flight. Or a flock on their way out to search for food. Or a young fellow on his way to court his love. How many like that? How many *thousands*? Ten thousand? Fifty? Five *hundred* thousand? Will we ever even *know*?"

"No," she said softly. "No. We will never know."

I stared at her. I had wanted her to deny it. To say everything was all right; that it wasn't like that. That I had it wrong. Instead she said. "We will all learn to live with it, Kel, just as we all learn to live with the idea that one day we ourselves will die. You didn't kill them. Morthred did. Morthred-Gethelred, Lord of Skodart, he murdered them. He murdered them the moment he dunmagicked their grandparents and great-grandparents into birds, ninety years or so ago."

I struggled for words, whispering because it was all I could manage. "I didna believe it, y'know. Not really. I didna believe all ye said about dunmagic. I thought I knew better. There was science, and it had all the answers. Dunmagic was an illness. Dustels had never been human, that was just a myth. Therefore, killing the dunmaster was going to change nothing. I was so certain . . ." I paused. "So arrogantly certain that I knew it all." I blinked back tears. "But *they* knew the truth, Blaze. Ruarth. The Xolchas Dustels, Comarth and the rest. So why did they keep flying? *They all knew Morthred was going to die yesterday.*"

"They were birds, Kel. Perhaps they could not conceive of being unable to fly . . ."

"It's got to be more than that."

"I've tried to talk to the ones who are still alive. I wanted to find Ruarth. But it's hard to communicate. They haven't learned to talk. They keep trying to—to cheep, to flutter their wings." She swallowed. "It's ghastly. They don't even *recognize* one another. They have no concept of what their own families look like. They can't find their loved ones. They can't say their own names. They don't even know their own faces." She took a deep breath. "Xetiana organized the guard into rescuing all the—the children stuck up on window ledges and rooftops. And adults too. Not everyone died, you know."

I shuddered, imagining all the things that must have happened that day, all over the Isles. "Creation, Blaze," I whispered, "a body falling from the sky can do so much damage. It wasna just the Dustels who died yesterday." I gestured helplessly. "There were others in the hospice . . ."

She dropped her gaze to look at our clasped hands. "I know."

"And the Fin. I didna kill Morthred soon enough for the people on the Fin . . . How—how do I go on living?" *How do I live with the guilt of that?*

She was silent for a while before answering. Then, "You did your best. How can anyone do more?"

Our eyes met and held. I asked quietly, "Blaze, did you *know* what was going to happen?"

She shook her head. "I did ask Ruarth. Of course I did. So did Flame. Do you think we didn't all think of this, long ago? He told us not to worry about it. He told Flame it would happen slowly enough for any flying Dustel to come down to land . . ." She looked down unhappily. "She believed him. I wasn't so convinced. They became birds instantaneously; why wouldn't they change back the same way? He took me aside later and told me that many Dustels believed that they would never be anything but birds. *They* hadn't been changed by dunmagic, you see, only their grandparents and great-grandparents had, and those older generations were dead. So, many Dustels thought killing Morthred would bring back the Islands, yes, but they themselves wouldn't change because they were born birds . . ."

"And they were wrong."

"Yes, they were wrong." She dropped her gaze. "Ruarth did once mention to me that all Dustel birds were prepared to die so that the human Dustelfolk could go home . . . I didn't think much about it at the time, but now, now I think he meant just that. If they did die when Morthred did, then they were prepared to accept that. But they couldn't stop flying. They were birds. It would be like telling us not to walk because it may kill us."

"He told me he'd kill Morthred himself, if he could. And that I wasna to look back. I didn't know what he meant. But he knew then that I might be the one who had to kill the dunmaster . . ."

"Wise words." She looked back into my eyes. "Kel, if they could accept it, then so must we."

I think that was always one of the things I liked best about Blaze: her brutal honesty. She never did clothe things in fine words and hypocrisy. *They died, Kel. Learn to live with it.* And I have tried. For fifty years, I have tried . . .

"What do ye think happened to him?" I asked her.

"To Ruarth? Tor and I, and Dek—we've been everywhere, looking. Although we might not recognize him, I am sure Seeker would."

"And?"

"There was a Dustel who was flying down the cliff face into Xolchasport when Morthred died. People saw him fall onto the rocks and then into the sea. They couldn't find his body, but there's no doubt that he was killed. We—we think that was probably Ruarth . . ."

"Why? What makes ye think that?"

"Because he would have followed Flame."

And then I remembered why we were all there in the first place. "Flame?" I asked, astonished that for a time I had completely forgotten her. "Where *is* Flame? *How* is Flame?"

She hesitated, and I scented distress. Grief.

Another wave of terror washed over me. Another moment of not wanting to know, of not being able to accept the unacceptable. "Oh, selverspit," I said, and felt sick again. "She's *dead*?"

"No, no," Blaze said hurriedly. "No. We think she left on the *Amiable*."

I stared at her, stupefied.

"You know she vanished on the way back to her room from the viewing platform. It was deliberate . . . she must have used illusion. The *Amiable* sailed away shortly afterward. The two subverted sylv women were still on board—you know, the ones who couldn't swim—and all the enslaved crew. We think Flame must have been on board as well."

"Did the port authorities not *stop* them? I understood there were guards with crossbows who had orders—"

"They didn't see the ship leave."

"Illusion again."

Blaze nodded. "I think it must have been her, not the other two."

"But *why*? Why would she go?"

Blaze shrugged. "Maybe she recognized you, and knew she was going to be rescued soon. The dunmagic part of her wouldn't want to become a sylv again, remember? So she ran away. Or maybe she had no idea rescue was so close. Maybe it was just that she wanted to escape Morthred, so she did. And I guess the sylv part of her recognized that sooner or later she was going to betray Ruarth. By running away from Morthred, she could also save Ruarth, or so she thought." She gave a half-grunt of reluctant admiration. "She always had guts, Flame. She's one of the most courageous people I've ever met. Maybe she left, not knowing Morthred was going to die, calmly stole his ship from under his nose anyway, and sailed away." She shook her head in wonderment.

I said flatly, "And ye think Ruarth tried to go after her, and that was the moment I killed Morthred."

She nodded. "I don't think she would have allowed Ruarth to leave on the *Amiable* with her. She was running away from him, as well as from Morthred." Her voice was husky.

I bowed my head. "She's lost to us then, Blaze." I remembered that Flame had been her closest friend. The only woman friend she'd ever had. I felt her pain, mingling somehow with my own, the aroma of it reinforcing my own grief. For a moment I could not separate the two of us. She laced her hands into mine, sharing unreservedly what she felt, her way of saying that she understood.

I said, "Even if we were to find her again, it would probably be too late."

She shook her head in a worried fashion. "There's something we're missing. I know it."

"Aye," I said. "I think ye're right." I tried to pinpoint what exactly was bothering me. "Those other ex-sylvs—all of them, the ones at the Mere, the ones here—they have dun in them that smells like Morthred. But Flame's dun is different. Just as Ginna's was."

"Ginna?"

"The child I told you about, the sylv who was raped by one of the Mere dunmagickers."

"What are you trying to say?"

"I don't know. But I thought, well, maybe that's because it was Morthred who contaminated all of the others. But someone else who subverted Flame. And Ginna . . . she was different again."

She looked blank. "You mean after we left Gorthan Spit? But who—? Where would Flame have met someone who could do that without me knowing?"

"When ye were in jail, perhaps?"

She thought about that. "It doesn't seem possible." She was frowning, her gaze intense. "Kel, tell me everything you read about dunmagic. Everything you can remember. You said that there was something that puzzled you . . ."

I fetched my notes on what I had discovered in Garrow's papers and books, and started to tell her as much as I remembered. Halfway through, she stopped me. "Wait a moment. What did you say just then?"

"That sylv women have dun children in the event of a liaison with a dunmagicker."

"Yeah, that. Duthrick once told me that too. I didn't think anything of it then, *but I do now*. Kel, don't you remember? Flame told us that sylvs can stop conception. In fact, she as good as told us that she had done so when she was raped by Morthred."

I nodded. "I remember."

"So how is it sylvs give birth to dun children? No sylv would ever willingly bed a dunmagicker, believe me. So it would have to be rape, and the woman concerned would stop conception."

"Aye. If she could," I agreed, and my heart seemed to be blocking my throat. "Ginna was pregnant. And she was a sylv. She obviously couldn't."

There was a short silence. Then, "You didn't tell me that before."

"I didn't think it was so important . . ."

"Oh, *shit*," she whispered. "Oh *shit*, Kel, Flame is pregnant with Morthred's child! *That's* what he meant. His legacy . . . His legacy will span the archipelago. His child will be the heir to both Cirkase and Breth. Flame doesn't have to get pregnant by the Bastionlord: she's *already* pregnant! Morthred was going to fool the Bastionlord into accepting *his* child, his own dunmagicking bastard." She looked at me with eyes that contained all the horror I heard in her tone. "The child's a dunmagicker . . . *that's* who subverted her, Kel. Her own baby! That's why nothing smelled the way it did before. She betrayed us because her own child subverted her from within. The child, not Morthred."

Appalled, I couldn't speak.

She jumped to her feet and started pacing. "Damn your eyes, Gilfeather. What sort of a lousy physician are you? You are supposed to recognize things like a pregnant woman!"

Useless to tell her that it was the women in my family who handled most of the pregnancies and childbirths. I kept silent.

She did a quick calculation. "It's been four months since she was raped. She must know. She must have known for ages . . . Oh, saltwater hells, if she'd said something, you could have done something!"

"Possibly. But, Blaze, the Bastionlord would have to be unbelievably gullible to accept as his own a child that's going to be born in just five months time."

"Once she's married, she could coerce the whole damn court into accepting the child as his . . . that was that Morthred planned, I'm sure of it." She sat down abruptly and sank her head into her hands. "How can this have happened?"

"Easily," I said, and smelled the bitterness of my own stupidity. "No sylv is going to be raped by a dunmagicker unless he is stronger in power than she is. And if he is stronger in power, then he has enough magic to circumvent her attempts to prevent conception."

"Without her even being aware he has done it."

"Apparently."

"Damn him to the Trench and beyond, that *bastard*. That utter bottom-crawling slug of a man! Even dead he is going to haunt us."

"Blaze, we don't know how she feels . . . this is Morthred's child. She was raped. He coerced her to obey him. But now he's dead and she's free of him . . . We don't know what effect Morthred's death has had on her. It may make things easier for us to—to convert her back. Maybe she will not even go to Breth."

"She's free of Morthred, true. *But not of his get*. Not free of subversion. The subverter is alive and well inside her body! Hells, Kel, the baby must have somehow protected itself. Stopped her from telling us . . ."

"It's hardly a rational human being at the moment. It's only an embryo!"

"I'll believe anything of Morthred's bastard."

We gazed at one another, two people shattered by their realization. Blaze's eyes were blurred with tears. She wiped them away angrily with the back of her hand. "We have to make plans. Tor wants to speak to you about that, by the way."

"Ryder? Talk to me about what?"

"He's going to take the next packet boat from here back to Tenkor. He wants you to go with him."

I groped for sense in all this. "Why Tenkor? Why *me*? Surely he should be going after Flame!"

"He thinks there's a better way. He dreams of finding a cure for dunmagic. He thinks the two of you can do it together. He thinks a cure is the only way we will ever save Flame. And just because Morthred is dead doesn't mean sylvs are safe from subversion. Plenty of his henchmen could know how to subvert. There'll never be a certain end to it, Kel, till there's an end to magic."

I gave a bark of laughter that had no humor in it. "Now there's an irony for you, lass: I've come to believe in magic, while Ryder thinks it's a disease that can be cured." I shook my head at the insanity of it all.

"Well, he doesn't exactly think there is no magic. But he has come to believe that magic is passed on like a disease, and can therefore be cured like a disease. He wants to work on that idea back in Tenkor."

"And you? The Keepers have put a price on your head. Ye'd be safe in Tenkor too."

She snorted. "Can you imagine me among all those patriarchs? I would be bored out of my mind in a week. No, Dek and I are going after Flame. I don't know what we will find. I can't be sure where she's gone. But I will find her. And then . . . then we'll see. Xetiana has agreed to fund me. She's worried sick about having a dunmagicker married to the Islandlord of Breth, so she's willing to pay me to keep an eye on things."

I stared at her. "I canna help but feel it's unlikely that Flame will still have gone to marry the Breth Bastionlord of her own volition."

"She's a dunmagicker, or nearly so. What would a dunmagicker want more than anything else? *Power*, Kel. The power to hurt and maim and kill. Yes, I think she's gone to Breth. I think she'll marry him, and after a while, she'll kill him. Her child will be the next Bastionlord and she will be regent. Eventually her father will die and she'll be able to claim the throne of Cirkase. And she will have the black powder for cannon-guns."

It was hard to remember she was speaking of Flame. I continued to stare at her, and felt ill. "Ye're going to kill her."

"If there is no other way. I made her that promise."

"And if Tor and I find a cure for magic?"

"It may still be too late for Flame. Tell me, Kel, how long will it take you to find a cure, if there is one to be found? A year? Two? Six?"

"We could always try Keepers and sylv healing again—"

"As a last resort, of course. But I'd rather Keepers didn't know yet a while. They would see her dead rather than risk a dunmagicker on the throne anywhere. Well, perhaps I would too—but at least I would make sure that we explore every way we can think of to save her first. Keepers may not be so . . . careful."

"So they will be after her too, if they find out what happened?"

"They will. And I will have Duthrick after my hide as well, as soon as he finds out what happened here. The Keepers have spies everywhere, damn them." She gave a rueful smile. "Don't worry, Kel, I wouldn't know what to do with myself if life were too easy . . ."

I choked on the tragedy of that, and turned away so she could not see my face. "Ye've got it all worked out, then."

"No one's pushing you, Kel. You can go where you like. Do what you will. Talk to Tor. I know you don't like him, but he's a good man."

I wanted to say: Skies, Blaze, not anymore. We saw to that, you and I. He's an angry man, filled with rage at the two of us. A hard man, hardened by the dun we put within him.

What was it the ghemph had said? *We did more evil than we knew.*

But I didn't say any of it. I couldn't burden her with more than she already had to carry. I sighed. None of what had to be done was going to be easy. Or even safe.

I thought of Jastriá, and the Sky Plains. Of my exile and my family. I thought of all the Dustel Islanders and the people on the Fin who had died because of what I had done, and I knew that I would spend the rest of my life trying to make amends, and still have trouble sleeping at night. I thought of Ruarth, who had loved so long and so well and so tragically. I thought of Flame, subverted by her own ill-gotten child, sailing to a future so bleak it was unimaginable. I thought of Blaze, pledged to kill the friend she loved. Blaze, hunted by those she had once served. I felt shredded by despair.

"What time is it?" I asked.

"Late. Let's have some supper, and then bed. You are exhausted." She stood and held out her hand. "Come, Gilfeather. We have plans to make. Places to go. Things to do."

I didn't take her proffered clasp. Instead I asked curiously, "Halfbreed, d'ye ever give up?"

She cocked her head to one side and thought about that. "I spent the first thirty years of my life largely friendless. And then I met Flame. And Tor. And you. And Dek. In a few weeks—no, from the very day I met Flame—my whole life changed." She gave a wry smile and a shrug. "I guess what I'm trying to say is that I'd cross the Glory Isles from one end to the other twice a year if Flame needed my help. No, I'm not going to give up on her. Not yet. And if I ever do, it will be to kill her. To put her out of her misery, because I made her a promise that I would." She was silent a moment, then she added, "Does that shock you?"

I shook my head. "I killed Jastriá, for just that reason, remember?"

"You've come to terms with that, I think."

"Aye, I think I have. I dinna think I deserved the way she wanted to hurt me, but I canna blame her. She is to be pitied, not blamed. People are . . . more complex than I once thought. I've learned a lot in a very few weeks."

"So have I. And it hasn't all been good. I—I've lost a friend because I wanted to save his life. And now I plan to lose another by killing her. I am so profligate with my friends, one could assume—wrongly—that I have plenty to spare." There was more dry humor than bitterness in her words, but their poignancy still stirred me.

"Ye'll always have me," I said lightly.

"Will I? The way I'm going right now, I shall probably do something horrendous to you too."

"Ach, lassie, ye already have. You did that right at the beginning of our relationship, remember? Ye stole my selver and wrecked my life." I smiled at her. "And yet I'm still here.

Somehow I dinna think ye'll ever find anything worse to do to me, so doubtless ye're stuck with this friend for life."

She didn't smile back. In fact, she bit her lip and looked away. "That—that means a lot to me. Thank you."

"Ye mentioned food," I said, wanting to change the subject.

She held out her hand again, and this time I took it and clambered to my feet. I was desperately tired. She said, "Kel, will you be all right?"

I knew she wasn't talking about my fatigue. I said honestly, "I don't know. One day at a time, I suppose. What happened to the Dustel birds—I was the instrument, even if I wasna the cause. It wasna my fault, and it would have happened one day anyway, I suppose. Morthred couldn't live forever. I could wish I'd done it sooner, though. Then those people on the Fin would still be alive." Saying it didn't change anything, of course; the fact remained that an action of mine had killed thousands of people all over the Isles, and it would haunt me for the rest of my days. She knew that, and so did I. "Blaze—"

"Yes?"

"I'm sorry. That I put ye through all that, when ye were on the Crumble, I mean. Because I didn't have the stomach to kill him earlier. Because I kept waiting for ye or Tor to happen along and do it for me."

Her face broke up into a smile. "Ah, Gilfeather, what's life without a bit of excitement? You had two seconds to spare. Plenty of time."

I didn't know what she meant. "Two seconds?"

"The dun he threw—most of it was directed at the Crumble, where I was standing, not at the Fin. But it never got there. Because you hit him over the head, he lost control of the magic and it dissipated in all directions, more or less harmlessly. Unfortunately for them, the Fin was closer to where he stood, so the edge of the power reached it first. It was that close, Kel. If you'd hit him two seconds later, the power would have reached me and powdered the Crumble out from under my feet. And it was a *long* way down. I wouldn't be standing here now."

I stared at her, shocked. "Two seconds."

She nodded.

"I almost killed ye." My heart stopped, just as it had when

I had watched the stack fall and thought it was going to land on her. I wanted to tell her the truth then. I wanted her to know so badly. I wanted her to know that it had never been Flame that had attracted me, but her. That ever since that night up on the meadow of the Sky Plains, when she'd spoken to me of Jastriá, and the friend she'd killed, and we'd smelled the moonflowers together, she had filled my thoughts. In the end, by the time we'd reached Xolchas Stacks, I loved her as much as I'd ever loved Jastriá. More.

I wanted so much to tell her now, as I had wanted to so many times: but what was the point? At first I had misinterpreted the nature of her love for Flame, then Ryder had come on the scene and I had seen the way her eyes followed him, confound the wretched man. And he was everything I wasn't: handsome, competent, well-traveled, a man of consequence. A man who had saved her life, several times. Who could match her, step for step. Not a red-headed physician who tripped over his own feet every time he stood up.

I'd been jealous of him, of course. And I'd saved him for her, not because I cared all that much for a Menod priest. To buy Tor's life I'd let twelve new dunmagickers go on their way into the world—because she loved him. I had not yet worked out if that made my action morally more reprehensible, or less . . .

I smiled. "It's just as well ye can run *verra* fast, isn't it?"

"It is indeed, you clod-hopping selver-herder," she said amiably. "Let's go get supper. Xolchas mutton is *very* good."

Behind the teasing, I scented the fondness she held for me, and had to be content with that.

A letter from Researcher (Special Class) S. iso Fabold, National Department of Exploration, Federal Ministry of Trade, Kells, to Masterman M. iso Kipswon, President of the National Society for the Scientific, Anthropological and Ethnographical Study of non-Kellish Peoples.

Dated this day 15/1st Single/1794

Dear Uncle,
Sorry, I don't have another packet of translated papers for you yet. Nathan has been busy with some transcriptions of other documents that are now needed by the Ministry.

Uncle, there is something I need to ask your advice about, concerning Anyara. As you know, our relationship had developed to one of deep affection. I had in fact "popped the question," as they say in today's vulgar parlance. But, alas, things are not well between us at the moment. She was pressing to accompany me on this voyage to the Isles of Glory. If she were my wife, it would indeed be possible to include her, for it is an entitlement of the expedition comptroller that he may take his spouse on board. But I feel that an expedition of this nature is not appropriate for a well-bred lady. When I told her this, though, and asked her to be patient, she was not pleased. Whatever understanding there was between us has now been terminated. I understand that she has since gone to the Minister for Trade. She has not told me this, you understand, but I have heard from other sources that she is trying to get herself included in the expedition in some capacity or another.

I was wondering if anyone has approached our Society about this? For an opinion, perhaps? I am deeply alarmed, for I feel that I will end up looking like a fool, especially if she manages to obtain the patronage of the Protectoress. I need your advice. Is there some way the National Society can recommend that her application for any post be disregarded?

Truly, Uncle, in one way I feel I have had a narrow escape. Miss Anyara isi Teron is obviously hoydenish in the extreme, and far too wild. I have never been so deceived in all my life. It appears she even gained access to the Society's library and began reading the Blaze-Gilfeather papers in their unabridged state after you had lodged them there! I am sure you cannot have been aware of this. What was our librarian thinking of, allowing this? I have never been so appalled. When I think of some of the anthropological works lodged on those shelves, so inappropriate for gently bred ladies! And now Anyara seems obsessed with meeting Blaze Halfbreed; can you imagine? Uncle, it is my fervent hope that you will lend your support to me, and try to rectify this state of affairs in any way possible.

About the next set of papers: I will have them to you as soon as possible. More about Blaze and Gilfeather, of course, but there are some other people I interviewed as well, in particular one of the tideriders of Tenkor. Fascinating fellow, who had a foot in both camps, so to speak. In addition, I was given access to the Patriarch Histories and to papers of the governing Keeper Council—interesting reading, all of which shed light on the myths and beliefs and history of the Glory Isles.

There has never been a problem of too little information. The problem always has been to separate the pearl from the shell . . .

I remain,
Your devoted nephew,
Shor iso Fabold

GLOSSARY

Glorian terms and people extracted from a compendium compiled by Anyara isi Teron, 1794–95, with reference to situation of 1742. Original lodged with the National Society for the Scientific, Anthropological and Ethnographical Study of non-Kellish Peoples.

Alain Jentel: Menod Patriarch from the Spatts, killed in the bombardment of Creed. Friend to Tor Ryder.

Anistie Bittlelyn: Friend of Garrowyn Gilfeather. Resident of Porth Island, Mekaté.

Arnado, Syr-sylv: Wealthy Keeper Isles sylv and swordsman who works for the Keeper Council, specifically for Duthrick. Blaze's one-time mentor and fencing teacher.

Asorcha: Chamberlain to the Barbicanlord of Xolchas Stacks.

Awareness/the Aware: The Aware are people born with the ability (Awareness) to see and smell magic. They cannot perform magic themselves, nor can they be directly harmed or deceived by magic.

Barbicanlord: Ruler of Xolchas Stacks (*see* Xetiana).

Bastionlord: Ruler of the Breth Island group. Bastionlord of 1742 is a known pedophile.

Blaze Halfbreed: A citizenless half Fen, half Souther Aware woman, born and raised in the Hub, Keeper Isles. Parents unknown. Worked for the Keeper Council under the guidance of Syr-sylv Duthrick in her capacity as one of the Aware, including as an assassin of dunmagickers.

Castlelord: Ruler of the Cirkase Islands.

Castlemaid: Name given to Castlelord's heir, if female.

Creed: Small cockle-farming village on Gorthan Spit that was taken over by dunmagickers, then bombarded by the Keeper ships.

Dek/Dekan Grinpindillie: Illegitimate son of Inya Grinpindillie of Mekatéhaven and Bolchar, a fisherman of the Kitamu Bays, Mekaté.

Dih Pellidree, Exemplar: Leader of the Fellih-worshippers in Mekaté.

Domino/Dominic Scavil: A very short Fen Islander from Hethreg Cove, henchman of Morthred.

dun/dunmagicker: Red (or red-brown) magic and the person who uses it. Harmful powers include the ability to kill others, to destroy property with explosive power that varies from individual to individual, or inflict sores that are ultimately fatal. They can also heal themselves, disguise themselves with illusion and erect protection wards. Dunmagic is only visible to the Aware, or to the dunmagicker using it, although the effects are obvious to all.

dunmaster: A dunmagicker who is particularly skilful and powerful in the use of dunmagic.

Dustel Isles: Vanished islands of the Souther group. Believed to have been submerged in 1652. The area is now known as the Reefs of Deep Sea.

Duthrick, Councillor Syr-sylv: Executant Councillor of the Keeper Isles. Powerful sylv. In charge of much of the covert activities of the Keeper Isles outside of their own islandom, particularly when intervention is needed to protect Keeper interests. Given name: Ansor, rarely used.

Emmerlynd Bartbarick, Lord: Keeperlord of the Keeper Isles in 1742.

Eylsa: One of the ghemphs, water bouget pod. Died helping Blaze near Creed in 1742. Spirit name: Mayeen.

Fellih-Master: God of the Fellih-worshippers, not to be confused with the Menod God, who is seen as a false god by Fellih-worshippers.

Fellih-worshipper: One who worships the Fellih-Master, or who is born the child of a Fellih-worshipper. The religion was centered on Mekaté, but spread widely, especially in the Souther Isles.

Flame Windrider, Syr-sylv: Name taken by Lyssal (*see also*) after escaping from Cirkasecastle.

Fotherly Bartbarick, Councillor Syr-sylv: Son of the Keeperlord, Emmerlynd Bartbarick. Also known as Foth the Foppish or Bart the Barbaric.

Garrowyn Gilfeather: A selver-herder physician from Tharn Wyn on the Sky Plains of Mekaté.

Gethelred, Syr-sylv: A sylv member of the Dustel royal family before the disappearance of the islands. One of the twin sons of the Rampartheir Willrin in the mid-seventeenth century. Escaped being murdered by his uncle Vincen. Believed at one time to have died in the subsequent civil war or in the sinking of the islands.

ghemph: Non-human race. Responsible for tattooing the citizenship tattoos into earlobes of all Glorian citizens. Gray-skinned, hairless, with webbed and clawed feet, but possessing no outwardly visible distinction between the sexes.

Gorthan Spit: The only island outside of all the legally recognized islandoms. A place without real government and no easily recognized leaders. Has only one main town: Gorthan Docks. The only place where the citizenless can remain without harassment.

Great Trench: Believed by many to be a place in the deepest parts of the ocean where all dead souls go; sometimes thought of only as the final home for the soul of any sailor lost at sea; equated by the religious with hell and the home of the evil Sea Devil. Generally thought to be cold, dark and unpleasant.

Havenlord: Ruler of the Mekaté Island group.

Holdlord: Ruler of the Bethany Isles. In 1740s, the Holdlord had two sons: Tagrus (deceased by 1742) and Ransom, Holdheir.

islandom: An island or group of islands that forms an independent administrative unit, or country.

Janko: Waiter at The Drunken Plaice, Gorthan Docks. (*See* Morthred.)

Jastriákyn Longpeat: Kelwyn Gilfeather's wife.

Keeper Council: Elected body that rules the Keeper Isles under the leadership of the Keeperlord.

Keeper Fair: Name of Syr-sylv Duthrick's ship.

Keeperlord: Elected ruler of the Keeper Isles. Present lord is Emmerlynd Bartbarick.

Kelwyn Gilfeather: Sky Plains physician from Wyn, Mekaté.

Lance of Calment: Rebel known for his daring during the uprising of the poorer landless people of Calment Minor in the 1730s. Still has a price on his head in the Calment Isles. Identity largely unknown. (*See also* Tor Ryder.)

Lyssal, Castlemaid of Cirkase, Syr-sylv: (*See also* Flame Windrider.) The only child and heir of the Castlelord of Cirkase. Raised in Cirkasecastle and ran away in 1742 to Gorthan Spit, where she had an arm amputated after contamination by the dunmagic of Morthred the Mad.

Menod: A contraction of Men of God, used to designate the religion as a whole, or all worshippers/believers (male or female) of their God. Centered on the Keeper Isles, but widespread on all islandoms and generally seen as the religion of choice for most islandom ruling houses.

Menod Council: A body elected at an annual Synod, comprised of patriarchs and matriarchs, which rules the Menod faithful of the Glory Isles through a network of patriarchs and matriarchs. Administrative center on Tenkor Island, Keeper Isles.

Morthred: Dunmaster believed to be responsible for sinking the Dustel Islands and changing the islanders into birds in the year 1652.

Niamor: A Quillerman who formed a friendship with Blaze on Gorthan Spit that eventually resulted in his death.

Rampartlord: Ruler of the Dustel Isles prior to the sinking of the islands. The position was not revived among the survivors or their descendants.

Ransom Holswood, Holdheir: A Menod who came to the position of heir to the Bethany Islands when his older brother died, thereby thwarting his ambitions to be a Menod patriarch.

Roof of Mekaté: Another name for the Sky Plains.

Ruarth Windrider, Syr-aware: A Dustel bird descendant, through the female line, of the last Rampartlord of the Dustel Islands. Born and raised on the roofs of Cirkasecastle, until he left in the company of Lyssal in 1742.

sea-pony: Very large amphibious sea creature that leaves a slime trail on land. Reputedly blind or with only poor eyesight. Can be used to transport goods or people, but needs to return to the sea every few hours or it will die.

sea-dragon: Large sea creatures, possibly mythical, that have a reputation for eating sailors, wrecking ships, etc.

Securia: Name given to the post of the head of security in several islandoms. (*See* Shavel.)

selver: Domesticated animal found only on the Sky Plains. Can be ridden. Young animals produce very fine wool, much in demand throughout the Glory Isles, called wool-silk.

selver-herder: Any person born to a Sky Plains tharn.

Shavel: The Securia of the Barbicanlord of Xolchas Stacks, in charge of the safety of the Barbicanlord and the islandom's general security.

Sky Plains: That part of Mekaté Island which is found at the top of the Scarps. Home to the Sky People, or selver-herders.

Spitter: Anyone who lives on Gorthan Spit.

stack: Any island of the Xolchas group.

sylv: Blue (or silver-blue) magic that enables healing, and the construction of illusions or protection wards. Sylvmagic cannot be used for destruction or to inflict physical harm on people or things. Sylvs are born, not made, but have to be taught how to use their powers, otherwise it simply leaks away. Sylvmagic itself is only visible to the Aware or to the sylv using it, although the effects are obvious to all.

Syr: Courtesy title given to anyone with status, usually qualified by the reason for that status: e.g. Syr-aware, Syr-sylv, Syr-patriarch, etc.

Tor Ryder, Syr-aware patriarch: Menod patriarch Stragglerman, onetime scribe, rebel and swordsman. Was an active leader of the failed Calment rebellion. (*See also* Lance of Calment.)

Tunn: Tapboy at The Drunken Plaice inn in Gorthan Docks. Killed by Morthred's dunmagic after helping Blaze.

Xetiana, Lord: Barbicanlord of the islandom known as Xolchas Stacks.

Glenda Larke is an Australian who now lives in Malaysia, where she works on the two great loves of her life: writing fantasy and the conservation of rainforest avifauna. She has also lived in Tunisia and Austria, and has at different times in her life worked as a housemaid, library assistant, school teacher, university tutor, medical correspondence course editor, field ornithologist and designer of nature interpretive centers. Along the way she has taught English to students as diverse as Korean kindergarten kids and Japanese teenagers living in Malaysia, Viennese adults in Austria and engineering students in Tunis. If she has any spare time (which is not often), she goes birdwatching; if she has any spare cash (not nearly often enough), she visits her daughters in Scotland and Virginia and her family in Western Australia.

You can find out more about Glenda at her website
www.glendalarke.com

Book One of The Isles of Glory

The Aware
by Glenda Larke

0-441-01277-9

A halfbreed's search for a mysterious slave woman
leads her to a lawless land of dark dunmagic and an evil
that poses a threat to all the Isles of Glory.

"A EXPERIENCED AND GIFTED WRITER...
A RIP-ROARING TALE." —*VISIONS*

"WITTY, GRITTY AND ENTHRALLING."
—TRUDI CANAVAN

Available wherever books are sold or at penguin.com

b948